CAMELOT'S COUSIN

An Espionage Thriller

by

David R. Stokes

TELEMACHUS PRESS

Cover Design by Mike Zizolfo

Published by Telemachus Press, LLC
http://www.telemachuspress.com

Visit the author website:
http://www.camelotscousin.com

ISBN: 978-1-938135-75-0 (eBook)
ISBN: 978-1-938701-37-5 (Paperback)

Version 2012.09.17

Printed in the United States of America

10 9 8 7 6 5 4 3 2 1

"For my Dad and hero, Dr. Gerald W. Stokes, with immeasurable and inexhaustible gratitude for a lifetime of love, wisdom, and never-to-be-forgotten conversations about the past, present, and future."

"*It may take ten years for an agent to manoeuver himself into a post where he has access to policy decisions. Temperamentally the Russians are prepared to wait that time. Temperamentally the Latins and the Anglo-Saxons find this waiting very hard.*"
John Bruce Lockhart (1914–1995)

"*But it was thou, a man mine equal, my guide, and mine acquaintance.*"
Psalm 55:13

Preamble

This is a novel—a work of fiction. The story is the fruit of the author's imagination. Though it includes familiar (even famous) people, and whenever possible I have tried to stay close to the actual historical record and timeline, the narrative is my invention.

That said, when a character refers to actual authors or books in this novel, the passages quoted are indeed accurate—as are any suggested clues. For a partial list of nonfiction works I used to create this story, see the "Author's Note" at the end of the book. But don't read it now; it will spoil the fun.

Once again, please know that the story I have written is fiction.

I made it up.

Really.

David R. Stokes
Fairfax, Virginia

CAMELOT'S COUSIN

Prologue
Near Shrewsbury, England—January 1985

CHARLOTTE OLFORD STOPPED her bicycle on the side of the road and pulled the hood of her dark blue jacket up over her head. She tied the string in place under her chin and rebuked herself for having wrongly calculated. Certain that she would be able to make the ride home before any rain began, her judgment had proved to be flawed. However, she was still reasonably sure that she would be home by the time any serious downfall happened and well before sundown, which she reluctantly acknowledged was also approaching more quickly than she had judged.

Ready to resume, she checked the basket on the front of her having-seen-better-days machine and ensured that it was secure. Then she was again on her way. Charlotte had been shopping in town that Friday, picking up a few last minute provisions for the weekend. The weather had finally turned toward the mild side, after beginning the year bitter cold. She couldn't escape the thought that if this were the fifth of January instead of the twenty-fifth she might have needed more provisions from the store because of snow. *Oh my*, she thought—*that was so beautiful.* But it appeared that this weekend would be clear, after the evening rain of the moment, and make for a wonderful few days of home and hearth in a little place called Emstrey, England, located just a few miles from Shrewsbury, which was a much bigger spot.

No one was on the road, but then this little pathway was barely a road, more of a lane, actually. The major arteries in, out of, and around

Shrewsbury were likely filled with travelers at that moment, with many of the people making their way from London to Wales. It was a well-traveled route. This was the reason she was somewhat startled to hear the sound of an automobile approaching from the rear—wait—it was two automobiles and they seemed to be operating at full throttle.

Charlotte stopped her bicycle again and moved a few feet off the road to wait for the cars to pass—they seemed to be in such a hurry. In a moment they raced by her. She thought the first one looked like a fancy sports car of some sort—maybe a Jaguar? The second one, following all-too-closely behind, was a make unfamiliar to her, an odd looking motorcar, for sure. Both drivers, neither car had any extra passengers that she could see, had intense looks on their faces. Was one of them after the other?

She watched them disappear around a bend in the road about a quarter mile ahead—they had made it that far in what seemed to her to be a mere second or two. Again on her way, she labored against a wind that had now picked up and found herself wishing she had left town much earlier.

When she reached that bend in the road, she negotiated the curve and immediately saw something ominous ahead—about another quarter mile, just as the road entered a patch of woods. Charlotte tried to accelerate to get to the scene.

There was smoke and the smell of petrol. It was the Jaguar. The car that had been trailing it was nowhere in sight. The driver of the Jag was slumped over the wheel and covered in blood.

Her first instinct was to stay clear because of the possibility of the fuel exploding, but she overcame that and carefully opened the driver's door and tried to communicate with the man. He was alive and groaning in pain. She pulled him away from the steering wheel and caught the first glimpse of his face. It was well known, not only in these parts, but the entire nation— even some parts of the world.

Charlotte gasped and felt completely at a loss as to what to do. She told the driver—"Lord ... Lord! We need to get you out of this car." She summoned all of her strength and marveled that she was able to pull the much larger man out of the vehicle and drag him to a safe distance from the unstable car. She looked the man over more carefully, particularly at his head wound; it was bleeding profusely. And she noticed for the first time that the wound looked a bit queer—not all that much like the man had hit his head hard—actually it looked like, well, a wound that might come from a bullet. Rather curious, she thought.

She leaned forward to look a bit closer just as the petrol exploded with a powerful force, but they were far enough away and sheltered, at least in part by a large tree. She nearly shouted in the wounded man's ear: "I'm going up the lane to ring for help. Someone will be here in a tick. Keep your chin up!" She immediately cringed at having used the cliché in such a perilous moment.

Finding a phone a little way up the road, she notified the authorities, told them what she had seen and the name of the well-known man in the accident. They told her to wait by the phone, which she did for what seemed hours, just her and a red telephone box, well into the night. Finally, a nice officer came and took her statement and thanked her for calling the accident in.

"How is he?" she asked, referring to the man in the Jaguar.

"He's been taken to hospital over in Shrewsbury, but it looks pretty bad."

Shaken, Charlotte finally arrived home around ten o'clock. She had called her husband telling him what had happened and he had put the little ones to bed. He had a cup of Earl Grey tea and a cheese sandwich waiting for her. She devoured the sandwich and asked for a glass of whisky. Then another. But nothing would help her sleep that night.

The next morning she had the cup of tea she had passed on the night before and opened the local paper, wondering if the accident had made the news yet. It had. The front page of the venerable *Shrewsbury Chronicle* told the sad story about that famous man she had tried to help. He had, in fact, died overnight. She found herself tearing up, but then as she read the rest of the story her mood changed from grief to frustrated anger.

The paper simply had it all wrong. It described the accident, but didn't say anything about another car chasing the man and not a word about any bullet wound or her part in the story. The article stated that the man had run off the wet road and into a tree. And it said that the man who had died was on his way from London to Wales. But that didn't fit what she knew to be true. The fast cars that passed her were driving the opposite way—*away* from Wales. Besides, the road to Wales was on the *other* side of Shrewsbury.

It all made no sense to Charlotte, but then again, she regularly found many things in the local paper that didn't make much sense. She made a mental note to pick up one of the London papers, but never actually got around to it. She also thought briefly about calling the newspaper or writing a letter or something, but soon she was caught up in the delightfully routine and deliberately sedentary activities of a quiet English weekend. And that was that.

Chapter One
Clifton, Virginia—Present Day

RANGER HAD BEEN part of their family for nearly a dozen years. He was just a pup back when Vince and Elizabeth brought their first child home—a beautiful daughter they named Cynthia (after Elizabeth's mom's mom). And he was a vital part of the greeting party when baby sister Monica moved in about three years later, and then again when yet another girl, this one named Miriam, joined the family two years after that. You'd be hard pressed to find any family photograph without the dog somewhere in the shot. Ranger was what you might call a mutt, but such demeaning words were never uttered around the Benton place. They once counted that he probably had six breeds in his DNA, but to every member of the family he was a prize-winning thoroughbred. To them, his blood ran pure blue.

Vince stood just under six-feet tall and carried a little over two hundred pounds of somewhat flabby weight. His hair was nearly black with no hint of gray, though he had recently turned forty, and his eyes were deep blue. His skin bore evidence of significant dermatological problems in his youth.

He was usually the first one up in the morning, his day usually starting around four AM. On this day that would turn to out to be so particularly sad for his family, he found Ranger lying all too still on the floor as he looked in on the older girls who shared a room before heading downstairs to make the morning coffee. Actually it was ready to be made, just took the push of a button; no one had ever taken the time to figure out how to use the device's timer.

Normally the dog quietly got up, sensitively seeming to know that he wasn't supposed to awaken the girls. Then he would follow Vince downstairs to the back door and out to do his first business of the day. When he didn't move *this* morning, the dad tiptoed in and gently scooped up the dog, pulling him into his arms.

And then he knew for sure. Ranger was dead.

He went downstairs and opened the back door. Walking out into the brisk early autumn air, he didn't notice that he wasn't wearing a robe, or even slippers. He was determined to make his way to the shed out back and was already beginning to be overcome with emotion. Silly, he thought, but sadly real.

Actually, it was much more than a shed. The structure was the size of a garage, minus a car. Vince used it as a combination workroom and studio. He kept some radio equipment there, using the space for occasional free-lance work. The walls had some makeshift soundproofing. It was a pretty good place to record. The room was seldom cleaned because Liz rarely graced the space. It was his "man cave"—at least that's what the ladies in his life called it. He laid Ranger down and covered him with an old brown, and already smelly, blanket all the while trying to figure out how to tell the girls the bad news. He made his way back to the house.

The Benton family lived on a beautiful piece of property. Some would say it was downright pastoral but for the fact that it was not very far removed from the congested bustle of modernity. Most of the homes in this area of historic Clifton, Virginia were on five-acre sites, but Vince and Liz had fallen in love with this plot consisting of more than eleven. The house was smaller than many of the others in the area, particularly the newer estate homes that had been built after tearing down earlier structures on the same sites. At first they thought they'd expand the house in the years to come, or maybe even build a whole new one—plenty of room for it—but they never got around to it. So what if theirs was more of a cottage surrounded by mansions? It was home. And it had everything they needed. The place breathed contentment.

The girls especially loved the yard, if you can call eleven acres a yard. There were daily deer sightings. The occasional fox, too. Sometimes they'd just know a skunk was nearby. And when the wind was just right, they smelled more than a hint of horse. Several of the neighbors had stables and sometimes the girls would be invited to visit the "horseys," as they still called them.

But without a doubt their favorite feature of the place was the large tree that towered behind the house, slightly off to the left. Truth be told, when Vince and Liz looked at the home more than fifteen years earlier, it was the tree they saw first. They moved to the area from New York so Vince could take a new job with a Washington, DC radio station—some tech stuff, production, but the occasional opportunity to do some writing work with the news department. Seeing the tree was almost a metaphysical moment for them as they instantly envisioned it as a hub of familial fun, with kids—as yet unborn—running around, swinging from it and climbing its low hanging limbs. They didn't tell the talking-too-much realtor, but she had them at *cherry tree.*

The house was fine enough—quite nice, actually. There were four bedrooms, two baths, a partially-finished basement, new heating and cooling systems, and that edifice about thirty feet from the house (Vince immediately called "dibs"—at least in his head). The entire site looked like a quaint cottage scene in the English countryside.

Through the years they indeed enjoyed the home, especially that tree. They loved its beautiful blossoms in late March. But the best part of it was the annual ritual—usually early in June—that always began with the girls bursting into Mom and Dad's room announcing (okay, yes, yelling), "The deers are at the tree. Wake up! The deers are eating the cherries!" And this was no time to lecture the little ones about singular and plural when it came to deer. Immediately Vince and Liz would spring into practiced action.

Now, some men might instinctively go for the gun—see a deer, get a gun. That's the logic, right? But this day was never about harming any animal, and Vince had never been much of a hunter, even though he did have a man cave. It was all about guarding the fruit and then picking it. Soon the Benton kitchen would be filled with nectarous delights. The succeeding days would be sweet! Liz would make homemade cherry pie cobbler. One year she got creative and made a cherry upside down cake (something she never repeated, for which the family was quietly grateful). Even Ranger joined in. He loved cherries. But he never bothered to spit out the pits and the girls would laugh when they saw some of his "deposits" in the grass.

"Daddy, there are pits in his poop!"

Vince decided that the death of the family dog was enough of a crisis to warrant at least going in late, so he sat down at the desk in the family room and signed on to his gmail account. He knocked out a quick note to Valerie Doling, who ran the office: *"Gonna be late today—Ranger died, don't know how I am going to tell the girls!"* After he sent it, he scanned his inbox to see if there was anything urgent. There wasn't, just some news items, which he could read later, and seven items in his spam folder, which he deleted without review. He started to get up and walk away, when a new email popped up. It was from Valerie. Was she already at work? It said, *"Oh, that's horrible! Not to worry, I'll tell Temp and the gang, give a hug to the girls, V."* Then he noticed the tag, *"Sent from my I-Phone."* No, she wasn't at work—yet—but she was always working, or so it seemed. Good for her.

In fact, he wouldn't make it to work at all that day.

While waiting for the coffee maker to produce the delivery mechanism for Vince's drug of choice, he reached for a couple of mugs. For him, he selected one with an image of legendary broadcaster Edward R. Murrow and his quote: *"A Nation of Sheep Will Beget A Government of Wolves."* This was the preferred coffee container these days for most of the staff at the radio station. Using it made him feel a little better somehow for not going to work on time this day. Of course, Liz always used the same cup, but it was not in the cupboard. Vince looked in the dishwasher instantly remembering that he had forgotten to turn it on before going up to bed the night before. That Liz would not be happy was a gross understatement. He found the coffee cup bearing the images of their two daughters and hand washed it as the coffeemaker beeped three times announcing that the brew was ready. After pouring two cups and adding cream to hers, he turned on the dishwasher, better late than never, and walked quietly upstairs, passing the girls' room. He placed Liz's cup on the nightstand beside her bed. Liz was beautiful, he thought. He wondered, frankly, what she ever saw in him. She was about five feet, four inches tall, weighing around a hundred and thirty pounds, brown hair, green eyes—with a contagious smile that she wore nearly every waking moment. He was sure glad everyone said the girls looked like *her.*

She opened her eyes and smiled, then quickly sensed something was wrong.

Vince seldom brought coffee to her.

"What is it?"

"Ranger didn't wake up. He's dead."

"Whhhaaaaaattt???" she asked. She rubbed her eyes while trying to adjust to the light from the lamp Vince had so suddenly turned on. "Are you sure?"

"Yes honey, trust me, I'm sure."

"Oh my, the girls, have you told them?"

"No, they're still asleep. I sent a note to Valerie that I'd be late, but we need to talk about how we're going to handle this."

Soon Vince and Liz were sitting at the kitchen table drinking their *second* cup of coffee and devising a strategy. They agreed that the wisest way to deal with this was tenderly, but firmly. Get it all out today, that would be best. They'd talk to the girls, keep them home from school, maybe watch some home movies, and probably bury Ranger somewhere on the property. They'd let the girls find a nice spot on their eleven acres and have some kind of farewell ceremony. Of course, even as they planned all this it was pretty clear to both of them that they were just as upset at the loss of this great family friend as were their little girls.

Cindy, Monica, and Miriam were heartbroken when they heard the news, instantly crying and doing so throughout the morning. They didn't want to watch movies. They didn't want to talk; they just wanted to cry. Finally, they asked where Ranger was? Vince hemmed and hawed and started to say something about "a better place," when Cindy said: "No, Daddy—where is his *body?*"

"Oh, well … um … I put it somewhere safe and I wanted to talk to you about where we should bury him."

All three girls cried and said through their tears, "By the cherry tree!"

Amazingly, neither Liz nor Vince had thought of that, but it was perfect. That tree was the heart of their property. They had gathered there through the years, now they would grieve there. They'd grieve for a dog.

As the Sun's angular autumnal rays bounced off fallen leaves and recently dormant grass, the family made their way in a procession of sorts, one led by Vince holding a brown blanket bearing the body of Ranger out to the cherry tree. Liz carried the shovel. Cindy carried Ranger's dish, Monica tightly gripped a ball worn ragged over time by Ranger's playful teeth, and Miriam tagged along behind with a security blanket of her own. Vince chose the spot slightly behind the tree and far enough away not to dig into any roots—this needed to go flawlessly—and quickly. He began to dig as the girls and Liz wept. Truth be told, so did he.

When he had reached a few feet down, he began to feel something with the shovel. A root? A rock? No, it was not hard like a rock. He moved the shovel from left to right and it was still there. Whatever it was, it was a pretty good size. His eyes met Liz's, hers clearly asking, "What's the matter?"

Thinking quickly, he said, "Girls, I'm sorry but there's a rock down there and I'm gonna have to find another spot ..."

"But Daddy," Monica cried, "Ranger wants to sleep by the tree!"

"I know, honey, and he will. I just need to dig the hole in a different spot by the tree, Okay?"

And he did. After what seemed to be an eternity, the blanket, bearing Ranger, was placed in the new hole Vince had dug and the dish and ball were put there, too. Words were spoken, tears were shed, and then Liz said, "Hey, girls, I think I have some frozen cherries left from a few months ago, how 'bout we make a nice cherry pie?"

"Yay!" They yelled and smiled through their tears.

Vince of course, hadn't been able to get out of his mind just what he had hit with his shovel. There was a little daylight left, so while Liz and the girls made their way to the house, he took the shovel back to where he had first started digging. He worked at it for a bit, then noticed something that looked like leather. His first thought was that he had managed to find the burial site of one of the pets of the previous owners, but after a little more excavation work it became clear that it was a briefcase or suitcase of some kind. Now he was really curious. Maybe it was a hidden stash from a 1920s bank job; he smiled at the clearly stupid thought.

Finally he was able to extract the item from its resting place and it was, indeed, a *case* of some kind, wrapped in clear plastic. A very nice one, actually, and it also bore some initials. It appeared to be brown and it was bulging, its contents obviously significant for its size. It was caked in dirt. It was also *very* heavy.

Vince looked toward the house and saw Liz and the girls through the window. They were in the kitchen doing whatever it was you did to make a pie. He decided not to take his buried treasure into the house. It was too dirty anyway. He made his way over to his man cave where there was a table for him to open this strange container and see what was inside. Entering the small structure, he switched on the lights, which included a hanging fixture centered over a large conference-like table. The table was completely covered with books, newspapers, file folders, magazines, paper plates, and paper coffee cups. It all had the look of some kind of paper pusher's unkempt laboratory.

He put the crust-covered case on the floor and began moving the material on top of the table to make room for his examination. After clearing an area about three feet by three feet he placed the case there. He carefully tore away the plastic wrap—or whatever it was. Now, in the light he could see that the case was definitely made of leather and it was locked. He also could make out the initials—"H.A.R.P." Were they for a person, or an organization, or what? Interestingly, and actually surprisingly, he thought, the case bore no evidence of any kind of water damage. It had to have been there for at least fifteen years because they had not noticed any case burials while they lived there, so that would date it back to at least the 1990s. But it actually looked much older than that. It was a style of case he had never seen and it looked like it could be fifty years old, or more, he thought.

He wanted to open it, of course he did, but not in a way that would destroy the case itself. He tried using a paper clip as a make shift lock pick, but he had no clue what he was doing. Finally, curiosity getting the best of him, he found a crowbar, and though it was probably overkill, used it to pry open his find. He looked inside and saw various papers, something wrapped in plastic (a book?) and a couple of other objects, all wrapped in some kind of once clear plastic—one was a small leather case about the size of a candy bar and a larger item, awkwardly formed. He carefully began to remove the items from the case. First, the papers, which he placed neatly on the table, then the little leather case. Next the larger item, then finally at the bottom of the case he found the book, also wrapped in plastic.

He turned the little object over and around to get a look at it from all sides, then he applied a small amount of pressure and to his amazement it opened easily. Inside was a small metallic object and pulling it out he immediately recognized it as a miniature camera, bearing the name *Minox*. What had he stumbled onto here? He found his adrenaline pumping. This was really cool!

Vince's cell phone rang and he looked to see that it was Liz calling.

"Hello?"

"The pie's in the oven and the girls are asking for you."

"Sorry Liz, I'll be there in a couple of minutes, just cleaning up out here."

"What're you doing?"

"I just wanted to fill in that other hole and got distracted," he said. For some reason, he wasn't sure why, he opted not to tell her what he had found. In fact, he wasn't all that sure what it was, anyway. The short phone call over, he gathered the things he had taken out of the mysterious case and put them back in. He then took it over to a shelf on one of the walls and placed it on the floor beside it, covering it with some old newspapers and magazines. And he still wasn't sure why he was doing this. He just had a sense that he had found something quite interesting.

Chapter Two

TEMPLETON DAVIS'S JOURNEY en route to becoming a media star in two areas—broadcasting and writing—was more of an odyssey. After all, someone with a PhD, who had also been a Rhodes Scholar, was an unusual suspect when grouped with most of the other "talkers" filling the mostly AM airwaves with animated noise every day.

He was born in January of 1960 in Eureka, Missouri. Back then it was a sleepy little village nearly 30 miles west of St. Louis—but since Temp was about 11 years old it had been the home of a major regional amusement park that helped the area to grow significantly. Most summers the family pitched their tent (literally) near Branson, Missouri and beautiful Table Rock Lake. This was long before Branson became, well, Branson. Back then it was somewhat like Eureka, barely on the map. But it was a great place for camping, swimming, fishing, and summer fun.

Davis was an excellent student with the potential for scholarships at some fine institutions far from home, but he opted to stay close. His father died of a sudden heart attack when Temp was 13 and being an only child he found it very hard to leave his mother alone. So after graduating from the local high school (valedictorian of the class of 1978), he enrolled at the University of Missouri at St. Louis. He majored in history—assuming at the time that he would teach—but also minored in journalism. He developed an interest in broadcasting, as well. This began with a part time job at the university's radio station, KWMU, which also happened to be affiliated with *National Public Radio*.

Though his work at the beginning involved little more than errand running, he made it a point to carefully observe everything around him—from the work of technicians and their handling of the large reel-to-reel tape recorders, to the on air personalities. Before long, he was thought of as a member of the team and was even given the occasional "on-air" opportunity to read a line or two during a break. His interest in journalism and flare for language—even as a student—impressed those around him. And it didn't hurt that he had a good natural voice for radio. He loved everything about broadcasting and because radio was thought by many to be a thing on the way out, very few others even tried to intern at the station. Temp had great latitude and freedom to learn all the aspects of broadcasting. Early on he decided that this would be his main career focus—much to the chagrin and disappointment of many friends and would-be mentors who saw this as a waste of brains and talent.

By the time he graduated (with honors), young Templeton Davis was a very familiar voice to the more than 200,000 KWMU listeners around the region. And on his last day before heading to his next adventure, the staff surprised him with a pretty neat going away gift: an hour-long show featuring callers and station people with words of thanks and encouragement. He was a young man who was going places and, frankly, many at the university assumed, or at least hoped, that he would make his way back to them one day. But that was not to be. Temp's mother passed away during his junior year in college—after a long battle with lung cancer—and following that he decided it was time to find out about the world beyond the American Midwest.

During the first semester of his senior year one of his professors suggested that he apply for a Rhodes scholarship to Oxford in England for graduate work. Such things were always long shots—and no one from the UMSTL had ever made the cut, though several had applied over the years. He put together an application package and was more than surprised when he was invited to an interview with the American agent for the program. He was accepted and a couple of months after graduating from UMSTL found himself on his way to England and Exeter College at the University of Oxford. They would be two years filled with academic challenge, the broadening of horizons, and personal growth.

The focus of his research was Winston Churchill in the years after World War II, a time period largely ignored up till then by scholars in favor of the Winnie's more famous and stellar moments. Temp paid great attention to the elections of 1945. Churchill's successful war government was defeated and succeeded by the Labor Party and Clement Atlee. He would eventually leverage his research about and interest in Churchill into his first bestseller. But his time at Oxford was about much more than research and the pursuit of a prestigious academic degree (and accompanying pedigree); it was also a period for emotional, intellectual, and political formation. He became a bit of an anglophile and over the ensuing years had made his way back to the picturesque city of spires and scholars on the Thames whenever possible. Once he even debated at the famous Oxford Union, taking the "pro" side of the question: "Is the British Monarchy relevant and should it be preserved?" He was amused at the local reportage and all the comments about an American defending the Queen and her heirs.

When Templeton Davis returned to the states following his studies at Oxford, he attended Georgetown University in Washington, DC, earning his PhD in political history. During his year and a half at Georgetown there was an attempt (he didn't realize it until later) to recruit him for the CIA. But more significantly, it was then and there that he met Carolee.

Templeton Davis and Carolee Hamilton were soul mates from the start. She had fine, soft red hair and blue eyes, a combination that never ceased to draw Temp in. They married a week after Temp finished his studies at Georgetown. She was an heiress of sorts. Raised by her father after her mother died when Carolee was seven years old, she, also the only child, inherited controlling interest in her Dad's chain of fast food restaurants in the Midwest, based in Chicago, which made for a very lucrative business.

The couple moved around a lot as Temp was getting his broadcasting career up and running—climbing the ladder, such as it was. He turned down an offer back in St. Louis, one that combined work at KWMU and the promise of eventual airtime on National Public Radio (NPR) and a light-load teaching schedule that he would be able to invent to his liking. But he didn't see much future in the public broadcasting side of things and sensed that the real future was in commercial radio. Along the way, he worked for stations in Richmond, Virginia, Buffalo, New York, Charlottesville, Virginia, Scranton, Pennsylvania, and Detroit, Michigan, before landing the job at WBVY in Rosslyn, Virginia, just across the Potomac from Washington, DC, not far from where he and Carolee had first met.

Broadcasting to an audience in the nation's capital, it wasn't long before he began to be noticed by more than commuters in their cars. His moderate approach—tilting some to the conservative side, but never with the stridency of the more doctrinaire talkers—became increasingly popular. His NPR background served him well as he tried his best to give the program a cerebral feel. Within a year of his arrival in Washington, his program was picked up for syndication in a few "test market" cities and the results were positive. He had become a creative alternative for listeners weary of the scorched earth broadcasting style of many talk radio hosts. Of course, he was also criticized—by voices on the right and left—but that just seemed to reinforce his philosophy often crystalized by one of his trademark witticisms: "The middle of the road is a good place to be if there is a wreck on both sides!"

Temp was on his way to success in his chosen profession and enjoying life with Carolee. Then came the accident. She was driving home alone one January night after dinner with a few friends in Fairfax—sort of a girl's night out—when her BMW skidded on a patch of ice and hit a telephone pole. She died instantly. Whatever success he had following this—some of it significant and substantial—there was part of him that could never fully enjoy its fruits without Carolee.

By now, his live morning program, which ran three hours, from eight AM until eleven AM in the east, called, not surprisingly, *Templeton Davis Live*, aired on more than a thousand stations, a mix of AM and FM across the dial, as well as Satellite Radio and Internet Streaming. There were some estimates that his audience was more than 35 million at any given time.

He was blessed with a melodious voice, though minus the typical radio announcer inflections. Some called it soothing, an unusual quality for someone in the sort-of-conservative trench warfare business. His highly developed vocabulary (he worked on this all the time, always trying to find ways to work in his latest acquired obscure word into the conversation—and he had some help) combined with the blue-blood-sounding voice—no doubt cultivated via the environs of public radio and Oxford—gave off an unmistakable air of erudition. There was the hint of patrician in the way he talked.

Davis stood a little over six feet tall with brown hair, graying at the temples, and blue eyes. His weight hovered around 200 pounds, but it was a constant battle for him, especially in recent years. He usually appeared somewhat rumpled, even though he could afford, and regularly purchased, well-made clothes. On him, they sometimes looked as if he slept in them. This tended to bring out the mother hen in some of the women in his orbit, but he never seemed to notice. His hair always looked like he missed his haircut appointment the day before.

Occasionally someone would mention that he sounded a little like the late T.V. actor William Conrad, though with a hint of William F. Buckley (that'd be the patrician part). He relished the comparison, because Conrad had been a broadcasting hero to him. He would regularly remind those who mentioned it in his presence that Bill Conrad was first and foremost a great radioman before the days of television. In fact, he was the radio voice of U.S. Marshall Matt Dillon on *Gunsmoke*. But when the show made its successful leap to the still primitive television tube, Conrad was left behind in the Dodge City dust, replaced by a guy named James Arness, tall, handsome—thin—who looked the part. Conrad was also the voice of the classic 60s TV series *The Fugitive*, as well as the narrator for the Cold War cartoon show, *Bullwinkle and Rocky*. Davis was so enamored of the late great Mr. Conrad that he named his production company *Dodge City Media*, in a nod to Conrad's radio portrayal of Marshall Dillon.

Davis's broadcasting formula had evolved into an eclectic blend, somewhat unusual for a sort-of conservative talk show host. He did some interviews—actually letting the guest do most of the talking. He learned the art of the interview growing up in the St. Louis, Missouri area in the 1960s listening to KMOX and though he would never be involved with sports radio, his hero as far as interview skills was concerned, was Jack Buck, broadcaster for that city's baseball, the Cardinals. The guy never asked a question, but rather made brief, leading, statements and then paused, letting the guest take it from there. It was so seamless and Templeton thought, so very cool.

Along with the radio interviews the show occasionally included some sketch humor. He had a creative team under contract, a group skilled at parody. And, of course, there was ample Davis commentary, a stream of consciousness about whatever was happening in the news. It made for an entertaining three hours. Many who listened to him didn't agree with him, but they liked him. He was too nice of a guy, they thought, to be on talk radio. This was in evidence anytime he appeared in public—crowds flocked to his engagements, most of which were sold out a few days after being publicized. He was paid very well for these personal appearances.

His most recent book, written with the help of a dedicated staff, made the *New York Times* best-seller list almost immediately, as had several prior works, mostly about politics and history, with just a hint of mystery to make it interesting. In fact, several of his books became *New York Times* best-sellers—beginning with a popular tome about Winston Churchill's life during the period between his surprising election loss in 1945 right after the war, to his command performance at Fulton, Missouri in 1946 and the quickly famous "Iron Curtain" speech.

His favorite writing, though, was fiction—particularly the spy-thriller novel. The genre was a taste—better, an obsession—he had acquired at Oxford. He had also picked up the odd story and rumor while at Exeter and hoped one day to dig into it all more—tales of real-life spies and intrigue. Reviewers had been hard on him for his fiction, but he was determined to do it and do it well and was actually getting noticeably better at it. None of his novels had become blockbusters—yet, as he regularly reminded himself—he loved getting lost in the creation of a complicated and compelling story.

But for whatever reason, he hadn't written a word in nearly six months.

Davis was a celebrity, more than a mere broadcaster; he was a fully evolved *personality*. He was also well off, having carefully managed his income and investments over the years, yet he didn't live like it. Sure, he flew from place to place in a private jet and seldom settled for less than the best. It's just that he really didn't get out all that much. He wasn't a recluse per se, but certainly a homebody. Possibly this is the reason those who knew him well never thought of him as a rich guy. He had managed without effort to keep his sense of simplicity.

And as far as the private jet was concerned, it was the one indulgence—toy, if you will—he allowed himself to luxuriate in. Davis learned to fly just a couple of years after he learned to drive a car and he had a lifelong love for flying and airplanes, beginning with an extensive collection of model planes when he was a kid. So when he had the chance to scoop up his own—a beautiful 1997 model Hawker 800XP from some hedge fund former billionaire when the economy started to tank in 2008, he jumped at taking over the lease without batting an eye. It was so worth it, he thought.

That was also when Templeton Davis met and hired Milton Darnell, a guy who had flown combat missions in the second Gulf War and was then serving as an agent in the FBI en route to flying planes for the Bureau. That is, until Davis made him an offer he couldn't refuse. Soon Darnell, who had grown up poor in the Detroit, Michigan suburb of Inkster, was working personally for Davis as a security man, personal assistant in some logistical matters, and of course, co-pilot when they flew the Hawker, named *The Carolee*.

Darnell was a tall—well over six feet—strikingly handsome African-American man. He was married to a wonderful lady named Kacie and they had a son named after him—Milton Jack Darnell, Jr. But everyone called the young boy Jacky. Kacie loved her husband's new job, having never warmed up to Milton working for the FBI. Sure he'd be flying planes—eventually—but that was only after the requisite few years in the field. Frankly, it kept her awake at night. Now she slept very well. After all, how dangerous could it be to guard a radio host and fly with him here, there and everywhere? Sometimes she and Jacky tagged along for the ride, which was always fun and they'd wind up spending a few down days in this city or that where Templeton Davis happened to be doing his celebrity thing.

The other good thing about her husband's job was that he worked from his home a lot, which meant he was around. He was always on call, mind you—and in touch with his boss. But he didn't keep regular hours at an office, per se. In fact, most of his duties took place outside of regular office and broadcast hours—trips and such.

So Milton Darnell was nowhere around when Templeton Davis saw Vince Benton walk by his always-opened office door and he called to him, "Hey, Vince!" Benton turned and walked back a few steps to his boss's office and popped his head in.

"Heard about your dog—bummer. How're the girls doing?"

"They're fine, went back to school today. Had time for some closure yesterday. Thanks, by the way, for understanding. Good show today," Vince said, trying to change the subject. "I thought the callers were top notch."

Ignoring the comment about the show—callers were not his favorite feature—Davis chose to keep talking about the dead dog. "No prob. Had a dog once when I was a kid. Ran off. Cried for three days."

Vince made his way to a chair in front of Temp's desk and sat down.

"So—you have a funeral or something?"

"Actually, we did and then the girls and Liz made some pie."

"Ah, yes—cherry pie. Wouldn't mind some of that myself."

"Well, funny you should mention that, because I was thinking of asking you out to the house tomorrow, if you have any time. I found something you might find interesting, what with your love of intrigue and spy stuff. Not sure what to make of it, maybe you can give me a hand."

"Really?" For the first time Temp was actually interested in this conversation. "What ya got?"

"Well, when I was digging a hole, you know to bury the dog, right by our cherry tree, I hit something. Had to actually start a new hole. Then after we buried Ranger and the girls were back in the house, I decided to see what I had hit. Turns out, it was something buried back there. Probably been there for years."

"What was it?" asked Templeton, his attention now completely focused.

"Well, a briefcase of some kind ..."

"You found one of those legendary briefcase nukes from the Cold War?"

"No," Vince laughed, "Not that—but it had a camera in it and tripod and some kind of odd looking book wrapped in plastic."

"You got my attention. What time do you want me there—how about I come over for breakfast?"

"Well, uh, better make it later—I don't want Liz to freak out, we move a little lazy and slow on Saturdays. How 'bout lunch time?"

"I'll be there. Any markings on the case?"

"Yeah. It had the word 'HARP' on it."

"HARP—you mean like what angels play?"

"Yep."

"Hmmm … what's that line from *Alice in Wonderland*? *Curiouser and Curiouser.*" Davis smiled as his mind instantly flashed back to Oxford and to conversations in pubs like the *Eagle and Child* and the *Lamb and Flag* over lukewarm pints of ale about the likes of Lewis, Tolkien, and that very twisted man, Charles Dodgson, a.k.a. Lewis Carroll.

Vince went back to his office and called Liz. "Honey, Temp is gonna drop by tomorrow around lunch time—that OK?"

"Well, I *was* gonna take the girls shopping. Wasn't really planning to make a fancy lunch for your boss. Can you play host without me?"

Vince actually liked that idea, since he hadn't told his wife about the mysterious briefcase. He wasn't sure why. He just hadn't gotten around to it. Now, it could wait a bit longer.

Chapter Three
June 1951

IT WAS A beautiful day for a drive through the scenic Northern
Virginia countryside. The driver had no way of knowing that the curves and
hills along the road he traveled—U.S. 29, Lee Highway—would one day
become a virtual gauntlet of housing developments accompanied by bur-
geoning commercial sprawl. In June of 1951 all of that was beyond anyone's wildest imagination.

Having left his Washington, DC home at 4100 Nebraska Avenue NW,
he proceeded along MacArthur Avenue, then Canal Road, traveling not too
far from the familiar restaurants and taverns of Georgetown he had grown
to love during his brief sojourn in the United States while serving as First
Secretary to the British Embassy and as liaison between the Embassy and
America's intelligence services.

Crossing the Key Bridge he raced south along Lee Highway trying to
put sufficient distance between where he had been and where he was going,
both geographically and figuratively. Soon Arlington was far behind—Falls
Church, too. He wasn't actually all that sure exactly where he was going. He
just knew that he had to find *that* spot he had scouted out in late March,
though the previous trip was in weather not nearly as pleasant as this gorgeous day.

He remembered that there was a left-turn onto a narrow road, then a
certain bend of the road somewhere the other side of Fairfax, that's what he
recalled. And there was a fairly large cherry tree a few hundred feet or so

from the road. It had been covered with beautiful white blossoms. That was
what stood out that day in his mind's eye. He loved cherry trees. They
reminded him of his boyhood days when there was an old *hedelfingen* cherry
tree outside his bedroom window. Once, during a drive around the
Shenandoah area over by the Blue Ridge Mountains, he found several
dozen such *prunus avium* trees. But finding one this far from there, a solitary
tree eschewing the crowd to live and stand alone, well this was something.
Now if he could just find it. It was the perfect spot. In a way, the tree
reminded him of himself.

The driver's mind was racing even faster than the car. Just that morning his world had been turned upside down—no small feat for someone
who daily managed to navigate his own personal wilderness of mirrors.
There was a meeting in his office, followed by his abrupt announcement, "I
think I'll go home and have a drink …" He did. Then another—a double.
But by now the alcohol was barely felt, having been forced from his blood-
stream by surging adrenaline. He drove the powerful dark green 1941
Lincoln Continental Convertible sans top and the wind massaged his face,
while his usually in-place hair flapped from side to side. The machine's
powerful 12-cylinder engine seemed to be happy to be out on the open
road, having sat idle for several weeks since its *real* owner had boarded the
Queen Mary for England.

Finally, after what seemed to be hours, but in fact, less than one, he
saw the spot up ahead. It was just as he remembered it. The tree no longer
bore the blossoms of spring. Its branches were now abundantly covered
with dark, sweet fruit. He guided the large automobile off the road and
began to move it toward the site, but was slowed down by the soft earth.
Deciding not to chance getting stuck—the last thing he wanted or needed
was any other eyes on him—he stopped the car at a point less than 50 feet
from the road and went immediately to the boot, smiling at the Americans
and their odd word for it—"trunk."

He reached in and grabbed a large leather bag almost the size of a
small suitcase. He knew it as a *portmanteau*, but his American friends
wouldn't have a clue as to what that meant. It was a Gladstone bag, a very
nice one he had acquired years back at a fine leather shop in the
Westminster area of London at home. The case had two sections and a

place for secrets, of which this man had many. He earnestly hoped he wasn't seeing the last of it. Then seizing a shovel he had taken from his garage back in the city, he began making his way toward the big tree. Reaching his destination, he looked left and right seeing no one around or on the road. It was a nearly isolated spot. He removed his tweed sport coat, loosened his necktie, rolled up his white shirtsleeves, and finding a spot partially concealed from the road by the tree, he began to dig. He wanted to go down at least four or five—maybe six—feet, creating a hole large enough for the leather satchel.

Not used to this kind of work, he found himself further energized by the digging. Then, sensing he had created a sufficient void, he dropped the shovel, removed his handkerchief and wiped a small amount of sweat from his brow. As he folded the cloth to place back in his pocket his eyes rested on his initials, all four of them, embroidered on it—noting that those same initials were actually also on the leather satchel—H.A.R.P. Reaching for the bag, he wondered if he should try to remove them. But he thought better of it. After all, he was sure to come back to this spot to retrieve what he was burying as soon as—how did the Yanks say it?—the coast was clear, that's it! This was to be a temporary stash; he was sure he'd be working with the contents of the case again very soon.

He placed the satchel in the hole, grabbed the shovel and went to work replacing the soil. Eventually, satisfied that he had buried it well, he picked up his jacket and shovel in hand and started back to the car. Then he stopped abruptly and reached for a dark cherry from the tree, allowing himself a momentary indulgence. Eating it, he spit out the pit and took another, then another. The burst of flavor triggered his memory and for an instant he was back in England; then he heard his father's severe voice reprimanding him—his old man at once scared and fascinated him (he had that effect on many people). After a few moments, he went back to the Lincoln and soon he was heading swiftly north on Lee Highway wondering what the next few days held for him. Would he be able to come back soon to this beautiful and quite delicious tree by the road? If not, had he buried all the material safely enough? Had he double-checked everything? For someone used to stealthy work, he found himself very nervous. He was glad to be alone. To engage even in small talk just now, as shaken as he was, would only magnify his problem with stuttering. A problem he could—and did—no doubt blame on dear old Dad.

Of course, he had every reason to be concerned. The news he had received earlier that day was unnerving. "The bird has flown" hadn't bothered him that much, he was braced for that. But not what followed. The "bird" was a reference to a fellow named Donald MacLean—someone who had been long suspected of being a spy for the Soviets with the code name HOMER. Now came word that MacLean had run. No news there. In fact, that was good news, something the driver himself had helped to arrange. Then he was told, "And what's worse is that Burgess is gone, too!"

"Burgess?" And he braced himself for the storm certain to come.

Harold Adrian Russell Philby, known to one and all as "Kim," didn't have to conjure up feigned surprise at this revelation. Years later he would write that he was shocked by this—stunned in fact. But he knew what was happening and had, in fact, had a hand in it all, though holding out hope that Burgess would stop short and not make life a living hell for his good old friend, Kim. He had given Burgess a message for MacLean—that MI-5 was close to arresting him, believing him to have been passing secrets to the Russians. The message also contained instructions for Burgess. But, frankly, you never knew what Guy was going to do; he was the poster-child for unpredictable and contrary.

Guy Burgess had, in fact, lived at the house on Nebraska Avenue with Philby and his wife. He was now driving Burgess's Lincoln, his pride and joy purchased just a few months before for the sum of $1,145 from a Virginia dealer. They were *known* to be friends. Now surely suspicion would be cast on Kim Philby. Was he a spy, as well, the Yanks and Brits would surely wonder? This was what he faced and hoped he would be able to survive. Thus the need to get some of his "tools" out of the house. It wasn't stuff that was easily disposed of, and he was very much hoping he'd have future occasion to use it in America—but for now he had to try to bury it somewhere. Somewhere far enough away, yet close enough to retrieve should the need arise. *Sure it would. Sure it would,* he tried to tell himself.

Then it hit him—he had forgotten the shovel! But he decided not to return to the scene just yet, the shovel would be there waiting for him when he went back to dig the case back up. Actually, it'd be pretty convenient.

But in fact, Kim Philby would never go back to the big cherry tree for its fruit or the stash buried beneath the shadow of its branches. Within days he too would be on a ship headed home to England, having been unceremoniously and unofficially deported as someone quite unwelcome in the States by the CIA and FBI. J. Edgar Hoover himself had demanded it of the British Embassy, or else things would grow quite cold between the allies. Hoover's threats were effective. Philby would never again set foot on American soil. And in the fateful year 1963, he would join his comrades in espionage, MacLean and Burgess, in Moscow.

Russia, for whom they all had secretly worked most of their adult lives, would be his home for the rest of his pathetic days. He would live and die as a British pariah, though a Soviet hero—they would even print a postage stamp in his honor. The cause of death would be a decades-long overdose on the drug of deceit.

And he would never know the ultimate fate of the personal treasure he buried that day in the Virginia countryside.

Chapter Four
Georgetown—Washington, DC

TEMPLETON DAVIS LIVED in Georgetown just a short ride over the Key Bridge from his radio studio in Rosslyn, Virginia, an unincorporated area of Arlington County, and the home of several media outlets. When he wrote that first bestseller about Churchill, he used the money to buy a town house just a few blocks from the heart of the busy shopping area. He loved being close enough to walk to everything he needed. He acquired other homes soon, one a farm just outside Charlottesville, Virginia (which he turned around and sold for a hefty profit before the real estate bubble burst—he nearly doubled his money in the over-heated market), another with a view of the ocean a bit north of Palm Beach, Florida, and of course, there was his midtown Manhattan apartment near Carnegie Hall in New York City. But the Georgetown domicile felt the most like home to him—elegant, yet quaint.

Occasionally, when the weather was just right, he even walked to work—took him about forty minutes. He particularly loved this time of year, when the air turned crisp and cool and the leaves morphed into comforting colors. Temp's two-story home on N Street NW was spacious by Georgetown standards, and since he lived by himself now, it had more than enough room for his needs. But there wasn't a day when he didn't miss Carolee.

They had no children and no real ties to the community out in Fairfax County, so he sold their home in Vienna and bought the town home about six months after her death—now almost five years ago. But he wished with all his heart that he could share it all with her.

Well meaning friends had tried to fix him up with potential love interests, but it was almost as if something had been disabled in his heart by the death of his wife. He found himself channeling all his energy and interest into work and career. At first friends thought it to be therapeutic, then some began to whisper that it was becoming somewhat unhealthy. But they knew better than to push their friend. Possibly this was the *secret* of his success.

To most on his staff it was obvious that Valerie Doling was devoted to her boss beyond the emotional bounds of employer/employee matters, but Davis was clueless. He would occasionally invite Valerie to lunch and he'd talk about the show with her, totally unaware of how her feelings toward him had grown. She spent a lot of time thinking about the nature of hope.

On this particular Friday evening, Temp—alone—stopped by *Martin's Tavern* at the corner of Wisconsin Avenue and his own N Street NW as he did regularly for their excellent prime rib. He loved places like this in Georgetown. They had character, not to mention history. Davis was an espionage buff—he had more than 1,000 books in his personal library related to the subject. And he enjoyed the legends about intrigue taking place at the tables and bars of such places—places such as *Martin's Tavern*, which lays claim to be where Jack Kennedy proposed to Jackie way back when. Of course, the fact that the restaurant was just a few blocks from his house didn't hurt either.

He sat down at the bar and the bartender—a man who looked well past retirement age named Gus (really)—brought him his usual, an Arnold Palmer. Temp was not much of a drinker. Maybe he would indulge in an occasional glass of Merlot, or once in a while a bit of single malt Scotch, or a rare Guinness, but never to excess.

"Heard your show today, Mr. Davis," Gus said.

Templeton had long given up trying to convince Gus, who was about three decades ahead of him in age, to stop calling him "sir" or "Mr. Davis." Had to be one of those old-school bartender things, like the slightly stained vest and well-worn bow tie.

"Thanks for listening," Temp said, not really wanting to re-hash the broadcast's talking points. "Pretty slow tonight for a Friday," he said, looking over the room and gently changing the subject.

"Yes sir, I 'magine folks are enjoying the great weather—it's a beautiful night."

"Indeed it is," Davis replied, strongly hoping to end this tortured light banter.

He reached for a cocktail napkin and pulled out his outrageously expensive fountain pen and began to doodle—writing HARP, then H—A—R—P, then H.A.R.P. He found himself lost in thought about his conversation with Vince Benton earlier. Those letters meant something. But what? He ordered the prime rib, with a baked potato, a Caesar salad with extra anchovies, and of course the restaurant's signature popover pastry, and continued to doodle, now on his third cocktail napkin. When the salad came, he picked at it, fully absorbed in what he was writing and trying to figure out.

Then a thought came to him and he had the urgent desire to race home to his study to look something up. Surprising himself, not to mention Gus, he asked for his food to be wrapped to go. Quickly, the fine meal was placed in various manifestations of Styrofoam and then a large shopping bag. He paid the bill and was out the door, zigzagging with his head down so as not to be easily recognized; he moved in and out of pedestrian traffic toward his home a few blocks away. Ten minutes later, he entered the house, disarmed the alarm, then quickly armed it again behind him, taking his food into the kitchen.

He made his way to his study—the heart beat of his house—by far his favorite room. When he bought the place, he loved that the previous owners had taken out one of the upstairs rooms, making the main floor living room area larger—higher ceiling and all. But Templeton Davis knew the moment he saw it that this would not be any old, ordinary living room. It would be his study—or, better yet—his *library*. Bookshelves were installed, custom made, of course, and eventually they became home to his nearly 3,000 volumes of history, politics, and—yes—hundreds of books known generally as spy novels. From Le Carré, to Forsythe, to just about every author in the genre, the library was an archive of espionage writing. He cultivated this aspect of his library, even receiving regular emails and calls from used booksellers here and there peddling something they had found.

He had read most of them, but not all. One day, though—one day, he promised himself. When he retired he'd never leave this room. The whole spy thing was something he had enjoyed even as a kid, but since Carolee had passed he had immersed himself even more deeply in stories of intrigue, mystery, and daring.

He reached into his pocket and pulled out several crumpled napkins containing his scribbling from the bar and placed them on his cluttered desk. He turned on the lamp. How many times, and ways, could one write the letters HARP? Quite a few, as it turned out. The meal in the kitchen would have to wait a bit now as he began his hunt in the library. It was moments like this that made him regret that he had never taken time to actually organize his books. They were shelved randomly and chaotically. A novel might be next to a biography, a work of history next to the latest Daniel Silva book (his favorite author at the moment).

But he knew what he was looking for by now. It was a small paperback he had picked up a few years before. A yellowish orange paperback. He smiled as he thought that, because it meant that he did have his books organized in his head—by color. The book was called, *My Silent War*, and had been written in the late 1960s by a man who had defected to the Soviet Union a few years before, a Brit named Philby, "Kim" Philby.

Temp was somewhat familiar with the story, though he hadn't actually read *that* book. He knew that Philby had been a deep-cover agent for the Russians during the Cold War, having been recruited as part of a now infamous spy ring at Cambridge University in the early 1930s. Templeton was trying to recall Kim Philby's actual full name—something told him that his first name started with the letter "H." "Howard?" "No, that's not it," he actually muttered out loud.

The bookshelves covered much of all four walls in the room, and because the ceiling was so high, they required a ladder to reach the top shelves. It was, of course, on one of these upper shelves that Temp finally found what he was looking for—after nearly an hour of searching. In the mean time, he had come across several other books about old Mr. Philby, and they formed two unmatched stacks on his desk.

Right about then he began to notice that he was very hungry. So he left the books on the desk and went back to the kitchen to warm up his meal in the microwave, returning in a few minutes with his food and a large ice water. Clearing a place in the center of his desk for the food, he began to cut into the beef, smearing some horseradish on it. Then he grabbed the little book by Philby. He searched for anything that might help and noticed almost immediately on the back cover the description: "In the annals of espionage, one name towers above all others, that of H. A. R. P. 'Kim' Philby ..." There it was—H.A.R.P., the initials of one of the most famous spies in history.

But what were they doing on something that Vince Benton had dug up in his backyard?

Intrigued, Templeton Davis quickly finished his meal and made his way to his oversized leather chair, complete with ottoman. He took Philby's little book with him. Turning on the lamp by the chair, he began to read what "Kim" Philby had written more than forty years earlier. First though, he read introductions to his edition of the book written by espionage journalist Phillip Knightley and novelist Graham Greene. Knightley asked the reader to decide if the book was a "frank confession" or rather "an insidious piece of Communist propaganda." He also wrote that, "In the history of espionage there has never been a spy like him, and now with the Cold War over, there never will be." For his part, Graham Greene, clearly an admirer of Mr. Philby (apparently, they were friends in the old days), pronounced that the book was "honest" and, insofar as propaganda was concerned "it contains none."

Hmmm ... Temp found himself thinking, why hadn't he read this one before? A wave of excitement swept over him. He was wide awake, though it was now well into the evening. Usually a man early to bed, sleep would evade him for now—he was hooked on this book. He read Philby's introduction:

This book has been written at intervals since my arrival in Moscow nearly five years ago. From time to time in the course of writing it, I took counsel with friends whose advice I valued. I accepted some of the suggestions made and rejected others. One suggestion, which I rejected,

was that I should make the book more exciting by heavier emphasis on
the hazards of the long journey from Cambridge to Moscow. I prefer to
rest on a round, unvarnished tale.

By midnight, Templeton Davis, a fast reader, had pretty much
devoured Philby's two hundred-page memoir. And he had learned some
fascinating things along the way that possibly connected to the topic of
conversation with Vince Benton hours earlier at the office. Most notably,
that just before "Kim" Philby had been booted out of America by the intelligence community, under suspicion of being a Soviet spy back in 1951, he
had disposed of some of his equipment in the Virginia countryside. The
only problem was that what Philby had described in the book as the location of his stash was nowhere near where Vince and Liz lived. Philby wrote
that he wrapped several items "into waterproof containers" and drove out
into the country to an area he described as around Great Falls, Virginia,
where he then buried the evidence.

Great Falls was a long way from Clifton in Northern Virginia. Was
Philby deliberately trying to mislead in this account? Davis scratched his
head then he rubbed his eyes. Now he was tired. He decided to try to get
some sleep before researching a bit more in the morning before driving out
to see Benton.

Chapter Five
Clifton, Virginia

LIZ MADE A large breakfast for the family on Saturday morning, eggs, sausage, even pancakes, served with very real Vermont maple syrup, though the family had never actually been way up there. She even let everyone finish off the last of the cherry pie. The girls loved that. Then she and the girls got dressed and left around ten AM to go to the Fair Oaks Mall over in Fairfax to shop. She told Vince that they'd return around two PM, but Vince knew better than to count on such exactitude when it came to Liz and the whole time-space continuum. She tended to lose all track of time when on such outings with the girls, and that was just fine. Before they left she told her husband to say hello to Templeton Davis and the girls told him to say hi to "Uncle Temp."

Vince poured a large mug of coffee and exited the back door of the house and walked briskly, sans coat, to his man cave, all the while hoping he'd left the heat on out there the night before. Entering the glorified shed he immediately smiled at the warmth. It was actually very warm, something that Liz wouldn't have liked, since she was the one tasked with paying the bills. He turned the light on, put his coffee mug down on the table and began to revisit the curiosity that had been hidden in his backyard for who knows how long.

Just as he started to sort through the satchel, he heard a car drive up. Moving over to the window, he saw that it was his boss. Kinda early, he thought, but Temp tended to keep his own time, not to mention counsel, so he opened the door and called out to Templeton Davis as he walked toward the house. The boss was wearing khaki slacks and a sweatshirt bearing the name and emblem of the University of Michigan.

"Out here, Temp!"

Davis entered the building and quickly surveyed it with a look that indicated he was less than impressed with the place. It was no book-lined library, for sure, but to each his own.

"Nice place," he said, sort of rolling his eyes.

"Well, it serves a purpose," Vince said, almost defensively.

"No, no—didn't mean anything by that. You got any more coffee?"

"Yeah, it's in the kitchen in the house, I'll grab a cup for you. Meanwhile, here's what I found last night in all its glory. Pretty weird, huh?"

"Yes ... weird," said Davis, his eyes fixed on the satchel on the large table and the various items surrounding it.

"Whadaya think it is, Temp, any idea?"

"Well, go get that cup of coffee and I'll take a quick look. In fact, I've an idea what it just might, be."

With that Vince exited his man cave and walked quickly back to the house. He found the perfect coffee mug for his boss, one that bore the words, 'History Buff,' something he had picked up at the Detroit Airport's *Henry Ford Museum Store*, and poured the coffee, moving quickly back out to the man cave. When he got back, he noticed that Temp had started to unwrap one of the items and it looked like some kind of stand or tri-pod, with a place on top for something to be attached.

Temp set the tri-pod up and then removed the little camera from its case and put it on top of the metal stand—it clearly fit.

"Know what this is?"

"No idea."

"It's a mechanism for photographing documents or papers, the kinda thing that was used decades ago by spies."

"Russian spies?" Benton inquired.

"Well, spies on both sides used cameras, but based on the markings, this looks like it was made behind what used to be known as the Iron Curtain."

"Seriously?"

"Yep, pretty sure—I've got some books on this back at my place ..."

"I'm sure you do," Vince quickly countered, knowing of his boss's penchant for espionage stuff. Some of the staff even suspected that Templeton Davis was pretty good friends with some of the high ups out at Langley.

"Fascinating," said Temp, "Simply fascinating!"

"Last night I did some research at the house, the whole 'H.A.R.P.' thing, couldn't get it out of my head and then it hit me where I might've seen it, so I started digging around in my books. Sure enough I found what I'm pretty sure the initials stand for."

"You kidding me?"

"Nope, dead serious and it's a big deal."

"Well are you gonna tell me, or what?"

"Yes, of course, but first I want us to have an 'understanding.'"

Not having a clue about anything his boss was talking about, Vince replied, "Understanding?"

"Yes. I wanna make sure that if this turns out to be what I think it is, that we are clear on what it all means."

"Temp, I usually know where you're going, but you've lost me."

"Sorry, Vince—not trying to be heavy-handed or mysterious here, but you may have stumbled onto something of historic interest and I'd like to be part of whatever steps you take from here on out."

"Well, Temp, you're the historian here, I am just a tech guy, so I have no problem following your judgment and I trust you completely. You've never done me wrong in all the years I've worked for you."

"I know that, Vince, and I appreciate the vote of confidence, but this thing could have some monetary, as well as research value."

"Research?"

"Yes, and that's my interest. I have more money than I need, but I'd love to be able to dig through all this and study it and I'm more than willing to pay you for the privilege."

"Hey, Temp, we're friends, you don't have to give me anything ..."

Davis interrupted Benton, "I'm not trying to insult you, Vince. I just want to make sure we have some clear parameters here ..."

"Temp, I just invited you over to look at something I dug up, I didn't plan to start negotiating the Treaty of Versailles with you," Benton chuckled.

"How 'bout this," Davis countered, "I give you a check for, say, $2,500 right now and we write up a little agreement, just something hand-written, that gives me the right to study these objects and be part of any decision you make about their disposition?"

"Disposition?"

"Yeah, like if you sell them or give them to a museum, I wanna be part of that."

"A financial part?"

"No, you're missing my point, Vince. I'm not interested in the money aspect, if there *is* any to be made. I'm interested in the research value and maybe I'll write that dream book I've been waiting for."

"Then you'll make money," Vince smiled.

"Okay, then I'll make money, but trust me, you know how 'into' this kind of thing I am. I'd study this for free."

"Okay, Temp, Okay, whatever you want, but keep your money, you can study all this stuff on one condition."

"That being?"

"What the hell are you talking about? What is this stuff?"

"Fair enough. Anyplace to sit out here other than that beat up chair over there?"

"Sorry. This ain't a fancy Georgetown library," Vince laughed sarcastically.

Temp suggested that they go inside and that Vince bring the items in the case with him. While Benton put the items in a clean box to take into his house, Temp made his way out to his car to fetch a few books he had brought with him.

Chapter Six

VINCE SPREAD THE items from the satchel on his kitchen table and quietly hoped Liz and the girls got lost in time and wouldn't return too soon. Temp came in carrying a stack of books. He put those on the table as well. Vince decided to make a fresh pot of coffee, this time the good stuff, a Costa Rican blend, nice and bold.

As the aroma of the fresh brewing coffee filled the room, Vince asked Temp, "So, what're we talking about, what'd ya find out?"

Reaching for a little paperback book, Temp said, "Vince, I think you may have discovered one of biggest finds of the decade."

"It's a case with a camera, Temp. How big a deal could it be?"

"Yes, but the initials, H.A.R.P. could be very significant, they could stand for Harold Adrian Russell Philby."

"Philby? Wasn't there a spy way back when named Philby … I think Kim Philby?"

"Wow, Vince, I'm impressed. I thought I was the only one on our team who'd know that."

"Well, it's a famous story and I saw a movie on BBC America a few years ago, some special mini-series they played over in England about some spies from, what was it, yeah—Cambridge University? *The Cambridge Spies,* that's it. Actually I think we have it on DVD, Liz and I both liked it, pretty well done."

"Yeah, I saw that one, too, and have been meaning to watch it again. Yes, that's the guy—Kim Philby—one of the most notorious traitors

during the Cold War. Well this is the book he wrote after he defected to
Moscow in the 1960s, 1963 I think it was, when he went from Beirut,
Lebanon to Moscow, and it was a best seller here and in England. Of
course, that was during the time when the Cold War was the dominant
generational conflict, something that touched and defined so many aspects
of life."

Temp opened the book and found the passage about Philby burying
his spy equipment and read it to Vince. When he came to the part about
Great Falls, Vince countered …

"But this is a long way from Great Falls."

"I know that Vince, but remember that this is a book written by a
master deceiver. Some people—heck, a lot of people back then—believed
that it was filled with disinformation and misdirection. It could be that he
wanted to make sure that what he had buried would never be found. And
to the best of my knowledge, which is admittedly limited, I don't think his
stash has ever popped up. Of course, I could be wrong. But think about it,
you have dug up a brief case with a spy camera in it, a case bearing Philby's
initials—coincidence? I really doubt that."

"So—you think I, or we, have Philby's stuff?"

"I really do. But, as I say, I'd like to study it some more and it's
important, in my opinion, that we keep this very quiet. Does Liz know
about it?"

"Nope. Didn't tell her, yet."

"Well, you mind waiting on that? It might be better to know what we
have before we start noising it about," Temp suggested.

"Sure, no prob."

Templeton Davis looked at the pile of material on the kitchen table
and grabbed what looked like a book—a book wrapped in some kind of
protective plastic, and began to tear away at the wrapping. With all the discussion about agreements and cameras and spy stuff, it struck him that they
hadn't even checked this tidbit out.

"What do you think it is, Temp?"

"Looks like some kind of journal or diary … Wow … this could be
gold!"

Though the bookish looking item had been completely wrapped, it still seemed to bear some signs of wear and tear, possibly even water damage. Or maybe it was just old. The material buried by super spy Kim Philby back in 1951 would be more than sixty years old.

There were no markings on the cover, and it now very much appeared to be a journal; this conclusion was confirmed when it was opened as each page, or at least most of the pages, had been written on in cursive, likely with a fountain pen, indicated by the widening and narrowing of the letters written on the pages. Davis preferred fountain pens, so he was familiar with the look of prose written with one.

The final item pulled from the mysterious satchel was a small booklet of sorts, about twice the size of a standard passport. Its pages contained column after column of numbers and letters in random order.

"Hey," Temp said. "Ya know what this is?"

Vince's relatively blank stared vacated the need for actual words in response.

"This looks like it's what was called a 'one-time pad.' Spies used them to decipher coded messages. I read about these all the time in novels. Primitive, but very effective, as long as the key doesn't fall into the wrong hands. Some of them I've read about were actually printed on 'flash paper' for quick burning, but this book seems to be on regular paper."

"So, what does it all mean, Temp?"

"Well, at the least, it means that we definitely have the stash from a spy from a long time ago, and I'd bet a month's salary that all this shit belonged to Mr. Kim Philby."

"Well, your salary is bigger than mine, Temp," Vince said. "I'll wait a bit before I put my money down." Their eyes met and they both smiled.

Just then the phone rang. Vince answered it. It was Liz in the car with the girls to say they were on their way home. They'd be there in less than ten minutes. Vince told Temp that he'd prefer the stuff be put away before she got home.

"Sure, let's get it all in the box. Hey, would you mind if I borrowed this journal for the weekend? I'll bring it to work on Monday. I'm intrigued by it and would love to read through it back at home where I have my spy laboratory of books," Temp smiled.

"No problem. Have at it. Lemme know if you find any atomic secrets."

"Mind if I take this possible 'one time pad,' too?"

"Not at all. It's not like I've got a clue about any of it."

They gathered all the "evidence" and walked the box back out to the man cave, securing it in a corner under some blankets. By the time they exited the building, they heard a car horn honk and Vince and Temp waved at Liz and the girls in the White Ford Expedition that was approaching the long driveway. It pulled up next to Temp's Burgundy Range Rover and Liz got out and gave Temp a hug.

"Stay for dinner? I'm making a big pot of my special chili—maybe even some cornbread."

"Sounds tempting, Liz. Rain check? I've got some research to do."

"Always working, Temp. Ever make time for some fun?"

"Liz, you know I love and live for my work. In fact, Vince and I were talking about my idea for a new book. Another bestseller for sure."

"Okay, well, let us throw the book party and then I'll make a *big* batch of chili!"

"You got it," Temp smiled, "Hey, Vince, I'll catch you Monday, remember, we have that former CIA spook in studio to talk about his new book."

And the Range Rover headed back to Georgetown.

Chapter Seven
Georgetown

THE DRIVE HOME to Georgetown took about forty minutes, including the stop at a *McDonald's* drive thru in Arlington. His wealth and success had never been able to trump his taste for fast food. When Templeton Davis got home that Saturday afternoon he returned to his library, this time with the items from the mysterious case in tow. He wanted to go through it page by page, but first he fired up his Mac desk top computer and spent a while searching the internet for articles about Philby and what had happened back in 1951. He was sure he knew the basic elements of the story, reinforced by what he read the night before in Philby's book. It was the stuff of espionage legend and had been popularized by that British mini-series, but he wanted to make sure that there weren't any holes in his grasp of the story.

What he found was a labyrinth of often-contradictory articles. There were references to a "third man." Davis recalled seeing an old black and white movie starring Joseph Cotten and Orson Welles, with that name— *"The Third Man."* It was set in Vienna, Austria he thought he remembered, sometime after World War II, something about spies—and he made a mental note to watch it again.

He was hooked and embarking on a journey into obsession. It was familiar territory for him. Even as a kid, he'd get an idea in his head and soon find himself reading everything he could about it, becoming a self-styled expert. He had read as a boy about the great inventor Thomas Alva

Edison and how he'd go to a library each week and use a ruler to measure a
foot of books, checking them out for reading over the next several days.
Davis started to try to do this, but instead of it becoming something random, he'd seize on a subject and exhaust his local library's supply of information. Then it'd be on to the next one. Lots of time it was sports, which is
how he had become such a boxing trivia buff.

Now, for the first time in a very long time he found himself feeling the
same way. As he visited site after site dealing directly or indirectly with his
research about Kim Philby, he noted books that were referenced or advertised and bounced back and forth between what he was reading and an
order page at his favorite used book source web site, adding several titles to
his 'shopping cart.'

This "third man" reference he kept seeing seemed to be pivotal in
understanding Philby's story. Apparently, in May of 1951, two Brits fled to
Moscow—two men who had been involved in espionage, Donald MacLean
and Guy Burgess. At the time, Burgess had been living at Philby's house in
Washington, DC—some place on Nebraska Avenue NW. Kim was stationed in America's capital by MI-6, Great Britain's 'CIA,' though they'd
very much resent the comparison since they had been in the spy business
for decades before the "Yanks" started with the Office of Strategic Services
(OSS) in World War II, then the Central Intelligence Agency (CIA) being
founded in 1947. The reality was that the Brits had their MI-5, sort of like
our FBI, dealing primarily with domestic matters, and MI-6, the arm of
their intelligence services that dealt with international stuff—like our much,
much younger CIA. Of course, their long-time use of something called 'the
Official Secrets Act' ensured that much of the sordid, even lurid stuff of the
spy game never saw the light of day.

At the time, Kim Philby was the rising star in the world of British
intelligence work, someone, it was said, who was being groomed for the top
job—'C,' the cryptic, yet honored title of their spy czar, the head of MI-6.
But all of this was to change because of an episode that seemed to be so
very amateurish—at least for those who prided themselves on a reputation
for being the best at the great game.

Apparently, Philby, MacLean, Burgess, and a few others were part of a
group of spies recruited at Cambridge University in the mid-1930s. They

were tapped and trained by Soviet Intelligence to become "deep penetration" agents as part of a grand scheme to infiltrate the upper echelons of British life and power. Up until then, much spy work was carried out by lower-level employees, clerks, secretaries, and minor functionaries. But there were limits on what these agents could obtain or had access to. So the idea was to find some men who were on the obvious fast track to power positions, and in that day this meant the sons of aristocracy—young men "to the manor born"—who could be persuaded to work for the Soviets. Accordingly, they targeted fellows with father issues who had doubts about the future of capitalism.

By all accounts Cambridge, and its usual suspect school, Oxford, became hotbeds of socialist—even Marxist—discussion and ideas. There were recruiting agents in place, those who knew how to exploit this interest to the benefit of the Comintern (the Communist International), a movement dedicated to the global spread of Marxist-Leninism, but controlled by the Soviets. Premier Josef Stalin envisioned an unprecedented network of highly placed spies.

Templeton Davis starting making some notes on a yellow legal pad with his rather expensive fountain pen. He wrote about how Philby had been privy to some information shared by the Americans about a project called 'Venona,' and how the Yanks had been able to decipher some intercepted communications between Moscow and its agents in the U.S. and Britain. As the material, some of which had been lying around for a few years before the code was cracked, was analyzed it became apparent that there was a high level spy or mole in the British Foreign Office, this at a time when atomic secrets were being leaked to the Russians.

The evidence pointed to a spy with the code name HOMER and more clues indicated that he had a contact in New York. Before long, Philby knew that they'd be hot on the trail of his college friend and fellow Soviet spy, Donald MacLean. MacLean had been First Secretary at the British Embassy in Washington, DC at the end of the war and for a few years after and had also acted as Secretary of the Combined Policy Committee on Atomic Development. What's more, his pregnant wife, Melinda, had lived in New York (she was American born) with her mother and this gave MacLean the pretext to travel from Washington, DC to New York City every few days to meet with his Soviet controller. This would be the crucial clue that would ultimately lead investigators to Donald MacLean, of this Philby was certain.

By this time MacLean was working back in London and there was no real way to warn him of the impending danger. So the story goes, Philby tasked Burgess to find a way back to London to warn their mutual friend. But how to get Burgess back to London? They concocted a scheme whereby Guy Burgess, a man known for his often flamboyant, even outrageous behavior, would get effectively kicked out of America. So he embarked on a series of episodes closely related, traffic violations, overtly homosexual propositions, drunkenness, all with the claim of 'diplomatic immunity' finally prompting the Governor of Virginia to file an official complaint with the British Embassy.

Next thing you know, Guy Burgess had a ticket on the *Queen Mary*, a ticket home to England where he could warn Donald MacLean and tell him to flee before he was arrested. It was a well-executed plan. And when friends Kim Philby and Guy Burgess said goodbye as the Queen Mary was about to sail, Philby, half-jokingly, but also half-seriously, remarked to his comrade, "Now, don't you go, too!" Of course, he must have had a premonition about what was going to happen.

For whatever reason, still one of the great mysteries of the Cold War as far as espionage history is concerned, Guy Burgess didn't just warn Donald MacLean to run, he ran with him, setting the stage for a major crisis for Kim Philby, because he knew that suspicion would fall on him that he was involved in tipping off MacLean. And pulling a phrase from popular culture, the title of that well known 1949 movie, *The Third Man*, the tag was soon applied to Philby, first in whispers, then ultimately in public accusation, that he was the "third man" in a vast conspiracy. At least that's how the story had been told and pretty much accepted as gospel.

As Temp read the various articles on the web, printing out the most helpful, he wrote a note to himself: "Seems like pretty sloppy work on the part of the Soviets, considering that Philby was being groomed for something as big as becoming 'C.'" And with that he found himself scratching his head over something that has puzzled historians and amateur sleuths for decades: "Why did the Soviets allow this fiasco to happen, when so much of what they did exemplified precision and mind-numbing patience?"

Remembering that he hadn't touched his fancy McDonald's lunch, now two hours cold, he quickly went back to the book order page and finished, picking several titles to be sent from various booksellers around the country (one from the U.K., actually). He hoped they'd help him along in his new cause du jour.

Chapter Eight
Stowe, Vermont

THE OLD MAN dressed in jeans and wearing a University of Maryland sweatshirt finished his glass of amber ale and looked around at the crowd gathered in his favorite watering hole on this Saturday afternoon. The place was packed and he hated it, frankly. He loved drinking virtually alone, not so much at home, but with just a *few* other customers in the joint. So he decided to call it a day. He had no interest in the four college football games playing on the various televisions or in listening to the annoying crowd reactions to the latest fumble on the three-yard line. Motioning to the attractive woman tending the bar, he put down some cash and said, "Catch ya tomorrow, Betty—wait—there's football tomorrow, too, right?"

"Yes sir, you know that Bill—how many years you been coming in here, Honey?"

"Too many, Betty. Okay, I'll see ya Monday for lunch, think I'll have a Reuben."

"Want me to put the order in now?" Betty smiled.

"Nope, just like to plan. Can't help it. Always thinkin' ahead—force of habit."

With that he grabbed his ever-present cane, something he resentfully needed these days, and was out the door and walking back over to his shop and hoping that the kid hadn't made too many mistakes while the boss was away. He could still walk pretty briskly, even with the cane and being eighty-six years of age, though people who happened to see him on the street thought he was much younger.

Some locals wondered if he had some secrets in his past. There were times when he would have a little too much to drink at that favorite drinking and dining establishment, the bar at the *Green Mountain Inn* up the street from his bookstore, and he would get a bit loud and loquacious. He would never say too much, but just drop hints here and there. Sometimes he went off about the commies and Kennedy—he didn't seem to like President Kennedy too much, but he'd stop himself before saying too much. And Castro—he hated Castro and would tell folks, "Ya know, ol' Fidel and I are the same age!" Which didn't seem to make much sense to most who heard him say that. Frankly, some found his mysterious side off-putting, but those who interacted with him the most—like Betty at the bar—well, they knew he was harmless, if maybe haunted by a painful past.

In his prime, Roberts had been handsome enough. A little over six feet tall and never all that heavy, he had a presence back then that was clearly intimidating to anyone who dared to get in his way. And there were days when people—bad people, in fact—got in his way. His hair had thinned over the years and grayed a bit at the temples, but not completely. His hearing was still great—unusual for a man his age—and his eyesight, too, though he did have to use glasses for reading. Most people who knew him these days assumed that he used the cane because, well, he was *old*. But every step Bill took reminded him of what had happened years before in Berlin, the fight, gunfire, the brutal pain in his left leg.

Local Vermonters thought he was just old, but Bill knew that he was in pain because something bad had happened to his leg. Yet, Bill Roberts never used pain meds. He was an old school, bite-down-on-the-bullet kind of guy. But sometimes during the dark days of those Vermont winters he would wonder if his toughness was the right choice. It hurt so much. But wasn't that why God made amber ale and Scotch whisky?

He walked in the front door of his shop and shouted immediately, "Any customers, Kenny?" His young "associate" was Kenny Starwood, a junior at Stowe High School who used to come into the store regularly to find graphic novels or vintage comic books. Roberts one day decided to make the relationship official and offered the kid a job. So he came in for a

couple of hours after school and most of the day on Saturday. Worked out
pretty good for both of them. Roberts got to work on the Internet side of
things, while Kenny minded the store. Kenny loved the job because he got
a great discount on what he bought.

"No sir, Mr. Roberts," Kenny responded to his boss. "Just one phone
call, some lady wanting to know if we had any movies on DVD."

"You tell her that this was a *book* store and not an entertainment
center, Kenny?" Because that's for sure how the old man would have
handled the call.

"Pretty much, Mr. Roberts," Kenny said, though he really hadn't handled it quite that way. He never liked to cross the old man.

Such was the conversation on a slow autumn Saturday afternoon in
Stowe, Vermont. Though the foliage was just about peak, there didn't seem
to be as many tourists out and about this year. Probably the economy,
Roberts thought. Summers were good, autumns were fair, but the winter
ski-crowd, that was the biggie. And some of the fellow travelers (he loved
that term), those in the vacationing parties who didn't ski, loved to sit near a
fireplace and read. Good thing there was the perfect place for such sedentary endeavors called *MINT CONDITION—Used Books* right on the main
drag in town. In a few days he'd close shop for a while, during the break
between the foliage and ski crowds—he was looking forward to that.

Of course, like most used booksellers, the lifeblood of Roberts's business was actually the Internet, which is why he listed his books at various
major sites. Back from lunch, he turned on his computer—password protected—he wasn't sure he trusted Kenny. Then again, his life had been built
around a lack of trust. He typed the word LITTLEHARRY—his own private, *very private*, joke (it was his codename in another life)—and went
immediately to his mail.

There were eight notifications, all had come in since he had gone to
lunch and all were sent from the same customer, someone with the screen
name "Conrad." He instantly knew who it was. They had talked once on
the phone and Roberts had immediately recognized the voice. It was one he
heard regularly on the radio. Any morning, Monday through Friday,
Templeton Davis Live could be heard in every nook and cranny of the dusty
and somewhat chaotic bookstore. But ever the discreet one, it was part of

his training, if not his DNA, he didn't let on that he knew who it was. He did, however, pay special attention to *this* customer, even paying a little extra out of his own pocket to make sure everything got to his famous client post haste.

Bill Roberts specialized in books about history, with also a pretty good supply of fiction, particularly spy fiction—even some first editions of famous novels. He supposed this was why he found himself filling so many orders for Mr. Davis, just listening to him on the radio over the years you could guess that the guy loved mysterious stuff, he seemed to be the only guy doing talk radio—conservative talk radio—who would interrupt the latest predictable rant about tax rates and take the better part of a show to talk to writers who spun tales of intrigue, Brad Meltzer, Daniel Silva, Brad Thor, Robert Littell, or even Tom Clancy. Roberts only wished Davis would do this more often.

Of course, Roberts had his own reasons for stockpiling books in the spy genre, since he used to be a spy *himself*. A real one. But that was in another life, ages ago. He was young and idealistic, the world was simpler, we had only one real enemy—the Big Bear, the Soviet Union—and in retrospect, the world was actually a safer place than today. Funny, huh? He thought, *a world obsessed with nuclear "Mutually Assured Destruction" (MAD) was actually safer than this new world of terror in the hands of so many potential enemies.*

Roberts had even tried his hand as a spy novelist, a fairly common retirement pursuit of former spooks. His old friend, the late E. Howard Hunt (yep, *that* Howard Hunt of Watergate infamy), had written several dozen and many old copies adorned the shelves of the Vermont bookstore. Bill, though, had just written two potboilers—one a story woven around the building of the Berlin Wall back in '61, the other based on his experiences as a spy even before there was a CIA, in the days of the old OSS. He used a pseudonym, or as fancy-schmancy writers call it, a *nom de plume*, and pretty much managed to fly beneath the radar of his former employer in Northern Virginia. But few wanted to read about those long gone days anymore. Like the black and white movies of that era, it was a time that now seemed so unreal, almost surreal. Bill knew, though, how very real it had been. He even knew the odd secret or two, things that had never been made public. He also had some hunches—pretty good ones, in fact—about things that never seemed quite right from back then. And he had made and kept some records, though he wasn't at all sure what he or anyone else could do with what he had put together. *Maybe someone, some day,* he thought.

Roberts looked over his email orders and noticed that all eight titles ordered by "Conrad" were, in fact, about espionage. No surprise there. There were two books by the late John Costello. He was an author who died suddenly of food poisoning on a trans-Atlantic flight at the age of 52. Because of the nature of his work, some had wondered what *really* happened. The books by Costello that Temp was interested in were *Mask Of Treachery*—about the spy Anthony Blunt, and *Deadly Illusions*, co-written with the help of a former KGB guy named Oleg Tsarev. The order included three books about good old Kim Philby. *Ah Philby* ... Roberts wondered if Davis would be interested to know that he had actually met and interacted with Philby several times when he was stationed in Washington. Of course, this was long before anyone suspected Philby of being "the third man." Those were the days. The old man allowed himself a brief smile at the memory.

Rounding out the order were books about Donald MacLean and two about a defector by the name of Krivitsky. Yep, Roberts thought—*Krivitsky, now there was another interesting story.*

The bookseller could not help wondering what inspired Templeton Davis's purchase. What was his interest in this stuff? He printed out the list of books and made his way through the stacks to the section in the back corner of the store. It took him only a few minutes to locate all eight of the titles and soon he had the order boxed and ready to go, doing it all himself, this was no job for Kenny. He'd send it out Monday, express. Templeton Davis didn't pay for expedited shipping, but he had learned from experience that this particular bookseller, for whatever reason, seemed to send orders to him that way.

Chapter Nine
Georgetown

DEVOURING HIS BIG Mac and fries pretty quickly, Temp was back at his desk reaching for the plastic wrapped journal that had been found by Vince Benton in what now very much appeared to be master commie spy Kim Philby's briefcase. His adrenaline surged as he carefully opened it to the first page. He leafed cautiously through several more pages, trying to make out the writing.

It was definitely made with a fountain pen—black ink—and the penmanship was excellent, though the words themselves were, not surprisingly, rather cryptic. A name here, a word there, incomplete sentences, and seemingly random numbers—it would take a while to make much sense of it all. If ever. He was sure that the one-time pad also found in the case, though it was very brittle because of age, would come in handy, if he ever figured out how to use it.

He wanted to make some notes, but of course preferred to avoid defiling the journal itself, convinced that its very existence made it very valuable, irrespective of what it contained. Templeton Davis was growing more and more confident that he had in his possession something that he could exploit into a book that would be a major bestseller—*Philby's Private Diary*, or some such title. But more than the idea of notoriety and financial reward was the sheer joy in being on the trail of discovery. What secrets did this book hold?

Davis looked at one of the bookshelves behind him and saw a journal of his own—a blank one, practically brand new, something he had picked up when he had done one of his book signings at the *Politics and Prose Bookstore* on Connecticut Ave (NW) in town. He would use this book for his notes about Philby's journal.

The first thing he did was to look for any markings in the book that would further verify that this had been, indeed, Philby's property. And he pretty much found that in a small scrawl in the upper left corner of the inside of the front cover.

H.A.R.P.

There it was again—so unless this case belonged to some member of a symphony orchestra somewhere with a penchant for cloak and dagger, there was little doubt that this was the material Philby said he had buried by Great Falls, but in a should-have-been-predictable-case of misdirection, had instead squirreled away in another pastoral area of Fairfax County. Temp found himself wondering if, after the release of Philby's book in 1967, any of the people from Langley had spent any time whatsoever searching for the stash using the "treasure map" clues in *My Silent War*. He smiled at the thought of such a waste of time. His mind conjured up a scene like that of FBI guys digging up that Michigan farm a while back looking for Jimmy Hoffa's body.

He continued carefully turning pages looking for anything that might jump out as recognizable. He'd examine every inch of it more carefully later, now he just wanted to survey it.

About six pages in he saw a reference to HOMER with the initials DDM nearby. Davis was well enough acquainted with the story to note this as a reference to Donald Duart MacLean, the man Philby hastened to warn back in 1951. MacLean was a Soviet mole in the British Foreign Office who had been passing secrets to the Soviets. Some of the secrets, Davis seemed to recall, were directly related to the atomic bomb and the Soviets development and testing of their own device in 1949, forever changing the world.

A page later he saw the name "Guy"—this must be a reference to Guy Burgess, he thought. Strange fellow that Burgess. From his reading, Temp learned that Burgess and Philby were fast friends and that when Burgess had been transferred by MI-6 from London to Washington in 1950, he lived at Philby's house on Nebraska Avenue in Washington, DC. It was assumed after the fact that this was because Philby might be able to keep the volatile Burgess on a short leash. He was an alcoholic and a homosexual with a penchant for extravagant and absurd behavior. And it turned out that he made things pretty sticky for the otherwise smooth operator Philby.

Famously, one cold night in early 1951, Kim Philby and his wife Aileen hosted a dinner party for several of the higher ups at Langley. James Jesus Angleton and his wife were there. He was a mover and shaker in the field of counter-intelligence, who would become famous in the 'Company' (many thought infamous) because of his near-obsession of searching for a Soviet "mole" in the agency. No doubt, Kim Philby's treason rattled Angleton. He had befriended and trusted Kim. They met weekly for lunch and to swap stories, likely the odd secret, too.

Also at the dinner was Winston Scott, later to become chief of station for the CIA in Mexico City, becoming entangled in the web of Lee Harvey Oswald intrigue, and Bill and Libby Harvey. Sometimes referred to as "America's James Bond," Harvey had worked for the FBI, only to be fired by J. Edgar Hoover, reportedly for drunkenness. He was soon hired by the young CIA and became a legendary force in the agency. Years later, President John F. Kennedy would insist on meeting this colorful agent.

He was also one of the first Americans to have suspicions about Mr. Philby.

As the story goes, the dinner party was going along great. The food was good and the booze flowed like water from an open fire hydrant. Those guys drank like camels. All of a sudden in walked Burgess, who lived at the house, but had specifically *not* been invited to the party. He was crude, vulgar, and unpredictable and, at any rate, preferred to spend his evening prowling around the homosexual sub culture, as it then existed in the American capital.

Before long, Burgess withdrew all the oxygen from the room with his outrageous behavior. An amateur caricature artist, he asked Libby Harvey if he might draw her. She agreed and Burgess went to work on a large sketch-pad. When the drawing was finished, he showed it to everyone and Libby was horrified, as was hubby Bill—and everyone else, for that matter. The caricature revealed the usual exaggerations common to such drawings, but in this case, it showed her skirt pushed up around her waist and she was wearing no underwear.

Well, that was enough to set Bill Harvey off and he was close to mopping up the floor with Guy Burgess before Philby intervened and apologized profusely, blaming Burgess's behavior on the alcohol. Not assuaged, Harvey and Libby quickly left and the party pretty much deteriorated from there.

A few months later, when MacLean and Burgess flew the coop en route to Moscow, the head of the CIA, Walter Bedell "Beetle" Smith (he had been Eisenhower's assistant during World War II) asked for opinions about Kim Philby. Angleton wrote a report basically arguing that Philby was *not* a spy. Certainly this is what Angleton hoped, since he had been so close to him and had shared so much information. But Harvey, who had never gotten over the insulting and offensive behavior of Philby's crony, Burgess, and had long held suspicions about Kim, wrote a report that made the case that Philby had been working for the Soviets all along.

Smith was persuaded by Harvey's argument and put pressure on the Brits to send Kim Philby packing. And though it would be nearly twelve more years before he would himself flee to the Soviet Union, Philby's life on the upwardly mobile fast track was effectively over at that point.

Temp made a note of the reference to Guy Burgess. No surprise there. But it was more confirmation of the legitimacy of the satchel as belonging once to Philby. That part of this case closed, so to speak.

Davis worked late into the evening that Saturday, making notes of things he saw in the excavated journal. And Sunday it would be the same, rising early and knocking back two pots of coffee losing all track of time. By the time he dropped his pen to watch the Redskins game that afternoon— they were playing Dallas, couldn't miss that—he had managed to recognize several things that begged for research. There was no narrative to read in the book, but yet there was a flow to it and page after page bore names and references.

"Angleton" appeared several times, as in James Jesus Angleton. The aforementioned HOMER, too. And, of course, Burgess. Also, there were some other names—unfamiliar references such as, SCOTT and OTTO—

and BUNNY. Next to the word BUNNY were the letters DOG. Made no sense (as if any of it did at this point). Then he remembered the earlier reference to HOMER with the nearby letters DDM. He knew that HOMER was Donald MacLean's code name with the Soviets, so it followed that possibly BUNNY was a code name and DOG were the initials of the person. A lady spy? Davis scratched his head and rubbed his eyes, growing a little weary.

On the next page after the one bearing the word BUNNY there was a reference to 'Oswestry,' and Davis made a note of it. Lots of stuff to look up and Templeton Davis, though now ready for a break, relished the prospect of digging more into this interesting story.

Then there were several pages with what could only be described as gibberish, things like:

KJEUFWWJHCNHHGFSAOLI QUHPN

He had noticed similar, but far from identifiable, markings in the little passport-size booklet.

Meanwhile, the Redskins lost to Dallas in overtime.

Chapter Ten
Rosslyn, Virginia

THE GROUP GATHERED in the small conference room every-
day—Monday through Friday at six AM sharp and Templeton Davis's staff
went over the plans for that morning's show, which began just after the
news at eight AM, Eastern Time. Vince Benton was there, Valerie Doling,
too. They were joined by several other members of the show's staff.

On this Monday they discussed the plan for each hour. During the first
hour, Temp would hit the big news of the weekend. The President of Iran
had once again defied the rest of the world with nuclear threats. Surprise,
surprise. Davis would talk by phone on the air with America's Ambassador
to the United Nations, Sheila McIntire, about the nutcase in Tehran.

Or was the guy crazy just like a fox?

During hour two there would be open phones. Temp liked doing this
on Monday, letting folks talk about whatever they wanted after the weekend.

But Davis was really looking forward to the final hour that morning,
especially in light of his weekend sleuthing activities. Joining him in the
TDL studio for the bulk of the hour would be a guy named Richard
Holcomb, a retired CIA employee. In fact, he had been pretty high up in
the agency. Holcomb had written a book about the ethical and moral
dilemmas involved in clandestine work. There was a chapter or two on
torture, another on lying, yet another on the use of sex as a weapon; that's
pretty much all Temp knew as the staff met.

He usually read the books of authors he was planning to interview, at least he tried to, and in fact, he had taken the book, called *Fair Enough— Espionage and Ethics*, home with him on the weekend. But he had been otherwise occupied and had never gotten around to reading it. Fortunately someone on his staff, a young man named Gilbert Hobson, had. The guy was his full-time research assistant and part-time court jester—complete with a Master's degree in history from George Mason University in Virginia, though he was originally from a little town called Moberly in Missouri. Hobson looked the part, horn-rimmed glasses, bow ties, v-neck sweaters and all. He was rail thin and some wondered if he had ever had to shave—such a baby face. Since coming to work for Templeton Davis two years earlier, he had traded his clean-cut hairstyle for a more unkempt hair mop. Most saw it as a benign attempt at sucking up to the boss, who apparently seldom met a barber, or comb for that matter, that he liked.

Gilbert was off-the-charts smart. He had a nearly photographic memory, at least near enough that most around him thought he had the capacity for total recall. Davis would pick his brain almost daily—sometimes several times a day on this or that and they had almost immediately developed a working chemistry. Temp loved it when anyone comparing him to other talk show hosts up and down the radio dial would comment about Davis's clear intelligence (he actually had a Google Alert set up—by Gilbert, of course—so he could be notified whenever someone mentioned his name and the word "erudite" in the same article). But the boss knew that a lot of what he was able to say was due to the work of his young in-house tutor. Their conversations were very much under the office radar. Not even Valerie Doling had much of an idea what they talked about when Temp's door was closed (a fact that bugged her, frankly).

One of the biggest secret gems between the boss and his young research geek was the whole "word of the day" thing. Every morning Gilbert would hand his boss a small index card with a word—usually multiple-syllabic—written on one side and the definition and an example of usage on the reverse side. The idea was that Temp was to try to work the word du jour into his broadcast and every time he did Gilbert would get a $50 bill. This sometimes worked out to close to a couple thousand dollars a month—all paid out of Davis's pocket, in cash. Sort of a daily dare or wager. This helped Hobson with his student loans. Of course, the research assistant cringed when he listened to his boss misuse whatever word it was—then he laughed. Even geniuses have a sense of humor, usually though they get jokes no one else does.

The boss knew he could count on Gilbert to provide a synopsis of Dick Holcomb's book that morning and he wasn't disappointed. The glorified book report included some biographical information about Mr. Holcomb. He was seventy years old and had served at the CIA in one manner or another from 1963 until his retirement in 1988. Following that, he continued to help the agency on a regular basis with consultant work. His career had taken him around the world, from Vietnam to Berlin, to several postings in South America. Certainly there were things he couldn't (and didn't) divulge, but the things he could were in themselves fascinating to Temp as he read through the bio.

"Gil, have you met this Holcomb guy?"

"Yes I have. He spoke at a symposium over at Georgetown University. They did a seminar on Richard Helms to mark the donation of his papers to the university by his family. Holcomb was one of the speakers along with Henry Kissinger and some old warriors from Cold War days. I talked with him a bit at the cocktail party afterwards. That's when I asked him if he'd be interested in coming on the show. He listens to you regularly, so he jumped at it."

"Seems like an interesting guy. Would you do me a favor?"

"Certainly."

"When he gets here, could you check with him and see if he could hang around for a few minutes after the show? He's in the final hour and I'd like to pick his brain about something."

Vince Benton looked over at his boss with a smile and a slight nod, and a pretty good idea about why Temp was interested in talking with the former spy guy. Gil noticed the eye contact between his boss and Vince and wondered what it was about.

"You got it, Boss. Wanna do an early lunch with him?"

"Yeah, that'd be great, or just coffee somewhere."

After the meeting broke up, Vince Benton followed Temp back to his office and once in, closed the door.

"So, what did you dig up about what I dug up?" he smiled as he asked, proud of his turn of the phrase.

"Well, some interesting stuff. Lots of things I want to research. Mind if I keep that journal and the other little booklet a bit longer?"

"Hey, like I said Saturday, Temp—I trust you and I know you'll keep me in the loop. I do think, though, that I need to tell Liz about it. I really don't like keeping secrets. In fact, I am not at all sure why I have kept this one."

"No problem. I just think it is something that shouldn't be talked a lot about until we know what we are dealing with."

"Are you going to talk to this Holcomb guy about it?"

"Nope. Not gonna mention it specifically, but I have a couple of questions that I think he can help me with, how to decipher something, things like that. I'll just tell him that I am researching for a book, a new novel I'm writing. He'll understand."

With that, Vince left for the control room and Temp finished his show preparations as he usually did, reading the front sections of the *Washington Post, New York Times*, and *Wall Street Journal.*

A few minutes before eight he was seated in his studio chair setting up his computer screen, opening windows to *FoxNews.com*, and *CNN.com*, while once more checking his email, something he almost compulsively did throughout his radio show. And at 8:05 he heard his theme song, a riff derived from the theme from the academy award-winning movie from 1970, *Patton.* At just the right moment the music faded a bit and Templeton Davis's voice boomed in the studio and around the country.

"Hello Americans, this is Templeton Davis in Washington, stand by for the Monday edition of *Templeton Davis Live!*" The final words were boosted by a bit of reverb by Vince Benton, the producer.

The show that morning went by quickly. The U.N. Ambassador was an excellent guest and the President of Iran was correctly characterized as a buffoon, without using that specific word. It was clearly implied. And the callers in the second hour were above the usual grade, not a dud in the bunch. So as the third hour of *Templeton Davis Live* got underway, the show was on a roll.

Chapter Eleven

WHEN VALERIE DOLING ushered Richard Holcomb into the studio while the ten AM news feed from *ABC* was playing quietly in the background from the wall monitors, Templeton Davis immediately realized that Gil's briefing paper about the man and his book failed to deal with one important detail. The guy was a giant—easily six feet, six inches tall and likely weighing well over three hundred pounds. He was an imposing figure.

"Good morning, Mr. Holcomb, glad to have you aboard for the show today," Temp greeted his guest, though not sure why he had used the maritime reference—"aboard." Did he really say "aboard?" Yes, the visitor's first impression was a little rattling.

Until he smiled and said, "Hey, drop the 'Mr.' stuff, call me Dick—everyone else does, though some may mean something different than my name."

Temp laughed. So did Valerie, covering her mouth with just a hint of embarrassment and with that she was on her way out of the studio, leaving the two men alone.

"Well, I'm Temp—no formalities here. I'm looking forward to our conversation. You done many of these?"

"Oh, sure, Temp—I guess I've been interviewed about a hundred times since the book came out four months ago. But frankly, I'm really excited about this interview. I'm a big fan of your show and catch it whenever I can."

Davis was used to such comments and usually didn't give them much weight, just talk. But something about Holcomb gave Temp the feeling that this guest was, in fact, a loyal listener and he thought that was cool. Heck, maybe he had a whole ring of TDL fans over at the CIA.

"Well, lemme knock a few preliminary liners and such out of the way and a couple of comments holding over from that last caller before the break at the top of the hour, and then I'll come to you. It'll just be Temp and Dick chewing the fat about espionage."

"Great."

"By the way, did Gil, my assistant who met you back at that Georgetown thing, ask you about hanging out for a bit after?"

"Yes he did and I'd be glad to. I have another interview at 2:30, a phone-in show, but I'm good until then. Wanna grab an early lunch?"

"That'd be great, there's a terrific place down the street with very good sandwiches," Temp replied just as the theme music started up and Vince Benton signaled twenty seconds to go.

"Holcomb nodded and gave him a thumbs-up sign." Wow, even his thumb was huge!

Dick Holcomb listened and watched as Templeton Davis opened the hour with a few one-liners and a final word to the last caller from the previous hour. Then Davis began his segue to their interview.

"I know a lot of people have not-so-good opinions about the CIA, but I for one am persuaded that, by and large, it's an agency that has been filled with heroes throughout its history. And for every supposed mistake or misdirection, there have been dozens—even hundreds of successes. And frankly, I'd also like to think that we'll never know the good things good people have been doing for decades to keep America free and safe. That said, so you know how I feel about it all, I of course know that there are challenges. And many times those challenges are moral and ethical. Just what is justified? What can a free society permit in the name of intelligence gathering and operations? Joining me today to talk about this is someone who ought to know—he's been in the trenches—a career man with the CIA, and someone who's recently written a fascinating and important book called, *Fair Enough—Espionage and Ethics,* his name is Richard Holcomb. That's your real name, right?" Davis chuckled.

His guest smiled and said, "Well, except, like I said off the air, call me Dick."

"First off, when you write a book about the CIA as a former employee, how much of it do you have to run by or get cleared by them?"

"Great question, Temp, because clearly there are boundaries. Some issues and specifics are off limits. What I've tried to do with this book is not deal with actual cases, but with scenarios. However, there are scenarios that have, of course, a relationship with real life. But like I say, it's something that has to be watched."

"Did anyone at Langley ask you to pull anything from your book?"

"Yes."

"Care to elaborate?" Temp prodded.

"Nope. Next question."

"Gotcha," Temp smiled.

"So, what's the most common personal conflict people who go into clandestine work have?" And with that the conversation morphed into a pretty thorough discussion of right and wrong and just when the ends actually justify the means.

"Interesting stuff. We're talking with Richard, I'm sorry—Dick—Holcomb about the moral dilemmas of spying," Temp said as the bumper music started for a soft break, Temp having signaled Benton that he was going out a bit early for this one. "I'm Templeton Davis in Washington, more of our conversation—fascinating stuff, frankly, or is it just me? Straight ahead."

The hour flew by, as Davis and Holcomb bantered back and forth about the ethical challenges surrounding spying. They took a couple of calls; one involved a question about the early days of the CIA, the other a bit more provocative turned into a rant about torture, accusing the CIA of being guilty of the most egregious human rights violations in the world. Holcomb handled himself very well, "Really? Is anything we've done worse than, say, North Korea or even Cuba—or the old Soviet Union? Dear Mr. Caller, you haven't a clue what you are talking about." About that time Templeton Davis made a signal to the producer to cue the bumper music—though it was, again, a bit early for a break—but a great way to lose a nutty caller. Thank heavens for soft breaks, the safety net of talk radio.

Soon Temp was in countdown mode, saying good-bye to his guest and his audience and off the air, another edition of Templeton Davis Live for the archives.

"Dick, let me drop these notes back on my desk and we'll head out. How's a good Reuben sandwich sound?"

"Great! But make mine a club."

Chapter Twelve

EXITING THROUGH THE revolving doors of the building, Davis and Holcomb walked up Wilson Boulevard to a place called *Reilly's*, a combination bistro and Irish pub, never quite figuring out what it wanted to be when it grew up. They sat down at a booth in the far back corner, Davis positioning himself so that he could see the room, a quirk of his.

They both ordered iced tea and scanned the menu, finally settling on what they had already decided—the Reuben for Davis, and the club sandwich for his new friend (at least he hoped), Dick Holcomb. Very quickly they were engaged in an animated conversation.

"Dick, it's interesting that the staff booked you for today's show, because I spent the weekend researching an idea for a new book—this one another spy novel, thriller, something like that. It's tentative. I'm just getting started. I've been fairly successful with my writing and this book will be pretty good, I think," Davis said matter-of-factly.

"Fairly successful?" Dick countered, "You say, fairly successful? That's like saying Babe Ruth was fairly successful at hitting home runs. I'd say you're a literary star and I only hope my book sells five percent of the copies you've sold of yours—then I could retire for real!"

Davis smiled and admitted his unusually self-deprecatory understatement, "Yeah, well …"

He was very careful in the conversation not to give up any specifics about the book, or anything about what had been dug up out at the Benton place—certainly nothing about that. There was mainly one thing he wanted to learn from this espionage expert, something that would help him along at this stage of the project—that's what he was thinking of it as now, a project—though he knew it had already become an obsession.

"Dick, in my reading and research into the old days of cloak and dagger stuff, I keep coming across something called a one-time pad, and I'm curious about what they were and how they were used. I was never very good at math and puzzles of any sort, heck, have a hard time doing the Monday *New York Times* crossword—you know, the one for beginners?"

Holcomb smiled at the reference, having himself mastered such puzzles every day of the week and even the famous *London Times* version. He found himself feeling momentarily superior to the best-selling author across the table. And he liked it.

"Wow, you're getting into the nitty-gritty. One-time pads, huh?"

"Yeah, what can you tell me—can you give me the *Reader's Digest* condensed tutorial over a sandwich? I'm buying." Davis smiled.

"Well," Dick sort of sighed, "It's simple, yet complicated. But I'll give it a shot, let me finish this sandwich—can you ask our gal for a few extra napkins?"

"Penny?" Temp called over to their waitress. "Can we get some extra napkins here?" She grabbed some and came to the table expecting to help two helpless men clean up a mess, but there was no mess and she handed them to Davis, while giving her regular customer a puzzled looked.

"Thanks Penny, hey could I get a cup of coffee from ya? You want one, too, Dick?"

"No I'm fine," he said while chewing on a large bite of his now-almost-gone sandwich.

"So, you want to go to spy school, Temp?" Dick teased. "Okay, here's lesson one—relaying secret messages. For centuries, people have been trying to devise better and better ways to communicate in code. In the business, we call it cryptography. It just sounds more mysterious and smarter."

"That's right. In laying out this book, there are some messages that need to be passed along and I have seen this one-time pad thing pop up in books, so I thought I'd use it. But I gotta understand it first!"

"Well, people have been working with numbers and letters, as I say, for a long time. I even read somewhere that one of the Roman Caesars actually had a code he used based on changing the alphabet as it was back then. The idea is to set up a pattern—any pattern—as a code and then make sure only the one sending the message and the intended recipient have the key to decipher it. So if I wanted to send you a message that said, 'It's going to rain tomorrow,' I'd disguise it by scrambling the letters in a seemingly random way. But the important part would be that which I'd already given you, and only you, which is the key so you could figure out what it said."

"Yeah, I get that part—it's a secret code—but what's the code?"

"Well, that's where the one-time pads come in. You would have a book or booklet of seemingly random keys, but only one of those pages would match the message I sent. There'd be some prearranged signal such as, 'On October 20th use page five,' or some such thing and that's the page you'd use to decipher the code. The vital piece of the puzzle, so to speak, would be knowing the page to use."

"Okay, I get that—but couldn't anyone figure that out eventually by finding the right page by the process of elimination?"

"Well, theoretically it is unbreakable. That's where the 'one-time' part comes in. Both parties have to destroy that particular key page after that one use. In fact, sometimes in the Cold War such keys were printed on something called flash paper, which was designed to burn in, well, a flash." Dick smiled. Temp told him that he'd heard of that.

"Give me a couple of those napkins, Temp."

Davis handed Holcomb two paper napkins and watched as his friend pulled out his pen (not a fancy fountain pen, Temp noted) and began to make some markings. On the first one he wrote something, but hid it so Temp couldn't see it, then he folded it in half. On the second napkin he allowed Temp to see what he was writing, not that it made any sense whatsoever:

XLRTZPRLONYCMBQ

"Okay, what I have done here is to arrange fifteen random letters all in a row, because I want to send you a message of the same length, no punctuation, you just have to figure out the word breaks. I know the message I want to send you. I've written it on this other napkin. These letters are random, I just wrote them down as they came to mind, no specific order. This would be the key on the one-time pad."

Temp nodded and the clueless look on his face had given way to one that indicated he was beginning to catch on.

"So, what's the message, Dick—that I should drink more *Ovaltine?*"

Dick stared back blankly.

"You know, that Christmas flick they play non-stop on Christmas Day, the kid with the glasses—Ralphie?"

"Never saw it," Dick said, and he was beginning to wonder about Davis. Did he really want to know this stuff? Holcomb had an impatient side to him, one that tended to show when he was in teaching mode.

"Sorry," said Davis, "Please continue."

"Well, now I want you to go away for about five minutes—hit the restroom, go buy a paper, flirt with the waitress, I don't care what—just give me some time to encrypt my message for you using this random code, then I'll show you how to crack it. Off with you, my lad, and be quick about it," Dick said, now smiling and trying to sound like Clarence the Angel in *his* favorite holiday movie, *It's a Wonderful Life.*

Temp got the reference and the joke and got up from the booth and walked away.

Chapter Thirteen

TEMPLETON DAVIS WENT over to the bar and pulled out his *Blackberry* to check his latest email. The bartender started his way and Temp put out his hand with a motion that indicated he didn't need anything. There were two messages on his device from Valerie Doling about guests for upcoming shows, another from Gil, his research assistant, giving him a link to an article about North Korea, the topic he'd be discussing on one of the upcoming shows, he couldn't remember what day, *yadda yadda yadda.* He looked up from his handheld convenience-slash-annoyance and glanced across the room toward his lunch partner. The guy was scribbling on another napkin, then another. Temp thought, *hey we're gonna need more napkins.* About half of the seats at the bar were filled and he noted that everyone was drinking Guinness. What, was it some kind of national stout day, or something?

As he pondered this important matter, he heard Dick Holcomb call him back over to the booth and he rejoined the cloak and dagger table for part two of his lesson, *Ah grasshopper …*

As he sat back down across from Dick Holcomb, the former spy pushed a napkin across the table—a napkin bearing some made-no-sense scribbling:

DBVTSVLPGGRXPBO

A single line eye chart, he thought to himself and smiled.

Dick instructed him, "Now, I want you to decipher this code for the special message of the day!"

Temp looked at him and said, "How in the world am I gonna do that?"

Dick handed him the napkin he had written on earlier, bearing the letters: **XLRTZPRLONYCMBQ**. The only thing the two sequences had in common was that they both contained fifteen letters. And Temp scratched his head as Dick chuckled a little.

"Okay, now there is another piece of the puzzle you need."

"Really? I had no clue," Temp replied sarcastically.

"You need to understand how this all works."

"Ya think?"

"Now here on this napkin," Dick said as he produced yet another defiled paper napkin, "I have given you the most basic of codes. It's the English alphabet with each letter being given its numerical equivalent in sequence. 'A' is zero, 'B' is one, and so forth."

"So," thinking he now had it all figured out, "I simply figure the number for each letter and that's it?" Temp asked.

"Not quite, there's more to it. First, remember that you have to translate your message with the key on this other napkin, so **DBVTSVLPGGRXPBO** can only be understood with **XLRTZPRLONYCMBQ**. And that's the beauty of the one-time pad. In the espionage world, only two people, the sender and the designated recipient, theoretically, would have the key. To anyone else it'd all be just so much gibberish."

"I know the feeling. Hey, you said 'theoretically.'"

"Yes, we'll get to that, but first I want you to translate or decipher the message based on what I've just told you. I'll do the first letter for you to show you how," Holcomb said.

"Okay, but, again, I gotta warn you, I was day dreamin' during math class back in school and I can barely tell time when it comes to numbers," Davis said sheepishly.

"No problem, a child of five could do this," then Dick tried to be funny and sound like old Groucho Marx with his famous line, "Someone fetch me a child of five." They both smiled.

"The first letter in your message is 'D,' right?" Dick asked Temp.

Davis nodded.

"And the first letter in the key, which only you and the sender would ideally have, is 'X.' So you simply calculate their total numeric value, remembering your table and how 'A' is zero and so on. Like this: 'D' is '3' and 'X' is '23.' You subtract '23' from '3' and get '–20,' or a negative number. When you get a number below zero, add 26 back in (the number of letters in the alphabet). We're using something called modular arithmetic. In other words you wrap around the end of the alphabet and go back through. Sort of like military time versus the way civilians read a clock. In this case, you'd add '26' to '-20' and get what?" Dick asked his pupil.

"Um … let's see, '6'?" Temp answered like a tentative third grader.

"Correct you are. You get a star today Mr. Davis. Now if you want a whole constellation, figure out the rest of the message. Take your time, but I've gotta leave in twenty minutes," Holcomb said teasingly.

Opting to draw on the back of one of the paper place mats (why didn't they think of that in the first place?), Templeton Davis went to work, putting a portion of his brain—was it the left part or right part?—he rarely used for work, and he found himself enjoying it, if only because he was that much closer to figuring out some of the cryptic stuff in Philby's mysterious briefcase.

With each letter he found the next one a bit easier to process. The second letter in the message turned out to be 'R.' Then came 'E' and 'A.' Finally, he completed the message bearing the fifteen-letter run-on word: **GREATGUESTTODAY**. He chuckled as he found it easy to see where the word breaks were. And he thought about how indeed, Holcomb had been a great guest and a big help.

"Hey thanks, Dick, this was very, very helpful. I think I've figured it out, so the person sending the message would reverse this process, using the key to create a coded message?"

"You're correct. In this case I added 'G' to 'X' and got '29,' then I subtracted '26' and came up with '3,' which is 'D' and the first letter in the coded message."

"So this is hard to break?"

"More than hard to break, it is theoretically *impossible* as long as the key is destroyed and never seen by anyone else. Ever hear of a guy named Claude Shannon?"

"No, can't say that the name rings any bells."

"Well, he's probably the most important, if not most famous, man you've *never* heard of, I can tell you that!"

"Really? How so?" Temp asked, almost afraid not to, what with Holcomb's emphatic way of saying it.

"He was a scientist with *Bell Labs* back during World War II and wrote a paper that was classified at first, but later published, well after the war. In it, he laid the foundation for much of what we still use today in the transmission of information. That *Blackberry* in your pocket? It functions, like any computer, thanks to groundbreaking work done by Shannon more than half a century ago. And he, in fact, did some work on the whole 'one-time pad' thing and proved that, when used correctly, they're unbreakable."

"Used correctly?"

"Ah, that's the key. Always is. The human factor. Shannon argued that there were several factors that had to be in place for messages using one-time pads to be unbreakable: The key must be truly random, never reused in whole or part, and kept secret. I actually had the chance to meet him back in mid-1970s before he retired from MIT. Some of us from the CIA visited up there to hear him lecture on cryptography—he even invited us to his house for an evening. It was quite an interesting night, I'll say that."

"OK, well, clearly you want to tell me this story, so I am all ears, you have been so generous with your time today."

"Thanks, I don't get to tell some of these stories very often," he smiled. "Well, we had heard that Shannon had, shall we say, somewhat of a reputation for eccentricity. It was rumored that he sometimes navigated the corridors at MIT on a unicycle—or a pogo stick!"

"Sounds like that guy in *A Beautiful Mind*. Was Shannon nuts?"

"Not at all. Though he did develop Alzheimer's long after he retired— died about ten years ago in a nursing home up in Massachusetts."

"Sad."

"Yeah—my mom died like that, very sad—heart-breaking, really," there was a pause in the conversation, one driven by unspoken respect. Then, after a few moments, Holcomb continued, first clearing his voice.

"Ahem ... as I was saying. So we go to this guy's home and it's like Edison's house, or what I'd imagine that'd look like. Gadgets and books everywhere. On Shannon's desk there was this box, a simple wooden box, with a switch on the side. It sat front and center on the desk just begging for attention. So I took the bait and asked him about it, like a dummy."

"What was it?"

"Well, Shannon smiled at me and said: 'I call it my *Ultimate Machine*. Why don't you flip the switch, Mr. Holcomb, and see what happens?' Of course, just the way he addressed me put me back in college being intimidated by one of my professors. So I flipped the switch!"

"And ...?"

"The lid slowly opened and an artificial hand came up—like on that old *Adam's Family* TV show? And the hand reached over to the side of the box and flipped the switch off and then receded back into the box, the lid then closing!"

"What the ...?"

"I guess it was his idea of humor and come to think of it, everyone did laugh quite hard, as I recall. The guy also had a machine that played chess, but I declined the match. I'd learned enough at the feet of the good doctor."

"Funny stuff. I guess there is a thin line between genius and going 'round the bend."

"Yes, I suppose. But at any rate, back to the matter at hand, the idea of a one-time pad being theoretically unbreakable. The fact is that there have been times when spies have been sloppy and the keys were discovered, giving an adversary a way to crack the code. This was how we wound up with the 'Venona' project back at the end of World War II, helping us track down and identify those Soviet spies, Donald MacLean and Kim Philby."

At the mention of Philby's name, Templeton Davis was caught off guard and coughed a bit, looking for words. Holcomb just observed.

"Yeah ... um ... I've heard about Philby, wasn't he here in the states for a while?"

"Sure was. He was the number one intelligence officer for the Brits here in Washington, DC in 1950 and '51, but we were on to him even before that, of that I am convinced."

"Really? I didn't know that."

"Yep, and there are still some people alive and kicking from the old days, men who actually knew old Philby. In fact, one old bird I met while researching my book, a guy who lives these days, up in Vermont of all places, an old Cold Warrior living in the land of the lefties, has a whole bunch of stuff on Philby and his comrades. He has made a hobby of it. Former company man—runs some kind of used bookstore up there."

The reference to the bookstore caught Davis's attention, as did the reference to Vermont, seeing as Temp was pretty sure he had a speaking gig up that way in a few days. An interesting coincidence.

"Reeaaally?" he said, drawing out the word for emphasis. "Got a name on this guy?"

"His name is William Roberts, known now by most as just plain old Bill, but back in the day I think they in the agency called him 'Wild Bill.' Hey, I gotta run. It's been fun, hope I helped you. Thanks for plugging my book today on the show and if I can help you anymore, lemme know. I look forward to reading *your* new book."

They shook hands and exchanged business cards, then Richard Holcomb went on his way. Templeton Davis, however, lingered at *Reilly's* and went to the bar.

"Guinness, please."

Chapter Fourteen
Rosslyn, Virginia—Langley, Virginia

TEMPLETON DAVIS WENT back to his office after lunch with former CIA agent Richard Holcomb, and his pint of Guinness, a rare daytime treat. Anytime, for that matter. Valerie was waiting for him with a list of calls to return and some promos he needed to record that afternoon, a lot of network stuff, "Hello, Americans, this is Templeton Davis, join me for *Templeton Davis Live* Monday through Friday at six AM here on the intelligent voice of Nowhere, Kansas, K-O-R-N," or at least that's how these things started to sound to him after doing this job for so many years. Still though, he was grateful for the job he had, the money, the celebrity, and always felt quickly guilty when he indulged in such selfish cynicism. He didn't like being—even for a moment—that cynical guy.

After doing about a dozen show promos, along with a commercial for some home alarm company, he called for Valerie and asked her: "Do we know anyone over at Langley who'd know something about the history of the place?" Of course, Temp himself had many contacts—high level ones—but this wasn't the time for that. He needed to fly under the radar, at least to the extent possible, while poking around a story that had so much explosive potential.

Valerie Doling missed her calling. She should have been running the White House switchboard. She could find anyone, anywhere and had a razor sharp memory for important, heck, even unimportant contacts. She had worked for Davis for six years now, after a lengthy stint with a Scranton, Pennsylvania television station right out of college. She even became a bit of a minor local media celebrity up there. Having studied communications at Syracuse University, many back in the day at school thought she was destined for one of the networks—certainly as an on-air personality. She had the looks for it for sure—drop dead gorgeous could-have-been-a-model looks. But for whatever reason, she took the job with the Davis team, one that turned out to be very fulfilling.

Frankly, many people wondered why she had never moved on—or married, for that matter. Now she was pushing 40 years old and outside offers coming her way (on either the career or amatory fronts) had slowed down significantly. But she loved the team and her job and it became her comfort zone. And she loved Temp—simply stated. Even when he gave her one of these "hey, do we know someone at …?" tasks. Over the years several people from CIA had been on the show and whenever she needed to book a guest for a comment on something—not an easy thing to do with the people at Langley—she called her old college roommate Lauren Schmidt. Lauren had been recruited by the agency back at Syracuse, where she had majored in public relations. And she was the perfect fit for the CIA's usually awkward PR department.

"Hey Lauren, it's Valerie—been a while since we talked. When you get a chance could you give me a buzz over here at the office? Temp needs some help with something, not necessarily show related—at least I don't think it is. Call me," and she hung up after leaving the voice message.

Lauren called her back less than ten minutes later.

"Temp is wondering about talking with someone who knows the history of the CIA—do you have an official historian?"

"Sure do. He's a great guy with a small staff. They work on a lot of things. Back when General Hayden was DCIA (Director, Central Intelligence Agency) the department expanded. Hayden was a history major and he was the driving force behind some of the public symposiums we had, like one for the late Richard Helms, another about some Polish spy, I think. And there was also one a while back about the Korean War. What's your boss up to?"

"Dunno exactly, it's some new project of his, all pretty hush-hush. I'm not completely in the loop, but that'll change soon, I'll make sure of it," she laughed. "So who runs the history thing there?"

"Guy's name is Stevenson, Albert Stevenson, a PhD from University of Chicago. He's been here for many years, his great uncle was Adlai Stevenson, the guy who ran unsuccessfully for the presidency for the Democrats against Eisenhower a couple of times, long before we were around. He's a nice old guy and he loves it when anyone shows him and his department any attention. Frankly, since Hayden left there has not been much for them to do down there."

"Lauren, could you do me a favor and ask your Dr. Stevenson if he'd have a few minutes for Temp today or tomorrow, a few minutes for a phone conversation."

"On the air?"

"No, sorry, not that kind of call, but we'll sure keep him in mind. No, this is more of a personal interest with Temp, I think he's beginning to work on another book, which means I become a copy editor for a while again."

"Oh, sorry girl."

"No, no. I actually like it. A bit tedious sometimes, but it's interesting work."

"Lemme call you back in a bit, or first thing tomorrow on the history thing. I think I'm about to make Dr. Stevenson's day, heck, month for that matter."

As it turned out, Dr. Stevenson jumped at the chance to talk to Templeton Davis, even off the air, and before long Valerie Doling popped into Davis's office and told him that the CIA's official historian was holding on the phone for him.

"Really? Great job, Val, I knew I could count on you. Thanks! Could you close that door on the way out?" he said, hoping that he wasn't sounding rude. He knew that Valerie was not used to being in the dark and soon he'd bring her into his loop. As soon as the loop started to make more sense to him. She told him that if he needed her, she was heading down to the coffee shop in the lobby of the building. "Want me to bring you back something? Oh, and also, we need to chat about your quick trip to Vermont this Friday to speak at that insurance thing." She loved pleasing him and, yes, hated being out of his loop.

"No on the pie," he said. "Unless the pie today is blueberry. Where exactly am I going in the land of the liberals on Friday?"

"You'll be up in Stowe—ski country, but now it's all about the foliage. The gig is at some very fancy resort and you should be talking to a couple hundred insurance people—sales and management types," she advised him.

"Got it. We'll talk in a bit—I may want to extend my stay a day or two up there. Stay tuned," he said with a big smile on his face that just annoyed Valerie who also hated it when her boss played little games.

Then Temp picked up the phone. "Dr. Stevenson, thanks so much for calling, sir. I'm very grateful that you took the time to talk with me. I won't keep you long."

"No problem Mr. Davis, I've heard your show many times and I read your book, the one about radical Islam. It was pretty good," the compliment given with a grudging hint. After all, the guy was a *real* historian, the kind of man who was likely institutionally and constitutionally suspect of the work of rank amateurs, especially celebrity amateurs like talk show hosts, not to mention novelists.

"Well, thanks a lot and since you mention books, I'm heading in a different direction with my next one, probably another novel, not sure yet, though. But I do know that it's gonna involve some Cold War spy stuff. And that's why I wanted to talk to you. I'm told that you're the man."

"Well, I don't know about that, but I'm glad to be of service. You say Cold War spies, huh? Always an interesting genre. I'm sure I can help you some. Any story or people in particular?"

"Yep, I'm interested in the Kim Philby story."

"Philby, huh? Well, he's sure the big kahuna when it comes to spies and espionage stories. In many ways he did more damage to the agency after he left America, even after he fled to Moscow, than he did while he was here, though there is ample evidence of his treachery while the guy was in the U.S."

"You don't say? How's that?"

"Well, the place sort of went nuts for a couple of decades during the toughest part of the Cold War. There was always talk of a Soviet mole here at Langley. And a guy named Angleton, who was actually the head of counterintelligence here, conducted what turned out to be a nearly twenty-five-year witch-hunt. When he was finally pushed out by one of the directors, Colby I think it was, things calmed down and, of course, that was when the congressional committees were looking closely at us—mid '70s."

"Uh huh, I remember that. Senator Church's thing, right?"

"Yep, that's the one, led by Frank Church from Idaho. In hindsight, it pretty much looks like Angleton's paranoia came from his betrayal by Philby. They were actually friends and who knows what the head of counterintelligence had told the Soviet spy over four-martini lunches at Harvey's Fish House in DC."

"Fascinating. Now the old Soviet spies had code names, right? Wasn't Philby's later found out to be STANLEY?"

"I think you're right, but I'd need to look it up."

"Great, Dr. Stevenson and while you're digging around, could you check out some other code names for me?"

"Sure, I suppose I could. You got a list?"

"A short one, two code names that I've come across in my reading," Temp continued, comfortable now in describing the book he was starting to develop as a work of fiction, when in fact, he already knew that it was going to be all too true. "There's a code name for a Soviet agent named SCOTT, and yet another with the name, BUNNY."

"BUNNY? Seriously?" Stevenson asked skeptically. "Sounds like an unusual code name."

"Yeah, I think it must be some lady spy. Speaking of lady spies, could you also see what you could dig up about another name I came upon: Kitty Harris?"

"You got it, Mr. Davis—BUNNY, SCOTT, and Kitty Harris. Can I have a couple of days on this?"

"Oh sure, and please call me Temp and I'll call you Albert—how 'bout that?"

"Works for me," said the historian.

Though their conversation was over, within a short time the dialogue between the historian and the broadcaster would become the topic of discussion where secrets—deep dark secrets—were guarded with particular vigilance, even half a world away. And one old secret in particular, one that still had the power to shake the world, would become vulnerable to exposure. This was something some people would never allow to happen—at least not without a fight.

Dr. Stevenson assembled his staff and asked, "Guess who that was?" Their looks indicated that they either had no clue, or didn't at all care; he wasn't sure which and decided not to try to find out.

"That was Mr. Templeton Davis, the radio celebrity. And he'd like our help."

With that the historian filled his staff in on the details and gave a couple of them specific assignments. Dr. Stevenson felt, at least for a fleeting moment, like he was back in the halls of academia and tasking his hungry-for-attention graduate assistants with an assignment for a project that would ultimately bear his name. It was a familiar feeling, though one long gone these days. Frankly, nothing very interesting or important ever happened in the history department at the Central Intelligence Agency.

For whatever reason, the historian never even thought about talking to someone in the agency's public affairs department, though that should have been protocol.

Chapter Fifteen
Georgetown

TEMPLETON DAVIS SPENT the late afternoon and early evening in his library. He had a lot of reading to do and immersed himself in every reference he could find among his books related to the Philby affair. He marked pages containing possibly relevant factoids with post-it notes, used as bookmarks and occasionally wrote in his notebook—usually a note to himself about another trail to go down. He was taking it all in, making notes, mental and literal, about items requiring further exploration. It was how he processed information, first the overview—read as much on a subject as possible—then go back and start to sort through it. He was looking forward to his shipment of books from his friendly Vermont book dealer, hoping it was expedited, as was usually the case. More grist for the mill, he thought.

Was that guy up there in Stowe—the same town where he was scheduled to speak to those insurance guys in a few days? He wondered.

Around eight PM he opened a can of chili from his special order stash sent to him by a friend from *Tony Packo's* out in Toledo, Ohio and found some saltines in the pantry for his dinner. He finished the bowl quickly and downed a glass of ice water with similar dispatch. That *Packo's* stuff was spicy. Five alarm spicy.

He decided to try his hand at code breaking and revisited the journal from Philby's case. Locating the page with the gibberish—words that made no sense and were obviously in some kind of code—he wrote the first line at the top of a clean page on a legal pad:

KJEUFWWJHCNHHGFSAOLI QUHPN

Remembering the lesson Dick Holcomb had taught him hours earlier, he pulled out what clearly was one of those one-time pads that Philby had left behind in the case. He was pretty sure that Philby had probably translated the coded message from his Soviet contact and also passed it along somewhere, and had also likely destroyed the page of the one-time pad that had been used to decipher it. But as he looked closely at the booklet of code pages, he could not find any evidence that any pages had been torn out. Had the master spy been sloppy, or was he just so sure that he wouldn't be caught? Everything in the case, in fact, its very existence suggested that Kim Philby had only intended its contents to be beneath the sod for a brief time. It seemed to speak of unfinished business.

So Templeton Davis decided to go page-by-page using the skills Holcomb had shared to see if any of it translated. He figured all he had to do was the first few letters on a page, because if the first word was gibberish, that clearly wasn't the right page. It was a bit of a needle-in-a-haystack kind of thing, but Davis found himself enjoying the prospect of discovery. *Better than a crossword puzzle, for sure,* he thought to himself.

And potentially more lucrative. He smiled at that thought.

There were to his count twenty pages in the booklet, all bearing columns of letters—random letters. So he began at page one, coming up with the word: FMXTH. Now, that would be challenged for sure in a scrabble game. Then he went to the next page, getting better at the process along the way, page after page. By the tenth page he had a major headache. In fact, he was quite tired. He put a mark in the booklet and promised himself to come back to page eleven in the morning.

He grabbed a handful of saltines from the torn open sleeve still on the kitchen counter to help with the lingering but pleasant effects of the chili and got yet another glass of ice water and went up to bed. He stabbed the TV remote control with his fingers and found something on the history channel to his liking. It was a documentary about the Bay of Pigs fiasco in

1961, and set the timer on the set to turn off in an hour. But the ill-fated invasion of Cuba by CIA trained exiles hadn't even started before he was mercifully sound asleep.

A thunderstorm roared through the Washington, DC area about three AM and one particular clap of thunder shook Temp awake. He tried for a few moments to doze back off, but soon realized it was not worth the effort. Besides, all the ice water he had consumed was beckoning to be released. Getting up, he took care of the used water problem and then headed downstairs to make a pot of coffee. And just then the thought struck him that he could resume his super-secret-decoder-spy-stuff work. He laughed out loud, surprised by the almost childish glee this new project made him feel. He was instantly awake. Like-it-was-noon awake.

Cup of coffee in hand, he made his way back to his desk in the library and turned the lamp on, ready for round two. Page eleven in the one-time pad book was where he had left off on what was, he admitted, probably a wild goose chase. But as he translated the first few letters of Philby's gibberish using the key on the eleventh page of the booklet, he, for the first time, had formed what looked to be an actual word: CENTRE. Sure it was spelled wrong, but then again, he seemed to recall that the word CENTER was in fact sometimes spelled CENTRE. He had seen it like that before, he was sure of it. And the word itself was one likely associated with espionage, as in a message coming from the CENTRE or headquarters, wherever the heck that was.

His adrenalin surging by this point, he took another sip of coffee, though he wasn't in any real need of caffeine. He pulled his reading glasses off and rubbed his eyes as if preparing himself to focus on a valuable piece of art or jewelry. He had to leave for work in about ninety minutes, so he had no time to waste. He was determined to translate the entire message, one that looked to be about twenty-five words long, give or take.

Turns out that with all the lines of code, the message was actually closer to fifty words long. And Davis was nearly trembling with excitement when he finished it and read the words out loud:

CENTRE WISHES MADCHEN CONTACT HOMER AND ESCORT TO MOSCOW VIA STOCKHOLM AS SOON AS

POSSIBLE STANLEY SHOULD POINT ATTENTION AT DDM
BUNNY HIGHEST PRIORITY MUST BE PROTECTED ALL
COSTS THIS NUMBER ONE CONCERN OF CENTRE STANLEY
SHOULD PROCEED WITH CAUTION BEWARE GOOD LUCK

Davis drew a line from the first mention of STANLEY to the side of
the page and wrote, "Stanley is Philby." Then another from HOMER on
the other side of the page where he noted, "HOMER is Donald MacLean
or DDM." Then he drew a line from MADCHEN and penned the words,
"This is Guy Burgess." Finally, he circled the word BUNNY on the page of
the legal pad and drew a line to the top of the page where he wrote: "Who
is BUNNY?"

All the while he wondered if he was reading it all correctly? For years,
the accepted story had been that Guy Burgess had fled to Soviet Russia
with Donald MacLean as a last minute thing, more of a panic, one that
messed everything up for Kim Philby. Now, here was a note, apparently
sent from whoever was directing the spy efforts of Mr. Philby, instructing
him to tell Burgess to go to Moscow. What's more, something was indicated that had never appeared anywhere to the best of Davis's knowledge—
that the highest priority the Soviets had at the moment was *not* to protect
Kim Philby, the man ever since assumed to be collateral damage from
Burgess's mistake, but rather to make sure no attention was paid to another
spy with the code name BUNNY.

Davis was very glad now that he had asked CIA historian, Dr.
Stevenson, to research that code name because whoever BUNNY was, this
person was clearly of great importance to the Soviets back in the day.
Important enough for them to be willing to sacrifice not just two of their
fabled agents, MacLean and Burgess, but also apparently, Philby himself.
This was quite a find.

He needed to get back in touch with the Langley history guy right
away. He gathered his notes, the napkins with scrawl, the one-time pad, and
Philby's journal and put it all in a large manila envelope, which he then
sealed. He then held the bulging package in his hands and looked around
the room. For whatever reason, he had the sense that this material should
be squirreled away somewhere. Maybe it was the subject matter itself, or the

genre, he wasn't sure, but an almost primal instinct seemed to drive him to hide it all.

Climbing a ladder up to a top shelf, he pulled out three books from a series on the American Civil War, written by Bruce Catton and tucked the envelope containing the fledgling fruit of his research in the area behind. He then put the books back in their place. After climbing down the ladder, he removed it from that section of shelves and hooked it onto the track of the shelves directly across the room. As he did so, he laughed out loud, and uttered the words, "Temp, you're getting paranoid, old boy!"

He showered and dressed for work and soon was in his Range Rover headed toward the Key Bridge in light traffic. It would certainly be hard to focus on the radio program this day. The buried treasure Vince Benton had found a few days back contained what now appeared to be a treasure map in a sense, only it was very unclear where the destination marked by "X" was located, or even what it all meant.

Chapter Sixteen
Rosslyn, Virginia

THROUGHOUT THE STAFF meeting and then the entire show, Templeton Davis was preoccupied with his new "project." A few times he was asked, first by Valerie, then Vince Benton, if he was feeling all right or is "everything okay?"

"Yep. Finer than frog's hair split four ways and parted in the middle," one of his pet responses, which most of the team just found annoying, "It's all good." And he kept in motion, not letting himself get into any kind of real conversation with anyone. He wasn't in the mood. He wanted to chew on his discoveries. Stick and move.

Since his show started at eight AM, a bit early to try to reach Stevenson at Langley, he would need to wait until after eight AM to make his call. And the wait was, frankly, slow torture. But he was elated when during the final hour of the show Valerie sent him an instant message that popped up in the upper left hand corner of his computer screen telling him that the historian had, in fact, already called *him*. Did he have some valuable information, Temp wondered?

The last half hour of the show seemed to drag on, a phone interview with historian Victor Davis Hanson about one of his articles, this one about the latest misstep by the vice president, a man who seemed destined to be dumped from his party's ticket next time around. Usually, an engaging interview—one of his regular favorites, in fact—there were a couple of moments when he seemed to lose his train of thought and the silent pause was deafening—a real radio no-no—soon he was hearing music in his ear leading him to a merciful break, during which the guest asked the producer the question du jour, "Temp alright today?"

"Says he is," Valerie told Hanson while a commercial for *Ovaltine* was playing. And finally, Templeton Davis was signing off of an edition of his show he knew ranked among his worst broadcasting efforts ever. He left the studio and raced back to his office and closed the door, raising even more eyebrows and red flags for his staff. He located the number for Dr. Albert Stevenson at the CIA and after one ring he was finally talking to the guy he'd wanted to speak to ever since that early morning storm roared through the area.

"Dr. Stevenson, this is Templeton Davis, thanks so much for getting back to me so quickly, I got your message—what were you able to find out?"

"Well, Mr. Davis ..."

"Temp, remember, call me Temp."

"Okay, well, Temp, yes I dug around some, made a few phone calls and did a search internally here in our files, specifically on the idea of Soviet agents code-named SCOTT or BUNNY and also about one the woman, Kitty Harris. I was able to put something together for you in memo form. It's sort of the way I process things, the researcher in me—so what I'd like to do is send it over to you and let you look at it and if you've got any questions or need more information you can ring me back. How's that?"

"That's super, Albert—send it to my private email address: carolee17@gmail.com. And please don't give that out to anyone. I guess I can trust the CIA to keep a secret, right?"

The historian laughed and said, "If you can't trust us, who can you trust?"

"Great. Send it over and I'll read it at lunch today and, again, I'm deeply grateful. We need to get you on the show sometime. Any events or historic anniversaries coming up that we could discuss?"

"Sure, let me check with the PR people. Gotta get clearance for everything that goes out to the public, but I imagine we can come up with a thing or two that'd be of interest. By the way, good luck with the book. I was, though, wondering what the two code-names you asked about had to do with Kim Philby?"

Temp paused to think and then replied, "Well, I came across them in one of the books and I'm thinking about weaving a story around code names or something." It was a pretty lame answer, but the historian let it go and they said their goodbyes.

After hanging up the phone, Stevenson was struck by the thought that he was about to send information to a media person without consulting the very PR people he had just referenced to Templeton Davis. He instantly felt anxious and for a moment or two considered calling Davis back and begging off. But in the end he decided there was no harm in what he was doing and he attached his memo to an email to Templeton Davis. He also put it in a special file folder, sensitive to Davis's desire for privacy and secrecy.

The ironic thing, however, was that this communication and, in fact, the whole process of Stevenson's search for information was actually not all that much of a secret. His recent research activities had been monitored by listening ears and prying eyes at Langley. And a report had already been filed in another place, far away. This simple search for two names began to arouse a hibernating bear out of a decades-long slumber.

That bear was none other than America's old Cold War foe, Russia. And by the time Templeton Davis opened his email at his Rosslyn, Virginia office around 11:25 AM that very morning, the communiqué, complete with its attached memo, also popped up on a computer screen in an otherwise dark, dank, and nearly forgotten room. It was in an old building known far longer for its own association with intrigue and secrecy than even the venerable CIA Northern Virginia headquarters itself.

The building had been built just as the nineteenth century was drawing to a close, originally designed as the headquarters of a large Russian insurance company. When first constructed, its style was Neo-Baroque and it featured breathtakingly beautiful parquet floors. The front façade was adorned with a large clock fixed directly in the center. However, nearly twenty years after it was built the beautiful building was transformed. And just as a human being's physical beauty can be betrayed by ugly character, internal evil that eventually makes its mark on once lovely external features, similarly this building became something hideous. This had nothing to do with periodic renovations and upgrades over the years, but rather to what went on there, making it a very infamous place.

A notorious placed called Lubyanka.

Chapter Seventeen
Moscow, Russia

WHEN THE BOLSHEVIKS took over Russia in the autumn of 1917, they promised things like freedom and justice. Gone were the days of the autocratic czar and his dreaded secret police force, the *Okhrana*. Members of *Okhrana* regularly terrorized citizens who threatened, or were perceived to threaten, the monarch's rule. They were especially aggressive and vicious when it came to tracking down and punishing revolutionaries— men and women who had become enamored of the writings of a certain man, Karl Marx.

Vladimir Lenin himself had felt the wrath of the czar's agents. He was a victim of guilt by association, his brother having been involved in the plot to kill Alexander II. That czar eventually succumbed in 1881 to a bomb attack, an ornate church now standing on the spot where he died. The future Bolshevik leader spent a lot of time away from Russia in those days, always rationalizing his apparent cowardice, while letting others pave the way, and often shed their blood for the revolution he envisioned.

Likely the most enduring legacy of the *Okhrana* was the creation of the most infamous forgery in history, a document called *The Protocols of the Elders of Zion*. Purported to be the written evidence of a secret plan by Jewish plotters to rule the world, one that fed Adolf Hitler's anti-Semitism and continues to be popular reading in the Muslim world, it was actually a document developed by members of the *Okhrana* to give the czar a scapegoat for his many political problems. Pogroms—organized persecutions of

the Jews—became a regular experience for Jews in Russia in the early part
of the twentieth-century under the czars.

But with all rhetoric about overthrowing the czar and his corrupt and
violent regime, Lenin and his gangsters soon had their *own* secret police,
first called the *Cheka*, activated within a month of the great "revolution,"
before the fateful year 1917 had ended. Over the years it would change its
name and acronyms, but it was always essentially the same—an organization devoted to the control of the Soviet people through any means neces-
sary, first as the *Cheka*, then the *State Political Directorate* (GPU), then the
NKVD and eventually—KGB. Under Lenin, and later Josef Stalin, it would
expand its role and involve itself in the global spread of communism,
working through the *Comintern*, a highly effective organization in Europe,
even America. Its stated goal was to work "by all available means, including
armed force, for the overthrow of the international bourgeoisie and for the
creation of an international Soviet republic."

Though the names changed over the years, the basic nature of the
organization varied little, even after the end of the Cold War and the demise
of the Soviet Union itself. By the early 1990s, the KGB was broken up and
its mission divided between two agencies—the SVR (*Foreign Intelligence
Service*) and the FSB (*Federal Security Service*). Sort of like the division between
the British MI-5 (domestic) and MI-6 (foreign). However, over the years,
the lines between the domestic and foreign practices of the successors to
the KGB have become increasingly blurred, with the FSB emerging as the
stronger of the two. And those familiar with KGB history and methodology
have no doubt that what exists in Russia today is not all that different from
what Stalin had created in the 1930s. One constant, of course, has been that
macabre venue called Lubyanka.

Part operations center and part prison, this mysterious place is where
accused traitors have gone to die and sinister secrets have been buried. And
on this autumn day in yet another October, one seemingly far removed
from revolutionary 1917, but in reality not all that much, in a small dimly-lit
room with three desks and only one computer to share among those working there, four people hovered around one desk and a single computer
screen. They were reading a report from a source inside the American
Central Intelligence Agency. It described, nearly word for word, the source

having an obvious flair for precision, the memo written by Dr. Albert Stevenson, the official paid historian of the CIA, to a famous American media personality. The Russian quartet, in unison, understood exactly what the words on the screen meant. They were back in business—actually in business for the first time ever. Like sleeper agents serving various causes and countries, people who live routine lives, waiting in boring anonymity for some day to come when they might be called upon to perform a trained-for task, one of vital importance for their masters; these comrades had been awakened from a tag-team slumber that had begun more than half a century before. They were successors to other successors, knowing only that they had been tasked to guard a matter of great importance and secrecy. They likely felt that they would eventually retire and pass their charge on to another group of soon-to-be-bored-to-death civil servants in the bowels of the haunted old building. But this day they knew that their lives were about to become very interesting, at least for a little while.

Georgy was the leader of the group, though he had never had much opportunity to assert himself as such. Having spent most of his days in the office chain smoking *Java* cigarettes and sipping (on the sly) vodka, he kept his fellow workers occupied with a virtually constant game of *Durak*, a Russian card game where the goal is to get rid of the cards, the last one to do so being tagged as *Durak* or "fool." Ivan, Grigoriy, and Svetlana never gave him much trouble, as long as he didn't flaunt his superior rank. At any rate, such superiority would only become an issue in the case of a real emergency.

Like, possibly, *this* one.

Georgy and his team read the Stevenson memo and said not a word to each other, though clearly they were each lost in thought. Georgy soon had the presence of mind to place a call to his superior, a man named Nikita, who in turn called his boss, Sergei—the man who would wind up briefing the man who would brief Vladimir Putin about it all, very soon. This was how such information was designed to flow.

"Sir, a most urgent item has come to our attention."

"Yes? What is it? Where is it coming from?"

"It comes from one of our friends in the United States, in Northern Virginia," Georgy blurted out, almost unintelligibly, though his boss discerned the salient point. This was a clear indication to Sergei that the item coming in was from the headquarters of the Central Intelligence Agency and was, ipso facto, a drop-everything-else-and-focus-on-this matter.

"Okay Georgy, calm down and slow your speech, take a breath and whatever you do put out that foul-smelling cigarette!"

Georgy, having just inhaled some of its acrid smoke, immediately smashed the remaining part of the cigarette on the desk, which was fortunately made of metal, wondering how his boss knew he was smoking. "Yes sir, I am fine, please let me explain."

While Georgy Mahklovich exhaled, filling the immediate airspace with the pungent odor of cheap tobacco, Templeton Davis was on the other side of the world downloading the document that had garnered so much attention in the depths of the Lubyanka. The file was titled, "Information for Templeton Davis." He pushed the do-not-disturb button on his telephone and prepared to read what his new historian friend had sent his way.

Templeton Davis's co-workers all immediately noticed the "dnd" light for Temp's line on their phones and their curiosity grew. It was so unlike their boss, usually a loquacious man who had difficulty keeping a secret, to be so cloak and dagger. What was he up to? Did this have something to do with the show? They were puzzled and, frankly, a little annoyed. Especially Valerie.

Chapter Eighteen

DR. STEVENSON'S COVER email was brief, just a couple of lines. He almost apologized for the length of his memo, blaming it on his historian's flair for detail. Davis, though, actually hoped what he was about to read was laden with detail—the more the better—to help him wrap his mind around what he was working through. He clicked to download the file and watched the screen. It seemed to take forever for his Word program to open and load the memo. Finally, there it was in all its potential glory. Much preferring to read such a document from a hard copy—an old habit and reminder that he was part of a generation that hadn't completely embraced all things cyber—he quickly printed it off. Skimming it on the screen while his way-too-slow printer labored to spit out page after page, he quickly noticed that his historian friend had, in fact, been doing his homework. Grabbing the pages from the printer, he used a small binder clip in the upper left corner to hold them together and he began to read:

MEMO

18 October 2011

FROM: Dr. Albert Stevenson, PhD, Staff Historian, CIA
TO: Templeton Davis
SUBJECT: Soviet Spies, Code-Names: SCOTT & BUNNY, and Kitty Harris

Regarding Soviet agents from the Cold War era, SCOTT and BUNNY, I have searched our database and referenced a few books and herein give you a synopsis. If you need more information or clarification on anything in this memo, please call.

The Soviet agent code-named SCOTT was a mystery character for a long time, until a few years after the Soviet empire fell apart. For a brief period of time in the early 1990s and for whatever reasons, the people of the old KGB opened their files, at least somewhat, revealing some important things. For example, though not your concern per your request, we were able to confirm that a certain Mr. Alger Hiss, the guy a young Richard Nixon went toe-to-toe with in the late 1940s, accusing him of being a Soviet spy, something Hiss denied until his dying day, was, in fact, working back then for the Soviets. In fact, he was doing so when he was at Yalta in early 1945 with the then dying Franklin Roosevelt. Yalta, as you may recall, was the conference involving FDR, Winston Churchill, and Josef Stalin, one in which the stage was set for Soviet domination of Eastern Europe, the catalyst for the Cold War.

We were able to also confirm much about Soviet espionage penetration of U.S. and British political and security agencies, including significant details about the famous Cambridge spy ring, which included your Mr. Kim Philby.

As for SCOTT, what I found very interesting as I dug into this last night was that this was reference to a Soviet agent recruited not at Cambridge University in the 1930s, but rather at the other big-name school in the U.K.—Oxford. It seems that there was a second spy ring operating out of Oxford, one that was a contemporary of the Cambridge network, but one of which we know very little. The bits and pieces of information we do know, however, point to some very interesting things that have never really been fully investigated. And agent SCOTT is very much a part of this, possibly the key to the whole issue.

The reference to Oxford almost took Davis's breath away. Why hadn't he heard about this? After all, he had lived there and that's where he really cut his teeth on espionage lore. He continued reading:

It turns out that SCOTT was eventually identified a couple of years back. Here's a link to an article in the *Times of London* (I have included a copy of this and a couple of other items with this memo):

www.timesonline.co.uk/tol/news/politics/article6276267.ece

His name was <u>Arthur Henry Ashford Wynn</u>, prominent medical researcher who died in 2001, and he was the first spy recruited at Oxford in the mid-1930s, around the same time that similar recruitment was going on at Cambridge. Some document came to light that described him in 1935 as "about 35 years old, a member of the CP [Communist Party] of England, graduated from Oxford and Cambridge Universities, radio expert." He was first brought into the Soviet espionage web by a man working for the communists by the name of Arnold Deutsch. His code-name was OTTO. You'll see his name pop up in connection with Philby, Burgess, MacLean, and later another spy named Anthony Blunt, a relative of the Queen of England.

What we know about SCOTT/WYNN is that he was a highly regarded recruit himself, who was successful at, in turn, recruiting others to the dark side. In fact, it looks like he may have influenced as many as 25 recruits for the Soviets, British subjects willing to spy for them. And this includes a single, cryptic reference to the other name you asked me to dig up—BUNNY.

According to what I have been able to dig up, SCOTT—who was regarded at the time as just as important to the Soviets as was Philby, interestingly—recruited this BUNNY. But as far as I know, the identity of BUNNY has never been revealed.

With regard to the woman known as Kitty Harris, she was a Soviet agent who operated under more than a dozen different code-names in the late 1930s. She was very involved with Donald MacLean, including a romantic relationship while working with him in espionage work for the Soviet Union.

As Temp read through the memo he was now confident that the names SCOTT and BUNNY found in the Philby journal in his possession were the very same people now being described by the historian for the Central Intelligence Agency. And what he was digging around now involved Oxford—possibly in a way that had been significantly overlooked by researchers and scholars over the years. He wanted to call Dr. Stevenson to disclose what he had found but resisted the urge. He would wait a bit longer, read up more on the whole thing. Hopefully the books he ordered from the store up in Vermont would be waiting on his doorstep when he got home after work.

Davis sent an e-note to his staff to let them know that he knew he'd been a bit preoccupied and was sorry if he had appeared rude, but he would bring all of them up to speed in the morning at their regular meeting. Then he shut his computer down, folded the Stevenson memo and put it in his back pocket and made his way to the parking garage. As he drove home he reviewed everything he knew at this point. Kim Philby had received instructions to make sure MacLean *and* Burgess took off for Russia, while making sure to guard the apparently more important spy, BUNNY. Now he knew that BUNNY had been recruited by SCOTT at Oxford University in the 1930s and, though SCOTT was now known to be the late Arthur Wynn, the identity of BUNNY had never been revealed.

He, of course, wondered: *Who was BUNNY?* And he wondered if there were any clues in Philby's journal. Whatever the case, Templeton Davis was wide awake, adrenalin in surge mode as he pulled up to his home in Georgetown. It would be another great night of amateur sleuthing.

Oxford, he thought, *it's about time for another visit!*

Chapter Nineteen

TEMPLETON DAVIS'S HIGH hopes for that evening were further stimulated when he saw a parcel sitting on his front stoop. It was indeed from the bookshop in Vermont. He took it inside the house and opened it. The first thing he noticed was an envelope with the words "A Personal Note For Mr. Templeton Davis" on the face. Inside was something written by Bill Roberts, owner of *MINT CONDITION—Used Books* in Stowe, Vermont, which read:

Dear Mr. Davis,

Please forgive this personal contact, but I have listened to you for many years and I have always appreciated your business. You have ordered several times from me, for which I thank you. As I was filling this current order I noticed the subject matter and wanted to let you know that I have many other items in which you might have interest. I also have a very personal perspective on some of what you seem to be researching and would welcome the opportunity to talk with you personally about all of it. My background prior to becoming a respectable old Vermont book monger might very well be of interest to you. If you would like to talk, I have enclosed my business card and have also written my cell phone number on it.

Best Reading,
WWR

He immediately remembered what Dick Holcomb had told him, something about an old guy living in Vermont who ran a used bookstore, could this be the guy? And he noted the name of the town as Stowe—where he would actually be in a couple of days, the thought energizing him. He couldn't remember the name Holcomb had mentioned so he went into the library, moved the ladder to the right spot, climbed up and retrieved the envelope he had hidden there. Once back down the ladder (he then carefully moved it to the opposite side of the room) and at his desk he sorted through the envelope's contents for the handwriting-covered paper napkins from the diner. Finding one, he saw the name William Roberts and next to it the notation, "Wild Bill." Looking back at the note from the guy in Vermont, he read the business card: **William Walter Roberts—Bookseller**. *Another cool coincidence*, he thought.

Ten minutes later, even before completely unpacking his latest shipment of espionage lore and literature, he was dialing Mr. Robert's cell number. After four rings, and just as Temp thought it was about ready to default to voice mail, and he pondered what message, if any, to leave, a voice on the other end answered with a one word question, colored in gravelly rasp, "Yes?"

"Is this William Roberts?"

"Who wants to know," the voice made to sound like something out of an old black and white gangster movie. Davis didn't know it yet, but the old man's bark was really very much worse than his bite. In fact, the whole rough sounding vocal stuff was a deliberate affectation Roberts liked to use when he didn't have a clue as to who was calling.

"Sir, this is Templeton Davis calling from Virginia. Thank you so much for getting the book order to me so quickly, I can't wait to go through it."

"Well," said in a clearly milder, different, voice, one that even had a friendly quality to it, "You're a good customer and I'm a big fan."

"Yes, I saw that from your note. I appreciate that and, frankly, I'm more than a little intrigued by what you mentioned about 'other material.' In fact, just yesterday I had a conversation with someone and your name actually came up."

"Would that someone be an old jackass named Dick Holcomb?" Roberts asked with a laugh.

"How'd you know?"

"Told you I was a listener to your show. Holcomb came up here about a year ago and we spent a day talking about the old days. He's a nice fellow, though his book tries, in my opinion, to balance things that can hardly be put right. Ethics and espionage rarely mix well. At least that's been my experience and since he mentioned me to you I guess you know that I used to be 'in the business.'"

"Yes he did, and in light of what I talked with him about off the air, and your note, I'd like to take you up on your offer and talk with you. As it happens, I've got a speaking engagement there in Stowe this Friday night at some resort up that way, and I could stay over and get with you on Saturday and pick your brain a bit."

"What ya workin' on—if you don't mind me asking?"

"Well, a novel of sorts, some Cold War stuff, spy stuff, you know ..."

"Yeah, I know ... I know ... been there, done that and have many boxes of old, unsold books to prove it. Of course, I'm sure whatever you write will be a smash hit and if there's anything this old retired has-been can do to help, well, I'm at your service."

"I doubt you're anything resembling a has-been and I'm sure you can give me a hand. I've been dialoguing with the historian at Langley and ..."

"Historian at Langley? Now there is a great fiction writin' gig for ya," Roberts sort of snorted. "The company has never been very good about writing, hell, even keeping track of its own history."

"Seems like a nice enough fellow, he's related somehow to Adlai Stevenson."

"A wimpy liberal pinko democrat, that's what Alger, er, I mean Adlai was," Roberts chuckled. He had devilishly used a line made famous by the commie hunter, Joe McCarthy, deliberately, for audience effect, confusing the democratic governor of Illinois with accused Soviet spy, Alger Hiss. The old man wondered if his caller had any idea what he was talking about.

Temp was taken aback by the comment—not it's content, but the tone and realized that he was dealing with a complicated man, a real character from the old days. This was a guy who had been on the front lines of Cold

War intrigue, someone who likely knew where bodies had been buried and who may have, in fact, planted a few himself.

"Well, we can hash this all out this weekend, that Okay?"

"Fine by me."

"Great. I'll be at your store late morning on Saturday; look forward to meeting a real American hero," Temp said, deciding to go with it and pour it on a little thick for the old man, guessing that the guy was a little hungry for attention and affirmation. Turns out, he was.

Following the conversation with Bill Roberts, Davis returned to the parcel he had found on his doorstep. He unwrapped the books and put them on his desk. The titles were:

A Death in Washington: Walter G. Krivitsky and the Stalin Terror, by Gary Kern

Walter G. Kritvitsky: MI-5 Debriefing & Other Documents on Soviet Intelligence, edited, with translations, by Gary Kern

Deadly Illusions, by John Costello and Oleg Tsarev

Mask of Treachery: Spies, Lies, and Betrayal, by John Costello

The Crown Jewels: The British Secrets at the Heart of the KGB Archives, by Nigel West and Oleg Tsarev

The Cambridge Spies: The Untold Story of MacLean, Philby, and Burgess in America, by Verne W. Newton

Treason in the Blood: H. St. John Philby, Kim Philby, and the Spy Case of the Century, by Anthony Cave Brown

Kitty Harris: The Spy with Seventeen Names, by Igor Damaskin

My Five Cambridge Friends, Burgess, MacLean, Philby, Blunt, and Cairncross: by Their KGB Controller, by Yuri Modin

Some light reading for the evening, he smiled and thought. Temp went to the kitchen to find some sustenance and noticed a half-empty sleeve of saltines. He had left it open the night before and the first few crackers were rather stale, but he ate them anyway. He located the trusty jar of peanut butter in the pantry and decided to make do with peanut butter and crackers for his evening meal. Some friends would just feel sorry for him. A middle-aged guy with loads of money eating peanut butter and crackers and spending an evening reading books about spy stuff from the Cold War was just pathetic. But for him, it was turning out to be a bit of an adventure.

Some time that evening, he had the idea to turn his upcoming weekend trip to Vermont into a small staff getaway. He would invite the Bentons, Valerie, and Gilbert to join him—Milt's wife and kid, too. It would be his way of making up for being rude earlier.

Chapter Twenty
Moscow, Russia

"THERE HAS BEEN a very interesting development, Putka," said the man in the gray suit to his long-time friend who was wearing a tuxedo, the proper attire for a night set apart for watching the ballet at the world famous *Bolshoi Theater* in Moscow. But the rare night out with his wife had been interrupted even before it began when he was handed a note and immediately he had to come back to his office.

His office was deep inside a famous complex of very old structures. Their name came from a word meaning "fortress," and that is exactly what had been the defining quality of this fascinating parcel of planet earth—the Kremlin. Winston Churchill's dictum about Russia itself being "a riddle, wrapped in a mystery, inside an enigma" could be just as easily described to the Kremlin, the intriguing microcosm of the nation itself.

He was the President of the Russian Federation, having been reelected to his old post and holding the reins of power more securely than ever before—a czar-like hold. And only this close personal friend dared to call him Putka.

"Yes Vava, I assumed so and that you would not have called me away, this evening particularly, unless that was indeed the case."

The two men only used their childhood nicknames during the most private of conversations. In fact, very few had heard the names 'Putka' and 'Vava.' This was because very few actually knew how far back the friendship between the two men went. Official biographies, the kind found on the internet and enhanced in the security files of nations around the world, tended to miss the fact that though the accepted record indicated that these two men had met at the beginning of their careers, they had actually met years before as young boys growing up in St. Petersburg. And for some reason they decided to keep this childhood acquaintance a secret. For to know this would be to better understand the bond between the two men— the bond of a lifetime.

Over the years, the two men had shared so many common interests, from martial arts as boys, something called 'sambo,' a Russian form of judo, to their love for British spy novels and intrigue; they were soul mates on many levels. They were even both Beatles fans. Vava actually outranked Putka when it came to their old jobs, but Putka had emerged ultimately as the alpha-male in the relationship, though Vava was actually four months the elder. No matter that he was a retired Colonel and that Vava was a retired Lieutenant General in the Russian security services, Putka had actually once run the whole outfit, the FSB, and now Vladimir Putin ran the whole country. And he knew that his best friend, Vava, known to the rest of the world as Sergei Ivanov, would always be there for him, these days as Deputy Prime Minister of the Russian Federation.

And as the saying used to be "once KGB, always KGB," so it was with the new manifestations of Russian control and paranoia, the SVR and FSB. The two men in the office that evening were masters of the spy game, both never tiring from it. They had shared spy novels as boys growing up under Khrushchev and now they were living their youthful fantasies.

They were also both very intrigued by what they had just learned, because it held the potential of parachuting the both of them back into the middle of one of the stories they loved, when their nation was the most feared on the planet. Of course, they also knew that all of a sudden some-one in America was navigating close to a flame that could burn them all. The two men in the Kremlin saw themselves as guardians of that flame. And the fruit of their conversation that evening would set in motion a series of operations on the other side of the world. They needed to know exactly what was going on and the only way was to do some things the old fashioned way.

"Vava, please get me the file called, ⬚⬚⬚⬚⬚⬚.' We need to review everything, just in case this American media star begins to tread where he does not belong."

"Certainly, Putka. I will have the file about this BUNNY matter on your desk first thing in the morning. What time will you be here?"

"Quite early, Vava. I am not sure sleep will be my friend this night," Putin said as he stared at his friend and comrade with a famous look that most observers saw as calculatingly cold. Ivanov knew, though, that behind those eyes was the mind and heart of a friend and loyalist.

Vava went to a cabinet and withdrew a bottle of expensive Vodka and poured two drinks. Handing one to Putin, he said, "Let us drink to the success of what we are beginning."

"Success!" said Putin as they touched glasses. They both downed the drinks in a single, practiced, swallow.

Several hours later, as the next workday began in Moscow, a dark van, having made the trip from Brooklyn, New York, crept along Wilson Boulevard in Rosslyn, Virginia, in the middle of the Northern Virginia night, stopping near a rather ordinary looking office building. Working while no one else was around and before the early birds of radio would be reporting for work, three men got out, two stayed in the van, one of them in the back, where all the equipment was located. In fact, it looked like the cockpit of a space shuttle back there.

In about an hour the three men had returned to the van and it left the scene, circling the area for a few minutes. While driving away, the technician in the back gave a thumbs up sign to the other men, indicating that he was getting good readings from what the others had left behind. They stopped at an all night store, grabbed some badly burned coffee and various snack provisions, then made their way back to the scene. They drove the van into a parking garage across the street from their target and positioned the vehicle on the fourth level near the wall on the Wilson Boulevard side, the perfect vantage point to capture everything they needed from directly across the way. Then they took turns taking catnaps before the action began.

Several devices had been carefully planted in the offices of the famous *Templeton Davis Live* radio show, one in the conference room, another in the celebrity's office, and three phone lines had been tapped—Gilbert's, Valerie's, and, of course, Temp's.

Over the next several days, just about everything said by Davis and his staff would be recorded, transcribed, and the salient material sent far away to that fortress in Moscow, where two little boys in a candy store would consume it all with delight.

Chapter Twenty-One
Rosslyn, Virginia

"FIRST THINGS, FIRST," Templeton Davis said as he began the staff meeting, shortly after six AM. "I want to invite all of you, and Vince, this includes Liz and the girls, up to a beautiful place in Vermont this week-end. I'm speaking there Friday night and have decided to stay over and make a weekend of it—there's a man I need to interview for my research on this new book I'm putting together. We'll leave right after the show is done Friday and be back late Sunday night. It's on me—hotel, travel, food—sort of a way to say thanks for being such a great team and to bring you in on a project I've been working on the past few weeks. We'll take my plane."

They all broke into smiles and immediately accepted his offer, though Benton had to go through the motions of calling his wife. He knew she'd be cool with it. Just the chance to fly on a private jet (he'd been on trips with Temp many times, but never with Liz and the girls) and Vermont was supposed to be beautiful this time of year—what with the foliage and all—though they'd never been.

The men in the van also took it all in, though they bore no smiles, just the expressionless focus of men doing a job. And shortly thereafter they sent their first of many updates that day back to Moscow, where in just a few hours Vladimir Putin and Sergei Ivanov would review them.

"Valerie, call Milt Darnell and tell him to get the plane ready and make sure he knows that Kacie and the little guy are invited. Tell him we'll be traveling to Stowe, Vermont. And contact that resort where I'm speaking—

it's called the *Stowe Mountain Lodge* I think, and get rooms for everyone. Tell Darnell that we'd like to be wheels up from Manassas by one PM, and that we'll fly back home sometime after six PM on Sunday. And make sure we've got some candy and kids' snacks on board, as well as a movie that's kid friendly for all the kiddos to watch," he instructed as Valerie Doling made careful notes.

"Now, you're all probably wondering what I'm working on," Davis said, glancing over at Vince Benton, the only one in the group with any clue as to what had been preoccupying their boss. "It's a new book and I think it has the potential to be another bestseller. It's going to be a spy-thriller kind of thing, set in the Cold War several decades ago." He saw Benton smirk a bit. "And the reason I'm gonna stay over in Vermont is to meet a man up there who'll be able to help me. He's written a few of these himself, runs a bookstore in Stowe, in fact. But most importantly, he used to work for the CIA back in the day. He's a retired spy."

"Did this have anything to do with your lunch with Richard Holcomb the other day?" asked Gilbert Hobson, who had made the original contact with the CIA author.

"Yes, Gil—we talked about it and he gave me the name of this man up in Stowe. I'm gonna need your particular research skills soon for this project, we'll talk about it on the flight up on Friday, Okay?"

"Sure, in the mean time anything I can start checking out?"

"No, not at the moment—but soon."

Valerie spent the better part of the day, following Davis's radio show, making the arrangements for the weekend trip. She booked the rooms—the lodge was happy to accommodate Davis—plenty of space for everyone. She also made sure that each room would be stocked with ample provisions, treats and snacks. The people at the resort jumped at the chance to help. They were aware that Davis was speaking there, but had been told that he was planning to fly in on his own plane and then back home that night. So now knowing that the broadcaster/author would be around the hotel for a few days was big news that spread like wildfire around the resort and would be the buzz of the weekend for the guests.

Valerie also confirmed that they'd be flying into the Stowe-Morrisville State Airport, which was a little less than ten miles from where they'd be staying, and she reserved three SUV's, Ford Expeditions, from a local rental agency (the agency had them brought over from Burlington). Everything was set for a wonderful weekend in Vermont.

Davis decided to make one more contact with Dr. Stevenson that afternoon, letting him know that he had read the memo and was going to be digging deeper.

"Thanks again, Doc for the memo—very helpful. I wonder if there's one more thing you could do for me?"

"Sure thing, glad to, if I can."

"I plan to meet soon with an old guy, retired from there at Langley, and I wonder what you might be able to tell me about him. Name is William Walter Roberts, I'm told they used to call him 'Wild Bill.'"

"Sure, I've heard of him. He was one of the, shall we say, more colorful people to work here during the Cold War. Lives up in New England now, I think, gosh, the guy must be close to ninety years old."

"I don't think he's quite there yet, but close and he's still pretty active for his age. Also, from what I gather, his mind is very sharp. I'm actually heading to Vermont this weekend to meet with him and talk through my ideas."

"You know, that name 'Wild Bill' was actually quite an honor," the historian said.

"How so?"

"Well, back before there was a CIA, back in the Second World War, even before the existence of the old OSS, President Roosevelt tasked one of his college buddies, a guy named William Donovan, to do intelligence work for him. Sent him to England to gauge what Churchill was up to, and this guy developed the nickname of 'Wild Bill.' He then became the leader of the OSS when it was created in '42, but by the time the war was over, he was out—J. Edgar Hoover didn't like him, nor did Mr. Truman. But around the CIA, the man's a legend. In fact, there's a statue of him here in the lobby. William Casey had it put there. It's a shrine of sorts. So, for anyone else to be called 'Wild Bill' in this place, that itself is sayin' something."

"Interesting. Any idea what particular things he worked on? Was he around in the days when Philby was in the States?"

"Dunno. Let me check and get back to you. I guess I'm becoming your research assistant," the historian chuckled.

"Oh, sorry—I tend to get enthused about stuff I work on and forget that it might appear I'm trying to use people, my bad."

"No, no, you are not putting me out at all. It's been a pretty boring time in the history department of the CIA since the new president came to town with a new team. But please don't quote me on that," Dr. Stevenson cautioned.

"Gotcha, Doc, your discontent is safe with me," Davis chuckled.

Just as he hung up the phone, Vince Benton knocked at his mostly closed door.

"It's open. Come in."

"Temp, thanks so much for the invitation this weekend. Liz is excited and will tell the girls when they get home from school."

"It'll be fun for everyone, old buddy."

"I assume this all has something to do with what I dug up in the back yard."

Templeton Davis instantly realized that in all of his frenetic activity to feed his current obsession, he had pretty much left Vince out of the loop. Pretty shoddy, actually, considering that it all began with Vince's big find.

"Yes, and I've been meaning to talk with you about all of it, it's getting quite interesting." He spent the next half hour bringing Benton up to speed and he assured him that whatever this whole thing became, it would benefit both of them very much.

"You know, I haven't even told Liz about it yet. I don't really know why. It's like I'm not sure about it all, if maybe what we're on to may not be the safest thing."

"Sure, it's safe," Temp insisted. "It's not like Russian spies are going to swoop in and grab Philby's old satchel. Come on, Vince, this is a history thing— think of it like archaeology, or something. Dinosaur bones don't attack."

"Well, remember *Jurassic Park*?" Vince persisted, "There's still something about it all that makes me a little uneasy. And, I guess that's the reason I haven't said anything to Liz. But if you think …"

Temp stopped him, "Hey, that's your call."

"Yeah, I know."

"Bottom line Vince is that whatever happens, if I do write that book and if there's any real money to be made on it, trust me, I'm looking out for you and yours. Haven't I always?"

"That you have, Temp. That you have."

The mention of something called "Philby's satchel" changed everything in the van across the street. The men snapped out of the routine, almost-bored body language, sensing immediately that this reference was significant and they hastened to tell the people back home.

Chapter Twenty-Two
Oban, Scotland—September 1938

IN RETROSPECT, IT was an odd and inconvenient time for a fishing vacation in Scotland. The host was the former Colonial Secretary. He had stepped down from that office under Neville Chamberlain just four months earlier and then succeeded his father as Fourth Lord of Harlech, entering the House of Lords. Now, members of his family, and a significant entourage, including persons from various government offices, joined him in what seemed to be a last grasp at the straw of a fast fading summer. But more than that, this trip to scenic Oban, a coastal village about 65 miles northwest of Glasgow—"the gateway to the Isles" as the locals liked to call it when singing their village's praises—was hastily planned. And it was executed with the largely unspoken thought that there might not be much time, if any, for ventures of this sort for a while, maybe many years—if ever again.

The very large estate owned by the Colonial Secretary was an impressive setting for this getaway. It had been in his family for generations and he simply loved entertaining and just generally impressing guests with the home. Of course, he seldom felt the need to mention that the property actually came from his wife's side of things. She was a Cecil, from the politically prominent British family of that name. Her father was the Fourth Marquess of Salisbury and her grandfather had been Prime Minister.

From the front windows on the upper floors you could see the quaint postcard-ready sight of the sea, while in the foreground was the famous distillery around which the town had been growing for the past century and a half. Some of the finest single malt Scotch whisky in the world made its way the short distance from distillery to sea-going vessel, then to an ever growing and quite loyal market around the globe.

The political simmering that had been going on in Europe and much of the world was clearly about ready to reach full turbulent and toxic boil for the second time in twenty years. The mad man Hitler had again and again demonstrated his impudence with demands for territory and now it seemed like he was ready to consume that awkward creation made in the aftermath of the Great War, Czechoslovakia. And who would stand in his way?

But British aristocrats would see their holiday habits change only when they were wrested from them by a world turned upside down. So fishing it was, though the actual act of luring sea trout, the local fish called by some "the prince of darkness" because of its affinity for the night, from the water was incidental to the real agenda. The trip was really all about conversation—actually more gossip than anything—drinking, and generally forget-the-rest-of-the-world-with-its-problems merriment. Plus it rained most of the time, not all that unusual around those parts.

Donald MacLean, who worked in the Foreign Office was there. So was Kitty. They were lovers. Slightly tall, thin, and looking every bit the part of the young and ambitious diplomat that he was, MacLean had been recruited by the Soviets a few years before while he was studying at Cambridge. They were surrounded by so many people about their age that it was reminiscent of college days. Thinking about those college days brought memories flooding back to MacLean's mind, some painful, some exciting.

Cambridge was a place of privilege when he went there in the early 1930s, the son of a prominent Liberal British political leader, Sir Donald MacLean. The father was a deeply religious man and the son grew to resent him and reject his faith, both religious and political. He as much as renounced his father when he learned that Sir Donald had joined Ramsey MacDonald's awful National Government in 1931, seeing this as contrary to everything he was beginning to believe as a college student. He was a full-fledged communist by the time his father died in 1932.

Many students at places like Cambridge and Oxford were attracted to the toxic ideology during, and because of the ravages of, a global great depression. Even some who came from money and privilege found ways to protest against the very means that enabled them to live as they had become accustomed. Communism was presented to them as a path to utopia for mankind, with the Soviet Union leading the way. People like the writer Lincoln Steffens traveled there, seeing what the political powers wanted them to see, and telling the public back home in America and Britain that they had seen the future and that it worked. But they were being told and sold a lie of monumental proportions.

Soon, some in the intelligence services in Moscow came upon an idea to develop a network of deep-penetration agents, tapping into the disaffection of many of the young people who had grown up in privilege. The idea was bold and visionary—to recruit and train a network of young people who would one day rise to power following the well-trodden path of class and privilege. Donald MacLean was one of many "Oxbridge" students who signed on to a lifetime of treachery in the name of ideology.

Some would be very successful. Many would be discovered and discredited. Others would flee and live out their days in Muscovite squalor. And others would succeed undetected by anyone hidden even from the inquisitive eyes of history.

There was Guy Burgess, a brilliant young man with a photographic memory. He was a homosexual, tending to explain his near-predatory proclivities on the fact that he had been traumatized years earlier as a young boy when he had to help remove his dead father from off top of his mother, the old man having died during the act of intercourse. Burgess was a controversial choice for espionage work even in Moscow, for obvious reasons—his brusque flamboyance. But he was a good recruiter.

Of course, Kim Philby was the big catch and he committed to work as a Soviet intelligence agent during a brief meeting with a KGB recruiter on a park bench in Regent Park. Son of a famous Arabist and sometimes British intelligence officer in his own right, St. John Philby, a man who converted to Islam and embraced a radical version called Wahhabism in the pursuit of influence in Arabia. St. John had nicknamed his son "Kim" after the character in Rudyard Kipling's novel of the same name, a story about the great game, replete with espionage references. In retrospect, the nickname was presciently ironic.

The whole thing became fodder for psychologists with the common factor in most of the recruitments being serious "father" issues, manifesting themselves in rebellion and rejection of heterodox standards. Burgess's homosexuality and later that of fellow Cambridge spy ring member, Anthony Blunt—even MacLean "experimented" while in college—all of it seems to indicate a drive in these young men to reject their upbringing. This rejection manifested itself in various expressions of living double lives. And the thrill, even romance to them, of espionage to save the world from fascism, capitalism, and later nuclear holocaust, was very addictive.

Eventually, Burgess would find his way to the intelligence service via a stint at the British Broadcasting Company (BBC). MacLean would become a rising star in the Foreign Office, Philby would make his mark in MI-6, eventually and ironically leading the division of counterintelligence tasked with keeping an eye on what the Soviets were up to and being groomed to eventually replace Stewart Menzies as "C" or the head of the whole agency. And Anthony Blunt would work through the war at MI-5, then sign on to work at Buckingham Palace as the purveyor of all the royal artwork.

All highly placed men from the aristocracy, the best families and schools, fanatically dedicated to the spread of global communism and the hegemony of the Soviet Empire.

Chapter Twenty-Three

LORD HARLECH WAS an important man with access to title, office, and political power. He liked having young people around because they were predictably and sufficiently impressed. They sat at his feet listening to every erudite word from his lips and he fed off the energy they brought with them. These were young men who might be soon off to war. Young ladies who would kiss them good-bye and more, many of whom would one day mourn those who would not return. It was a typically British aristocratic gathering. There was lawn tennis, card games when it rained— as it did a lot that long weekend—and all sorts of frivolity. The music of Glenn Miller's band playing on the wireless and phonograph provided a lively backdrop for the weekend. They danced to "In the Mood" and "Jukebox Saturday Night," and petted to "Moonlight Serenade."

But not everyone there was British. Certainly not Kick, who was there with two of her brothers, Joe and John—though everyone called John "Jack"—they came from quite a large family. Kick was her nickname. Her given name was Kathleen. The family surname bespoke Irish ancestry, but that was back a few generations, these days they were American. Irish-American, not necessarily a passport to aristocratic fellowship in the Great Britain of the 1930s, but that *other* thing sealed the deal. Their father was the American Ambassador to the Court of St. James in London—Joseph Patrick Kennedy, self-made multi-millionaire, generous donor to the American Democratic Party, friend, or so he thought, of President Franklin

Delano Roosevelt himself, and a man with burning and unbridled ambition
for himself and his many children.

Father was not all that impressed with Kick's companions and was
glad her brothers were along to keep an eye on her, or so he thought, they
really didn't focus on protecting their sister and had other ideas. So Kick
had become recently enamored of a young man named Billy—that's what
she called him, Billy, even the name made her father's sphincter tighten. It
wasn't that Billy wasn't from a good family. He was. In fact, that he was
already, even in his early 20s, an aristocrat—the Marquess of Hartington, *or
some such nonsense,* Joe Kennedy thought—that was William Burlington
Hartington's full title. Not enough for dear old dad, though, Kick knew.
Billy wasn't Catholic; he was Protestant, one of those Church of England
Protestants. That certainly wouldn't do and Kick knew that she wouldn't
even find support from her usually sympathetic mother. For her father,
religion was about politics, power, and position—for that matter everything
was. Mother, however, was actually a deeply religious woman. At first Kick
admired her mother's piety, but as she grew she began to realize that religion had become an escape from reality. That reality was her father's philandering. As Kick watched her brothers, particularly Joe—though Jack didn't
do so badly for himself—chasing and nearly always catching the girls, she
knew that the flawed apple of promiscuity hadn't fallen far from her family's paternal tree.

She was wired differently, though. With her it wasn't about mere sex.
It was about love and even at her relatively young age and in a time when
many of her generation were behaving as if there would be no tomorrow—
a prospect not all that unreasonable—she had been so much more dis-
criminating in her choices and actions than her brothers, who were at times
quite reckless when it came to matters of amour. Simply rascals, she
thought, but she loved them nonetheless and very much enjoyed their
company and was so glad they were part of this new life that seemed to be
beginning for all of them.

Billy Hartington, the young man who had already won her heart—but
that was all thus far—was part of a group of fellows, young men all, who
watched the international situation from the vantage point of being lads to
the manor born, so to speak. And Kick and the other girls flitting about

enjoyed watching their young men, fellows they just knew would be running the world one day, watch the world for them. Many of the boys were
actually related, brothers and cousins and such. And the Kennedy's from
Massachusetts, across the pond, just seemed to fit in. Almost like family
they were, it was a real bond. Whereas the British rulers-to-be had gone to
Cambridge and Oxford, sometimes fused into the singular moniker
"Oxbridge," the ambassador's sons had gone to Harvard, located in a whole
other Cambridge. They had also recently enhanced their educational experience at the renowned and prestigious London School of Economics, sitting
under professors such as the avowed socialist, Harold Laski. The Kennedy
patriarch and wealthy capitalist now serving in his formal role in Great
Britain surely despised the political and economic theories being taught by
Laski and his ilk to his sons, but he loved what the connection meant for
their political pedigree, something the old man was always attentive to.

Joseph P. Kennedy viewed the gathering storm of potential global
conflict with deep fear, not only for the country he loved and represented;
but also because of his own sons who would most certainly be called to
serve. In fact, he knew his boys well enough to surmise that they'd
volunteer for the fight to come, seeing it all as a great romantic adventure.
Father knew better. There was no real romance in war. But then again, he
also knew that if war *did* come—and God forbid that it should—any
political future his sons might have would depend on them heroically
answering the call to duty.

Joe Jr. was the oldest of the Kennedy kids. He was handsome, charismatic,
and someone everyone just knew would achieve great things—the most likely to
succeed in any group. His daddy had been grooming his namesake for great
things from the day he was born. Of course, the Ambassador himself had his
sights on the great American prize, the presidency, and there were many back
home who saw the man representing Washington in England as an heir apparent
to Franklin Roosevelt who would, so the thinking went, retire to his Hyde Park,
New York home when his second term ended in early 1941. But of course, there
was a lot of water yet to flow under many bridges in the next few years. And he
still hadn't figured out that the crafty fox in that wheel chair in the White House
had sent Kennedy to London not to promote him, but rather to exile him. FDR
saw Joe as a potential political rival and had out maneuvered the businessman.

Chapter Twenty-Four

THE WEEKEND IN Scotland so long ago was designed to be about fun and forgetting all problems big and small. And the best part of the fun for Donald MacLean, who really worked for a whole *other* foreign office, being a Soviet spy and all, was sitting in the evening with the other young men—the ladies were somewhere else, who knew what they were doing—near one of the many fireplaces in the large estate, glasses of fine whisky in hand, a ghost-like haze of used cigar smoke filling the room, and listening to Lord Harlech go on and on about this and that. The old man's tongue had been steadily loosened by ample quantities of the local potent, olive gold, elixir. Several bottles of 14-year-old Oban Scotch Whisky were spread out on various tables throughout the spacious sitting room. There were also a few pitchers of water standing by. No ice to be found, though. It just wasn't done. And even using a splash of water would be conspicu-ous. It was certainly not something the old man would do.

That old man was now telling his juicy stories and regaling his young audience with all the inside things he knew, dropping this name and then that one. MacLean, of course, loved it for reasons different than the other fellows. This kind of thing was always grist for the information mill—an espionage agent's bread and butter. The subject this particular evening, chosen of course by the host and his alcohol-fueled musings, was once again the Prime Minister Neville Chamberlain, a man who enjoyed fishing in Scotland himself and had, in fact, been invited to be part of this weekend by the wealthy former Colonial Secretary. Another exercise in hospitable futility, he thought. It was about the tenth time—had to be—that he had invited Chamberlain to join one of these excursions and when this particular proffer was eschewed he vowed to himself never again to invite *that man*. But he knew deep down that he'd go back on that internal pledge. He was, after all, a politician and loyal Tory. You didn't survive very long in politics in the Conservative Party, or any party for that matter, by bearing grudges. Certainly not by acting on them.

"The PM seems completely paralyzed by that odd fellow Hitler," said Lord Harlech, now working on his fourth glass of Oban and just after relighting his cigar, which had gone out from recent neglect. He exhaled and continued.

"I have it on good authority that he still believes it is impossible for someone to be as evil as the man with the silly moustache clearly is. Neville is very naïve. Too trusting. He spent too much time trying to balance the nation's books when he was Chancellor of the Exchequer. Sees things in pure economic terms. He frets about how much better money could be used for things to enrich the nation culturally than for armaments of war, and all that. Poor man, he misses the point that we won't have much use for culture when our cities are bombed from the skies and the young ones will have to learn German as a *first* language."

Young Joe Kennedy, never one to be shy—that was more the manner of his brother Jack—spoke up. "So Mr. Secretary, in your opinion should Mr. Baldwin have anointed Winston Churchill as his successor instead of Chamberlain when he stepped aside? Clearly *he* is a man who wants war."

Not taking the bait, the older man took a sip from his glass and a puff on his cigar and stared at the young man (really, he probably was simply trying to remember who the boy was) before replying. "No, no, that is not my idea of what should have been, or should be done. Winnie is too unreliable and mercurial. Not a man to guide the nation during sensitive times. I'm just saying that I wish Neville would be more forthright. I wish he had some coherent plan. He seems to be lost in a London fog."

"Glad to hear you say that, sir," Kennedy replied. "I do not think Mr. Churchill should ever come to power and I'm sure my father feels the same way," he added for emphasis. With this reference, it registered in the old man's somewhat scotched brain that this handsome lad was one of

Ambassador Kennedy's sons. Joe Jr. continued, "There is nothing wrong with avoiding war. What does it really matter what Hitler does anyway—aren't his real enemies the Bolsheviks in Russia? Didn't he say so in that awful, awful book he wrote? What's it called, *Mein Kempf?*"

"Yes, my boy, that's about it. I think that we should be firm, but not to the extent of provoking Hitler to turn his attention this way. We should be allies, frankly. Communism is more of a threat to our way of life than is fascism. Though I'd, of course, prefer neither, thank you very much!" He pounded the armrest of his chair with his free hand several times to emphasize the point.

Several of the men, many of whom were barely out of boyhood, said, "Hear, hear!" raising their glasses. Donald MacLean joined in. He was just one of the boys this weekend taking it all in. Later he would make careful notes and Kitty—Kitty Harris—would pass them along to her handler. They would make their way to the inner sanctum of power in Moscow. MacLean wondered if Josef Stalin ever read his dispatches. He hoped so, that was *his* ambition.

Sitting in a corner and conspicuously *not* raising his glass or voice was Joe Kennedy's brother Jack. The fact of the matter was that he was an admirer of Winston Churchill. Maybe it was a sibling thing, some kind of rivalry for a father's attention, but he found himself enjoying the idea of having a viewpoint contrary to that of his older brother. And he saw the Colonial Secretary as someone not unlike his own father. An intimidating sort of man. Certainly when it came to the Ambassador there was no doubt that Joseph Patrick Kennedy Sr. clearly favored Joseph Patrick Kennedy Jr. as the apple of his eye and vehicle for his vast paternal ambitions. Jack resented this, though never really letting on. He tended to find other ways to express his individuality and resentment.

In the former Colonial Secretary's case though, *his* firstborn, an anointed lad not unlike Joe Jr., had died tragically in an automobile accident three years earlier. It was now left to a younger brother, someone without the kind of charisma possessed by the elder, someone who was more bookish and boyish and who made his way along with a sense of humor and wit, to carry the mantle for the aristocrat. In fact, Joseph Kennedy's second son and Lord Harlech's second son had much in common. They were about the same age—almost exactly the same age, actually. They were sometimes referred to as "slacker second sons" and both were quickly developing skills to enable them to surprise all who made the mistake of underestimating them. Jack looked across the room and saw his British counterpart, a fellow who already talked of a career in public life, following in his father's footsteps. The two young men had just met that weekend, but there was an instant bond. Even chemistry. Conversations about world affairs and the everywhere present ladies. It was fast friendship at first sight.

Meanwhile, the old man continued his stream of consciousness monologue, having moved on to a discussion about the fortress built by the French to protect their frontier, a network of bulwarks known as the Maginot Line. "It is a guarantee that Germany would never dare attack France, such a move would be the essence of folly," he pontificated.

Then in a quick moment, the old man was interrupted in mid-sentence as someone on his staff brought him a message. After a few moments of ear whispering while all others in the room looked on in uncomfortable silence and sipped their expensive but free-to-them whisky, the old man announced abruptly, "Gentlemen, I am afraid our holiday is coming to an end. I must return to London immediately. I have just received word that the Prime Minister has flown to Germany to meet personally with Mr. Hitler. I must tell you that this is a very interesting development." At that moment the young men all felt very isolated, here they were far north on the Island of Great Britain virtually cut off from what must certainly be a frenetic scene in London. They went back to their rooms and packed their satchels hoping to catch the next train south.

Within fifteen minutes, Donald MacLean received a telegram from *his* office calling for his return as soon as possible. The communication also informed him that he was being sent, transferred actually, to Paris. Events were beginning to move along. Kitty received no telegram, but she immediately planned to go with Donald. It would be romantic. She knew that it would also be helpful to the cause.

But before Kitty Harris left the house and made her way back to London with Donald, she disappeared for a bit to meet another man. Nothing romantic, mind you. Strictly business. Spy business. Kitty was what was called a "cut out," someone who passed information along and made contacts, but usually without those being contacted knowing of the existence or identities of other contacts. And in spite of the fact of their passionate love affair—something actually against the rules and for which Kitty had been reprimanded by her superiors—she had to keep Donald MacLean in the dark about her *other* contact that weekend in northern Scotland. He, too, was a young man, an idealist whose political and personal frustrations had provided the fertile ground for his recruitment by Moscow while he was yet a student at Oxford University just a few years before. He had been very useful, passing along the occasional morsel of information he was uniquely poised to access. But Kitty also knew that he was someone being watched by her superiors, watched closely with the idea that his greatest work might be many years down the road, seeds now being planted that would provide a vital espionage harvest much later.

Kitty never referred to this young man by his real name when communicating with her handlers, careful to use only his code name. And she felt a little bad not to be able to talk with Donald MacLean, a man she simply adored, about him. She just knew that he'd be amused at the code name the other young man had been assigned—BUNNY.

Chapter Twenty-Five
Washington, DC—Early March 1961

PRESIDENT JOHN FITZGERALD Kennedy got up from his rocking chair in the Oval Office at the White House and, cigar in hand, walked over to his desk. He had not yet grown tired of looking at this particular piece of office furniture. In fact, it could hardly really be called that. It was a slice of history. His wife, Jackie, a lady with a love for history and impeccable taste to boot, had done her research and insisted that her husband, the nation's thirty-fifth chief executive, use this particular desk in the Oval Office. The desk came complete with a compelling narrative.

About eighty years earlier, around 1880, Queen Victoria had given the desk to the nineteenth president, Rutherford B. Hayes. It had been crafted from the timbers of an old British ship called the *HMS Resolute*. The vessel had been built for Arctic exploration but became trapped in ice and it had to be abandoned. It was recovered and salvaged some time later and the Queen ordered a desk to be made from its wood. Hayes and many other presidents found uses for it in various places, hideaway offices, other rooms in the White House, but never in the Oval Office itself.

In fact, the Oval Office as it has long been known, the seat of presidential pomp and power, didn't really come to be, as we know it, until early in the administration of Franklin Roosevelt who needed a place to work that was accessible by wheelchair. So, though the White House has always had several oval shaped rooms, the Oval Office per se became part and parcel of the presidency in 1934.

It was Jackie Kennedy, with her passionate vision for style, who decided to find the *Resolute Desk* and make it a fixture in her husband's primary office in 1961. After all, he was a navy man and had grown up with a sailor's love for the sea in Massachusetts. Could there be a better choice for him? His PT-109 memorabilia would look great nearby, she was sure of that. Also, she knew that Jack had a deep affection and respect for Great Britain ever since he spent those years there when his father was the U.S. Ambassador to the Court of St. James. Truth be told, he was a bit of an anglophile. And then there was the simple fact that so many of their dearest friends were from England, trusted confidants, and people who were just great fun.

Certainly that was the case on this particular day barely six weeks into Kennedy's presidency. A good friend, one of those very good friends from Great Britain, had just presented him with a box of fine cigars. The kind you could hardly find anymore in the United States. Not just because they were rare, no longer made, or even all that expensive, but because of *where* they were made. Cuba—Fidel Castro's communist annoyance located just ninety miles from the southernmost part of the United States, Key West, Florida.

JFK's predecessor, General Eisenhower, had put that whole embargo in place a year before and tobacco lovers across the country were learning to do without admittedly the best cigars in the world. But not Jack Kennedy. He had a friend who could smuggle them into the Oval Office whenever he needed them. A good friend from way back.

"Ah, it's a beautiful desk, Jack," the friend said. "Jackie told me the story. She's quite proud of it and tells me as well that she has some right royal plans for the whole house."

Jackie was not all that fond of many of her husband's friends, or as she sometimes called them "cronies." They tended to be a rough and vulgar bunch, men who had signed up to help Jack in his early Boston campaigns and sort of hung around as he became something much more important than some obscure backbencher. Not a Brahmin in the bunch. She also got the feeling every once in a while that the men around her husband were almost trying to box her out, or was it maybe that they were just trying to cover for him? She was not stupid, she knew about her husband's extracurricular activities with other women, though likely she did not have the complete picture. She had simply decided early on in their marriage to accept it all as part of what it meant to be married to a great man— particularly one named Kennedy.

This particular friend, however, was different. Jack knew him long before they met and began their whirlwind march toward marriage; but this gentleman could never be referred to as a crony, nor was he ever vulgar or rude. Quite the contrary, he was the essence of civility, manners, grace, and charm. Sometimes Mrs. Kennedy found herself wishing her husband could be a little more like this friend.

Jack opened the top drawer of the desk and pulled out a cigar cutter, one adorned with the presidential seal.

"They put this silly seal on everything around here. I half expect to one day wipe my ass with toilet paper bearing the great image," the President chuckled and grabbing a book of matches—also bearing the same official seal—he lit his cigar, letting the flame linger as long as possible, twirling the cigar slowly to make sure the burn would be even. His friend was way ahead of him and very soon the smoke from two fine Cuban cigars was taking over the Oval Office.

A door opened and Jackie walked in as the President made his way back to his rocking chair and sat down.

"Oh Bunny, do you boys have to smoke those in here? It's such a nice day outside, why not go out there?" Bunny was one of the nicknames she used for her husband, but not one of his favorites. Their friend was more than a little amused at its use.

The men laughed, not at her, but in the way two schoolboys would if they got caught smoking in the boys' room. Not to mention that these were some of the best cigars in the world.

"Sorry dear, this is a men's club. Uh, no women allowed," JFK teased his wife.

"Now Jack," the friend interrupted, "that's no way to talk to such a beautiful lady."

Jackie smiled at their friend and replied, "Oh, you two do whatever you want, but Bunny, I just wanted you to know that the baby is down for his nap and I will be walking around this dilapidated old house trying to figure out where to start turning it into the Palace of Versailles."

"Well, just remember, dear—we're not royalty."

"I know, Jack—but this is the people's house. It may have been good enough as is for an army wife, but not me. Trust me, you'll love what we're going to do with the place. And when we're done, I think we'll be able to show the whole thing on all three television networks. It'll be great fun!"

Mrs. Kennedy bade farewell, waving her hands in a gesture reminding the boys that they were filling the room with smoke, and went out the way she came in.

Chapter Twenty-Six

PRESIDENT KENNEDY AND his friend began a conversation about politics and the state of things in the world, the kind of repartee they had regularly shared since back in 1938 and that weekend in Scotland. The once young students of public and international affairs had matured into men who were in positions to accomplish significant things. The friend, though, had an agenda for this visit and he tried to steer, as best he could while Kennedy bounced rapid fire from subject to subject—the man had attention deficit disorder long before the very term had been coined—to his intended subject.

"How are you enjoying your cigar, Jack?"

"It's splendid. Simply wonderful. Thanks for helping me stock up."

"No problem, old boy—many more where that came from. We don't have the same rules as you Yanks, you know," the friend smiled then segued quickly to where he wanted the conversation to go. "Pity about Cuba. That rascal, Castro has sure turned things upside down. I imagine over here on this side of the pond it's quite the sticky wicket for your new government."

"You're right about that. But there are things we can do. Trust me on that."

"I'm intrigued, Jack. You've been in this office just a few weeks and you're making plans for something big?"

The President reached for another match, as his cigar had gone out. Rekindling it, he looked at his friend and made a decision to bring him into his confidence.

"To tell the truth, I've inherited a plan, one that I think might work, and if it does, not only will Castro be out, but he might be dead and things can get back to normal down there."

"Well, I'm sure that would make a lot of people very happy, especially those who lost businesses and property. Not to mention, it would probably boost your political approval ratings in spades."

"Well, there is that," Jack smiled sardonically.

"Can you tell me about it?" the friend asked. "I don't want you to give away any state secrets or anything like that, but I think the world should be made safe for Cuban cigars."

"Let me show you something," said Kennedy as he bolted out of his chair and reached for a rolled up document that looked like a map. It was sitting on the credenza behind his desk. Clearing off a spot on the desk, he opened the map—it was one of Cuba. He pulled a pair of reading glasses from his pocket and put them on—something he rarely did when cameras were around.

"For a while," Kennedy began as both men stood by the Resolute Desk, "the CIA has been organizing and training a band of dedicated Cuban exiles, preparing them for an invasion of their homeland. These men are patriots and they are the real deal. And though it was Ike's idea and that of his men, it's one that I think has merit and I'm at the place where I have to make some decisions. Maybe it'd be good for me to have an outsider's opinion, I'm not sure I always get the straight shit from the military brass and the people at the CIA."

The friend looked down at the map, by now wearing a pair of half-glasses to help him actually read the small print on the map. He looked every bit the part of a British aristocrat. "Jack, I remember watching one of your debates with Nixon before the election and when you advocated something like this, Nixon argued the opposite."

Kennedy laughed out loud. "That son of a bitch didn't know what hit him. I totally played him. Allen Dulles had briefed me on the whole thing just a couple of days before that debate, though Dick Nixon did not know it. Dulles is a crafty old spy and he decided to hedge his bets on the election. The bastard probably voted for Nixon, but he sure wanted to make sure if I won, he'd not be out on his arse."

"Apparently, it worked," the friend remarked.

"Sure did. And I'm sure Nixon pretty much crapped his pants when he heard me advocate some kind of action, because he then had to protect the plan that was already in process. He prides himself on being a skilled debater, but I mopped up the floor with him on that and I guess it helped me get elected. I imagine Dick will learn from this. He's a clever guy who just got screwed, that's all."

"So how big of an invasion are we talking about?"

"Well, it looks like we have about 1,500 men, well supplied with weapons and aircraft. And they'll hit the beach at the break of dawn one day next month at about here," he said, pointing to a spot on the map on the south side of Cuba—a place called Trinidad. "The idea is that this invasion will be preceded by some carefully targeted sabotage, and then accompanied by a massive propaganda campaign with leaflets from the air and over whatever radio we can commandeer."

"Really? Hmmm," commented the friend, "Mind if I weigh in on this, old friend. You may remember that back in the war while you were letting Japanese ships run into your PT boat, I was part of a team called GHQ Liaison Regiment and our nickname was 'Phantom.' We were all about reconnaissance and military intelligence, often working behind lines, recruiting human intelligence assets. Just the thing you're, I think, trying to do in Cuba." He said, resisting the urge to pronounce the name of the country the way Kennedy did.

"Yes, I remember. You served with that snooty actor, David Niven, right?"

"Served under is what I did. He commanded 'A' Squadron. That was my unit. And frankly, Niven was, and is, an officer and a gentleman. I will introduce you to him first chance I get. You'll get on great with him. Great chap." This was an unusually defensive kind of remark for Jack's friend to make and the President instantly understood how important the work he did back in the war was to him.

"Sure, sure—show me what you think, just a preliminary read on the thing. I could really use your advice on this. Everyone in the meetings speaks in unison, it's almost as if the group has only one mind and I'm not sure I'm getting the best counsel."

"OK, well, certainly, I see a few things right off. I'm actually a little familiar with the area myself, visited Cuba a few times as a younger man. Look here," he said, pointing at Trinidad on the map. "This area is pretty heavily populated, as cities in Cuba go, not like your New York or our London, but certainly it'll be hard to pull off a surprise raid at dawn without sirens going off and I'd imagine that there's a fairly decent communication network in the town, so word will get back to Havana in no time. And also, I'm sure that Castro is even now on the lookout for any sign of invasion and would have a bias toward guarding the cities."

President Kennedy nodded at his friend and wondered why some of the bright generals and intelligence professionals hadn't mentioned any of this to him.

"So, if you were putting this operation together, where would you come ashore?"

"Well, first of all you need to do more than sabotage before the invasion, there must be some human intelligence work. That's what we did in the 'Phantom Regiment.' But let's assume you have assets on the ground there in Cuba for the sake of argument."

Kennedy actually had no clue whether or not this was the case, but responded, "Yes, okay."

"Take a look over here to the west, up the coast. See this place called Playa Girón? There's an inlet there called Bahía de Cochinos."

"Yes, but my Spanish is rusty, what's that in English?"

"It's translated, 'Bay of Pigs.'"

Kennedy chuckled, "What a piss poor name for a place to invade."

"Yes, but there's no one there and you don't have to do it at dawn. You could have the men on shore and well inland before Castro and his band of gangsters have a clue."

John F. Kennedy instantly liked the idea. In fact, he loved it. He had been uncomfortable about something every time the planning group met and now it had hit him, thanks to the help of his good friend. The place was all wrong.

"Might I ask you a question, Mr. President?"

"Knock it off, you can call me that when others are around, but not one-on-one you horse's ass," Kennedy said laughingly. "Sure, fire away."

"What happens if the boys in the brigade, the Cuban fellows, no matter how well trained, get bogged down and are in real trouble? Are you prepared to send in the Air Force and Marines?"

"My advisors have assured me that such a scenario will never happen."

"Mr. President, er, Jack, please don't take their word for it, you'll be asked to provide help, I can just predict that, it's the nature of conflict to escalate, things go wrong."

"The answer is no. I'll not send in the troops and I've said so and will continue to say so."

"Do your advisors believe you?"

"They'd better."

"Well, my friend, I can tell you that you're about to be tested early on in your presidency and I'm here for you."

"Speaking of here for me," Kennedy said, "Any way you can really be here for me? Want me to talk to MacMillan about it? The Prime Minister and I are on good terms and I think he wants to get back to the days of a 'special relationship' between our two countries, the kind of closeness we had when Roosevelt and Churchill were running the show. We're getting together in a couple of weeks down in Key West, Florida, you should hitch a ride with him," the President teased.

"No, no, please don't talk to him directly," the friend said, acting almost horrified at the idea of Kennedy talking to the Prime Minister on his behalf, "let me take care of it. If I need the reference, I'll call."

About that time there was a knock on the door and Evelyn Lincoln, Mr. Kennedy's long time secretary poked her head in and told the two men that Bobby Kennedy, the Attorney General of the United States, was outside. Soon the three men were reviewing the ideas the visitor had put forth and the President's younger brother quickly agreed with their analysis.

Two days later, in a meeting with those in charge of planning for the upcoming Cuban initiative, President John F. Kennedy insisted that the site for the invasion be moved from Trinidad to the Bay of Pigs. He also insisted that it not be done at dawn. He wanted it to be a low-key affair. The men at the table were puzzled, but found themselves unwilling to argue with the new president who, for the first time in one of their meetings, had taken the initiative and seemed to be quite sure of himself.

Around the same time as Kennedy's meeting with the committee about Cuba, a man made his way to room 716 at the *Mayflower Hotel* in Washington, DC, that had one hour before been vacated by its most current occupant. Using a passkey, and placing the 'do not disturb' notice on the door, the man quietly entered the room and used a small screwdriver to remove the grate from the heating vent high on the wall over the unmade king size bed and a painting of horses. Behind the vent was an envelope. He removed the envelope, replaced the vent and made his way back down to the lobby and out the door. He took a cab to the National Cathedral, then another to a restaurant across the Potomac in Arlington, Virginia, but he only ordered a cup of coffee, leaving less than five minutes later. Finally a third taxi deposited him two blocks from his real destination, the Soviet Embassy.

He handed the envelope he had extracted from the hotel room to his boss. Dismissing the courier, the official used a letter opener, adorned with the hammer and sickle, and removed a three-page document. It was a detailed analysis of what was being planned by the United States with respect to Cuba, complete with a time frame and the exact place invaders would be coming ashore. The document also stated with confidence that under no circumstances would the new, young President of the United States authorize the use of American military might to support the men now clearly already marked for defeat.

The document was signed, simply: BUNNY.

Chapter Twenty-Seven
Stowe, Vermont

THE FLIGHT TO Vermont on Temp's private jet was very exciting for the members of his team. Vince's daughters demonstrated their excitement the most, seeming to bounce from wall to wall and seat to seat, nonstop as they raced through the sky en route. Little Jacky Darnell, not yet two years old, was also having the time of his life, while his mom did her best to manage him. Losing battle, there. The little boy's dad was up in the cockpit with Temp. Valerie found the playfulness of the kids contagious and felt like doing the same thing and so did several others, but they knew it wouldn't be professional, or even grown-up, behavior.

A little before three PM they were wheels down at the tiny airport and just as had been planned, the SUVs were awaiting their arrival. Thirty minutes later the Templeton Davis party was checking into the Stowe Mountain Lodge, a large and elegant, yet surprisingly quaint, resort located in a beautiful alpine area at the base of a mountain slope called Spruce Peak.

The party caused a bit of a stir while in the facility's lobby as they tried to organize just who got which room. Several people recognized the fairly famous broadcaster and author and one passerby actually asked for his autograph. Being a radio "personality" didn't attract the instant recognition that came the way of a television counterpart, but it was clear that his arrival had been noised about a bit by some on the staff, a fact borne out by what appeared to be a modest, yet evident crowd. The fact that there were a few large posters on easels with information about the insurance group's event that evening, complete with large pictures of Templeton Davis, "Special Guest."

Even Gilbert experienced a touch of celebrity-by-association, as an attractive girl seemed to be giving him the eye. He was flattered and flushed all at the same time and wondered if his bowtie was spinning around as nervously as his heart was pounding.

A little later, as evening approached, Temp found it hard to focus on the first matter at hand—the speaking engagement before the insurance peeps. But the show must go on. He did this kind of thing all the time, an hour or so, more or less, on the platform, with set pieces, stories, and motivational stuff, followed by the standard "meet and greet" and book signing. He had four basic "talks" that he shared when on the stump, so to speak. One was about the great opportunities in America—good for college audiences. Another was drawn from his book about radical Islam bearing the title, *More Than A War On Terror*. Sometimes Davis would just do a commentary on the news of the day or week. He had seen Paul Harvey do this some years before and it was a nice way to use his radio preps on the platform.

However, even though his mind was elsewhere and already envisioning his Saturday at a little bookshop in the heart of picturesque Stowe, he had the clarity of thought to know that the insurance crowd would probably respond best to his favorite speech of all, one based on the famous phrase uttered by Theodore Roosevelt in Paris in 1910—*The Man in the Arena*. Over the years he had developed a series of motivational stories drawn from history demonstrating courage and persistence during crisis. He would talk about political leaders, business moguls, and somewhat less well-known heroes, weaving it all together into an inspirational tour de force. Of course, it helped that he had written a book with the same name that did quite well and that was supposed to be available in abundant quantities at the back of the room that evening, along with several other of his popular titles. Actually, that particular book was published privately by his media company, *Dodge City Productions*, and largely for just this kind of back-of-the-room sales—though it was available in many bookstores and just about all the internet bookselling sites, as well. *Walmart* stores around the country stocked it by the thousands.

The lodge had provided him with a beautiful suite—overkill, but nice. He showered and shaved. Choosing the khaki slacks to wear with his every-day issue blue blazer and, as usual, eschewing a neck tie (he simply hated those things and it mattered not if everyone else on the platform or in the room was wearing one—he avoided ties as if they were actual nooses), he dressed and then read over his file on the speech. He always spoke without notes and he had developed enough material over the years to speak for about six hours, so it was a matter of choosing a few places to start and then the talk would roll along with a familiar cadence.

The rest of his traveling party had already made plans for the evening, quaint suppers and such. So he was on his own. Valerie had offered to go to the event with Temp, but he knew that she'd much rather enjoy a quiet night off. Even Milt Darnell, his pilot slash security guy was given the night off to spend with his family. Besides, the meeting planners had all the details handled. That's what was nice about these events. Pretty much turn-key—show up, give speech, pick up check (or rather have check sent to speaker's bureau agent for him to take his cut and then direct deposit the rest into one of Temp's accounts).

While checking in earlier he picked up a brochure that described the group meeting that night. He already had a memo on it from the speaker's bureau, but always good to know the audience, he thought. The organiza-tion was the Ohio chapter of the *National Association of Insurance and Financial Advisors*. About 400 of the faithful—this group made up largely of upper-level sales management types—had made the trip and presumably were looking forward to a stirring keynote speech from Templeton Davis. One thing such groups liked about him was that, while he could certainly weigh in on political issues and often did on his radio program, he could branch out from that into matters of business and otherwise popular culture.

In Davis's view, listeners—all except the diehard dogmatists—were weary of more and more conservative talk radio being a fiercely partisan appendage of the Republican Party. Temp kept his show balanced and much lighter than most of the other well-known "talkers." And he was pretty sure that this was the secret of his success. He was the reigning king of the medium at the moment. This could change—and likely would—but he was enjoying the ride.

According to his notes, he was supposed to meet a guy named Phil Culbertson in the hotel lobby at 6:45 PM, so he made his way there a few minutes before—always liked to be early. He picked up a copy of the *New York Times* along the way and sat in an oversized chair, figuring that Mr. Culbertson would recognize him. He skimmed quickly through the paper and rested his eyes on an op-ed piece by Thomas Freidman about the Middle East (no surprise there). Just as he was getting to the third paragraph he heard someone say: "Mr. Davis?"

Of course it was Culbertson, a man who looked to be in his early forties, wearing a charcoal suit and tie and the obligatory gargantuan name tag hanging down from around his neck over said necktie.

"Yes—nice to meet you. I guess you're my host and I'm to follow you—so where do we go?"

"This way, Mr. Davis."

"Call me, Temp—please, I insist."

"Certainly, Temp. We're sure lookin' forward to hearing ya tonight. I listen to you most every day, at least the time I'm in the car, which tends to be a lot in my line of work."

"Lemme guess—you sell insurance?" Temp queried, tongue obviously in cheek as he flashed the a-bit-nervous guide a reassuring smile.

"Yep, though I'm also a sales manager in Findlay, Ohio—ya know the area?"

"Sure do. I've been through there a time or two on the Interstate—I-75, right?"

"Exactly! You've got a pretty good followin' in the town. Of course, I'm sure you hear that just 'bout everywhere ya go, right?"

"Pretty much—but it's still always nice to hear. The day I get tired of it is the day I should quit." By this time they were walking down a hall and toward a room—actually a suite—that would serve as his green room before he was introduced. When he entered the room, he noticed a full spread of appetizers and drinks. The room was pretty full—more than 20 people, mostly men, but a few ladies. Seeing the crowd was a bit of a disappointment, because it meant that he'd have to be "on" and work the room. *Ah well—price of fame*, he supposed, not to mention the cost of doing business.

Culbertson guided him, actually grasping Temp's elbow which was a little annoying, across the room toward an elderly man, the guy had to be at least 80. He was impeccably dressed complete with a red rose on his lapel. The older man reached out his hand: "Templeton Davis, my oh my, I've been looking forward to this for a long time. Name is Spencer, Ross Spencer, and they tell me that I'm the big kahuna in this organization, but I never really know for sure," he said, then laughing with enthusiasm at his inside joke. Like inside his head, joke. But Davis chuckled with reciprocity.

"Mr. Spencer, great to meet you and it's wonderful to be here, I just hope I can bring something memorable to the occasion. Where 'bouts in Ohio are you from, sir?"

"Drop the sir shit, and pardon my French—I'm from Akron, born and raised."

"Got it. Been there a few times. Great city."

"Yeah, well, it used ta be," the older man said with more than a hint of resignation.

Not wanting to get into a serious discussion about the decline of the industrial Midwest, Davis moved toward the table with the food and drink and found a bottle of water. Right about then, someone near the door announced that the program was almost ready to start and the room emptied expeditiously. Temp found himself alone with his thoughts and a table full of food. Just then, someone came back through the door holding a wireless microphone, the kind that went around the ear and curved toward the mouth, and said, "Mr. Davis, someone'll be here to get you in about 15 minutes for your speech. In the meantime relax and the program's broadcast on the internal TV channel of the hotel—I think it's three. Here's your mike. Need any help with it? You can go ahead and turn it on now and the sound tech will bring it up live when you get on stage."

Davis needed no help with the familiar looking microphone and he also had no trouble resisting the urge to tune in to the big insurance fest on the in-house television feed and quickly got lost in his thoughts, which were mostly about spies, a satchel, a journal, and a quickly developing and quite compelling story. His reverie was brutally interrupted when Phil Culbertson came back into the room. "Time to go, Mr. Davis." He just couldn't bring himself to use the familiar, Temp. "You're on in a couple of minutes. Need anything?"

Temp grabbed a fresh bottle of cold water from the table and said, "Nope—all set. This is all I need. Point the way." They went down a few hallways and soon came near what looked to be a small backstage area. He could hear someone clearly somewhere in the middle of introducing him … "Broadcaster and best-selling author. How many of you listen to *Templeton Davis Live* on the radio?" Applause.

Then it was his turn. He bolted up a couple of steps, out onto the rather small stage in the quaint theater-type room. It looked like just about every seat was filled and the welcome was more than warm. About 50 people stood as they clapped, obviously trying to spark a standing ovation that never quite seemed to catch on. He made a mental note to see if he got the full effect at the end of his speech. Now he had a goal that energized him.

"Ladies and gentlemen, I'm thrilled to be with you tonight in this beautiful setting. Isn't the Vermont foliage breathtaking?" More applause. Then he plunged into his theme. "A little over 100 years ago Teddy Roosevelt was in Paris. His presidential days were over and he'd had enough of the big game hunt in Africa. He was something of an international celebrity in 1910, having left office a very popular man— which is rather unusual for a President of the United States, as you may have observed." He paused for effect and there was some mild laughter. This was a good crowd and it was a very good room for speaking, he noted.

"One newspaper guy at the time said," Temp paused for a split second because he knew the quote he was about to use about TR, but couldn't for the life of him recall the name of the journalist—"'When he appears, the windows shake for three miles around. He has the gift, nay the genius of being sensational.' His speech at the University of Paris, aka, the Sorbonne, had been advertised for a few weeks and it was a sellout—several thousand showed up to hear the man who was introduced as 'the greatest voice of the New World.' Teddy shared a lengthy, though powerfully delivered address titled *Citizenship in a Republic.* He touched on a wide array of themes—big issues of the times. He even had a prescient word or two about the dangerous decline in the birth rate in some nations—something that many talk about today in relation to the war on terror and the attempt by some to take over cultures through sheer numbers. But, of course, the most famous part of his speech—what we'd called today a 'sound bite'—was this:

> *'It is not the critic who counts; not the man who points out how the strong man stumbles, or where the doer of deeds could have done them better. The credit belongs to the man who is actually in the arena, whose face is marred by dust and sweat and blood; who strives valiantly; who errs, who comes short again and again, because there is no effort without error and shortcoming; but who does actually strive to do the deeds; who knows great enthusiasms, the great devotions; who spends himself in a worthy cause; who at the best knows in the end the triumph of high achievement, and who at the worst, if he fails, at least fails while daring greatly, so that his place shall never be with those cold and timid souls who neither know victory nor defeat.'"*

Davis quoted the familiar passage from memory and said, "My father had me memorize that quote when I was about twelve years old, along with another longer piece, the one by Rudyard Kipling called 'IF.' Of course, I thought my old man was crazy with such a demand—but I did it, the guy had certain powers of persuasion—and it is one of my favorite memories of him. He passed away about a year later," he said. Then he paused for effect.

"How many of you," he asked the audience, "have ever been criticized for something you did or attempted to do?" Every hand went up. It was the same anytime he delivered this speech and its hook of a question. "Just what I thought," Davis continued. "You're not alone, people. Now I don't want you to raise your hands to this next question, but just think about it for a moment. "How many of you have ever been hesitant to attempt something—or avoided it altogether—because of the potential for criticism?" No hands, just a lot of knowing nods. "Well, it's the same with me. And some years ago I began to study a little about this and I spent some time reading biographies of people who accomplished stuff," Temp continued, always trying to keep his language conversational as he did on the radio. He saw the most effective public speaking as simply an animated conversation. "And I learned something that really impacted my life.

Without exception, anyone who has ever tried to do anything worthwhile—invent something, write something, run something—even sell something," he added, sensitive to his audience du jour. "They all did so while having to deal with criticism."

"How many of you remember a former Vice President of the United States named Spiro Agnew?" Again, good show of hands—though not unanimous, especially among the younger people in the chairs. "Well, the guy had his problems and had to resign the nation's number two office in disgrace. Certainly, old Agnew was no Teddy Roosevelt." Laughter.

"But long before he had his legal problems, he gave a speech about the media of the day. Of course, you know I'm a member of the media, but what I want to pull out of what Agnew once said is a little quote—the way he referred to some of the media of the day. By the way, the shoe could still fit today with some," he said smiling. "He described certain people as—are you ready? This is gold. This quote is gold, because you deal with these people all the time. Agnew called them, *'the nattering nabobs of negativism.'*"

"How's that for alliteration? The nattering nabobs of negativism. So with a nod to two former vice presidents of the United States, Mr. Roosevelt, who served in that office under William McKinley and became President when McKinley was assassinated in Buffalo, New York—and Spiro Agnew, who served under Richard Nixon—someone who, by the way, loved the whole *In the Arena* quote—I want to talk to you for a bit tonight about some people who learned how to deal with critics and criticism—those nattering nabobs of negativism—and pushed through to accomplish great things. How's that sound?" At that point the room burst into applause and this was repeated every few minutes, as Templeton Davis waxed eloquent on the subject for the next—it-was-over-so-quickly—42 minutes. And, yes, he got that standing ovation he wanted.

Following the speech, Culbertson led Templeton Davis to the area designated for the meet-and-greet and book signing. This went on for yet another hour and by the time Davis got back to his suite he was exhausted. He ordered a BLT and a bowl of chicken soup from room service and watched some quite forgettable Canadian television before drifting off to sleep.

Chapter Twenty-Eight

WITH A PROMISE to meet together for breakfast at eight AM, the Bentons went to their room to put the girls to bed, ordering some room service, PB & J's for the girls and sandwiches with actual meat for mom and dad. Same with the Darnells. Valerie and Gilbert gravitated to the Hourglass Bar, where they washed down their own sandwiches and burgers with a local brew.

The girl Gilbert had seen in the lobby was there; again paying obvious attention to him and by then Valerie noticed it. She suggested that Gilbert introduce himself, but he said that he was far too nervous. "Maybe tomorrow," he said. Valerie replied, "Hey, tomorrow may be another day and she may be long gone. This is about two ships passing in the night, you should at least say hello." But Gilbert, actually clinging to his beer glass, shook his head. Valerie rolled her eyes rendering any utterance of the word "whatever" redundant. Soon they both called it a night and went to their rooms.

At breakfast Saturday morning, Templeton Davis conducted a meeting of sorts—letting them all know what he was going to do and what he needed from them. He spoke glowingly about the night before and of how nice and receptive his audience was. He also mentioned that he was going into Stowe (about ten minutes away) to visit a gentleman at a bookstore.

Gilbert was happy and not a little relieved to see the same pretty girl in the restaurant that morning, though she now seemed uninterested—hardly a glance his way. At that thought, he turned a tad sad and angry for not making a move the night before. "*A move?*" he thought. "*Guys like me don't have moves.*" And while he was drifting along in such a thought pattern he didn't hear his name being called by his boss.

"Hey Gilbert!" The third time Temp uttered it was almost loud enough for the whole area of the restaurant to hear. Gilbert cringed at the thought of the pretty girl hearing it, but then quickly concluded "*At least she knows my name, now!*" The smile that thought gave him, though appropriate to his train of thought, seemed quite inappropriate to others at the table who were at once uncomfortable as Gilbert seemed to be ignoring the man who made the whole trip possible. Valerie, of course, smiled as well—she knew what was going on.

"Yes sir?" Gilbert finally replied to Temp.

"Did you hear my question?"

"Sorry, what was that?" Cindy and Monica giggled and Gilbert looked over at them and gave them what he thought was a scary cease-and-desist stare, but that just made them laugh out loud.

"I said—you wanna go with me to the bookstore, I think I might be able to use your research skills."

"Sure, Boss, whatever you need."

Nobody else seemed interested in tagging along, not that they were asked. Vince and Liz had already noted an alpine slide nearby and knew the girls would love it. Everyone else seemed content to just hang out around the hotel and relax while taking in the beyond spectacular views of fall foliage at its peak brilliance surrounding the resort. And it was a great morning for a walk, as well—temperature in the mid-50s—sunny and with just a hint of a breeze. Autumn in Vermont—it didn't get any better than this.

Chapter Twenty-Nine

BILL ROBERTS ROSE early that beautiful October Saturday morning, but then he was an early riser by nature and training, dating back to his old days at Langley and even before. He didn't need an alarm clock. His body almost instinctively knew when 5:30 AM came around. And no one would ever convince him that the fact that he set his coffee pot to brew at 5:25, and that the aroma of whatever blend he was using at the time permeated the place, played any role whatsoever in his ability to wake up on the mark. Nope. It was his training, he was sure—the coffee redolence was superfluous.

After the drill of shower and shave and such, picking out the college sweatshirt du jour to wear with his jeans (this day he chose Georgetown—go figure) he made his way downstairs from his apartment—the one over his bookstore on the main drag in Stowe. It was still early, but he wanted to be prepared for the visitor who had promised to be by at ten. He'd be ready for him much earlier than that.

Entering the store, he flipped the switch illuminating only part of the room—the part toward the back, away from the street. He didn't want anyone to think he was open for business yet (as if any bookstore would be open at 6:26 AM), nor did he want any prying eyes peaking through the front window to see where he was and what he was working on.

Bill had a special "collection" of books and materials hiding almost in plain sight, but not where just anyone could peruse or ultimately purchase. He had installed a shelf within a shelf. Actually, he had a couple of hiding places in the building for his "sensitive" material. On the face of it, it looked like any typical section in a used bookstore, this one marked as an area for romantic novels. Hardly ever did a *man* go back there.

Near the back wall of the store and the fourth shelf from the top (just low enough not to require the hassle of a ladder) he eyeballed a measurement about two feet in length and grabbed a line of romance novels, moving them to a stool that sat nearby. He then carefully removed a thin wood panel—one that looked like the back of a shelf—but which in reality concealed some precious private stock.

It was part of his special spy-stuff-stash.

But it was not books, per se—at least not the published kind. It was a collection of papers, folders, journals—and even old newspapers and magazines. All kept in a nearly worn out box squirreled away in the wall behind a shelf. "Wild Bill" Roberts had for years worked on a story, one that both troubled and fascinated him. It had to do with some of the deepest secrets and darkest moments in U.S. intelligence history—notable failures and the grist for notorious conspiracy mills.

Throughout his career at the CIA, Roberts was never in a position to know, but he was close enough to question. Now he wondered if his soon-to-arrive visitor had somehow happened upon information or a missing piece of the puzzle—he just *had* to know. And could he trust Mr. Templeton Davis with his primitive and yellowing database of detail? He believed he could. Though he'd never met the man, there was something about the broadcaster that connected with Roberts on a visceral level.

As a result of all of his years of research and reflection, Mr. Roberts had an interesting working hypothesis. But to him, it was more than a well thought through educated guess; it was something that rang very true. He believed he could identify someone from the past—known to spy catchers, mole hunters, historians, and conspiracy buffs only by a one-word code name. And if what Roberts suspected turned out to be verifiably true, he would be able to break the biggest story, at least involving the world of intelligence, of the 20th century. In fact, he was pretty sure that if he had really figured it all out, what he had was the clue to a story much bigger than the mere, shadowy world of espionage.

Roberts grabbed the box and put it on the floor, replacing the wood panel and the books on the shelf. He took the box over to the large table that functioned as his desk. He wanted to review some things. But first, he turned on the computer to check his email and noticed a note from Templeton Davis confirming that he'd be by that morning. Roberts smiled. He was really looking forward to this. Davis also mentioned that he was going to bring one of his assistants along. This took the smile from Bill's face and he thought for a moment about writing back and asking him not to do so, but he thought better of it, and assumed that they could talk privately upstairs if the conversation turned really, really interesting.

Reaching into the cardboard box, he pulled out an old, but not ancient, newspaper. It was a paper from Britain from January of 1985. The headline told the story of a once famous man, someone who had known access to power and influence during a now almost legendary period—the early 1960s. The detailed obituary talked of diplomacy and a momentous time in the special relationship between the United States and the United Kingdom. And there was a lot about the dead man's long time friendship with the late and lamented John Fitzgerald Kennedy, one that dated back to the days even before World War II. Not only that, the now deceased former celebrity had often been seen in the company of President Kennedy's widow, until she married one Aristotle Onassis.

Bill Roberts scratched his chin and wondered if anything Templeton Davis would have to say would connect at all with the man whose obituary he had just read once again. Then he took the bin filled with his special collection upstairs to the living quarters above the store.

He went to what looked to be an ordinary medium-sized freezer—the kind you'd keep frozen meat in fairly long term (though it was not big enough for anything like a side of beef). It opened from the top. The old man reached in and began removing various cuts of steak, chops, hamburger, two chickens, and a turkey. He then displaced a panel—a false bottom—from the freezer and it was clear that the actual bottom of the freezer annexed nearly a foot from below the floor itself—a cut out space that was not at all noticeable from the outside. He then put the box he had retrieved from downstairs into the freezer, replaced the panel and put the frozen meat back in place.

Chapter Thirty
Clifton, Virginia

AROUND THE TIME the Templeton Davis party awakened that morning in Vermont, the van that had earlier been in that parking garage across from the building where Davis's nationally syndicated radio show originated, pulled out of the shoulder of the road in Clifton, Virginia, just a quarter of a mile or so away from the home of Vince and Elizabeth Benton. The van had been parked well off the road and hidden in the woods along the road, with little chance of being noticed by anyone, especially law enforcement.

Three men had exited the van 90 minutes before, taking a back route through the woods toward the Benton property. They were dressed in black and carried some tools of the trade—that is, if the trade is breaking and entering. But they actually had no intention of entering the house proper. No, their destination and object of interest was the building the Benton family called the "man cave"—Vince's glorified work shed out back.

The lock on the door posed no problem whatsoever for this band of professionals; in fact they all smiled at how easy it was to gain entrance. Once inside, they used their flashlights to survey the setting. The building had few windows, none of which faced the main road, so there was little fear of their clandestine operation being noticed by any car passing by. There weren't many people out on the nearby roads at that hour.

They knew that they were looking for a suitcase or briefcase of some kind. That much was clear from what they had been able to glean from their eavesdropping at the offices of Templeton Davis Live. But there didn't appear to be any such item in the small building. Then one of the men noticed a blanket in one corner obviously shrouding something and sure enough it was exactly what they had been looking for. They grabbed it and quickly made their exit, not even taking a moment to look inside— they'd do that in the van and if they needed to return to the scene, they still had time.

Once back in their van, one outfitted with high-tech equipment, the kind you'd expect espionage operatives to travel with, they removed all the contents from the bag. There was a tripod, a camera, and that was it. They immediately sensed that this was not exactly what their superiors had hoped to find. And when they communicated across several time zones with those who had directed their operation, they were asked: "That's all? Was there no book of any kind? No papers? No journal?"

So they made a trip back to the Benton property. This time they knew that they had to be a bit more invasive and it would be hard for them to avoid the returning owners sensing that their place had been ransacked. But it was what it was—they needed to find some kind of book or journal. They searched the "man cave" first—from top to bottom. Then they broke into the house and went room by room to no avail.

Their bosses back home were very unhappy. And their next instruction made the men in the van a little unhappy themselves, though they were quite careful not to even hint about this to the people half-a-world away. They simply agreed to the new instruction with soldier-like submission and programmed the GPS in the van for their next destination, one that would take them much of the day to reach: the northern part of the Green Mountain State. They pulled through a fast food drive-through for provisions and coffee and soon were on I-95 heading north.

Chapter Thirty-One
Stowe, Vermont

TEMP'S FORD EXPEDITION reached the center of Stowe in just a few minutes and he found a spot to park behind the Green Mountain Inn, near a building with many shops, including a bookstore—one that specialized in actual *new* books. He and Gilbert went to a coffee shop located in the front of the building. Temp ordered a large black coffee with two shots of espresso added. He wanted to be more than alert for his meeting with Bill Roberts. Gilbert ordered a diet coke—presumably for the same reason.

Roberts' store, *MINT CONDITION—USED BOOKS*, was located just a block away from the coffee shop, so he took his time and picked up a local paper and sat down to enjoy his coffee. Some nearby were whispering in a kind of "hey, you know who that is?" manner. He paid no attention and fixed his gaze on the local news. After reading the tabloid for about two minutes, he realized that it was dated the week before. Talk about a place with a slow pace!

Sheepishly pitching the worthless newspaper in the trash receptacle, he exited the building with Gilbert scrambling to follow. Davis turned right and made his way to his rendezvous with a real life, old time spy. He looked around as he walked leisurely up the block. He made the mental note that he must have seen this place in a Norman Rockwell picture—it was all so perfectly New England. Stores and eateries were beginning to yawn and stretch to life on one of the last Saturdays of the fall foliage tourist season.

Most of the owners and workers looked forward to the coming break—about a month between the colors of autumn and the blanket of white that heralded the ski season. And this particular Saturday had all the makings of a boom day—big crowds and good business. The weather virtually guaranteed it.

After what seemed to be just a few steps, he found himself looking up at the bookstore sign over a door. He turned the handle to walk in. It was locked. The store was set to open at ten, but it was still about five minutes before the top of the hour. But before he could conjure up any feelings of disappointment—or just impatience—he heard the door click to unlock and a young man—clearly not Mr. Bill Roberts—invited him in, while turning the sign in the door window over so as to advise passersby that they were indeed open for business.

The young man stuck out his hand, "I'm Kenny Starwood. I work here for Mr. Roberts. Nice to meet ya, Mr. Davis." Davis shifted the large coffee cup from his right hand to his left in order to shake the boy's hand.

"Well, great to meet you, too—you listen to my show?"

"No sir, I'm in school during those hours, but Mr. Roberts tends to fill me in on what ya talk about," he said while slightly rolling his eyes, but trying not to.

Before Davis could ask about where Roberts was, he heard the words, "Well, welcome my friend to our humble hole in the wall. Looking for an old book—or do you have some to sell?"

Taken back by the question, Davis paused and then saw the smile on the old man's face and they shook hands enthusiastically.

"Let's go back over this way to my office, well sort of office. No walls, mind you, but there is clutter, so that's an office, right?"

"Yes sir," said Temp, though already less than enamored of the small talk and noting that the word "clutter" didn't do the area justice. Try catastrophe. If a man's desk was any indication of his mind, well, this guy's brain must be a maze—a maze of mirrors.

The old man surprised Davis by abruptly jumping into the conversational deep water: "So, why don't you tell me what you're writing about and we'll see if this old spook can help you."

"Wow, Bill, you get right to the point, don't you?"

"At my age, it's beyond a sin to waste any time. So you're writin' a spy novel—that what you said?"

"Well, funny you should ask that, 'cause I'm pretty much telling most folks that it is a work of fiction—but between you and me and one of the many, many fence posts in your beautiful town—I'm actually thinking about a book that deals with spy history, you know—nonfiction."

"Ah, I see—and what makes you want to do that—what's your area of interest, if not expertise?"

Templeton Davis was surprised at the forthrightness and sheer force of the old man's personality. Usually people fawned a bit in front of him, at least at first—the fame thing—but this guy was obviously not impressed with celebrity. He seemed to wave all the preliminaries off in a dismissive kind of way.

"Well, sir," finding himself unusually deferential all of a sudden, "I'm not exactly sure yet, but I've stumbled on to some things that I want to research further and I thought maybe a guy like you could possibly suggest where I might start to dig."

"Maybe … maybe," said the old man who was clearly waiting for more from his visitor.

"Of course, you probably have records of my purchases from you over the past few years—and you reached out to me the other day after my most recent order. So I guess you know that I'm digging into the whole Philby, Burgess, Cambridge spies, thing."

"Lots of people have dug around that," Roberts countered. "It's been pretty well picked over."

"I'm not so sure," replied Davis.

"Oh, really? And just what's been missed, Mr. Davis? What have all the researchers and theorists overlooked that you've miraculously discovered?"

Davis bristled at the almost belligerent tone—a fast and notable shift on the part of the old man. Then, as if catching himself, and before Temp could answer, Roberts said, "Oh Hell, I'm sorry my friend. Here you come all the way up here to see me and I go and just about bite your head off. Sorry 'bout that. Guess I still tend to get a little funny, maybe even defensive about the old days, especially when people start digging around. It's a minefield, you know. Even though it's history—it's still pretty risky, even dangerous."

The old man got up from his chair and walked over to a table where a pot of coffee had been marinating for a while, it had a strong, overdone and burnt smell to it. Roberts blew the dust or whatever out of a mug and poured a cup then he added four spoons of sugar.

"How could it be dangerous? Isn't that a little over the top?" Temp asked.

"Not at all over the top, as you say. In fact, there *are* some secrets—let me put it that way—secrets that've been buried so deep for so long because they were never intended to see the light of day. And if they ever got out they'd cause problems even now, all these years later."

"Fascinating, Bill—simply fascinating. But, and hear me out on this, what if I've possibly discovered something that just begs to be written about, to be told to the public. I mean, I may have the makings of another bestseller here and be on the way to answering questions that've lingered since the early days of the Cold War."

"Like what, for instance?"

"Well, before I even begin to talk in any detail about any of this, I'd hoped we could come to an understanding—you and me. I'm sure we can help each other. I'm sure there are some things you really can't divulge to me, but—well, remember the Watergate story and that Mark Felt guy, the one they called 'Deep Throat'?"

"Remember him? Hell, I knew the son of a bitch and didn't care a bit for him. He was a lousy, disgruntled man and when Hoover—J. Edgar Hoover, that is—died and Nixon passed over him and gave the directorship of the FBI to that idiot L. Patrick Gray, Felt got his revenge by working with that jerk reporter Woodward. And don't get me started on Bob Woodward. I mean the guy made up a whole story about interviewing William Casey in the hospital and getting all that supposedly insider shit. Problem was that Casey was a vegetable by that time, his nurse was a friend of my daughter's and told me that the director could have no more talked to Woodward than a necktie could."

He paused and immediately sensed that he was wandering a bit. He didn't want Templeton Davis to think he was off his rocker or something.

Roberts stopped abruptly, saying: "But I'm sure you don't need a lecture on all that from an old man ... now, yes ... well ... I do remember Felt. How does he fit into your information?"

"He doesn't."

"What the ...?"

"OK, sorry—here's the deal. What I'd like to do with you today is sort of what Woodward and Felt did in that Rosslyn, Virginia, parking garage, which is right near my studio. I'll tell you what I know and you just tell me if I'm moving in the direction of something important—or not. Simple as that."

"I can do that. Sure."

At that moment, a bell rang signaling that a customer had come through the front door. Roberts excused himself from Davis and looked around the corner and saw that Kenny was on top of things and helping the young lady who came in to browse.

Back at the table, he asked Davis, "Where do you wanna start?"

Chapter Thirty-Two
Key West, Florida, March, 1961

PRESIDENT JOHN F. Kennedy had already changed some things in Washington, DC, even a mere two months into his presidency. Gone was the leisurely pace so evident throughout the Eisenhower years—a pace largely having to do with the General's age, customs, and challenged health. In its stead was this almost frenetic hyper-activity of the new White House. And as with most new administrations, the insiders were inclined to believe all the good things being written about them. It was all part of a process called a political honeymoon.

But there were some very pressing and potentially bad things on the new president's plate, particularly issues relating to Castro's Cuba and problems brewing half a world away in Southeast Asia. That regional reference would ultimately be associated in the public's mind with Vietnam, but during the early weeks of Kennedy's tenure at 1600 Pennsylvania Avenue it was not Vietnam, but rather a nearby neighbor that was garnering attention as the hot button place in the ongoing Cold War battle against communism—a place called Laos.

Kennedy sensed that it was time to have a serious meeting with the leader of one of the nations closely allied with the U.S.—Great Britain. So the president invited Prime Minister Harold Macmillan to meet him at Key West, Florida on March 26th. By this time, JFK had met with the prime ministers of Canada, Australia, and New Zealand, as well as the President of Ghana, but this meeting at the southern extremity of the U.S. would really be Kennedy's first serious opportunity for a substantive summit of sorts with a real counterpart.

Ever since spending time in England during his father's tenure as U.S. Ambassador to the Court of St. James in the late 1930s, he had been a bit of an anglophile. Unlike his father, and now long dead older brother, who both supported Chamberlain's appeasement (older brother Joe, largely because that's what father wanted), Jack Kennedy was an admirer of Winston Churchill's powers of communication and leadership so in evidence during the build up to, and conduct in, the Second World War.

And John Kennedy and Harold Macmillan were actually relatives, at least by marriage—sort of. The President's older sister, Kathleen, who was called "Kick" by those who knew her well, had married Macmillan's nephew in May of 1944. His name was William "Billy" Cavendish, Marquess of Hartington, and the heir of the Tenth Duke of Devonshire. But the whole thing was painful for Jack Kennedy to recall. Neither he, nor most of the family, attended the wedding because Cavendish was Protestant. Only older brother Joe, who as it turned out had not long to live, showed up for the ceremony.

It also turned out that Billy Cavendish didn't have very long on the earth. He was killed in action just four months after marrying Kick. She retained the title "Dowager Marchioness of Hartington," though not for long, as she herself perished in an airplane crash in France in 1948.

Though the two leaders would eventually develop a good working chemistry, this first meeting of Kennedy's presidency was an uneasy one. Both men were unusually nervous. Macmillan was concerned that his much younger counterpart (Macmillan had first been elected to Parliament when Kennedy was but seven years old) would think of him as a funny old man, more of a relic than a relevant contemporary voice. Kennedy was at least a little worried that his British counterpart might view him as young and inexperienced, especially since Macmillan had such a good relationship with the much-older-as-well President Eisenhower.

At issue was Kennedy's strong desire to see the Brits support strong action in Laos to stop communist aggression. But he came across as somewhat pushy and Macmillan was put off. In the end, though, the British

Prime Minister conceded a commitment to act in union with the Americans in Laos, if it came to that.

But it was the postscript to the meeting that really had the most lasting impact on geopolitics. Before the two men parted company, and after the obligatory public statements to the press and world, Kennedy pulled Macmillan aside for a personal conversation.

"Mr. Prime Minister, if I may be so forward, I'd like to talk with you about the next Ambassador from your nation to ours."

"Well, this is a bit out of the ordinary, Mr. President—but seeing as we're family and all ..." Both men smiled. It was one of the few moments since their meeting began hours before that was not tinged with tension.

"Indeed. Indeed. Well, speaking of relatives, the man I'd like to recommend to you, if I could be so blunt, is someone who is actually distantly related to both you and me—someone we both know quite well."

"We do?"

"Yes. And frankly, Mr. Prime Minister, I think this man's appointment would go a long way to perpetuating and enhancing the very special relationship between our two nations. In fact, I'd go so far as to suggest that we might wind up living out some glory days of our own reminiscent of when Mr. Churchill had your job and Franklin Roosevelt had mine."

"Ah yes—I recall those days well," a not-so-subtle reminder to his youthful counterpart that he had been part of the leadership team even back in those glory days, when he had been Winston Churchill's star protégé.

Ignoring the potential dig, Kennedy continued: "Well, yes ... I'm sure you do."

"So just who is this mystery candidate—as if I didn't already know? I have my sources, you know," the older man teased.

"Of course. I'm not surprised at all. Our wonderful mutual friend David Ormsby-Gore is the man for the job, as far as we're concerned." Then, as if catching himself, he added, "But indeed we know that such a decision and the job for that matter is primarily your concern, Mr. Prime Minister. I know what I'm doing here is a bit unusual, but consider that it is part and parcel of this very special relationship that I'd like to see continue that brings me to this."

"Mr. President, I don't take your recommendation as an affront in any way, shape, or form. I'm aware of your long time friendship with Mr. Ormsby-Gore. I'm also cognizant of his many qualifications and assure you that he has been on our short list. Of course he has much experience, as I'm sure you're aware. The man has represented Oswestry in the House of Commons for more than ten years. He served under my predecessor, Mr. Eden, as Parliamentary Under-Secretary for Foreign Affairs, and is my Minister of State for Foreign Affairs. In fact, some men might consider appointment to an ambassadorship as a career step *down*."

"Well, sir, I don't think David … er … Mr. Ormsby-Gore would feel that way."

"You have particular knowledge toward that end, do you?"

"Well, yes, as you probably know, he came to see me a couple of weeks ago and, in fact, helped me think through a pretty complicated problem."

"You know," the Prime Minister added, "that Ormsby-Gore comes from good stock with quite a significant political pedigree. His father held many important offices back in the day and was Colonial Secretary for a time under both Stanley Baldwin and Neville Chamberlain. Lord Harlech is still alive and kicking. And David's great-grandfather was Lord Robert Cecil, Third Marquess of Salisbury and three-time Prime Minister of Great Britain."

Of course, Kennedy knew all this. In fact, he pretty much knew everything about his good friend, David Ormsby-Gore; at least he thought he did.

"Yes, yes, he has quite an impressive hereditary résumé," Kennedy affirmed.

Macmillan replied: "Well, I'll take your thoughts under advisement, as they say. At any rate, I imagine we'll be making some kind of decision and announcement on the ambassadorial matter in due course."

The President of the United States nodded respectfully. "Thank you, Mr. Prime Minister, for your graciousness, and I look forward to many future meetings with you—and to continuing the very special relationship between Great Britain and the United States."

"You're most welcome, my … friend," catching himself (he almost said "my boy" and that would have been scandalous).

In due course, it was announced that David Ormsby-Gore, heir to a political and aristocratic family, was being appointed as British Ambassador to the United States.

Chapter Thirty-Three
Stowe, Vermont

DAVIS DECIDED TO plunge right into it with Bill Roberts, sensing that the old spy was a pretty no-nonsense guy and not all that long on patience. "Well, as I said, I'm interested in the whole Cambridge spies thing, but even more so, I'm curious about what you might know about another spy ring that dated back to the 1930s—one that recruited young men at the University of Oxford, not Cambridge." He decided not to bring up his own personal connection to Oxford and wondered if the old man had done his due diligence and checked out *his* background.

"Yep, that's one of the great unresolved mysteries of that era. There was indeed a spy ring, or at least recruiting was going on back then at Oxford. The exploits and high profile defections of the Cambridge boys, you know, Philby, MacLean, Burgess and then the exposure of that weirdo Anthony Blunt made the whole Oxford story just sort of go away," replied Roberts.

"Yeah, I know—and there's not much out there on it. But I've been looking through some books and I'm developing a sort of working theory," said Davis.

Just then, Roberts looked past Templeton Davis at something that obviously caught his attention and he held his hand up just about half way up his shirt in a motion that said "Wait a sec."

The old man got up and walked toward the coffee table mumbling something about checking on the kid and that customer, but really he wanted to check out what was happening a couple of aisle's away. Sure enough, he saw her. The girl who had entered the store was alone in the romance novel section looking at the shelves. She was tall, likely in her mid-twenties, very attractive and something about her didn't ring true to the old spy.

"Help you find something, honey?"

"No, no, I'm just looking at books," her answer revealing the hint of an accent, one that *really* got a hold of Davis's attention.

"Well, you've come to the right place," Roberts chuckled. "Let me know if you need anything."

"You're so very kind. Thank you, sir. I will."

Bill Roberts made his way back to where Davis was sitting and when they made eye contact he rolled his. "Hey, it's such a beautiful day, let's get some fresh air—how 'bout a walk?"

"Sure, I guess," Davis surrendered, though clearly puzzled as to what was happening.

As the two men made their way to the door, Davis saw the girl and immediately remembered her from the hotel, she had been in the lobby when their party was checking in the night before. Seeing Gilbert browsing some of the titles in a section marked "European History," Davis tried to summon him over toward the door but not so overtly as to catch the attention of the girl in the romance books section. The young man took the bait and made his way over to Temp.

"Don't be too obvious, but the girl who came in a bit ago, wasn't she at the hotel last night?" Davis whispered to Gilbert.

Gilbert was at once ill at ease and even started to blush—he had seen her enter the bookstore and had been going over scenarios in his head, trying to figure out a way to strike up a conversation with her, convinced that the pretty girl was stalking him, and not in a bad way.

"Yep, I saw her."

"Do me a favor, kid, keep an eye on her, Okay?"

Gilbert shot his boss a puzzled look, "Sure, happy to—but what for?"

"Just do it and I'll explain later," Temp said as he followed Bill Roberts out the front door and down the street.

The two men turned off the main road and within a block they were in a quiet (though everything was pretty quiet in Stowe!) residential neighborhood and Templeton found himself lost for a moment in admiration of the beautiful homes, many with large wrap-around front porches—*it was like being in a time warp*, he thought. His quest, and now breakthrough, if that was what it was, had done that for him early that morning. And just a rather long block ahead was the Stowe Public Library, itself a beautiful old structure. They slowly walked toward it.

Roberts broke the silence. "Sorry about that my friend. I guess my years in the spy game turned me into a bit of a paranoid. But that pretty girl seemed to be interested in overhearing our conversation."

"Reeeally? I saw her last night at the hotel, that's why I asked Gilbert to keep an eye on her." Davis replied.

"Yes sir, never can be too careful, could just be a coincidence, but I thought it'd be best to take our conversation on the road—or sidewalk, as the case may be," Roberts said as he smiled and for a moment took in just how beautiful the day was turning out to be.

"OK, so back to what you were starting to tell me—you said something about a 'working theory'?"

"Yes and I guess I need to bring you in on something and I'm sure I can count on your discretion, but at some point I'd need to tell you this—so here goes," Temp said.

His curiosity sufficiently triggered, Roberts replied: "By all means. I'm all ears!"

"Well, a week or so ago, one of the guys on my team—he and his family are here with me this weekend, in fact, I brought several members of the staff up here as sort of a retreat and way to say thanks for all the great work they do—anyway, this guy on my team, Vince Benton, was digging around on his property out in Fairfax County in Virginia. The guy's got a beautiful place there, and he came upon something quite odd and very, very interesting. It seems that a satchel or case of some kind had been buried there years before and Vince dug it up and found all sorts of stuff in it."

"A case, you say?"

"Yeah—it had some initials on it and it is in the style of what a lot of men, particularly Brits, carried 50 years or so ago."

"You said it had some initials?"

"Yep—H.A.R.P."

Bill Roberts stopped in his tracks and looked off into the distance without speaking for several moments—then said slowly and with a certain accent of emphasis: "Harold—Adrian—Russell—Philby!"

Templeton Davis was startled. How did this old man immediately recognize the initials as belonging to the infamous Soviet mole in British intelligence?

"I'm impressed!" Davis said to Roberts. "Mind if I ask you how you made that connection so quickly—and I might add, I think—accurately?"

"Well, one hardly forgets the important things. And I don't know if I told you, but I actually knew Mr. Philby, at least I met him a couple of times."

"Seriously? That's very interesting."

"What's more, I was very involved in what you might call 'clean up and control' operations in the aftermath of Philby's departure from America in '51. He had a big house over on, I think it was Nebraska Avenue, in Washington, and we went through that place with a fine-tooth comb looking for evidence against him. Found nothing. Then about fifteen years or so later, I think it was, the guy, who by that time had defected to Moscow, confirming what we had suspected all along, well—he wrote a book and talked about burying some stuff and he described the area and all and we went there and looked and then looked some more, but it was like the whole needle in a haystack thing."

"Well, apparently Adrian was pretty good at disinformation, because the stuff we've found was nowhere near where he said he buried it—pretty much the opposite direction, actually."

Roberts smiled and then he chuckled, "That old son of a bitch!"

Davis smiled as well, feeling pretty good that he had already forged a relationship with the old man. "And among the things in the satchel ..."

"Yeah, what was in it?" interrupted Roberts. "Did it have the stuff in it he wrote about in his book, a camera—things like that?"

"Yes it did—but there was more. There was a journal of sorts and something called a one-time pad. And this is what has made this whole thing so fascinating. I've been learning a lot about codes and decoding—in fact, our mutual friend, the guy who was on the show the other day, Dick

Holcomb, sort of gave me a crash course. But he doesn't know why I was interested."

"That's good, Davis—best to not let many people know about this just yet. So what kind of secrets have you uncovered?"

"Well, actually, I don't know if I've uncovered any secrets yet, but I sure have a lot of questions. And I thought maybe you could help."

"Glad to—nothing else going on today and you have captured my interest, for sure. Where's this journal now?"

At that mention, Templeton Davis reached behind himself, under his un-tucked shirt, and pulled out an envelope containing the journal and the one-time pad he had found and used to decode the BUNNY message.

"You've been carrying it on you?" Roberts asked with an incredulous look. "Pretty risky."

"Well I wanted to bring it today, in case we hit it off and I felt you'd be able to help me. I realize that I'm no spy and know little of—what do they call it?"

"Tradecraft. That the word you're looking for?"

Davis just smiled and nodded. He was already becoming very enamored of his new friend. "Yes, tradecraft. I've got a lot to learn and I'm pretty sure you're the man to teach me."

By this time they had reached the library and Bill Roberts led Templeton Davis through the front door. An elderly lady was at the front desk and Bill greeted her immediately. "Martha—mind if I take a friend of mine back to that conference room. He has something he wants to show me."

Martha Meyers had worked at the Stowe Public Library for a little over 45 years and knew everyone in town—at least those who read books. She instantly and obviously assumed that this was just another one of Bill Roberts' book customers, or someone trying to sell *him* a rare find or some such thing.

"Sure, sweetie—take as long as you want. The room is unlocked," she said, before returning to her task at hand—going over the list of overdue books. She never minded it when Bill Roberts came along—he was a big supporter of the annual Stowe Library used book sale held every summer.

In fact, the old man's store was filled with titles that had once adorned the library's shelves.

Roberts and Davis made their way to the back of the library and up some stairs to the second floor and entered the first door on the left. It was a simple room, with a table and six chairs. Best of all, it was very private. Roberts switched the light on and both men sat down at the table.

"Lemme see the journal," Roberts began, clearly very interested in examining it.

Davis handed the envelope to the old man and watched as the former spy looked at the one-time pad, then turned page after page in the journal lingering here and there for a moment, but not saying a word. At one point he paused and smiled, looking up briefly and making eye contact with Davis. Finally, he offered a simple word, "Fascinating!"

"I also have some results from some preliminary decoding I've done and I think you'll find it to be of great interest and I'm hoping you can also shed some light on what it might mean."

At that, Davis pulled a paper from his side pocket, unfolded it and handed it to Roberts.

Chapter Thirty-Four

GILBERT HOBSON WAS determined to keep an eye on the pretty girl in the bookstore, but obviously for reasons beyond just an instruction from his boss. Sure he wanted to support his boss who had charged him with the task, but also because he saw a new opportunity to make up for not overcoming his shyness the night before in the hotel cocktail lounge. So he casually and carefully made his way over toward the aisle where the girl was looking at romance novels.

When she caught sight of Gilbert, she smiled at him and because she was clearly determined to make sure the young man didn't chicken out again said, "We have to quit meeting like this."

Taken aback, Gilbert paused trying to figure out what she meant—yes, he was that backward—but he finally smiled. She made her way toward him and stuck out her hand and said, "Hi, I'm Anna, Anna Kaplan—I saw you last night at the hotel and then again this morning at breakfast, right?" pronouncing her name "Ah-nuh," with her accent clearly showing and Gilbert loved it.

"Yes ma'am," Gilbert began, while instantly reproaching himself with an internal voice—*dumb, dumb, dumb*, "I mean, yes, I remember you, my name is Gilbert, but most people call me Gil." Smooth.

"On vacation?"

"Sort of … just a quick trip up with my boss and some on our staff."

"Really? What kind of work do you do?"

"I work for Templeton Davis, his radio show—sort of an assistant, but I mostly do research and create copy for him and his show."

"Wow," she said, with a hint of flirtation, "Impressive. I've heard of him. He's a pretty important media personality, am I right?"

"I suppose he is, but he's really down to earth, not a snob or anything."

Gilbert found himself becoming more comfortable, even sort of confident, with every word being exchanged and surprised himself when he said, "So, can I buy you a cup of coffee? There's a place just up the block."

"I'd love that," Anna replied, and they left the bookstore quickly and before long were sharing coffee and more scintillating conversation. She told him that she had come to Stowe to check out the hotel as a possible venue for her company to use for a small convention. She was in the public relations business, lived in New York City, and had moved to the states when she was about ten years old from Estonia and just loved America.

Gil was almost instantly smitten. She actually seemed to like him. Go figure.

She seemed to be fascinated with what he did and the whole radio show celebrity thing, sort of making Gilbert feel like he was a bit of an important player. And Gilbert seemed to want to talk to her about everything. In fact, in less than thirty minutes he had told Anna all about her boss's new book—the one he was researching and how it had a whole spy and CIA angle to it. Of course, Gilbert wasn't in the official loop yet, and Templeton Davis hadn't yet tasked him with any research, but to hear him tell it to Anna, well, he was immersed in a developing story of intrigue and danger.

Chapter Thirty-Five

BILL ROBERTS READ the single page of notes that Templeton Davis had given him and immediately knew that he was looking at something of great importance. The paper contained the decryption of one of the pages of the journal, based on the key from a page of the one-time pad. Roberts read the words several times:

CENTRE WISHES MADCHEN CONTACT HOMER AND ESCORT TO MOSCOW VIA STOCKHOLM AS SOON AS POSSIBLE STANLEY SHOULD POINT ATTENTION AT DDM BUNNY HIGHEST PRIORITY MUST BE PROTECTED ALL COSTS THIS NUMBER ONE CONCERN OF CENTRE STANLEY SHOULD PROCEED WITH CAUTION BEWARE GOOD LUCK

"You decoded this yourself?"

"Yep—I used the one-time pad," Davis said, explaining his hit and miss, trial and error experiment in the middle of the night a few days earlier.

"This is very, very interesting, Davis. Did you find any other references in the journal to the BUNNY mentioned in this note?"

"Actually, yes—and some other markings—some initials, I think. Whadaya make of the paragraph on this paper, though?"

"Well, now it's time for me to take you into my confidence, young man," Roberts smiled and said to Temp, who hadn't been called a young man in so long that it made him smile, as well. "What you seem to have stumbled upon here is something I've been speculating about for many years. In fact, for a while it became an obsession of mine. I've always felt that there was more to the whole 'Cambridge Spies' story than the various versions that have been written about over the years. Years ago, I developed some theories, mostly circumstantial stuff, but never had much of anything to work with other than my wild and crazy imagination. Now you may've just given an old spy a gift—one last chance to discover something that could really change the way history is read."

"Wow—I had no idea it could be that important," Davis countered.

"Davis, you're right—you've no idea. Now where are the other markings in the journal? Show me."

With that, Temp moved to the other side of the table to sit next to the Roberts, pulling a chair up close. He leafed carefully through the pages of the old book.

"Okay, here, for instance," Davis said as he turned a page. "Note here, there's the word HOMER, and even I know that this is a reference to the spy Donald MacLean, who eventually defected with Guy Burgess to Moscow."

"Correct, he was discovered through the Venona intercepts, a project that began back in the middle of World War II, about '43, I think—and it was designed to decode messages that were intercepted from the Soviets. Now, this was very secret, supposedly not even President Roosevelt knew about it, but personally I think the old guy knew what was going on, he was a fox in many ways. Bear in mind that in 1943 we were allies with the Russians, so to spy on them at that time would have been quite unsettling diplomatically. Of course, the fact was we suspected that they were spying on us and the Venona project was crucial to finding this out."

"Yes, I've read some about this and ..." Davis interrupted, only to be cut off. Clearly the old man saw himself as the experienced expert and didn't want to be interrupted by a rank amateur, no matter what that amateur might be bringing to the table.

"Well, I lived through it Mr. Davis. It's more than academic to me. So anyway, as the cables that were intercepted began to be decoded—painstakingly slowly, I might add—we came upon the fact that there was a Soviet mole in the British Foreign Office. And there were a few clues. For instance, his Soviet handler was in New York, though the spy was based in the embassy in Washington, DC, obviously requiring the agent to make regular trips to New York to report in. MacLean's wife, Melinda, was pregnant at one point and stayed in Manhattan with her mother, providing the spy with the travel 'cover' he needed. And that's a piece of the puzzle that we eventually connected. All the while, Kim Philby had been monitoring the thing—throughout 1950 and into '51—and saw that they were closing in on his friend. He'd actually go over to Arlington Hall, where the Venona Project was headquartered, across the Potomac from DC and snoop around—and we let him because we were so enamored of the Brits back then. They were more experienced at spy stuff, having been at it much longer than us."

"It's really hard to believe how sloppy some things were back then," Davis remarked.

A bit defensively Roberts barked, "Well, this was when we thought the Brits knew what they were doing—they were our heroes, the big boys in the great game."

"I know," said Davis, "I don't mean to be critical, just making an observation in hindsight."

"Yeah, well … anyway, so the official history goes that Philby had to figure a way to warn MacLean back in London and he and Guy Burgess, an odd fellow, decided to create a scenario through Burgess's bad behavior to get him sent packing to England, the goal being to warn their mutual spy friend. And then when Burgess disappeared with MacLean in May of 1951, suspicion immediately surrounded Philby, since he and Guy were good friends and Burgess had even lived at the house on Nebraska Avenue with them."

"That's when the press was speculating about a so-called 'Third Man'?" Davis asked, knowing the answer, but wanting to encourage Roberts to continue the tutorial.

"That's right. It was the title of a movie from back then, about spies in Austria, I think—never watched it myself. I lived the real thing and there was no way they could really capture that in a movie, at least not back then. So Philby was suspected of being that 'Third Man' and sent back to the U.K. pretty quickly. Old 'Beetle' Smith didn't waste any time. He wanted Philby out of the country."

"What puzzles me in the story, Bill," Davis reflected, "is how such a supposedly accomplished spy in such an important ring of spies could be so sloppy as to let another agent live with him, especially someone who was apparently as erratic as Guy Burgess. Wasn't Philby smarter than that?"

"I've always thought so and you've hit on a part of the official story that's always bugged the hell out of me."

Just then, Templeton Davis's blackberry signaled him that he had a text message. Not wanting to interrupt Roberts' train of thought he at first thought to ignore it, but then quickly thought it might be important, even from Gilbert back at the bookstore.

"Hold on a second Bill, I need to see if this is a message from Gil back at your store." Sure enough it was. Gilbert had texted: *"Will meet you back at hotel, met Anna, Very nice, no worries. Later, -G"*

No worries? Hardly. "Bill, the kid I left back at the store just went off with that girl you saw."

Chapter Thirty-Six

UNACCUSTOMED, EVEN SURPRISED, as he was at what was happening so quickly, Gilbert was enjoying himself, nonetheless. His new friend, Anna, had already captivated his attention and imagination, even after less than an hour's acquaintance. Now he was in her vehicle, a rented Jeep Grand Cherokee—something that seemed to fit her persona quite well—driving along the roads around Stowe. They made their way north on Route 100 and into Waterbury and pulled into the *Cold Hollow Cider Mill*—something that seemed so very right on the picturesque autumn day.

"Ever been here before, Geelburt?" Anna asked, her accent working resonant magic with his name, further drawing him to her.

"This cider mill, or Vermont?"

"Either?"

"No to both, this is my first trip, but I'm finding myself loving it up here already," he said awkwardly, while giving her an equally clumsy look. She smiled back. *Too good to be true,* he thought.

They bought a quart of cider and a dozen just-made-and-still-hot cider donuts and soon were making their way back toward Stowe. Finding a somewhat secluded turnoff on the road, they parked in a wooded area near a small stream and drank cider and munched on donuts. She told him that Anna was short for Anastasia, and he immediately launched into a monologue about the Romanovs and the legends surrounding their young daughter—that she had survived the mass killing of the royal family in the summer of 1917. It was a story that had always fascinated Anna, as well, or at least she said so, as their conversation and whatever it was that was happening between them was moving at breakneck speed, much faster than anything Gilbert had ever experienced. He knew he was in way over his head, but he liked it.

By mid-afternoon they were back at the hotel and in Anna's room, where their acquaintance was transformed into consummation and Gilbert fell into a restful sleep in her bed.

While he was soundly sleeping, she quietly got up and turned on the computer at the desk in the room and sent a detailed email update—a full report, really—to another computer, this one in a van that, at the moment, was passing the exit for Vermont's State Capital at Montpelier on Interstate Highway 89, less than an hour away from Stowe. Two rooms had been reserved for the five men in the van. Four of the men would share the two rooms and the fifth man would take his place where Gilbert Hobson now slept with visions of the past few hours dancing in his head. He and Anna had a long time thing going on—poor Gilbert didn't have a clue that what had transpired since he met Anna at the bookstore was far from real. It was all just a way to learn more about what Templeton Davis was up to—and on to.

Anna needed to place a device, one designed for eavesdropping on conversations, somewhere on Gilbert's clothing or in his personal effects. But where? After looking over everything from his ensemble, she determined that the best place would be on his belt, near the buckle, and she used some adhesive glue to attach the small device to the inside part of the belt. Then she moved across the room with a small receiver in hand and turned it on, noting that a light indicated that a signal was being received. She in turn sent a note to the van that was now exiting I-89, moving south down Rt. 100. She whispered something and in a minute or so received an email that she was coming in clearly.

Then Anna climbed back into bed and waited for Gilbert Hobson to wake up.

Meanwhile, the van pulled up to the hotel and the men checked in and four of them took a nap, while the fifth man waited until the contented young man asleep in his bed woke up and was sent on his way.

Chapter Thirty-Seven

THOUGH TEMPLETON DAVIS was concerned about Gilbert and wondered what was going on with him and the girl he referred to as Anna, with a familiarity that mocked the few moments the two had known each other, it didn't distract him all that much from his on-going conversation with Bill Roberts.

In fact, with Gilbert and the girl out of the bookstore, they made their way out of the library and back to where their conversation started, which was good because the things that Bill Roberts had to show Davis—the broadcaster wasn't the only one with some interesting "finds," after all— were stashed at his place.

Entering the store, he checked with Kenny Starwood, and learned that there had been only three customers and that no one had made a purchase, and yes, the young, pretty lady had left with the guy who came in with Templeton Davis. He thought he overheard that they were going up the street for coffee.

Roberts led Davis through the bookstore and past the desk where they had initiated their talk, up the stairs into what was clearly a living area. They went through a small hall—really an anteroom—and Davis hit his leg on what looked to be a somewhat beat up old freezer.

"This your place?" Davis asked.

"Yep, home sweet home. I bought the place—in fact the whole building, which includes several shops on the block, some years ago. It's been a good investment. The rents pretty much pay my bills so whatever I make from the bookstore is gravy and I can indulge my bibliophilic tendencies," he said watching Templeton Davis smile, did the old man know that Davis loved big words fitly spoken? "Plus I have a government pension, too. Not a bad life, all told."

Roberts went to the counter by the sink and emptied a coffee pot of remnants from earlier and soon a new pot of Green Mountain coffee was brewing. Its aroma quickly filled the small space. The two men sat at the kitchen table and resumed their conversation.

"Where were we, Davis?"

"You were talking about how the official story on Philby and Burgess and the sloppy job they did would be certain to point the clear finger of suspicion at Philby, and how the whole thing didn't sit right with you."

"Damn right! Supposedly this guy Philby was being groomed to be 'C,' their nickname for the head of the Secret Intelligence Services over there, all the while the guy's a Soviet mole, apparently also highly regarded by them as well, and then he crashes and burns in a scenario that's almost comical in its amateurishness. Doesn't pass the smell test. Never has with me. Problem is that I really couldn't counter it with facts. Had some theories, but no facts."

"Theories, like what?"

"Well, like exactly what seems to have been communicated in the item you decoded. There it says that protecting someone else was the highest priority, hinting that there was possibly a mole or spy more important to the Soviets than Philby was. And if Kim Philby was so highly thought of that they thought he'd be running all the intelligence services for the Brits, then what in the world did they have planned for this other spy?"

"Would the references to someone named BUNNY be about that other spy?" Roberts didn't answer, but rather he got up from his chair and said, "Wait here."

Templeton Davis watched as the old man went over to that old beat-up freezer. Temp rubbed his leg where he had hit it. He watched as Roberts removed several items—appeared to be ordinary meat from a freezer (though by this time Davis found himself wondering what was real and what wasn't). Then a box emerged and Bill brought it over to the table and began to go through the contents.

Temp looked over at a pile of frozen packages on the floor and asked, "That meat Okay just to sit there?" Roberts rolled his eyes and sheepishly went over to put it all away, remarking that he was getting forgetful in his old age.

"I doubt that," said Temp. "I think you're just preoccupied, my friend."

"Good point, Davis. Good point."

While Roberts was finishing up with the freezer, Temp took stock of the room concluding that it pretty much looked like what you would expect the kitchen of a man in his eighties and living by himself to look like. Simple, cluttered, and not all that clean. When the old man returned he reached back into the box.

"What's this?" Davis asked the old man.

"Well, my friend, this'll get your interest for sure. I've been collecting this stuff for nearly three decades now. Wanna know what I call this old worn out box?"

"Um—yeah."

"I call it my BUNNY BOX."

"BUNNY as in the name of a spy? You mean such a spy existed? Was it a woman?"

"Well Davis, I'm not sure of a lot and I'd like to take you through my theories, but I'm pretty sure it wasn't a woman. In fact, I think it was a man and I think I've figured out who it was."

"Really? Amazing! Who was it?"

At this Bill Roberts held up his hands and said, "Not so fast! We've got some ground to cover and I need to take you through this step by step. It may be tedious, but it's the only way anything will make any sense—if any of it actually does."

"Well," Temp replied, "You've got my undivided attention."

"How about I send the boy downstairs out for some sandwiches, I don't have much to eat up here."

Davis liked the idea and having looked around the kitchen felt much safer ordering out. Within 30 minutes Kenny Starwood had returned with a couple of large roast beef sandwiches from the deli up the street, complete with a potent horseradish sauce that could have passed for just about pure horseradish, at least that's what Davis thought after his second bite made his eyes tear up and overflow.

But as powerful as the horseradish was, it wasn't nearly as tantalizing as the story Bill Roberts was telling and the case he was making about someone who may have been the most important Soviet spy of the Cold War—someone who had never been discovered. Could it be, Temp wondered, that an old man and a radio broadcaster sitting at a simple kitchen table in a modest apartment in a town comparatively remote from places like Washington, DC, Moscow, New York, Berlin, or London were involved in something of historical importance?

The BUNNY box contained file folders, newspapers, yellow legal pads filled with handwritten notes, and several books. When it came to the books, Davis actually recognized some of the titles. In fact, he owned them and had recently looked at several of them. As Bill Roberts moved from folder to folder to book and back to folder, his theory was becoming very clear.

"The thing that has never really been thoroughly examined by historians and those who have written books about the great espionage stories of the Cold War," Roberts said, "is that there was an effort to recruit potential spies at Oxford University in England, every bit as involved, and I think as effective, as what happened at Cambridge," Roberts remarked.

"Yet it's Cambridge, with the infamous 'Cambridge Five' that gets all the attention. Why is that?" Davis wondered aloud.

"That's because, I think—and this may strike you as the ravings of a conspiracy nut—the Cambridge initiative was in many ways a cover meant to divert eyes away from whatever happened at Oxford around the same time—and we're talking about the early to middle 1930s," Roberts concluded.

"Well if that's true, then it turns everything I've been reading on its head. Does it mean that all the other stuff is wrong?"

"No, not at all—all that really happened, Philby, MacLean, Burgess, Blunt, Cairncross, they all worked for the Soviets while serving in high level positions in British government and life. It's just that the story doesn't end there. And too often, instead of asking the right questions, investigators—

even scholars—have simply settled for letting the facts be interpreted by what they *already* knew."

"For example, take the whole HOMER and Donald MacLean thing."

Davis looked at Roberts, "Are you saying that MacLean wasn't HOMER?"

"No, Davis, I'm not saying that at all. Clearly MacLean was HOMER, but in the investigation before, and in the follow up in the years since, several assumptions have been made and it's things like that that make me wonder. It's like they stopped the investigation with MacLean, Philby and company and decided that they must have been the premiere Russian agents and then pretty much closed the case."

"You said 'For example' before I interrupted you, sorry Bill," Davis apologized.

"No problem, I understand your question and interest—but back to the example. One of the key pieces of the puzzle on the whole MacLean story is the testimony of a guy by the name of Walter Krivitsky—you're aware of him, aren't you, Davis?"

"Yes—I read that book, *A Death in Washington*, about how he died in, what was it—1941?"

"Yes, '41. But there's more to his story and it's hiding even in that book in plain sight."

"Whadaya mean?"

"Well, of course, Krivitsky defected from the Soviets around the time of Stalin's paranoid purges in the late 1930s, and along the way he gave both MI-5 in Great Britain and the FBI here in America some interesting tidbits. In fact, some of what he said was the first anyone really knew about a major mole in the British Foreign Office. Krivitsky gave us some pieces of the puzzle, at least some of the pieces that he knew and later when MacLean defected it was clear that much of what Krivitsky had told us ten years earlier had been ultimately verified by events. But it's those pieces of the puzzle that have long intrigued me. Here take a look."

Bill Roberts pulled his copy of *A Death in Washington: Walter G. Krivitsky and the Stalin Terror* by Gary Kern out of the big box. He opened it to a dog-eared page, one that also bore many notes and marks, apparently by Roberts himself. The section of the book talked about the Soviet plan to recruit college students into their service, "to grow up agents from the inside," the passage said. The novel idea was to recruit young people from good families, some even with aristocratic backgrounds, "in the hope that they might eventually obtain diplomatic posts or other key positions in the service of the country of which they were nationals."

After reading that passage, Davis remarked, "Well, that fits the profile of Philby and MacLean perfectly."

"Absolutely, but read a little more," Roberts encouraged.

"In another passage on the page it detailed Krivitsky's admittedly limited knowledge about the Soviet mole, the one who would turn out to be MacLean. From previous sources, MI-5 had learned that this spy was a 'Scotsman' and 'from a good family.' Krivitsky had the impression that the agent was someone who was in some way related or had access to the British Committee of Imperial Defense, or as he had heard it called, the 'Imperial Council.' Other clues were that the young spy was 'a young aristocrat' who was 'under thirty' (bearing in mind this is about 1939) and that the man was not in it for the money and 'had plenty of money.' It was also mentioned that he had attended 'Eton' and 'Oxford.'"

"But didn't MacLean attend Cambridge, and not Oxford?" Davis asked.

"Correct you are, Davis. And he didn't attend Eton either. But this point was lost along the way, and explained away, after Don MacLean defected. In other words, they had their guy, so they had to make the evidence fit MacLean."

"How'd they work this out?"

"Well, for the most part they made the assumption that Krivitsky wasn't sufficiently familiar with the distinction between Oxford and Cambridge—hell, even back then people talked about 'Oxbridge' and often used the names interchangeably, like some Brits might do with our Harvard and Yale. So they just assumed that Krivitsky meant Cambridge, which might be true, but still its one piece they had to *make* fit."

At that, Temp decided to interject his own Oxford connection. "Well, not sure if you know this, but I spent some time at Oxford—did graduate work there many years ago."

Roberts replied, "Yes, I know that—checked you out and was just wondering when you'd get around to confessing." He smiled and then continued, "And look at this."

Davis skimmed the passage put in front of him, one that said that Krivitsky had suggested that the mole might have been the son of an official with the Foreign Office. And it also noted that, for whatever reason, Krivitsky was very interested in the father-son aspect.

"Of course, Donald MacLean's father was a member of the Liberal Party and served in Parliament, but was never associated with the Foreign Office or anything that could be described as an 'Imperial Council.'"

"So whadaya make of all this, Bill?"

"Well, some years ago I decided to step back and take a look at this whole story and approach it from another angle. Instead of having to find a way to make all the clues fit the spy who defected—Donald MacLean—I asked the obvious question that no one else at the time or since has seemed to want to ask: What if there were *two men* being described and what if those who gave the clues thought they were talking about only one spy, but instead their clues were right, but were related to two agents, not one? What if there was a spy who was a 'Scotsman' and from 'a good family' and his name was Donald MacLean? But there was also one who had been to Eton and Oxford and whose father worked in some way with diplomacy and the foreign office—that 'Imperial Council' idea?"

"Seems plausible to me," Templeton Davis said, completely convinced that what Roberts was talking about made a lot of sense. "So it's possible that these 'Oxford Spies' might have been as substantial as the better known 'Cambridge Spies?'"

"I'm sure of it!" Roberts said as he smacked the table with his right hand for further emphasis.

Chapter Thirty-Eight

THE OLD MAN drained his coffee cup and went to the kitchen counter to fill it up again. "You want some more?"

"Nope, I'm good—so do ya have a fix on just who this other spy might've been?"

"Be patient, my friend. I'll get to that, but I need to bring you along the entire trail, especially if you hope to write about any of this."

It was the first real mention of Temp's proposed book, one still very much in the imaginative phase. He hadn't wanted to push his luck, but knew that what he was hearing from Bill Roberts, the former CIA spook, was gold as far as an interview was concerned and now it seemed like the old man wanted to help.

"Why haven't *you* ever written about this? You've clearly been immersed in the story; you've done your homework. I think it'd be a great book coming from you."

"That's just it, Davis, it can't come from me, don't you see? Having worked for years in the business so to speak, I'm bound by many things. It's not likely that anything published under my name could happen, or at least be filled with sufficient detail, without passing by the folks in Northern Virginia. And trust me, they'd chop off about half of what I'd write."

"I see, but if you help someone else then that wouldn't apply?"

"Correct, but the key is to keep my name out of it, I gotta be one of those, what ya call, anonymous sources," Roberts insisted.

"Got no problem with that, Bill. And I think this has the makings of being a blockbuster, especially if you're my 'silent partner.' How about money—what about that?"

"Well, I'd never thought of publishing such a book for the money, per se, but rather as something that I think might be important to history. But that said, if you make some money on it and are inclined to cut me in on any, I'd like to set up some kind of fund or account for my great-grandson—he's five years old and lives out in Denver, my granddaughter's boy. Never was much of a family man. Blew my marriage up—career got in the way and all—years ago. Never really had much of a relationship with my two kids—or their kids. Pathetic really. In fact, I doubt that the boy even knows he has a great-grandpa. But maybe someday he will." Bill seemed lost in thought for a moment, looking down at the floor.

"Tell you what," Davis said, breaking up the pregnant pause. "I'll write up something and designate a percentage of the royalties and …"

Roberts cut him off. "Nah, don't write anything up—just gimme your word that you'll do something for the boy and that's fine with me."

"You sure? That's a lot of trust for an old spy!"

"Well, chalk it up to getting soft in the head in my old age. I've got some health problems. Not all that unusual for a guy my age, and who knows how long I'm gonna live anyway. At this point, I find myself much more trusting. So—we good on that?"

"Count on it, Bill. Count on it. I'll make sure it's all handled right. Now take me on that tour of the details—I want to know all of it. Mind if I record any of this? It's easier than taking notes for me—heck, I should've had this out much earlier, but let's turn this thing into a real bona fide research interview—how's that?"

"Sure—fine," the old man said as Templeton Davis pulled out a small recording device and set it on the table.

"Okay," Davis, now in interview mode, began. "Let's go back to the beginning of your research. Tell me some of the things you dug into."

"Well, like I said before, I had followed the whole 'Cambridge Spies' story pretty closely back in the early '50s when it all happened and read everything written on it, including at least a little access to some stuff back at Langley. And I kept running into this idea of a ring at Oxford that no one seemed to know much about. For example, there is a reference here ... where's that book?" Roberts dug through the bin and pulled out a well-worn copy of a book by Nigel West and Oleg Tsarev called, *The Crown Jewels: The British Secrets at the Heart of the KGB Archives.*

Seeing the volume, Davis remarked, "I've got that book."

"I know you do, I'm the one who sent it to you. I've actually been keeping an eye on your ordering patterns for a while and wondered what your level of interest was in this whole story. Look here," Roberts leafed through the book pausing at the postscript toward the back. "Note the reference here to an 'Oxford Group' and the name of Edith Tudor Hart."

"Sounds familiar from my reading, but I can't place her—who's she?"

"She was a key player back in the day in England and someone involved in both the Cambridge and Oxford recruitments. She worked closely with a guy named Arnold Deutsch—he's the Russian handler generally credited with recruiting Kim Philby, the spy always considered the biggest fish in the Soviet net. And it was Edith Tudor Hart who connected Deutsch with Philby in about 1934. But the interesting thing is that in this book, which was written using some sources being made public during the time of Gorbachev, there's indication that Hart was also involved in recruitment at Oxford. Look at this," Roberts directed Davis to a passage:

> There are considerable gaps, the principal being the story of what has become known as the Oxford Group. While the Soviet spies recruited at Cambridge have now acquired international notoriety, very little is known about the other network known to have been drawn at roughly the same time from Oxford University.

Turning the page, Roberts directed Davis to another passage, one that quoted a letter from the old KGB files dated in 1936:

> Through EDITH we obtained SOHNCHEN [Philby]. In the attached report you will find details of a second SOHNCHEN who, in all probability, offers even greater possibilities than the first. Edith is of the opinion that [name deleted] is more promising than SOHNCHEN. From the report you will see that he has very definite possibilities. We

must make haste with these people before they start being active in university life.

"So they're talking about another spy prospect who was more highly regarded than even Philby, who has always been regarded as the big cheese when it came to Soviet moles back in the day?" Davis asked.

"Yes. Clearly that was the case and, here—look at what it says next, and remember this is all documented from sources inside the old Russian intelligence apparatus. West writes here about the code name for the so-called second SOHNCHEN, and suggests SCOTT, which is apparently what was used. See here, the next paragraph," Roberts directed Davis's eyes to what followed:

SCOTT: I wrote to you about him in my last letter. Through him we acquired BUNNY.

"BUNNY? That's the name I found in Philby's journal and I did some checking on it myself with that historian at Langley—I think I mentioned him to you—name is Dr. Stevenson?" Davis hoped Bill wouldn't go off on a tangent about the guy again, but Roberts didn't notice, or at least he didn't take the bait. "He told me he found a single reference to a spy code named BUNNY and I'm pretty sure I recall him saying that he was affiliated with SCOTT."

Roberts nodded affirmatively and added, "We, of course, now know who SCOTT was ..."

"Right, some guy named Arthur Wynn who died about ten years ago," Davis interrupted.

"Correct. But again, those digging around this stopped short—satisfied that they'd found his real identity. What they failed to do was follow through with the next logical step. Ask the obvious question. If through SCOTT they acquired BUNNY, who was significant enough of a catch to be noted like this, then why has no one tried to figure out any more about BUNNY?"

Templeton Davis wasn't sure if the old man was actually asking *him* this question or if it was simply rhetorical. In a moment, though, Roberts continued, "There's another reference down the page I want you to look at.

It seems that our boy SCOTT was a bit too zealous for the commies and they wanted him to slow down. Apparently he was trying to recruit anyone and everyone to the Soviet cause. Look here:"

> There should be no mass recruitment on any account. From among the many and promising candidates, select the most valuable. Check ten times, do not be in a hurry and recruit only when you have sufficient data. BUNNY's recruitment, for instance, was much too hurried.

"Interesting," Davis commented, "So SCOTT recruited BUNNY. You think this EDITH was involved?"

"I do. Seems like she was a very effective worker for their cause back then."

"OK, Bill, then here is the $64,000 question, who the hell was BUNNY—you have a theory don't you?"

"My boy, I've got more than a theory. I've got a name and having looked through that journal your friend dug up, I think I now have something solid to back it up. Until now it's been a matter of my imagination and speculation. It hit me some years ago when I was reading a book about the Cuban Missile Crisis."

"In 1962?" Davis countered, "What in the world did that have to do with what we're looking at—what did it have to do with BUNNY? And just what kind of codename is BUNNY anyway? Doesn't seem to have the mystique to it that so many of the names do."

"Well," Roberts smiled, "Yeah, that was curious to me, as well, so I did some research and it turns out that BUNNY was a pretty well known nickname in the 1930s. In Scotland there was this comic strip called 'Billy and Bunny' about a boy who got into all kinds of trouble. And several baseball players were nicknamed BUNNY. Then there was the famous jazz trumpet player from the '30s named Bunny Berigan—played like Louis Armstrong, but drank himself to death when he was only 33. Pretty well known and tragic story back then. Oh—and there's this ice skater, famous guy back then, who was in the 1936 Olympics in Berlin and won a gold medal for the Brits. He actually gave the king a couple of lessons, pretty big deal back in the day. So, bottom line, it was a fairly common nickname around the time that this agent was being recruited and trained."

"Interesting—but now, what about the crisis in 1962, how does that relate to BUNNY? You suggesting that there was a spy working for the Soviets and he was somehow involved in the great standoff between Kennedy and Khrushchev?"

"Actually, I am."

"Who was it?"

"His name was David Ormsby-Gore and when John F. Kennedy was President of the United States he was the British Ambassador to the U.S. and a very close friend to the President and the First Lady. But his loyalty was to the men in the Kremlin. Can you imagine?"

Templeton Davis was speechless.

Chapter Thirty-Nine

NOT EXACTLY KNOWING protocol in such circumstances, Gilbert Dobson awoke from his surprisingly deep mid-afternoon slumber, at first not sure where he was, nor what to do. Stay? Go? Order room service? But Anna made it easy when she told him that she had a meeting before dinner—it was well after three PM—so Gil took the cue and gathered his clothes about him and kissed the girl goodbye with a smile of satisfaction. He couldn't wait to tell Valerie and the others about the afternoon—well, most of it. He wouldn't actually kiss and tell, completely. He smiled as he thought about the fact that he had never had to be such a gentleman before. Since the group was supposed to meet in the lobby at five-thirty to head somewhere of Temp's choosing for dinner together, he had some conversation fodder for sure. He left Anna's room and went to his to shower and get ready for dinner.

Just after he cleared the hallway, a man—someone who looked tired and weary from travel—knocked on Anna's door and was quickly drawn into the room. Anna briefed him on her day, in complete detail. It was all part of the job. She was an operative of the SVR and the Russian Federation, successors to the KGB and the Soviet Union.

She had been sent to Stowe the day before (she had the luxury of air travel, flying into nearby Burlington), after the men on the team—the guys just now showing up—had overheard the conversation about the trip via the bug in the *Templeton Davis Live* conference room. Her assignment was to keep an eye on the group, collect whatever intelligence she could and wait for the rest of the team to drive up. She saw geeky Gilbert as someone she could quickly wrap around her little finger. She was right.

Obviously the people half a world away were carefully monitoring and intently interested in what was going on in Vermont. They were concerned that something that had been buried away in the dustbin of history now had the potential to see the light of day. Very concerned. Those on the ops team didn't fully understand it all—just following orders—but Vladimir Putin and Sergei Ivanov, known to each other familiarly as Putka and Vava, knew that what was being discussed now in colorful northern Vermont involved one of the last great secrets of the Cold War, the role of a Soviet agent highly placed in an internationally important role. An agent who at a crucial time in world history had unique access to and influence on people and events, he had been recruited during the glory days of such things in the 1930s. He had come to maturity in the Great Patriotic War of the 1940s (as the Russians regularly referred to the war the rest of the world called World War Two). And at a time when tensions between the Soviets and the United States were at their height, he was the highly trusted insider and confidant of President Kennedy, while working for the British Embassy, but actually for the Soviet regime. His fingerprints were all over the great events of nearly 50 years ago, from Cuba, to Berlin, back to Cuba—even Dallas. The fact of his very existence, not to mention his identity, must never become public knowledge. The two men were sure and determined about this. And they were ready to issue instructions of the most severe sort to protect their interests.

By now, they knew that an American named Vince Benton had accidentally discovered a briefcase once owned by Kim Philby. And they were pretty sure that despite all of Philby's insistence over time that there was nothing in the satchel of any importance, nothing to point the finger at anyone, and that the items would at any rate never be found, they had been lied to by a master deceiver. But just what were the contents of the case? The men tasked with finding this out had indicated that there might have been a book, or journal of some kind. If so, what had Mr. Philby written down? And didn't those who handled him teach him at all about tradecraft and such things?

It was time to put a stop to things before matters spun out of their control. The decision was made and the order sent. The most important word in the communication was "terminate."

Chapter Forty

TEMPLETON DAVIS WAS growing somewhat impatient with the old man's meandering manner of making his points, but he did his best not to show it—he didn't want to interrupt Roberts' train of thought, or derail the train for that matter. So slow and steady it would have to be. He looked at his watch and it was now a bit after 3:30.

"Mr. Roberts, this really turns the whole accepted scenario surrounding the Cuban Missile Crisis upside down, doesn't it?"

"Well, my boy, not so fast, we have much ground to cover before that," Bill Roberts said smiling wryly at his new friend and confidant. At that, Temp did his dead-level best not to roll his eyes or facially portray any emotion that suggested anything less than a sitting-at-the-feet-of-the-master-like-grasshopper fascination.

"Got it. So tell me all about this guy, David Ormsby-Gore," Davis prompted.

"Well, he's been a subject of interest and not a little mystery for many years. He died in a car accident in 1985, I believe it was, but questions lingered in some minds at the time as to the cause of the accident. There is— or at least there was, it was years ago—a professor over at Oxford who had sort of made Mr. Ormsby-Gore, better known in those days simply as Lord Harlech after the death of his father, a subject of research. I don't know if what he was working on was ever published. At least, I never saw anything about it. What was his name?" Roberts scratched his head and then began digging through pages and scraps in the box, finally his face breaking into a beam of sorts that said, "Aha, here it is—the professor's name was Clive Foyle, taught history with a special interest in the Cold War back then and Anglo-Soviet relations."

Templeton Davis looked over at his recording device on the table and saw that it was faithfully humming along, but just in case, he pulled out his Moleskin notebook from his left front trouser pocket and promptly wrote the name: "Dr. Clive Foyle—Oxford." It was a familiar name. He thought for a second, then added: "Trinity College." He was pretty sure he'd actually met the man years ago and seemed to recall that this Foyle character was a friend of one of his professors at Exeter College—*certainly worth checking out*, he thought.

"The name rings a bell," Temp said. "Is that an article about him?"

"Not about him, per se, but he is mentioned. Let's see, this is an article from a Brit paper around the time Lord Harlech met with his untimely accident, and it quotes Foyle. Should be able to look him up, if he's still alive. I'll leave that to you."

Davis calculated that Foyle likely had to be well into his 70s by now, if indeed he was even still around. He vaguely remembered the professor from his days at Oxford. He finished making a note or two and then asked, "So, this guy, Ormsby-Gore, or Harlech, or whatever his name was, died in 1985, and you say that he'd been a Soviet agent?"

"Yes sir! I'm absolutely convinced of it. Especially after seeing that Philby journal. There are some markings in there that confirm it all—as least to my mind. And, my new found friend, you've got the ingredients in your hands to write a blockbuster of a story!"

"Well, Bill, of course that's great to hear, but how can you be so sure? What did you see in the journal that confirmed it all in the few moments you were leafing through it?"

Bill Roberts pointed at the Philby journal on the table and actually snapped his fingers, saying: "Here, give it to me again, I'll show you." Templeton Davis slid the old journal across the table.

Turning the pages carefully, Roberts finally stopped and said: "Okay, see this word here?" Davis got up from his chair and walked to where he could read over Bill's shoulder. "Right here, this word: Oswestry."

"What's Oswestry?" Davis asked.

"Not 'what,' but 'where'—that's what's important. It's the district our Mr. David Ormsby-Gore represented in Parliament at the time Kim Philby was feeling the full wrath of the American diplomatic boot. And look here, you see these initials, right—here they are, plain as day right after the word BUNNY, D-O-G? Well, David Ormsby-Gore. Voila!"

"Amazing, so you've had this theory for years and never had anything to directly connect BUNNY with David Ormsby-Gore?"

"Exactly! It was one gigantic hunch based on a lot of circumstantial stuff."

"Like what you've been showing me."

"Well, Mr. Davis, there's actually one more piece of the puzzle that I've been holding back and this one should seal the deal for you, because it certainly did for me."

"I'm all ears," Davis said, now not at all bothered by the old man's processing pace. In fact, when he went back over to his chair at the table, he literally sat on its edge.

"Well, let's go back to Krivitsky, the Soviet defector from the late 30s, we talked about him earlier."

"Uh huh," said Davis, "the guy who gave the information to MI-5 that was later used to figure out the whole HOMER story."

"Right. Well, there's one more nugget in the story," Roberts said, reaching again for his copy of *A Death in Washington*. Finding the spot he was looking for, he read a passage to Davis that talked about how, during Krivitsky's interview with MI-5, as the defector was being read a list of names of people who had attended Eton or Oxford, the name 'Cecil' was mentioned and Mr. Krivitsky reacted to the name.

"Cecil?" asked Davis. "Isn't that part of David Ormsby-Gore's family heritage?"

"Correct you are. On his mother's side, our friend the Soviet spy was related to the famous Cecil family, a very influential part of Great Britain's wealthy and political aristocracy for a very long time. His great grandfather, Robert Cecil, had actually been Prime Minister back in the days of Queen Victoria."

"What'd the interviewers make of Krivitsky's reaction to the name 'Cecil'?"

"Well, it's the most curious thing. They simply regarded it as a 'false reaction.' They took everything else the guy said at face value, but not that. Strange, if you ask me, almost as if they couldn't believe anyone associated with that famous name and lineage could ever be a traitor. There was a lot of that feeling way back then. Until Philby. But by then, most of them had likely forgotten about Krivitsky's testimony—at least such little details. They had MacLean, Burgess, then Philby—the third man—case closed, period."

"It's almost like they really didn't want to get to the truth."

"No, it's more like they had a preconceived idea that spies all came from the lower classes, not the wealthy and powerful set, so it sort of blinded them to certain facts that seem so obvious to us now in hindsight. What's doubly interesting about all of this is that the context of Krivitsky's reaction to the mention of the name 'Cecil' is a series of questions and answers about a son with a famous father who worked in some kind of foreign office job, and how the son passed on documents his father had brought home from work. All of this was later forgotten, even though none of it actually described the man they all eventually concluded Krivitsky was talking about—Donald MacLean."

"Was David Ormsby-Gore's father someone with access to such documents?"

"Well, you tell me. His old man, William Ormsby-Gore, served as Colonial Secretary in the 1930s under Prime Ministers Stanley Baldwin and Neville Chamberlain. It's a position Winston Churchill once held. So would such a man be privy to juicy information?" Roberts grinned widely.

"Yikes!" exclaimed Templeton Davis, whose smile matched that of the old man. "This is wild stuff! Where's it been all my life—in fact, where've you been all my life, Bill? This is the mother lode."

"Mr. Davis, you've only begun to realize what this meant—and what it means."

"Well, sir, as much as I'd like to keep going today, I promised the gang I brought with me that I'd take them all to dinner tonight, so we'll have to pick this up tomorrow, if it's alright with you."

"Fine by me. Let's get started earlier if you want. They serve a nice breakfast halfway between here and where you are staying on the Mountain Road, place called *The Gables*."

"I saw it when I was driving into town—how about we meet there at, say, eight-thirty?"

"Make it eight," Roberts countered.

"Eight it is—got any recommendations for dinner in town?"

"Many great joints here in Stowe, but if I were you, I'd take a drive up through the notch."

"Notch?"

"Yeah—it's a little narrow pass barely big enough for a vehicle to get through, but you can. It was famous for smuggling fur back in the early days of the country and then, in the 1920s during Prohibition, for getting booze down from Canada. So you go up through it and after you come down the mountain you go a few miles. You pass that monstrosity *Smuggler's Notch Resort* on the right, then after another mile or two, you'll see a quaint looking spot called *Three Mountain Lodge* on the left. Great food—and the ladies will particularly love it. Table cloths are made from quilts—gals love that shit."

Chapter Forty-One
June 1961
Air Force One—Vienna—London

PRESIDENT KENNEDY HAD tried to take a brief nap during the flight from Vienna, Austria, to London, but he was too keyed up to catch even a wink of sleep. Possibly the cocktail of pills and injections were messing with his sleep mechanism, he thought. They had taken his back pain away, at least temporarily, but all he did in the small but comfortable compartment in the Boeing 707, one that had been used by former President Eisenhower, and that flew with the call letters of Air Force One, was to stare at the ceiling and then the walls. As his mind wandered, he wondered what differences the newer jet he was being promised would have over this, though he'd have to wait for more than a year to actually find out. No, deep down he knew this sleeplessness wasn't due to any medicine or pseudo-medicine, but rather what had just transpired. It had so shaken him to the core that he was not only wide-awake; he was also an emotional mess. This for a man who so craved to present the public image of being suave and confident.

He now almost regretted having set up this quick visit to the U.K. to see Prime Minister MacMillan. The original idea was that this would be the prelude to a victory trip home, of sorts, one that allowed him to bask in the glow of having dealt so firmly with Mr. Nikita Khrushchev at a summit he now knew had not only been ill-advised, but also for which he had been woefully underprepared.

Air Force Colonel James B. Swindal was guiding the craft to its final descent when he received word from air traffic control of a message for the President. He had the co-pilot write the message down and it was quickly passed along to the President's cabin, where Mr. Kennedy was tying his necktie and preparing to meet the various luminaries who tend to congregate at the bottom of any stairway bearing the President of the United States. John Kennedy smiled for the first time in days as he read that his good friend, David Ormsby-Gore, was waiting for him on the tarmac and was asking if he might come aboard before the President got off the aircraft.

"Tell, the boys up front to let the soon-to-be-Ambassador on board as soon as we are parked. I'd like to speak with him before we head out to meet the crowd," the President told Kenny O'Donnell, his long time friend and current appointments secretary. Soon enough, it was just two old friends chatting familiarly in the cramped confines of the President's bedroom on the airplane.

"Mr. President, this may be a bit outside of protocol, but I wanted to welcome you on your first visit as President to Great Britain, and though your stay will be short, if you need anything please don't hesitate to call on me. I am at your service, sir." David Ormsby-Gore said to Kennedy.

"Cut the crap, David," Kennedy barked back, "you know you just wanted to see the airplane from the inside."

"Quite nice, but I won't tell you how it compares with what our PM flies around in," David smiled as he looked around.

"Yes, well, uh, sometime next year, uh, I'll be flying around in the most up-to-date and efficient, not to mention comparatively opulent bird in the skies, so don't gloat, you limey bastard," the President of the United States smiled while re-lighting a cigar that had died out.

"Now to important matters," Kennedy continued, "I'm down to just a handful of these wonderful cigars, which as you know is my real reason for this visit to your fine country." Both men smiled.

Within a few moments David Ormsby-Gore exited the rear of the plane, barely noticed by the crowd watching the front door for the appearance of the youthful president. When Kennedy moved through the doorway and onto the steps, he was cheered by what seemed to be a crowd of a thousand or more—and he was more than a bit surprised by it all. He was also encouraged. After the savaging he experienced at the hands of the Soviet leader just hours before in Vienna. It was great to be among friends.

Prime Minister MacMillan and his wife, Lady Dorothy, met President Kennedy and his wife, Jackie, at Heathrow that day. And their reception was refreshing after spending some less-than-quality time with Mr. Khrushchev. In fact, Jack found himself once again in a relaxed mode and mood, the kind one gets when around friends—or at least friendly people. And his wife was charming this crowd as she had De Gaulle and company in Paris just a few days before. Maybe he should have let the First Lady negotiate with the Russians he thought as he smiled, watching his wife pour it on during the ride from Heathrow into London. His talks with MacMillan would have to wait until morning. The President was beat. And in many ways he was also a beaten man.

After a fitful night with little sleep, no doubt due to stress, he made his call on MacMillan at his temporary residence, Admiralty House. The famous address, number ten Downing Street, was undergoing renovations. The Prime Minister listened as Kennedy unburdened himself, and MacMillan was more than a little surprised at this unguarded transparency on the part of the President. He was listening to, and looking at, a completely defeated man. He felt pity for Kennedy and invited him upstairs where they ate sandwiches and drank whisky—none of which seemed to help Kennedy's mood.

The President suggested that they invite David Ormsby-Gore to join them. Then the three of them talked about geo-politics and speculated about what the Soviets might do next. The subject of Berlin was very much on their minds—what would Khrushchev do to stop the flood of people leaving the Soviet sector for the western part of that torn city? And if he acted aggressively, what would be the response of the Yanks and Brits?

In that private meeting, one thing became clear. John F. Kennedy had no desire, or stomach, to go toe-to-toe with the Soviet leader. He resignedly told MacMillan and Ormsby-Gore that there was not much that could be done, really, with respect to Berlin.

The President's friend took note of this and filed it away in his mind for an important report he would file for other friends later.

Later that June day, there was a large gathering for the christening of Kennedy's niece, the daughter of Jackie's sister, Lee Radziwill, followed by a characteristically lavish reception. During the reception, Kennedy pulled Ormsby-Gore aside and they disappeared for another private chat. By all accounts, he had become a close confidant of the President of the United States, something quite unprecedented. Robert Kennedy would later say that, "He was almost part of the government." And Presidential Aide, Theodore Sorenson recalled that JFK regarded David Ormsby-Gore "as he would a member of his own staff."

"Mr. President, you need to get home and get some rest—you look terrible," David said.

"Well, ah, remember Mr. Ambassador-to-be, you are talking to the President of the United States," at which both men broke into sustained laughter, the kind that suggested that neither of them could really believe who they had become and what they were doing at this point in their lives. It was a long way from Scotland in 1938.

By the time the President of the United States and his lovely wife sat down for an official ceremonial dinner with Queen Elizabeth later that evening, a communication was en route to Moscow, where Nikita Khrushchev had already been basking in the afterglow of his epic meeting with the American president. He gave the usual sycophantic people around him a word-for-word account of his time with Kennedy—over and over again. Clearly he knew he had won that day.

In fact, before Khrushchev closed his eyes that night he received word from his highly placed agent in London about Kennedy's private remarks to the Prime Minister, complete with the part about how the President of the United States would stand by and do nothing if the Russians made a move on Berlin.

They, of course, did make such a move a couple of months later in the form of a crude, but effective, wall. It became the icon of the Cold War. And true to his private thoughts and words, John F. Kennedy did nothing, while Nikita Khrushchev advanced the Soviet international agenda with the kind of confidence a boxer has when he knows that the other guy is going to take a dive.

A few months later, on a beautiful October day, just as the fall foliage was reaching its peak of color in and around Washington, DC, Sir David Ormsby-Gore—the knighthood having been anointed by Queen Elizabeth just before David and his family sailed to America—President Kennedy's longtime friend, formally presented his diplomatic credentials.

At that very moment there was great tension between the United States and the Soviet Union over the testing of nuclear weapons in the atmosphere. In fact, Chairman Khrushchev seemed to be on a rampage of late, flexing his atomic muscles with test after test before the world and especially in the face of John Fitzgerald Kennedy, whom he regarded as a political lightweight and nearly unworthy opponent. The British government under Harold MacMillan was trying to intervene to get the two parties back to the table of negotiation.

This was very familiar territory for David Ormsby-Gore seeing as he had been the lead negotiator for the British at test-ban talks in Geneva prior to becoming the Ambassador in his earlier role as Minister of State for Foreign Affairs. And in that prior role, and now this new one, he was well-positioned to keep an eye on things for his friends in the Kremlin, though there were times when he—at least in his own mind, never uttered, mind you—questioned the mental stability of the Soviet Premier.

Though he was clearly a man of divided loyalties and several layers of mystique, he longed for world peace. He increasingly saw himself as a voice of reason uniquely positioned to influence not only the balance of power (which admittedly he wanted to tilt toward Moscow), but also world peace itself.

Chapter Forty-Two
Stowe, Vermont

TEMPLETON DAVIS ARRIVED back at the hotel with barely enough time to shower and change before the scheduled time to meet everyone in the lobby to go to dinner together. A little before 5:30 PM he found the team already there and waiting and he told them about Bill Roberts' recommendation for a place to eat. Predictably, the ladies loved the idea and everyone piled into two vehicles. Temp rode in the lead vehicle, letting Gilbert drive and Valerie joined them. It was time to bring his assistants up to speed and this would give them time for a briefing.

As they climbed up the mountain road and negotiated curve after curve, finally moving carefully through the notch—what they'd all later describe as the vehicular equivalent of threading a needle—Davis gave Hobson and Doling a sketch of the story, minus some of the more interesting, possibly dangerous parts. And of course, everything he said was heard loud and clear by the men in the van, as the eavesdroppers trailed along about a half mile behind, just out of sight, but not at all out of range.

"Wow, what a cool story!" Gilbert exclaimed as Valerie nodded in clear agreement. "It's got all the elements of a blockbuster. It'll read like fiction, yet be very true. What can I do to help?"

"Well, I'm still pondering that, but what would you think about taking a trip with me over to Oxford, England to interview a guy?"

"Seriously? Duh—yeah! Of course, I would. Who's the guy?"

"Well, I'm not even sure he's still there. Bill mentioned him—the guy was a professor back in the 1980s, but would now be at least seventy-five. I haven't even had a chance to look him up."

"Well, I could do that—I actually know a guy at Oxford. Come to think of it, he'd probably let me stay with him. Want me to contact him? Who's the professor we want to talk to?" Gilbert asked. He was now warming up to the subject so much that it was "we" instead of "you" all of a sudden. Davis had no clue that he had tapped into the unfathomable power of a research geek. He just looked over at his assistant as if waiting for Mr. Smart-brains to catch up. "Oh wait, that's right—you were at Oxford, sorry—I'm sure you have your own contacts."

Temp smiled at him. "Name is Clive Foyle, I imagine Dr. Clive Foyle, and back then he was sort of an expert on this fellow David Ormsby-Gore. Foyle taught classes on the Cold War, which was of course still ongoing at the time, and did a whole course on Anglo-American relations during that period, particularly the Kennedy years. Heck, maybe he even wrote a book about it. Why don't you check that part out—okay?"

"You got it. I'll go online as soon as we get back—or if I can get a signal wherever we're going, I'll see what I find out on my smart phone."

The dinner was delightful. The setting was quaint and the food was delicious. Temp had prime rib, no surprise there—Vince and Gilbert, too. The ladies, including the girls had a dish named for someone related to the owners, it was called Chicken Jessica, and they loved it. Gilbert enjoyed his lobster, but not nearly as much as he enjoyed being able to tell his boss that he had confirmed, via his *Blackberry* and Google that a Dr. Clive Foyle was still on the faculty at Oxford's Trinity College. He was a Distinguished Professor of History, or so said the official website.

After dinner, it was back through the notch to the hotel. Gilbert could hardly wait. He was meeting Anna in the hotel bar that evening and had found himself looking at his watch throughout the meal.

But it was worth the wait when he saw Anna a bit later. She was sitting at the bar by herself when Gilbert came in. He was once again struck by her beauty. Climbing awkwardly on to the stool next to hers, she greeted him with a passionate kiss that embarrassed him almost as much as it pleased him. He could taste the alcohol on her and asked her what she was drinking. She told him that it was a vodka martini—a *Stoli* vodka martini.

"You should try one," she said. And he did. Then another and a couple more. Before long he was regaling Anna on all the details—most of which she already knew—about Templeton Davis's new project and how he—Gilbert Dobson—was going to be famous.

"My dear Geelbert," Anna teased, "I am from Russia and have heard so many stories of those who seek to bring things out that leaders don't want to come out. There can be much trouble. Are you afraid at all?"

Though Dobson had never really thought about it—in fact, he didn't notice that she had said that she was from Russia, when earlier she told him that she was from Estonia—no time for that yet with things moving so fast. The booze fortified him and he dismissed Anna's question with a wave and some kind of noise that didn't come out right. They both laughed and ordered more drinks. Gilbert had pretty much forgotten all about his Oxford research assignment. Blood was flowing far away from his brain.

Anna knew what her job was. The Russian team had received strict new orders from the men in the Kremlin. And a little while later, after she led Gilbert to his room and he stumbled in, she led him to the bed—but he couldn't keep his eyes open and fell into a deep sleep. The sedative she had slipped into his fifth vodka martini helped this along, of course. By the time he would wake up, his ship in the night will have sailed.

While he was asleep Anna went through Gilbert's computer carefully, looking for anything related to her information gathering assignment. It was fortunate that the researcher hadn't yet tried to find out more about the Oxford professor and there didn't seem to be much useful material on his computer, but she copied a few files on a flash drive. Her work done, she contacted the men on the team and they quietly left the hotel via a back entrance so as not to be conspicuous. They laid low for a while; then they made a couple of stops.

First, around ten-thirty that night they quietly entered Bill Roberts' building through a back door. They were quite surprised to find no alarm system—pleasantly surprised. As they made their way up the stairs toward the old man's living quarters they heard a television. It was turned up pretty loud and tuned to a movie channel playing the blockbuster 1960s movie *The*

Great Escape. Bill Roberts was asleep in a large chair with his feet propped on an ottoman. As they quietly surrounded him they could hear him snoring softly. And while Steve McQueen hopped German fences on a motorcycle trying to evade Nazi captors, one man covered Bill's mouth with a chloroform soaked rag. Roberts awakened with bright fear in his eyes, then quickly drifted back off from the effects of the inhaled drug. Another man pulled out a syringe that had been filled with a toxin and injected it into Bill Roberts' neck. The men weren't really worried about the needle mark showing because they planned to cover their tracks (and his) in dramatic fashion.

A third man was carrying a fairly large case and from it he removed four identical devices. They were explosive in nature (though the noise put off would be minimal and was very unlikely to be heard by anyone) and each had a small timer. They were placed in various places in the building—two upstairs and two in the bookstore proper. The timers were set for four AM, by which time the men in the van would be long gone. There would be a fire. Bill Roberts' body (already dead by now) would be burned beyond recognition. And it was doubtful that anyone investigating in such a small town—with its limited resources—would question that what happened was anything other than a tragic accident. Just a case of a careless old man burning to death in an old building full of fire code violations.

Their work in town done, they then drove out toward the airport where *The Carolee* was parked. They left the van for a bit, tampered with the aircraft, and soon they were back in the van and their mission was accomplished. They headed south, toward New York and their safe harbor in Brighton Beach, Brooklyn.

As for Anna, Anna Kaplan (though her real name was Anastasia Kapilyich), she drove her rental back to Burlington and caught a flight to LaGuardia and was relaxing in her own place—also in Brighton Beach—while the men in the van were still plodding down the New York State Thruway toward the city.

By the time Gilbert awoke the next morning she was long gone and he felt very sick.

Chapter Forty-Three

TEMPLETON DAVIS PARKED the Expedition in the gravel
lot adjacent to a very quaint Vermont inn called *The Gables*. Entering the
building he saw eight or ten tables and several people enjoying an early
Sunday breakfast. Did he actually see chicken livers on one of the plates?

"By yourself today, sir?" asked the polite hostess.

"No, another man'll join me in a bit," Davis said, while looking at his
watch and noting the time as 7:56 AM.

"How about this table over by the fireplace?"

"Perfect. Thanks!" He ordered coffee and began to peruse the copy of
the *New York Times* he had picked up at his hotel. He saw a story about
Vladimir Putin and was so engrossed in it that he barely heard the noise of
sirens in the distance. He looked up from the paper and noticed some folks
coming in and they were talking excitedly. Something clearly had happened.
As the new party sat at the next table, he leaned over and asked, "Something going on?"

"Is there ever, we like to never made it out to breakfast this morning.
They've got the whole downtown area blocked off. There's been a gigantic
fire."

"Really? Right there on the main drag?"

"Yep—some old bookstore and the other businesses on that side of
the street in that block."

Davis's heart literally skipped a beat. "Bookstore, you say?"

"Yep, that's what we heard."

Templeton Davis threw a five-dollar bill on the table and started for the door.

"Hey mister, you ain't gonna get nowhere near the area," one man shouted. But Davis didn't hear it—or didn't care—he needed to find out about Bill.

Traffic was backed up for more than a mile from the center of town, an intersection with a four-way stop, no traffic light, just the stop signs. Davis pulled into a parking lot next to a pub and set off on foot toward the smoke he could now see billowing up in the distance and hovering like a cloud over the otherwise picture-postcard-like scene. He moved along at an almost running pace and soon was near the main intersection, which had been blocked by law enforcement.

He walked up to a man in uniform and asked: "Is it the bookstore down there—is that where the fire started?"

The man grunted something that seemed to indicate a "yes" and Davis knew instantly that he wasn't going to get anywhere with this clod. Just then someone tapped him on the shoulder. It was another man in uniform. "Excuse me, but aren't you Templeton Davis?"

"Yes, I am," he replied, not knowing where to go with this next, but then deciding to take full advantage. "I'm Davis. You a listener?"

"Sure am, name is Dave Standard and I work with the sheriff's office. I heard you were in town," the officer said, holding out his hand.

"Well, Mr. Standard, I spent most of yesterday with the man who owns that bookstore, we're good friends," Davis said, embellishing things a bit, "and I'm very concerned about him, his name is Roberts, Bill Roberts."

"Oh, trust me Mr. Davis, we all know Bill, he's a great guy. But I think you're in for some bad news. I just heard over the radio that they have a body. The fire is now under control and they found a body, not recognizable, but it's likely Bill. Poor fellow."

Davis found himself profoundly moved and wondering what the hell had happened and did it have anything to do with the story they had been talking about. After several moments lost in thought, Davis asked the officer, "Is there anyway you can get me down there, I really would like to, well, see what is happening?"

Standard looked around as if trying to see if someone higher up was watching and then said, "Sure, follow me!" The two men made their way through the crowd and got fairly close to the smoldering remains of what had once been a pretty fine old, used bookstore. The inventory had burned, so had much of the building, and about then they heard the door to an ambulance close and the vehicle began to move. There was no siren, though, because there was no hurry. The guy on the stretcher—or what was left of him—was dead.

With nothing more to do at the scene, Davis began to make his way back to his car—a long hike, this time uphill.

"Need a ride, Mr. Davis?" Dave Standard asked.

"Actually, that'd be wonderful. I had to park way up the road about a mile in a pub parking lot."

"Well, my car's just a few blocks up that way. Let's go and I'll drop ya. Sure proud to meet ya. Wish I had one of your books with me."

"Tell you what. Give me your card and I'll send you one. How's that?"

"Super!"

"And then maybe you could do me one more favor?"

"Certainly, whadaya need?"

"I'd love to be able to call you in a day or so to find out what the official story about the fire is—arson, accidental? Stuff like that."

Dave Standard hesitated for a bit, not quite sure where Templeton Davis was coming from and finding himself wondering if the radio star's interest in the fresh case somehow went beyond just wanting to find out the fate of a friend.

"Okay, yes, give me a call and I'll tell you what we know. How's that?"

"Great, thanks," Temp said while exiting the police car to go to his own.

Chapter Forty-Four

AS TEMPLETON DAVIS navigated the curves and incline on the Mountain Road en route back to the hotel he dealt with a couple of swirling emotions. There was grief about Roberts. Though they had just met, the time they had spent together the day before was so very intensive and productive—and he really liked the guy, even with the old man's quirks. Then there was fear. Yes fear, though he wondered why? What was it about the death of Roberts that made him at least a little afraid? Afraid of what? Of whom? He also felt some guilt. His mind was raging with confused and interwoven emotions.

Of course, having immersed himself in spy stories for years there was part of him that wondered if what happened to Bill Roberts had not been an accident. What if what Templeton Davis was digging into was triggering panic buttons somewhere? Was this just raging paranoia—or was it possible? He really didn't know, but by the time he parked his vehicle and walked into the hotel lobby he had made a decision. They needed to head back to Virginia—now, though it was not even noon. Time to get out of Dodge. He pulled out his cell phone and called Valerie, telling her about Bill Roberts and the fire and without going into great detail he said that he needed to head back and asked if she could round up the folks and contact Darnell to get the jet ready. In a flash she was all business—and more than a little concerned.

Within the hour most of the party, luggage packed and all, was ready to pull out—everyone was just waiting for Gilbert, who was uncharacteristically late. Temp verified that Valerie had talked to him.

"I did, Temp. But he sounded awful and said he wasn't feeling all that well."

"Hung over?"

"I dunno. Maybe. I think he was out with that Russian girl again last night."

"Russian girl? That girl was Russian?" Temp asked excitedly.

"Yes. Why—is that important?"

Temp didn't answer, he just seemed lost in thought and by that time Gilbert had appeared. He indeed looked like hell and everyone hoped that he was just hung over, because no one wanted to catch a bug from him.

When they arrived at the Morrisville Airport, the group waited in a small lounge area while Milt Darnell did the pre-flight checks on *The Carolee* and filed his flight plan. After about 20 minutes, the pilot came into the lounge, pulled Temp aside and they had a fairly animated conversation. Valerie Doling kept her distance but sensed that something was not quite right.

"It's the strangest thing, Temp. A couple of the gauges seem to be off—or not working at all—and as I did a walk around the craft, I saw some smudges near one of the access panels underneath. Probably nothing, but at first I thought someone might have been working down there."

"Working on what?"

"Dunno, your guess is as good as mine, that is, if anyone was even really down there. Could just be a hunch gone wrong."

"No, Milt—better to err on the side of caution." The pilot nodded agreement.

Davis called Valerie over to them. "Hey, we may have a mechanical issue on the plane and this being a Sunday, it's really gonna be hard to get anyone to look at it. Are those vehicles still here? We may need to head back to town."

"Sure, Temp—we actually had the Expeditions through tomorrow, since that was the earliest the people in Burlington would be over to pick them up."

Just then someone who worked at the airport came over. "You folks okay? Any problems?" Temp and Milt briefed the guy, who turned out to be one of the administrators of the place.

"Well, if ya need to get home tonight, we have a Gulfstream out there I can let you charter. It's not as fancy as your bird, Mr. Davis, but it'll get you and yours home safe and sound. And one of our guys is available to fly down and then back here. And we'll get your craft checked out. How's that?"

Templeton Davis looked over at his party. The kids were running around, the adults just looked bored. Then he told the guy, "You know what, let's do that. Put it on this card," he said as he handed the man his American Express Platinum Card.

"Super," the man said. "It can be fueled and ready to go in a half hour—that work for ya?"

"Yes, fine—thanks!"

While waiting for the Gulfstream to be prepped and ready and while Milt Darnell was getting acquainted with the pilot he'd be spending a few hours with in close quarters—the guy mentioned his name, but Darnell forgot it as soon as the nickname was mentioned: Sky King.

Davis thought more about what had transpired back in town. He decided that he would send everyone on ahead and stick around for a day or so, enough time to get what was wrong with *The Carolee* figured out and fixed. He felt drawn back to Stowe. He sensed that there was a story there behind the death of his new friend. And he couldn't help but wonder if the materials that Bill Roberts had in what he called his BUNNY box had somehow survived the blaze. He now knew he had to find out.

He went out to the Gulfstream and told Milt that he was going to stay back with his aircraft and his pilot understood completely.

"No problem, Boss. We'll get everyone home safe and sound and catch you in a day or so."

Then he briefed Valerie and the rest of the group and got the keys to one of the vehicles back from her.

"You want me to call the lodge and tell them you're coming back?" She asked.

"No, no—I'll take care of it, you just have a nice trip home. I'll call you tomorrow. Call one of our usual guest hosts to sit in for me tomorrow. You pick," he instructed Valerie.

Temp watched as the Gulfstream taxied and took off heading south toward home. He got back in the Expedition and drove toward Stowe. He decided not to reappear at the *Stowe Mountain Lodge*, opting instead to see if he could get a room for the night at the *Green Mountain Inn* right on Main Street—just a couple of blocks from the burned out bookstore. The streets were cleared by then and it turned out that many of the guests had left—no doubt due to the chaos in the heart of the little town—so there were plenty of rooms. Temp's was in the back of the facility and he parked the Expedition nearby.

After showering—more to refresh than anything to do with being short of clean—he dressed and made his way to the front of the place toward the restaurant and bar. He opted for the latter and took a seat at the bar. The bartender was at the far end doing very little, just sort of staring off into the vague distance. So Davis just sat quietly for a few moments, not wanting to disturb her. When she finally noticed him, she had a look of embarrassment and apologized, mumbling something about how bad of a day it had been. And she looked like more than a tear had graced her eyes.

"Yeah, that fire was something awful," Temp said as his eyes met hers.

"Awful is right. Just awful. What can I get you?"

"Oh, I guess a Guinness, if you have, and maybe a menu, I may have a bite to eat and hang out here a while, if you don't mind." He looked around and the place was nearly empty—as was the hotel, no doubt because of what had happened down the road.

"Sure thing," she said as she drew a pint of Guinness and let it settle while handing him a menu. "My name is Betty."

"Temp," he said in reply.

"Oh, I know who you are. Read it in the paper this morning, your picture and all. You have some fans here in town. In fact, one of them passed away today—in that terrible fire up the street." At that, she began to weep.

"Were you a friend of Mr. Roberts?"

Betty seemed surprised. "You know that old guy? Yes—I guess you could call me a friend. He was a regular. In fact, you're sitting in his favorite spot. He was in all the time—unless the place was too crowded and folks were watching football or somethin'."

"Well, yes I knew him. Had done business with his store for a long time and just spent most of yesterday with him, in fact. I was so shocked to hear about what happened. He was a very interesting guy."

"Yeah, I guess you could call it that—interesting, you say. He would tell stories all the time and most folks in town just assumed he was making it all up—been everywhere, done everything, ya know. But I think there was more to it than that."

Temp measured the moment and proceeded with caution, not wanting to go into too much detail with the barmaid. "Well, he was sure colorful, to say the least!" They both smiled and Davis continued, "I'm sure much of what he said was true. I happen to know a bit about his background and know some others who thought very highly of him a lifetime ago."

"Nice to hear. Very nice to hear. I just wish he would come through that door and tell me one of his whoppers one more time," Betty said, again with tears in her eyes. Then with the wave of her hand she motioned at the menu in front of her sole bar patron. "Hungry? What can we rustle up for ya?"

"How 'bout a Reuben?"

"Bill liked them, too. One Reuben coming up and let me know when I can pull you another stout."

A little while later, Templeton Davis made his way—circuitously—toward the charred remains of Bill Roberts' place. It was pretty easy to access and no one was around. There was a full moon and he knew what he was looking for—that beat-up old freezer. It didn't take long to find it barely hidden under a charred piece of wall or floorboard. He looked inside and quickly noticed that it was very wet and the contents already emitted more than a hint of decay. He tipped it sideways so as to let the moisture drain and moved the food. He carefully felt around for any hook to help him lift out the false bottom and found it. Amazingly, very little moisture had been able to make it through and there sitting safe and sound was Bill Roberts' BUNNY box. Temp smiled and scooped it up and soon was back in his room with the materials. He emptied the box onto a table in his room and looked over everything once more—further convincing himself that what he was onto was so very significant.

Just before Templeton Davis dozed off that night, his cell phone buzzed, indicating a text message. It was from Gilbert Dobson: "Boss, as you could probably tell, I'm somewhat under the weather—don't think I'm up for travel to U.K. right now, anywhere for that matter. The flight home was excruciating. I threw up twice! Maybe I could go with you in three or four days?"

Davis replied: "No problem, kiddo. You get your rest and don't worry about that. It's way down on my list now. We'll talk in a few days." As he finished the text, he had the thought that this might be the best way to communicate over the next few days. Maybe it *was* paranoia, but there seemed to be too many coincidences, and if in fact he had stumbled onto something that really ticked off some powerful people, then they had the means to keep one step ahead of him. Maybe *they* had been listening in?

Chapter Forty-Five

BY THE TIME Templeton Davis woke up early the next morning at *The Green Mountain Inn* in Stowe, Vermont—having slept fitfully, with his mind racing most of the night—he had made the decision to travel to Oxford, England himself, and to do so in a very under-the-radar kind of way. His radio show was already being covered for that Monday and tentatively for Tuesday. He would drive the rented SUV to Boston and find a flight to London that evening—just go to the airport, spur of the moment and all. He had his passport with him. He had gotten into the habit many years before of making sure to have it with him on trips even in the United States, just in case he lost his driver's license or credit cards. He thought of it as sort of a back up. So that wasn't a problem. He had some clean clothes in his luggage (two pieces, always perfect for carry on).

One thing that needed attention was what to do with the BUNNY materials—including the Philby journal and now the documents gathered over the years by Bill Roberts. Then it hit him, he could ship it to a person for safekeeping, someone nearly invisible and who would not pry all that much. He immediately thought of Estelle—Estelle Ferguson.

Old Lady Ferguson, as most in the neighborhood referred to her, but never in her actual presence, was a delightful woman. Now well into her 80s, she had the energy and health of someone several decades younger. Her yard—front and back—was her pride and joy. She grew the most beautiful flowers. And living just across the street and three doors down from Templeton Davis, they had become well acquainted. He watched her place and got her mail for her when she went to visit her kids and grandkids in Poughkeepsie, New York, a couple of times of year. And she faithfully baked a blueberry pie for Davis as a thank you every time.

As for Temp, he never needed anyone to help with his mail when he traveled. He maintained a post office box in Georgetown, and received a lot of his mail at the office, so the postman never stopped at his townhouse. And that's what made him think of Estelle. He'd call her along the way and ship a parcel to her for safekeeping.

The one thing he needed was cash—plenty of it. He looked through the telephone directory in the room and noted the addresses of a few banks in town. He visited several of them—hitting their ATMs for the maximum—then getting cash advances from several of his credit card accounts. Within an hour he was carrying nearly $20,000 in cash and wondering if any alarm bells were going off anywhere about his numerous transactions.

Before leaving the area, he drove back out to the airport to check on *The Carolee*. A full maintenance crew was giving it a complete going over and Davis told the airport manager that Milt Darnell would be back in the next day or so to fly the jet back to Virginia. He offered to leave them a deposit for the repairs and maintenance but his celebrity was enough for the manager. *Gotta love small towns*, Temp thought as he smiled.

As he started down Rt. 100 south toward its intersection with I-89, he stopped at the *Cold Hollow Cider Mill* and grabbed a half-dozen hot-fresh donuts and a quart of nearly freezing cold cider and then was on his way. The four-hour drive took him through some of the most scenic parts of Vermont and New Hampshire—somehow bringing a measure of peace to his otherwise troubled mind. It was a sunny day and the foliage was spectacular—so breathtaking, in fact, that he almost forgot about the BUNNY box materials. Stopping for gas near Manchester, New Hampshire, he saw an office supply store and bought a mailing box large enough to handle what he had to send. They also handled the mailing of parcels—but first he had to call his neighbor to make sure she was on board with the plan. He went to a payphone outside the store and, having horded change since Stowe, dialed information first to get Estelle Ferguson's number.

"Estelle, dear—this is Templeton Davis from down the street."

"I know your voice, Mr. Davis. You always announce yourself when you don't have to. You know I listen to you all the time. What are you calling me about on this beautiful Monday? And where are you my boy? I haven't seen you around the past few days—you on a holiday?"

"Something like that, Estelle. Actually, I'm calling to ask a favor and it may seem to be a bit unusual."

"Why, Templeton Davis, you know I'd do anything for you. What is it, love?"

"Estelle, I'm going to send you a package to keep in a safe place for me. You know I don't get mail at my place, and I don't want to send this to my house just to sit there. So I'm going to address it to you and my name won't be on it anywhere."

"My, my, Mr. Davis, aren't you the man of mystery. A package you say. Might I ask what's in it?"

"It's just a few items I picked up at a book sale—you know how I like to collect the odd old book here and there."

"Yes, yes, that's just what you need, another book to clutter your house," Estelle said and then chuckled like a schoolgirl. She really did love talking with Templeton Davis. It was like tonic to her.

"Thanks, Estelle. Now, this package will come addressed to you from a bookseller in Vermont named Bill Roberts—that Okay?"

"Whatever you say, my dear. What would you like me to do when it comes? Should I run it over to your house and put it on the front table?" she asked. He had given her a key to his place long ago, and kept one to her house, as well.

"No, no—don't bother with that. Just put it somewhere safe there in your house and I'll come by and get it in a few days when I get back. No need to fuss over it, promise?"

Estelle was a pretty uncomplicated lady, not given to suspicion or intrigue, very trusting and all, so nothing in this conversation bothered her. She was just glad to help.

"I'm at your service—when do think you'll be home? The neighborhood is not the same without you."

Temp smiled, then the smile was gone and he found himself hoping for a second that he wasn't somehow putting Mrs. Ferguson in harm's way.

"Just a few days, Estelle, just a few days. You take care, now—Okay?"

He packed everything into the box while sitting in the Expedition, then went back into the store and arranged for the parcel to be shipped that afternoon to his very kind neighbor. He also bought a disposable cell phone and a loadable credit card, which he put $2,000 on. The clerk handling his transactions asked no questions—he was preoccupied with the rather loud music being piped into his left ear while looking around to make sure that the boss wasn't watching him.

When Davis arrived at Boston's Logan airport, he parked in the daily lot, choosing not to return the car to the rental counter—he'd face those consequences and that bill later. Then he checked flight times on the board and saw that there was a Virgin-Atlantic flight leaving that evening at 7:45—in about three hours. He booked an upper class ticket paying the $3,200 fare with cash—raising an eyebrow and he was sure that he'd be flagged for extra scrutiny when it came time to go through security, but he didn't want a credit card paper trail for anyone to follow. And as for upper class, well it may not be his own plane, he thought, but he'd travel in style and needed the rest. He also converted $3,000 dollars into British pounds at the airport—he frowned when he realized that it worked out to well under 2,000 in pounds.

He actually enjoyed the flight to London's Heathrow Airport (surprising himself), watched a couple of movies, ate some great food, drank some wonderful wine and a couple of doses of Johnny Walker Blue Scotch Whisky, and dozed off for nearly three hours. After he landed and jumped through all the entry hoops, he found a public Internet kiosk and sent a note back to the team. *"Hi Gang: Quite a weekend, huh? I'm going to take a couple of personal days this week, back soon—make sure the show is covered. I'll talk with you all when I get back, Best, Temp."*

Valerie wrote back before Temp logged off: *"Temp, what is going on? Where are you? Are you back in DC or still up in Vermont? What's going on? When Vince, Liz, and the girls got home from the trip, they found that their house has been burglarized. Not sure what was taken but they said the place was a mess, just all torn up. They called the police who came out to investigate. Vince said that it almost looked like whoever did this was looking for something specific. Said an old briefcase had been taken from his shed. He was pretty shaken, you might want to give him a call."*

His heart sank when he read the thing about the Benton house. He was also sure that his own place in Georgetown was likely now a similar kind of mess. And he knew what the something was that the intruders were looking for—it was part of what was in a parcel now en route to Estelle Ferguson.

Just before his time expired at the Internet kiosk, he reserved a room at the *Randolph Hotel* in Oxford, letting them know he was coming to town that morning. It was always his favorite place to stay when on one of his many visits over the years.

He found car service directly to Oxford from Heathrow, saving him a train ride to London's Paddington Station for a connection. The ride cost 75£. He gave the driver a big tip.

Chapter Forty-Six
Oxford, England

THOUGH HE ARRIVED at the *Randolph Hotel* well before the customary check in time, he was greeted warmly by a young lady at the desk. And within a few moments a manager of sorts—at least he exuded the air of someone more in charge—came over to greet Templeton Davis. The American author and broadcaster had been a mildly familiar face for many years to many who worked at Oxford's premier hotel. On the car ride from the airport, Davis had tried to calculate in his mind just how many nights he had spent there since his college days and concluded that it had to be at least twenty-five, maybe more. He always enjoyed visiting the city and thought of it as a very special place.

He asked the concierge where he might access a university faculty directory, explaining that he was looking up an old colleague. It was a stretch of the truth but accepted as plausible and within a few moments he had contact information for Professor Clive Foyle, long time member of the faculty at Trinity College. He wondered if the good doctor would remember him—it had been years since they had crossed paths.

He got settled in his room—very nice and comfortable—took a shower and was soon out the door onto Beaumont Street, deciding to walk on a beautiful day over to Professor Foyle's office. He made his way to Broad Street and resisted the urge—or better, deferred it—to pop into *Blackwells Bookshop*, one of his favorite places on the planet. Soon he located the building that housed Foyle's office. It seemed to be a more recent addition to the campus, and clearly a departure from the stately dignity of the surrounding structures, parts of which had been around for more than 500 years. This building was rather nondescript and appeared to be a clumsy afterthought on the part of those who created it. The fact that it was partially hidden by some very large trees—likely by design—was at least a bit of redemption.

Entering the building, Temp went up a flight of creaky stairs and immediately noted the unmistakable smell of furniture polish. The fact that it triggered a memory of his student days at Oxford made him smile at the thought that using the same polish all these years was something of a metaphor for how time seemed to stand still—or at least creep along quite slowly—at the prestigious center of research and learning.

Temp finally located the right room, but it was empty. There was a woman at a desk down the hall, so he asked her about Foyle's office hours. "Should be there now," she said, "Can't tell you where he is, you're welcome to wait, there's a chair there in the hall," she said with a tone that strongly suggested that he not bother her again. Davis thanked her (anyway) and took up his post in the chair in the hall outside the door of Dr. Clive Foyle, Distinguished Professor of History, as it said on the door. The clock on the wall across the way showed the time as just after noon.

Having picked up a copy of *The Oxford Times* at the hotel, Davis indulged in his quirky traveling habit, one he especially enjoyed when visiting Oxford. He located the classified section and scanned the pages to see what flats were renting for and how real estate was priced these days. It was one of those back-of-the-mind things with Temp, because he lived by himself and there was more than a little wanderlust in him. When he found places that, well, comforted him, as did Oxford, he would imagine buying a place and spending time there. And living again, at least for a spell, in Oxford was somewhere on Temp's "bucket list."

He was reading about what seemed to be a wonderful home on Blenheim Lane, dating back to the eighteenth century, complete with stone walls, vaulted ceilings, three bedrooms, two fireplaces, and pulled out his pen to circle it, when he heard the sound of slow shuffling of feet coming up the stairs. Soon the unmistakable image of a very distinguished professor came into view. Davis instantly recognized the man as Foyle, though he looked much older than he remembered. He had to be over eighty, Temp thought. He was stooped over a bit, wearing a dark brown tweed jacket, oxford shirt and well-worn-and-fading bowtie.

"You waiting for me?" Foyle said as he eyed his visitor carefully, almost suspiciously.

"Yes sir, I am. My name is …"

"I know who you are. I remember you and I saw you debate a few years back at the Oxford Union. You're that American, Davis, right? What can I do for you?"

"Well, may I come into your office and talk with you? I've got quite a story to tell and I think you might be able to help me."

The professor paused and looked over the top of the glasses that rested somewhat with a tilt down his nose and replied, "Well, you have a way of getting a fellow interested. Certainly, right this way." They entered the room. Foyle took a seat behind the desk and Davis on a small couch across from him. He looked around. The office was rather small and very cluttered, everything one would expect from the lair of a professional and tenured member of academia. "Now, what can I do for you?"

"Dr. Foyle, I'm, as you probably know, not only a broadcaster, but a writer, as well."

"Yes, I believe a few of your books have been released over here and have sold well. I think I tried to read one of your novels once—but couldn't catch onto it, sorry," he said. Then quickly adding as if to avoid an outright insult, "Don't have much of a taste for fiction, nothing personal about your book—in fact, I rarely buy novels but I did pick up yours."

Davis smiled at the clear attempt at kindness and responded, "Well, I just thank you for noticing the work in the first place and I'm sure you have enough reading material to keep you busy for a couple of lifetimes. It's what I'm working on now that brings me to you. I'm doing some research on a former British ambassador to the United States, David Ormsby-Gore."

At this, the professor's face grew tight and serious and he just nodded and sat back in his chair and crossed his arms. Davis continued, "I've reason to believe from one of my sources in the States that you have done some, I think significant, research on him and I was hoping to, as we say in the U.S. 'pick your brain' a bit."

After a moment the professor replied, "Well, I don't know if I can help you. I haven't thought about him in years—that was research from my early years, oh my, must be nearly 40 years ago," the professor said as he seemed to drift off in thought. "You know he was educated right here at Trinity College back in the 1930s."

"Yes, I knew that," Temp answered. "What I'm trying to figure out connects likely to his college days then his career afterwards. Back then, if you don't mind me asking, back when Mr. Ormsby-Gore was so much in the news, did you ever think of writing a book about him? I mean, after all, this was a British ambassador who it seems was almost a member of the inner circle of the President of the United States. That, in itself, would, I think, warrant a deeper study."

The professor didn't answer right away, but just looked into Davis's eyes as if trying to read him—trying to figure him out. "Well frankly, I did work on such a project back then, but when your president was murdered back in '63 it all seemed to be passé. And it wasn't long until Ormsby-Gore left politics and diplomacy for good—became something of a media baron eventually. Did you know that here at Oxford we lost a giant on that very same day that President Kennedy was killed?" Foyle asked, almost as if trying to deflect, or at least delay, a conversation about Ormsby-Gore.

"No, I didn't—who was it?"

"None other than C.S. Lewis—first name was Clive, too, mind you," he said with a smile. "He died on November 22, 1963 and a good number of us went to the *Eagle and Child* and had a pint and more in his memory. We hovered around a small television that someone brought in so we could watch the coverage of the Kennedy story from the States."

Davis nodded and smiled at the professor allowing his mind to drift back to college days and his own visits to that celebrated pub where the so-called *Inklings*, Lewis and J.R.R. Tolkien would meet to read their work of the day to each other. "That must have been a day to remember—I was just a little boy at the time, but I remember my mother crying and my dad holding her in his arms as they watched all of it."

There was another pause, then Foyle got the conversation back on its original track. "What exactly is your interest—your angle, Mr. Templeton Davis from the United States?" Foyle asked in a professorial kind of way.

"Well, my angle is espionage."

"Espionage, you say? The stuff of spies, cloak and dagger, MI-5, MI-6, CIA and all that tommyrot?"

"Yes, exactly."

"Then you're doing research for a spy *novel*?"

"Well, that's where I began, but along the way I uncovered some intriguing details that began to convince me that I might be on to something more. What's now developing will have the feel of a spy novel—only it's, I think, a very true story. One that involves a group of spies recruited right here at Oxford."

"Really. And what do you think you know?" the professor asked, bluntly.

"Well, let me ask you, Dr. Foyle, in all your research about David Ormsby-Gore did you ever have any question as to his, well, loyalties?"

"Loyalties?"

"Yes—did you ever come across anything that made you even wonder if maybe he was one of those children of British aristocracy who got caught up in the romance of communism back in the day, in the way Philby and MacLean did?"

He had laid all the cards on the table and he watched and waited for an agonizingly long moment to see what this Oxford professor might make of it all.

"Mr. Davis," Foyle said, finally breaking his pensive silence, "I have a class to teach in a few minutes, but what you're talking about is something I'd like to pick up later with you. There's a pub called *The Lamb and Flag* on St. Giles Street. If you'd like to meet me there about four this afternoon and are willing to spring for a pint or two and some food should I be hungry, I'll let you, as you say 'pick my brain.'"

"What—not the *Eagle and Child*?" Temp asked with a tone of surprise?

"No—too many tourists. And after all in their later years the *Inklings* took much of their ale drinking to *The Lamb and Flag*, when they disliked some of the renovation work at their prior hangout."

Templeton Davis smiled at the professor and left the office saying, "I know the place well and shall see you there, sir, at four."

Chapter Forty-Seven
Oxford, England

SHORTLY BEFORE FOUR PM Templeton Davis entered the pub and looked around the room. His nostrils were quickly engaged by the eclectic fragrance of stale air, moldy must, and a hint of alcohol. Noticeably absent was the smell of cigarette smoke, one of the few changes from way back when. There were few customers in the place at the moment—a few booths were taken up with couples, there was a larger party more toward the back, and off to the side there were two rather large men seemingly absorbed in conversation. A few booths away he saw Dr. Foyle, a half-filled glass of something amber sat in front of him and a small empty glass next to it. As he made his way over to the professor, their eyes met, though the good doctor's were already a little red for wear.

"Been waiting long, sir?"

"Not all that long. Got here about twenty minutes ago, I s'pose and started without you," he said without a smile. He appeared to be brooding.

"Well, what are you having there, Dr. Foyle? I'll join you."

"A pint of this good local ale and a glass of Johnny Walker Black."

"I'll join you with the ale, but pass on the whisky, thank you though."

Davis went to the bar and quickly returned with the drinks. The two men made small talk. Soon they revisited the subject of Mr. Ormsby-Gore. "I must tell you that you caught me off guard back there in my office earlier bringing up that name," Foyle began.

"Hadn't thought about him in a while, is it?"

"Actually, though that's what I told you earlier, I really think about him quite a lot. There was a time when I thought my research and work were going to lead to a world-class biography and maybe more. But it all changed years ago."

"What changed it?" Temp asked, deciding that there was something the senescent professor really wanted to talk about, but needed some encouragement.

"First, before I talk any more about this, I need to know what you're working on. You said it had to do with espionage and it involves Lord Harlech ... er ... Ormsby-Gore?"

"Yes, I believe it does, but there are many questions and I'm not sure if there's anyone who can really answer them."

"I can," the professor quickly answered, then catching himself, "What I mean is that I s'pose I know more about the man than anyone, certainly anyone in academic life. In fact, I had several personal interviews with him, including one just a week before he had that dreadful accident—the one that took his life. He was very nice—quite charming, but always with a hint of the mysterious. There were times when I wondered."

Foyle took the glass of scotch and drank it down in one swallow, following which he took an ample drink of the ale to chase the whisky down. It struck Davis at this moment that the professor had the look of a seasoned drinker.

The whisky seemed to loosen Foyle's tongue a bit. "There were things Ormsby-Gore said to me in the weeks and months before he died that seemed to me to point to some kind of inner conflict, as if he had something he wanted to say, but never could quite pull the trigger," he said in a voice made briefly raspy by the liquor.

"How hard did you press him?"

"Oh, not all that hard—I'm an academic man, not one of those vultures from Fleet Street, but I can tell you that I've always felt there was a story there. It's just that I've never been much of a chancer."

"Why didn't you keep digging after his death?"

"Wanted to. That's for sure. I wanted to, but then I had a visitor, someone who persuaded me to leave it all be."

"What kind of visitor?"

"The official kind. This fellow was from Five."

"Five?"

"Oh, sorry old boy," Foyle said. "That's Five as in MI-5, sort of like your FBI across the pond, only our boys have a lot more latitude, official secrets and all that."

"You're saying that someone from MI-5 asked you not to dig any deeper into David Ormsby-Gore's affairs?" Davis asked excitedly.

"Asked me? That's funny. No, there wasn't much asking about it. My visitor made it very clear that it would, shall we say, not be in my best interest to continue working on material for an Ormsby-Gore book, or *anything* about the man, actually. And I got the message as you Americans say 'Loud and Clear.' And that was that."

"And you just rolled over and played dead on it?"

"Well, though the words were never actually uttered, it was obvious that there would be significant personal risk for me—my job and tenure and all that. Frankly, there remains a close relationship in our country between the universities, particularly Oxford and Cambridge, and the intelligence services. Again, I'm just not a chancer—or what you might call a risk taker."

"I understand that, Professor Foyle, but didn't it make you curious as to what they were so concerned about? You never found anything that would have raised any kind of security issue, did you?"

"Well, not exactly—but I did hear the odd rumor or two."

"Such as?"

"I'll tell you, but you have to promise to keep my name out of anything. I'm already past retirement age and plan to work as long as I can, then live the rest of my days on my pension. So I don't need any trouble at this point in my life."

"Professor, you have my word. I don't want to bring anyone else's name into it and I have my reasons," Temp said, deciding not to tell his new friend about the fate of Bill Roberts—at least not yet.

"Fine then. Well, long after I gave up on Mr. Ormsby-Gore as a research subject—after he was dead—people would still ask me this or that about him. I'd get the occasional call from a newspaper reporter hunting background details. Apparently I was on some kind of listing of experts. At any rate, even after I was done with the project, I'd get the random note, or call, or query from someone needing this information or that."

"Sounds like the normal course of business."

"Yes, I agree, except that a few of the questions were from, how do you Yanks say it? Left field?"

"What questions?"

"I can't recall the actual wording of the questions—but I had the distinct impression that there were some people sniffing around the memory of the late ambassador, Lord Harlech—and they seemed to have it in their minds that our friend was some kind of Soviet spy."

Temp just stared at Clive Foyle and nodded affirmatively.

"Well, Doctor, that's the trail I'm on—and I think I've got more than rumor on which to hang the story."

"You don't say?"

"I'm going to bring you into this a little, but before I do, I need to ask—do you happen to have the name or names of those who made such inquiries?"

"My oh my, I'm not sure. The last one came a few years ago—it was actually a letter from a bloke in America. I may have that somewhere back in my office in a file. I can check. Now you're saying that there may be something to such a story?"

"In fact, I'm fairly certain that the ambassador was working for and reporting to the Soviets the whole time he was representing the U.K. in the U.S.A. That's exactly what I'm saying."

"Do you have any evidence?"

At that Templeton Davis briefed Professor Clive Foyle on the major points of the story, though careful to leave the names of those involved out of it. He mentioned a journal and a reference that certainly pointed to Ormsby-Gore. The professor listened intently and then suddenly said, "Mr. Davis, let's go back to my office right now and look for that letter I mentioned. You may indeed be on to something."

And with that they left the pub and began to walk back to Foyle's office.

Just as they exited the door of the place, the two men Temp had seen when he entered *The Lamb and Flag*, left as well, though neither Davis nor Dr. Foyle noticed, immersed as they were in the subject at hand.

The rugged looking fellows had been sitting at another booth about fifteen feet or so from Davis and Foyle and they strained to pick up on at least part of the conversation. But eavesdropping wasn't so much their assignment as was following the men and reporting back to their superiors as to what they were up to. A third member of their reconnaissance team was waiting outside, sitting in the driver's seat of a black Range Rover, the car of choice for people like Russian mobsters, part of the large émigré community in the U.K., men who also did the occasional odd job for the men back in the Kremlin. The driver saw Davis and Foyle exit the pub followed by his comrades a few seconds later. They proceeded on foot down St. Giles Street back toward Broad Street and the cluster of buildings that housed Trinity College. He started the Range Rover and decided to follow along—discreetly, of course.

Chapter Forty-Eight
Washington, DC—October 25, 1962

ROBERT KENNEDY, THE Attorney General of the United
States, opened the door, while knocking softly, thinking that his brother
Jack, the President of the United States, was dining alone. Jackie and the
children had been staying out at their farm in rural Middleburg, Virginia for
a while. The place was called Glen Ora and the Kennedys had leased it just
after the election in 1960. Jackie loved horses and the farm, which was less
than a two-hour drive and just twenty minutes or so by presidential heli-
copter; it was really her place. The official story was that she and the children were on a vacation—but the real story was the chronic strain on their
marriage due to the President's nearly compulsive philandering. The First
Lady and the children had returned to the White House a few days earlier at
the request of the President and in the light of extraordinary circumstances,
which was well beyond an understatement.

So brother Bobby was surprised to see the President dining on a
roasted chicken dinner without Jackie—who had gone to her room early
and taken dinner there and spent the evening reading magazines and
watching television. In fact, he was eating with another guest, but then seeing this particular visitor, Bobby's surprise gave way to relaxed familiarity.
However, no matter how close the President of the United States was in a
personal way to the British Ambassador, Mr. David Ormsby-Gore, what
Bobby needed to brief the President about was something urgent—and
very secret.

"I've come from *that* meeting," he said, trusting his brother would pick up on the not-so subtlety. John F. Kennedy looked his brother in the eye as the Attorney General sort of half-nodded in the direction of the Ambassador with a look that said something like, *Get rid of him, we need to talk.* But the President surprised his brother.

"Relax, Bobby. I, uh, the President has no secrets from David." Which was quite a concession, especially in light of what was happening in the world at that moment.

Robert F. Kennedy sat down at the table and examined the platter of chicken looking for a leg and uttering a rare-for-him curse word when he realized that his big brother and his buddy had robbed him of his favorite part of the bird. "I just met with Bolshakov and I think there is a chance that we might be able to find a way to convince Khrushchev to back down and maybe even agree to withdraw his missiles," he said, plunging right in to one of the most serious matters ever faced by two nations and the rest of the world in history.

The Cuban Missile Crisis was approaching critical mass. The blockade, or as Mr. Kennedy preferred to call it—"quarantine"—in much the same way that Harry Truman had referred to his move into Korea as a "police action," was not working insofar as causing any change in the status of the Soviet missiles ninety miles off the coast of Florida. In fact, over the past forty-eight hours it was clear that crews were working around the clock in a race to bring the project to full operative functionality. And some of the now low-flying reconnaissance planes being sent over Cuba by the United States were being openly fired upon. It seemed to only be a matter of time before one was shot down, giving the hawks on the Executive Committee, nicknamed the "Ex-Com," more cause to advocate a full out, full-press, war action against the Soviets and the Castro regime in Cuba.

Bobby was still hesitating some to talk so freely in front of Ormsby-Gore. David was more his brother's friend than his. He knew him and liked him. But it was a mere acquaintance, not the kind of friendship Jack seemed to enjoy with the ambassador. And there were times when Bobby was a bit uneasy around Ormsby-Gore. This was one of them, but he followed his brother's lead, as he usually did.

"Well, Mr. President," he began, though they were siblings, he did his best to use the title whenever others were present, "I met with Georgi a bit ago and pitched him our idea—your idea—about the Jupiter missiles in Turkey and he seemed very interested in getting the information back to the people in the Kremlin."

The Georgi mentioned was one Georgi Bolshakov, a man who worked as a journalist and Soviet Embassy officer, but of course as with many, if not most Soviet diplomats, it was a cover; his real job was with the GRU (Soviet military intelligence). A short, somewhat plump man, who in some ways reminded Bobby of the cartoon character Boris Badenov, the two men had developed a strong relationship over the past year and a half.

Following the fiasco at the Bay of Pigs, the Kennedy brothers were determined to do things their own way henceforth. When possible (and it usually was), they would find ways to bypass official channels and find intriguing alternative methods of dealing with complicated problems. So when the Attorney General of the United States had the opportunity to get acquainted with Mr. Bolshakov—a meeting set up by an American newspaperman in May of 1961—he jumped at it. They went for a long walk, sat in a park to chat, ran back to the Justice Department when it rained, and finished their conversation in their underwear in a hideaway library while their clothes dried out sufficiently.

The groundwork for the Kennedy-Khrushchev meeting in Vienna was laid out that day, and subsequently Georgi Balshakov was the preferred method of communication between the White House and the Kremlin. Though this had been recently strained when in the run up to the missile crisis, Mr. Balshakov had told the Kennedys repeatedly that there were no Soviet plans to place offensive weapons in Cuba.

"Your Russian spy has deceived us before, Bobby. You recall that he, uh, misled us just two weeks ago."

"But Jack, I'm convinced that he was in the dark as much as we were. He was out of the loop."

"Well, what the hell good is a so-called back channel if the son of a bitch is not in the loop—answer me that?" the President barked at his brother, as David Ormsby-Gore took it all in.

"Mr. President," the Ambassador began, after there was a lull in the heated exchange between Jack and Bobby, "what is this about Jupiter missiles in Turkey? I thought you've always maintained that they'd be off the table, that you'd never negotiate them away."

"Well frankly, David, I've been trying for months to get those damn missiles dismantled and the Joint Chiefs just sit on their asses and drag their heels. Now it's all different, because if I put them on the table as a negotiating ploy I'll be destroyed politically by the Republicans who think I'm not tough enough to stand up to Chairman Khrushchev. That jackass Dick Nixon would love the chance to salvage his suicidal run for governor in California by being able to crucify me. Not a chance in hell that I'll give him that!"

"So what do you propose to do?"

"Well, David, if I had a way to convince the Soviets that I will, in fact, dismantle those obsolete weapons in Turkey in, say, six months, but that it could never be mentioned now and linked in any way, I could save face."

"What about the future of Cuba? Would you later invade? We know of your particular distaste for that Fidel fellow."

"You know, David," the President responding after a brief pregnant pause. "In all honesty, I'd be perfectly happy to ensure the security of Cuba and I'm not going to risk all out nuclear war over it, that's for sure. But there is no way I can put that on the table without appearing weak."

"Interesting. Interesting. Is there anything Her Majesty's government can do to help?"

"I wish, David. I wish. But this is one mess I'm stuck in by myself," the President said as he wiped his mouth and called for some coffee.

"Well, Mr. President," the Ambassador prodded, "once you're past this unpleasant business, and I know you will be soon, might it be time to again visit that old idea you and I've been chatting about for many years?"

"You mean that test-ban idea?" Kennedy asked and Ormsby-Gore nodded affirmatively. "Of course, you know how I feel and I appreciate your advice on this matter. I even know that you have, uh, lobbied Jackie some on this issue, not that she's all that interested in most issues of public policy. But of course, this matter is truly one of life or death and I know she worries about the future for John and Caroline and all the other children of the world."

"Yes, Mr. President. Your dear wife is not only elegant and graceful, she's quite wise."

"Indeed, Sir David. Indeed. Yes, the idea of coming to an agreement with the Soviets on banning the testing of atomic weapons in the atmosphere is very much on my agenda. The question is whether or not it's on Mr. Khrushchev's agenda."

"But possibly some unilateral action on your part, Mr. President, might indeed pave the way."

"Well, David, why not let us get past this missile thing in Cuba and then our mid-term election here and maybe then—maybe—we might have something to talk about and work on."

Following the meal and after leaving the White House at a rather late hour, David Ormsby-Gore walked over to the *Mayflower Hotel*. He found a pay telephone and dialed a number well known to him. When the party on the other end answered, Ormsby-Gore said: "We must meet now." The urgency said it all.

Within an hour, the British ambassador had made his way across the Potomac River, taking great care that he was not followed, and to a very ordinary looking house in Falls Church, Virginia. It appeared to be just like every other house in the tree adorned neighborhood. An elderly couple— the locals assumed they were from Poland or some such place—lived there and they had occasional houseguests. There was certainly nothing going on to warrant any suspicion. Certainly not.

The dwelling was a safe house of sorts, hiding in plain sight. And that night, just before midnight, David Ormsby-Gore had a rare meeting with his Soviet handler. Such meetings were uncommon because they were, of course, risky. If the two men were ever seen together or connected in any way, there would be monumental trouble. Normally an agent such as the ambassador would communicate and receive instructions via a 'cutout,' an intermediary, someone who just served the cause by relaying messages. The ambassador's usual 'cutout' was a waitress at the *Occidental Restaurant* in the *Willard Hotel*. Her name was Lydia and she was purportedly from Hungary (she was really from Minsk in Belarus). But there had been no time this evening for usual processes.

His handler was already in the house, sitting in the living room drinking a cup of Russian Caravan tea. He was a serious looking man, impeccably dressed, and as-ever, a portrait of poise. His name was Aleksandr Semyonovich Feklisov, a veteran of the spy wars. He had handled some of the most important agents ever to pass information along to the Soviets, including Julius Rosenberg, Harry Gold, and Klaus Fuchs— all names associated with seeing to it that the atomic secrets of the United States made their way to Soviet laboratories in the early days of the Cold War.

These days, he went by the name of Alexander Fomin, someone also assigned to the Soviet Embassy, but who really worked for the KGB. He knew Georgi Balshakov, but didn't really care for him and part of his role in the States was to keep an eye on him. For some reason, the men in the Kremlin—particularly Khrushchev himself—were not always sure of his competence, or on occasion, his loyalties. Balshakov was one of those Soviet diplomats who seemed to relish the luxuriousness of life in the United States compared to that of Mother Russia.

"And to what, my good friend BUNNY, do I owe this rather unusual meeting?" Fomin asked, allowing himself the use of Ormsby-Gore's code name. "You have some information of value for us—something that might help resolve this terrible international tension?"

"Yes, old boy, I think I do. I was at the White House earlier this evening. I had dinner with the President. His brother came by and he'd apparently just met with Mr. Balshakov."

"Yes, I'm aware of where you were and of that other meeting this evening, as well," Fomin said, as he stared stoically at the Ambassador. Ormsby-Gore, usually the essence of poise and grace was intimidated, as he was any time the two met. He was very glad such rendezvous were rare. Did the guy ever blink, he wondered?

"Well, it's pretty clear to me from that conversation that Mr. Kennedy is perfectly prepared to give away his missiles in Turkey and promise not to invade Cuba in the future, but it has to be done in such a way that he can save face. You realize that the Americans have an election coming up in a few weeks and his party stands to lose a lot of ground, especially if he appears weaker than Chairman Khrushchev."

"In your opinion, is the President sincere—will he really keep such a bargain?"

"Yes, I'm sure of it!"

"Thank you, Mr. Ambassador. This information is most helpful. I'll work on how we can exploit this."

"My dear fellow, please know that we all want to avoid war, it's hard for us to even fathom the consequences of getting this very wrong at this crucial moment. Please let me know if there is anything else I can do. I have unique access to the pinnacle of power here in the United States these days and I want you to know that you can count on my service in the making of a more peaceful and just world."

Fomin continued his expressionless stare for a moment and then allowed himself the hint of a smile, "Yes, BUNNY, we're very aware of your strategic placement and you'll remember that we put you on such a course many years ago."

"Yes, of course, I'm very aware of this. I just ..."

"Let me finish, my friend," Fomin said, while holding up one hand in a gesture that admonished the ambassador to listen rather than speak. "We have great plans for you and you'll be crucial in the aftermath of this whole unfortunate episode. You made sure that we knew what the Americans knew well before they think we knew—and there's no doubt that you'll help us stay ahead of them in this great game of power and diplomacy."

A few hours later, as Ormsby-Gore was safely back at the British Embassy and trying to catch a few hours of sleep, he wondered what Fomin would do with the information he had been given.

Several hours later, as the lunch hour approached, Alexander Fomin called a journalist he knew, John Scali, who worked for *ABC News*. They met at the *Occidental Restaurant*—and yes, Lydia was their waitress. Fomin recruited Scali to take a fresh proposal to the highest levels of government—meaning President Kennedy. And thus the wheels began to turn to diffuse the situation and resolve the Cuban Missile Crisis. The world had been brought to the brink and had not plunged itself into the abyss. David Ormsby-Gore very much enjoyed being part of the history's sub plot.

Chapter Forty-Nine
Oxford, England

BACK AT THE professor's office, Davis stood helplessly by as Foyle almost seemed to ransack his own room. He was a man with a mission—and apparently in a hurry. During their walk from the pub, the professor had shared a lengthy monologue that seemed, for him at least, to connect the dots on the whole story. It was almost as if he had found the proverbial piece of the puzzle, something that turned the frustration of a longtime quest into the fruit of fresh discovery. Now he was looking for that file—or as he was referring to it: "Where is that bloody file?"

Davis was not unaccustomed to clutter. His own work areas—at the office and the ones in his various homes, in Palm Beach, the apartment in Manhattan, and of course, his main domicile in Georgetown—bore evidence of the occasional cyclone passing through, but Foyle had taken it to a whole other level. It's a wonder he could find anything.

But he did. After just five or six minutes he exclaimed, "Ah, here it is!" He opened a file that looked, from across the room where Temp stood, to contain at least twenty-five pages. He watched in silence as Dr. Foyle went through it carefully, page by page.

Breaking his silence, Foyle said: "Here you go, old boy. This is the one I was talking about. It came in back in 2007. Take a look." Davis grabbed the page from the professor's hand and read a letter to Foyle written by someone on the faculty at New York University in Manhattan, a Gregory Raspitov—someone who taught in the school's Russian and Slavic Studies department. The letter was an inquiry about whether or not Dr. Foyle knew of any possible connection between David Ormsby-Gore and a fellow named Aleksandr Feklisov.

"Dr. Foyle," Temp said, breaking his silence. "There's a reference here to a man named Feklisov—why's that name so familiar to me?"

"It should be familiar, if you're the espionage buff you claim to be. He was a Soviet spy associated with the Rosenbergs, Ethel and Julius, the couple executed in the States back in the 1950s for giving atomic secrets to the Soviets."

"But what connection would this Feklisov have with David Ormsby-Gore?"

"None that I can think of, which is likely why I never wrote this guy back," Foyle replied, quite careful not to say the name out loud.

"Professor, could I ask a big favor of you? Could I borrow that letter?"

"Sure. In fact, you can have it. Not much use to me."

"That's incredibly kind of you, Dr. Foyle—can I do anything for you? How about you let me pay you for this? You've already heard me admit that I have too much money," Davis said smiling at the academician.

"Tell you what," Foyle responded. I'd like to visit the States one day and you can help me then.

"Count on it. In fact, when you're ready to 'hop the pond' as you all say over here, let me know and I'll fly you over—first class—and make sure that you have a fabulous time for as long as you want."

"I just might take you up on that," the professor said and then he paused and looked first into Davis's eyes, then up at the ceiling. He took a deep breath and continued, "I'm not sure why I'm going to do this, but something tells me that you need a little bit more." At that Dr. Foyle went over to one of his many bookshelves and retrieved two bulging files from what was clearly a hiding place. "These are what files I have left on the man you want to know about. I've kept them all these years and I really don't know why. I want you to have these and if you can make sense of them, please use the material—but no one can ever know where you acquired this material."

Davis took the files and was at a loss for words. He was almost emotional. He was also almost gleeful. What he had just put his hands on was beyond significant and helpful. He put the files in the case he had carried with him from the hotel—an oversized leather briefcase.

The professor didn't allow the moment to get awkward. He just said, "Now, you need to be on your way. I have a class to teach this evening." They shook hands and parted.

Templeton Davis was excited about the new lead he had, the name on the letter now is his pocket, and the files. He now knew that he had to get to New York as soon as possible, but he was determined to spend the rest of the evening enjoying himself in Oxford. And his idea of an exciting time there always included a visit to *Blackwell's Bookstore* on Broad Street—one of the oldest such establishments in the world. Entering the familiar facility, just a short walk from where he had met Dr. Foyle, he smiled and inhaled deeply. He also experienced an adrenalin rush. Books were his addiction.

He hated to admit it, but whenever he went to a bookstore (or library for that matter) he checked to see if any of his titles were on the shelves and he was not disappointed on this visit. Four of his books, including several copies (paperback) of his early-on book about Churchill were stocked. It was one of life's little guilty pleasures for him.

He decided to see if there were any books about John F. Kennedy, particularly ones that bore mention of David Ormsby-Gore. He selected three biographies from the shelves and made his way to an over-sized chair in a corner. One of the books was a large paperback by American historian, Michael Bechloss. Temp had interviewed him a couple of times and enjoyed his work. Scanning the index for Ormsby-Gore's name he found a few mentions, but nothing major—except how the British ambassador seemed to be a presence in the White House during the Cuban Missile Crisis in 1962. He already owned a copy of the book, so he just made a mental note to read more of it when he got home. He never even opened the third book, one by Chris Matthews, because Barbara Leaming's book about Kennedy was filled will dozens upon dozens of references to Ormsby-Gore, some as early as the 1930s. He read a few of them, but decided to purchase the book and take it back to the *Randolph* with him.

As he was checking out, he noticed a reflection in a small mirror behind the counter; it struck him as interesting because he thought it looked like someone who had been sitting in the pub a while earlier. Coincidence, he wondered?

He exited the bookstore and made his way a few blocks back to his hotel and that was when he noticed the same man—again. He was about a block away, but it was unmistakable. Because he was such a spy novel junkie, he knew a thing or two—amateurishly—about what was called "tradecraft" and he decided to be circumspect for the rest of the night. He went briefly to his room, then down to the hotel's *Morse Bar*, one of his favorite spots in the city. Named for the fictitious character Inspector Morse, the bar got much of its more recent reputation as a favorite watering hole of novelist Colin Dexter, the creator of the Oxford policeman, and the inspiration behind other "spin-off" manifestations.

Usually enjoying a seat at the bar in drinking establishments, this evening he opted for a table near the fireplace and settled in for a little relaxation time. He planned on leaving early for Heathrow to head to New York. He asked for a single-malt scotch and they brought him a glass of Oban 14 year-old—no ice. He nursed it for about 30 minutes and then asked for one more.

It was as he was finishing his second drink and just about ready to retire to the room that he noticed—he was almost certain of it—not only the man in the bookstore, but now the fellow had been joined by what looked to be the other man with him earlier at *The Lamb and Flag*. This had to be no mere coincidence—he was being followed, or at least watched. Not quite knowing how to play it, he decided to try to get word to someone with the hotel, assuming there was some kind of security staff. He took a small notebook from his pocket and wrote a note explaining that he thought he was being followed—gave the description of the men and then called a steward over and whispered that he wanted a note passed along. Then he placed it discreetly in the young man's hand to give to whoever was in charge. He also gave the young man a twenty-pound note as a tip, which virtually ensured the missive's prompt delivery.

About five minutes later two men entered the bar. Temp ascertained that they were with hotel security. Shortly thereafter, he got up to leave and his eyes met those of one of the men from the hotel. Moments after Davis exited the *Morse Bar*, the two men who had been watching him made their exit as well, followed fast by the men from hotel security. As Davis got on the elevator to head to his floor, he noticed the security men approaching the other men—just as the elevator door closed. He resisted the urge to double back to see what was happening and assumed that he'd be contacted if he needed to be briefed.

Sure enough, twenty minutes later the two men with hotel security knocked on his door and came in to talk with him. They said that the men denied they were following Davis, but the hotel men didn't believe them. They told Temp that both of the mystery men spoke with heavy accents—Russian accents—and clearly were out of their element. The security men asked Davis what he was up to and he mentioned that he was investigating a story for a book and really couldn't talk about it. They followed with a query as to whether the fact that the men likely were Russian was significant—to which Temp rolled his eyes and said, "Oh yeah."

Davis asked if hotel security might keep an eye out for anyone else who didn't quite fit in. Also, he wanted to check out in the morning and needed transportation back to Heathrow and wondered if there was a way he could be spirited out of the hotel without being noticed. The men were glad to help and, in fact, enjoyed a little cloak and dagger work—so much better than the routine at the otherwise quiet hotel.

True to form, Dr. Foyle returned to the very same pub for a nightcap or two. A man took a seat near him at the corner of the bar. When Foyle went to the privy after his first pint and shot, the man, while no one was looking, put a couple of drops in the professor's pint glass.

By the time the professor left the pub a half-hour or so later, he was feeling sick and slightly disoriented. The man followed him slowly in the Range Rover. After a couple of blocks, Dr. Foyle collapsed on the sidewalk and no one was around to offer aid. In fact, within five minutes he was dead from poison. Meanwhile the beer glass was already in the dishwasher removing any trace of evidence.

Very, very early the next morning Temp left the *Randolph* through a service entrance, got into a BMW and made his way—uneventfully and undetected—to Heathrow Airport. He booked a Lufthansa flight to New York—first class. A few minutes before his flight was called, and as he drank yet another cup of coffee and read yet another magazine, he heard a name jump out from the drone of the television and the overnight news on the other side of the room. All he heard was "Foyle" and his heart seemed to skip a beat. He went over toward the television monitor and caught the end of the story, one about a beloved professor dead on an Oxford sidewalk from an apparent heart attack. The word "apparent" made Temp's own chest tighten. Sad was the fate of the late Dr. Clive Foyle, Distinguished Professor of History.

And Templeton Davis surmised that his newfound friend in Oxford was the latest to meet with a tragic end and he wondered how close he came last night, as well. He thought about the files now in his possession and felt both guilt and gratitude—an odd and confusing mix. He also wondered how it was with the team back home. He felt guilty not having called in the past day or so, and hoped with all his heart that by keeping his distance he was, in fact, keeping the people he loved out of harm's way.

Once the flight reached cruising altitude, Davis pulled out the letter the now late professor Foyle had given to him. As he read it again, he suddenly shuddered at the thought that the document was likely very dangerous to have, in light of what had happened to Professor Foyle. Then he reached for the Kennedy book by Barbara Leaming and used the index to read and mark every reference to Ormsby-Gore. By the time Davis landed at JFK he had a pretty good idea about how close the relationship between John F. Kennedy and David Ormsby-Gore had really been. As for the files, he really didn't want to dig too much into them until he had somewhere to work—and a seat, even a large one in first class on an airplane, was hardly a good research workspace.

Chapter Fifty

ALSO DURING THE flight, Templeton's desire to phone home reached fever pitch and he decided that he must talk to Valerie Doling, no matter what the risks. They all must, he thought, be freaking out having not heard from him for such a protracted period.

Noticing that the aircraft he was on was equipped with satellite telephones, Temp grabbed the information card. The big question was just how to get in touch with her without prying ears—which he assumed were now everywhere—picking up on the conversation. He couldn't call the office, nor could he call Valerie's cell. He thought for several minutes about how he might contact her—then an idea came to him.

Valerie Doling was a creature of habit and every day around 5:45 AM, or shortly thereafter, she stopped at the coffee shop on the main floor of their studio's building for a cup of coffee and whatever the pastry du jour happened to be. Sometimes she asked Davis if he wanted anything. Occasionally he did and sometimes they passed through the coffee shop at the same time en route to another morning of preparations for the broadcast. But usually if he wanted anything, she'd bring it to him. His favorite was blueberry pie—even for breakfast.

Temp calculated that it was about time for Val to be in the coffee shop, so he pulled out the satellite phone, swiped his recently purchased credit card, and called information. "Yes, thank you—I'd like the number for a place called Starburst Coffee Shop in Rosslyn, Virginia." He smiled as he gave the operator the name, recalling how the proprietor, a curmudgeon named Sullivan, had actually been threatened by the famous coffee concern of similar name, but had stuck to his guns. His defense was that his coffee was better—and it was—but also his establishment was much more than a coffee shop. After all, you couldn't get a cheeseburger at Starbucks, right? "Thank you, Operator—could you connect me? Thank you." He listened as the automated voice called out the number and he wrote it down while the call was being placed.

"Starburst, this is Rita—how can I help you?" Rita was a coffee shop waitress who looked like someone direct from central casting, complete with the pencil and pad, gum chewing, and more than a hint of attitude, which is probably how she survived her boss for so long. She was a fixture in the lives of so many who worked in the area and regularly frequented the Starburst.

"Hi there beautiful, this is Templeton Davis."

"Why good morning Mr. Davis, how are you? Haven't seen you around the building in a few days and we've missed your voice on the radio."

"Thanks, Rita. I've been away, but I'm heading home soon, so we'll catch up. Save a piece of blueberry for me, Okay?" He wasn't really in the mood for such light banter, but he wanted to make sure that there was no hint of urgency in his voice. "Is Valerie there by any chance?"

"No, Mr. Davis, she hasn't been in yet, but I'm sure she'll be here in a bit. Need me to give her a message?"

"Yes, if you would. Tell her that I'll be calling back in ten minutes on this line and if she'd wait for my call, I'd appreciate it."

"Sure will, sir. Is everything Okay? You calling from a tunnel some-where—sounds funny. Why not call her up at the office?"

Davis laughed lightly, "Nope—actually I'm calling from an airplane. And we have a new phone system being installed upstairs in the office, not quite up and runnin' yet," Temp said, proud of himself for thinking so quickly.

"What ya doing up in your airplane at this hour—it get fixed alright?" Apparently word had gotten around about the problems with Temp's jet.

"Yep, it's flying great. Hey, make sure Valerie waits for my call."

Davis placed the satellite phone back in its carrier and returned to the letter given to him by Clive Foyle. Then, after a few minutes, he reached for the satellite phone, swiped his credit card once more and dialed the number. Rita answered again.

"Hey there, Rita. It's Templeton Davis again. Valerie there yet?"

"Yep. Coming right up. She came in right after you hung up. Been waiting here, but not all that patiently. Hang on." She gave the telephone to Valerie who pretty much grabbed the thing and nearly shouted, "Temp, where in the hell are you? Don't you know how upset everyone here is?"

"Calm down, Valerie. Yes, of course I know how upset you all are. I get it. Now I need you to listen very carefully. Things are spinning out of control and I need you to remain calm and I need your help."

"What things are spinning out of control? What things? Where are you and what are you doing—what's going on? I mean it, you need to tell me."

"Valerie, please you're going to have to believe me on this," Temp said, in a voice just above a whisper because he was concerned that other passengers might hear. "I've apparently stumbled on to something in my research for this new book that's raising alarms in some, well, very dangerous places. I think it got the old man killed in Vermont. And more stuff is happening." He didn't go into detail or even bother to mention Dr. Foyle.

Valerie Doling found herself trembling as she listened, or tried to listen—the coffee shop noise, even at this early hour, was making it difficult, that and her boss was talking barely above a whisper. But rather than argue or press him, she decided that the best thing was for her to listen and follow instructions. "Okay, Temp, not sure what it all means, but whadaya need?"

"Good, thanks Valerie. I'll be home tomorrow, I promise—I'll be there for all of you—for all of us. Now, here's what I need. I'm on my way to New York and I need you to get a hotel room for me."

"But, what about your apartment on West 57th Street?"

"Not safe there, I'm afraid. I need to visit the city under the radar as far as is possible. So I need you to make a reservation for me in the code name we use when I travel sometimes, so people don't bother me."

"You mean, Mr. Dwight Chapman?"

"Yes. Do that. Put me at the *Marriott Marquis*, under that name, talk to the manager or security there, or whatever and use *your* credit card—I will pay you back. Just make it look like I'm trying to visit the city and that hotel without being a celebrity. They know the drill. But you've got to do this from a phone other than your office, home, or cell number, Okay? That's important, very important."

"Got it—it'll be done."

"I also want you to pick up a disposable cell phone and leave a message for me at the hotel with the number, so I can contact you when I arrive. I already have one—my smart phone is off and is going to stay that way, I even removed the SIM card."

This was really upsetting Valerie, but she tried to keep calm and sound business like. "Anything else?"

"Yes—you need to brief Vince Benton on everything I've told you—everything! He'll know some of the story already. Tell him that he needs to move his family out of their house for a few days, do whatever he needs to do, including bringing Liz up to speed. They need to disappear. Frankly, I think they could be in danger."

"I'll call him as soon as I hang."

"Okay, Valerie, you be careful and I'll call you from New York on the number you leave for me at the hotel."

"You be careful, too, Temp."

"Trust me, Valerie, I'm learning how to be invisible."

As soon as Valerie hung up the phone she went up to the office area and caught Vince Benton just as he was getting off the elevator. She brought him up to speed, scaring him significantly enough to convince him to take immediate action at home. En route to Clifton, where what had started out as a novel curiosity was now turning out to be a nightmare, he called Liz. They were already rattled because of the burglary of their home. And Vince knew that the satchel in his man cave was the only thing missing. So by the time his vehicle was in the driveway, she had packed and was ready at the door. Within minutes, they were on their way to Gettysburg, Pennsylvania where Liz and the girls would spend some quality time with her parents, who were surprised at the short notice visit, but so excited that they forgot to ask any questions. During the drive they talked in hushed tones careful that the girls wouldn't hear the details. Vince told Liz the whole story from the day Ranger had died. She scolded him for keeping secrets, but her tone wasn't all that intimidating. It turns out that there was good reason for concern about what he had dug up in the yard that day, after all.

After Vince dropped Liz and the girls off, he drove back to Virginia and checked into the *Marriott Key Bridge Hotel,* located just a few blocks from the radio studios.

When he checked in, the clerk asked how many nights he'd be staying.

"A couple for sure—let's just leave it open ended, Okay?"

Entering his hotel room, he felt instantly lonely and called Liz to check on her and the kids and she was glad to hear his voice.

Chapter Fifty-One
New York City

AFTER JUMPING THROUGH the usual enter-a-country hoops
upon landing at JFK Airport, Templeton Davis took a taxi to mid-town
Manhattan and the *Marriott Marquis* hotel. He looked for a front desk atten-
dant who looked somewhat supervisory and introduced himself and
explained that he was using a pseudonym for security reasons and that his
assistant had called. The clerk checked the computer and sure enough
everything was in place. The room was pre-paid, in fact significantly over-
paid in case he needed incidentals. And the clerk recognized Davis, so that
helped. His account was flagged in their system as a V.I.P. He was given the
key to a room on the 42nd floor, with access to the executive lounge and
amenities, as well as an envelope containing a message. It was the number
for the disposable cell phone Valerie had acquired.

"I'm in my room," he said when Valerie answered on the second ring.
"I'm beat but sleep'll have to wait—I've got someone to look up. I'll call
you back tonight. Keep this phone with you at all times. How're Vince and
Liz?"

"They're good, he shuttled Liz and the girls up to Pennsylvania, where
her parents live and he's got a room for a few days at the hotel up the road
from our studios."

Within an hour Temp had showered and changed clothes and enjoyed
a quick, but hearty breakfast at *Juniors Cafe,* across from the hotel on 45th
Street. After briefly talking again with Valerie by phone as he finished his

breakfast coffee, he caught a cab down to Greenwich Village and New York University. The letter from Dr. Foyle was in his pocket and he carried the large briefcase, which contained Foyle's files, the book about Kennedy, and a few personal items.

Having spoken at events a couple of times at NYU, he had no trouble finding his way around and caught the tail end of Professor Raspitov's lecture. As the students raced for the exits following dismissal, Davis made his way to the front against traffic and stood in a short line behind people venturing a comment, trying to flatter, or in at least one case taking issue with Dr. Raspitov's whole line of thought. Finally, and after all others had left the room, he stood face-to-face with the professor.

"I'm sorry, are you a student in my class? You look a little old for this undergrad group."

"No sir, I finished college long ago. Name is Davis, Templeton Davis," he paused to see if there was any recognition as he said it. There was.

"You the Templeton Davis from the radio?"

"That's me. You a listener?"

"Not at all, but I've seen you on CNN or something. What can I do for you, sir?" He said this in a dismissive sort of way, one that suggested that Templeton Davis's brand of talk radio was not nearly erudite enough for him.

"Well, I don't really know where to start except to say that I flew all the way from England yesterday to see you this morning."

"What in the world were you doing over there that would lead you to me?"

"Does the name Clive Foyle mean anything to you?"

Raspitov looked up and to the right a bit and said, "Yes, isn't he at Oxford? I had some correspondence with him a few years ago, as I recall."

"Exactly! In fact, I have that correspondence right here," Davis said as he pulled the page from his hip pocket and handed it to the professor.

"Where'd you get this?"

"From him, just two days ago in his office at Oxford. I was there to interview him on a matter and he let me borrow this letter where you ask for information about the late and former Ambassador, David Ormsby-Gore."

"I recall sending this. Sure do. Not sure I got a reply, though. How is Dr. Foyle these days?"

Choosing to ignore the question so as to avoid talking about a mysterious death so soon in their conversation (is there ever a good time for that?), Davis added, "I don't think he sent you a response. In fact, he tended to ignore requests like this."

"But why? You'd think he'd want to help a fellow academician." Raspitov said, as he smiled slightly.

"Well, turns out that he'd been muzzled for quite some time by their security services, particularly MI-5. Apparently, the subject of Mr. Ormsby-Gore was something certain people didn't want investigated much."

"That's rather odd, wouldn't you say?" replied Raspitov. Temp noticed how clear his English was, barely the hint of a Russian accent. "What were the spies afraid of? That sounds more like the old KGB than MI-5, frankly."

"I certainly agree and I'm not sure what their reasons were, but I do have a theory and since you had expressed a particular interest in the ambassador, one that involved a hint of suspicion, well, I thought I needed to see you as I continue *my* investigation."

"What kind of investigation, Mr. Davis?"

"Well, I'm interested in exactly what you asked Professor Foyle about in this letter. What sparked the question about the man's loyalty, or potential disloyalty? And what about this part about wondering if Ormsby-Gore was in any way connected to a fellow named Aleksandr Feklisov?" Davis asked, expecting to be enlightened.

"Sorry to disappoint you Mr. Davis, but I was asking that question on behalf of a student."

"A student?"

"Yes, as you might imagine, students from mother Russia tend to gravitate to my classes for obvious reasons and a few years ago there was a bright young girl—journalism major, I think, yes, journalism major—who asked me to write to Foyle. She was a little afraid to do so herself. From what I know about her—she graduated a few years ago—she came to this country after her father had been imprisoned in Russia. He was a wealthy man, not quite an oligarch, but he had become rich in the years after Yeltsin came to power. Before that, he had been in the KGB and from what I understand was a pretty high ranking officer. But I gather that he and a fellow named Vladimir Putin had never gotten along. He's much older than Putin and this girl is his daughter by a young mistress. I think the man must have been well over fifty years old when she was born. Probably close to eighty now, if he's even still alive. Russian prisons can be pretty brutal. At any rate, as I understand the story, Mr. Putin—someone who more and more reminds me of old Stalin himself—put this girl's papa away on purported corruption charges, but his real crime was that he spoke out against what old Vladimir was doing by consolidating power in his hands."

"What was this girl trying to find out with such a request regarding the old British ambassador—and have you kept in touch with her at all since she left NYU?"

"I believe she was working on a story having to do with Soviet espionage in the Cold War and somehow had it in her mind that the British ambassador to the U.S. back then had ties to the Soviets. And, yes, I hear from her every once in a while."

"Why would she suspect something like that—Ormsby-Gore being a Russian spy and all? Did she have any hard evidence?"

"I suspect that it was a story her father told her. As I mentioned, he was in the KGB and had been stationed in Washington, DC during the early 1960s. Probably worked at the Soviet Embassy under some kind of diplomatic cover, that's how it was done back then. For that matter, it's still done that way to a certain extent. He was probably around thirty years old then and likely trying to climb the ladder, such as it was in those days."

"Listen Professor, I know you don't really know me—but you know *of* me and I can assure you that I'm just doing research for a book I want to write, so nothing nefarious, mind you. Could you tell me where I might find her—well first, how about her name?"

The professor stared at Templeton Davis for a few seconds as if sizing him up and then volunteered, "I guess it couldn't hurt. Her name is Valeriya Kostikov—but I don't know where she lives, just where she works most every day."

"Well, that's a start. Where might that be?"

The professor looked at the clock on the back wall of the large class-room. It was just after 11:30 AM. "Mr. Davis, if you hurry, you might catch her as she begins her shift. She's a hostess at *The Russian Tea Room*."

"Know it well. I've dined there many times. It's a wonderful place. But I thought you said she was a journalism major." He left out the part that he had an apartment on the same block, one that was likely being watched even as they spoke. The coincidence was curious and a bit unsettling.

"She was and graduated near the top of her class. But the economy being what it is, it's hard to find work with the changes in the newspaper business and world of writing."

"Thank you, Professor, you've been very helpful. Here's my card, maybe we can have you on the show sometime, especially when I need to dig into Cold War stuff, I'm a bit of a buff myself."

"I'd love to help you Mr. Davis, just let me know—anytime!"

Chapter Fifty-Two
February–March, 1963
Palm Beach, Florida—Washington, DC

BY EARLY 1963, David Ormsby-Gore had not only become an unofficial part of the Kennedy administration, even family—he had also become somewhat of a frequent flyer on the presidential airplane. The previous October, while the world was busy watching developments in the Cuban Missile Crisis, a new Boeing C-137 Stratoliner entered the service with the call sign SAM 26000, unless the President of the United States was on board—then it was, of course, Air Force One.

Kennedy and Ormsby-Gore boarded the aircraft and left on a Thursday evening for a long weekend of relaxed conversation at what had become the president's winter White House, his father's home in Palm Beach, Florida. The luxurious Mediterranean style mansion, with red-tiled roof and six bedrooms, sat on a 1.6 acre site on the water, complete with more than 200 feet of beachfront.

Now that the world had been made safe for a while with the settlement of the Missile Crisis, David Ormsby-Gore used his face time with Kennedy for an intense lobbying campaign about the virtues of a nuclear test-ban, something the two of them had talked much about since the mid-1950s. This matter was high on Prime Minister MacMillan's agenda, but more importantly to Ormsby-Gore, it was the current machination of the Soviets, with Mr. Khrushchev trying to find a new way to score points before a watching world. Talks had been ongoing in Geneva for quite some time, in fact, Ormsby-Gore had been highly involved before being appointed as Ambassador, but every time the two sides got anywhere close to an agreement, Khrushchev managed to up the stakes or change the game.

"David, I'd love to come to an agreement with the Soviets," President Kennedy said to his friend as they had breakfast outdoors in view of the Atlantic. "But I always have to consider the domestic political situation."

"You mean the supposed Republican plan to make the idea of a test-ban treaty a major issue in '64?"

"Nothing supposed about it. It *is* their plan. You read the *New York Times*, don't you? A few weeks ago there was a front-page story all about it. It quoted that nuclear physicist, Edward Teller, saying that any attempt at such an agreement with the Russians would be tantamount to another Munich," Kennedy said with emphasis on the word "Munich."

The very mention of the word—not a place—but as a metaphor for a moment, an event, one that turned out to be a watershed, but could have possibly been a final moment to stop Adolf Hitler in his tracks before he blew up the world, took the two friends back to another time. And it was clear to Ormsby-Gore that he had his work cut out for him that weekend and in the months to come. John Fitzgerald Kennedy wanted to be Winston Churchill, not Neville Chamberlain. He saw himself as a cold warrior, not as an appeaser, the murmurings of his many critics aside.

"Jack, no one knows better than I do about your feelings regarding appeasement. We were in agreement twenty-five years ago in Scotland, and we are now, of course. But your Churchill-Chamberlain is somewhat outdated. You should also consider that Winston himself was arguing for détente with the Russians during his second premiership just ten years ago—this from the man who coined the term 'Iron Curtain.'"

"I know, I know, David—but that's a subtlety likely to be lost on the Republicans, if not the average citizen next year when the campaign is on. I have some political capital right now because people think I stood up to Khrushchev. Thankfully, all the back-channel stuff will never come to light—or should I say, hopefully?" The two men smiled.

Ormsby-Gore continued, "And as regarding that buffoon, Edward Teller, he has become the science guru for the extreme right wing here in

the States. You can't take him seriously. You saw what he did to Robert
Oppenheimer, right? He's worse than McCarthy was."

"Yes, of course, but the fear of communism is *very* real in America.
And remember that old Joe was a good friend to my family."

"I suppose," sighed David Ormsby-Gore.

Later that evening, just before going to bed, the British ambassador
wrote a handwritten note to Prime Minister Harold MacMillan. In it, he
stressed how close Kennedy was to getting on board the test-ban band-
wagon, but was concerned about domestic politics. Ormsby-Gore suggested that the Prime Minister reach out to Kennedy with a detailed
personal letter. This handwritten note rode back to Andrews Air Force as
that weekend came to a close and by Monday was en route to number ten
Downing Street via diplomatic pouch. Shortly thereafter, MacMillan began
to craft his letter—one of the lengthiest of his career. It arrived at the White
House on March 16th and five days later so did David Ormsby-Gore, on
March 21st.

"What did you think of the Prime Minister's letter, Mr. President?" the
ambassador began as they eased their way into a serious conversation after
some coffee and small talk.

"Impressive. He really poured it on—all that stuff about 'before it's
too late.' Was he talking about for the world or for him?"

"Probably both, Jack—the old man is weary and there are a few things
brewing across the pond that could spell political trouble for the Tories."
This was a reference to a major political scandal that was ready to blow up
in the U.K., one involving a high-ranking government official accused of a
relationship with a prostitute who was also seeing a Soviet agent, raising all
sorts of security concerns.

There was a pause in the conversation for a moment as Kennedy
seemed to be thinking about whether or not to delve into an unpleasant
subject, something he was sure David knew about, but more of a private
matter, yet one that in many ways related to what was going on over in
Great Britain.

Then Kennedy began, "I've been receiving regular reports from David
Bruce about what's going on and I see where, uh, some member of

parliament raised a question recently, one that was directed, uh, at John Profumo—any idea what'll come of it?"

"Well, the guy is a Labor MP named George Wigg and the word I have is that Mr. Profumo is preparing a statement to be made in the House of Commons tomorrow, one in which he'll deny anything improper. Mr. MacMillan already has the statement and is making a couple of recommendations for wording," David replied.

"It's been a tough year for you fellows, hasn't it? I see where you've lost track of your Mr. Kim Philby and the thinking of our boys at CIA is that he's gone over to the dark side, disappeared from Beirut in January, was it?"

A bit surprised that Kennedy had brought Philby's name up, or for that matter that he knew anything about Kim's disappearance, he replied: "Yes, well, Kim Philby has been a problem of many year's standing."

"Ever meet the guy?" Kennedy asked.

"No, don't believe I ever did, or at least don't remember," Ormsby-Gore replied, trying not to smile because he had not only met Philby, but they shared the same Soviet "cut out" for a while back in the United Kingdom, and were recruited for the Soviets around the same time. Most importantly, the Russians had made Kim's life miserable for the past decade or so all in the effort to keep Ormsby-Gore's covert work secret. In other words, the Soviets had rolled the dice back in 1951 and displayed a willingness to sacrifice Philby for Ormsby-Gore.

Of course, Kennedy had his own secrets, or so he thought. He was watching what would come to be known as the "Profumo Affair" with interest, not because of his celebrated penchant for gossip, but because he knew that there was every chance that his name might somehow be dragged in. After all, the girl Profumo who had been involved with—one Christine Keeler—was friends with a few of Jack's old consorts, particularly a couple of gals named Maria Novotny and Suzy Chang.

Of course, these matters were not really all that much of a secret to the Ambassador. He knew all about Jack's dalliances and, in fact, had been instrumental in putting one particular one in his path, Ellen Rometsch, who was really a Communist spy, as well.

Chapter Fifty-Three
New York City

TEMPLETON DAVIS WAS pretty sure that whoever had been following him had yet to catch up to where he was and what he was up to. But just to be sure, he took a rather circuitous path from the *Marriott Marquis* to NYU and he determined to do the same thing en route to the *Russian Tea Room*. The fact that he was going to be on the very block where he owned an apartment—one that was possibly being watched by nefarious characters—at the least meant that he'd need to be extremely careful. His place was at the end of the block in the towers above Carnegie Hall, but still the door was painfully close to the restaurant and much would depend on the vantage point of those tasked with the surveillance.

Yet, the more he thought about it, the less comfortable he felt about making any appearance on that block. Maybe it'd be better to meet somewhere else—that is if Valeriya Kostikov even agreed to a meeting in the first place. What if his call scared her? He found yet another pay phone, called information, got the number and placed the call.

The Russian Tea Room had been a New York landmark since the 1920s. Madonna had once checked coats there and countless stars and celebrities had graced the place. In fact, truth be told, the place was one of Davis's favorites, and not just because it was such a short walk from his New York home away from home. He loved caviar—one rather expensive luxury he regularly indulged—and he loved the way the restaurant prepared tuna, pan searing it with sesame, black olives, and capers. Just thinking of it reminded

Temp that he had not been eating much the past few days, with his whirl-wind of travel and intrigue. And they knew him pretty well there. He racked his brain to try to envision the young hostess, but nothing came to him.

"Russian Tea Room, this is Victor, how may I help you?"

"Hello Victor, this is Templeton Davis, I come in there every ..." but before he could finish the sentence, Victor said, "Of course, Mr. Davis I know you well—it's been a while, what can I do for you today—will you be coming in for lunch or dinner?"

"Possibly, Victor, but I wonder—is Valeriya working today?"

"Valeriya, um, yes she is, would you like me to get her for you?"

"Please if you would, I'd appreciate that," Davis replied, hoping that his request wasn't too out of the ordinary.

After a pause, a voice—he noticed it immediately as a lovely voice—came on the line, "This is Valeriya. How may I help you, Mr. Davis?"

"I'm not sure you remember me ..."

"But of course, I do Mr. Davis. We've talked about your radio program before."

Davis literally scratched his head at that one and couldn't for the life of him remember this girl, but it was great that she knew who he was. It would be disarming to her when he popped the question about meeting. Deciding to be a bit bold and putting two and two together, he ventured a comment, "That's right, we talked about your journalism work. Didn't you go to NYU?"

Flattered that he'd remember, she almost giggled and said, "Yes, we've talked about that, how nice of you to remember." By now Ms. Kostitov was wondering what the call was all about.

"Valeriya, I was wondering if you'd be able to meet me for coffee or something today and before you get uncomfortable, it's all professional. There's something I think you might be able to help me with."

"How can I help you, Mr. Davis? Can you give me some idea of the subject?"

Davis had to think quickly, and he did and came up with: "I'm working on an article about the future of journalism, especially for young people out of college. And, well, I thought of you working there at the restaurant and not in the field in which you've been trained and I thought you'd have an interesting perspective," he said, hoping she'd buy it.

She did. "Do I ever. I'd love to talk with you about this. What's your schedule like?"

"Well, the thing is that I'm finishing the piece and need to get it turned around by the morning. What time do you get off work today?"

"They only have me working the lunch shift today, so I'm clear a little before three PM. Can I meet you somewhere?"

"Yes, certainly, let's meet at three or a little after at the bar at *Mickey Mantle's* up by the park, just a couple of blocks from you—do you know it?"

"Yes, I know the place. I'll see you there at three and I look forward to it," she said cheerfully.

For the Brighton Beach based team that had tracked Davis and his party to Stowe, Vermont, and that had tried to fulfill their mission of termination, the trail was cold. Their most recent instructions were to try to figure out where Davis was and what he was up to, but without much to go on. The information made available by the operatives in Great Britain wasn't very helpful, either. They had only been able to find out that he had flown to New York, so he was presumably in the area. A check of major hotels yielded nothing and a couple of them were watching the building on West 57th Street where his apartment was located. Nothing going on there, though. For a middle-aged, overweight amateur sleuth, Templeton Davis was proving to be pretty good at basic tradecraft.

Then they caught a break, much to the disadvantage of Mr. Davis. It was one of those odd coincidental things, but in retrospect there was actually a certain elementary logic to it. After all, this was a block where Davis owned a residence. Add to that, the presence of a world famous eatery featuring *Russian* cuisine and culture. Throw in a fair number of regular patrons—even staff at the establishment—who were expats from the old country, and you have the kindling ready to be lit by a spark of recognition or mention. This was the case that day at the *Russian Tea Room*.

As already noted, two of the men who had tracked Templeton Davis from Virginia to Vermont were watching the building where Davis had his apartment. Actually, they were taking shifts of a sort, with one or the other killing time at the conveniently located little taste of home a few doors down the block. And when Victor came looking for Valeriya, who at the moment of Templeton Davis's call was standing near the corner of the bar chatting with the bartender—a beautiful girl named Natanya—while sipping a Diet Coke, the man at the bar perked up when he heard, he was *sure* he heard it, the name of Templeton Davis mentioned a few feet away.

He tried not to look too conspicuous after the young lady who had been sipping the Diet Coke left her drink and hurried away, but he needed to get close to her—close enough to find out what was going on. Finding her near the hostess station talking on the phone in quiet tones, he tried to hear what she was saying, but to no avail. He took out his phone and sent a text message to his comrade down the block: *Heard a mention of name Templeton Davis just now … think he was on the phone with a hostess here. Will keep an eye on her.* A few moments later, his smart phone vibrated indicating an incoming text: *Do u know her name?* He typed one word in reply: *Nyet.*

He went back to the bar and positioned himself nearer to the corner where the hostess and the bartender had been conversing. He looked across at the mirror behind the bottles and was pleased that he could see the hostess at her station. He hoped he could keep this spot for as long as it took to see if and when the hostess left the restaurant. So he settled in for a leisurely lunch.

"Another drink?" Natanya asked the man now sitting on a different barstool.

"Yes, please, another vodka and tonic."

"My name is Natanya. Can I get you a menu?"

"Yes, thank you, I believe I will eat something—my name is Leonid, most just call me Leo." They shook hands as Natanya handed a menu to him. He took a few minutes scanning the menu and saw so many items he wanted. When she brought him his drink he said, "I think I will start with the red borscht then have the kulebiaka."

"Very good, Leo—the salmon is excellent today," she said as she smiled at the man who was at the moment only one of three customers at the entire bar on an unusually slow day for the legendary restaurant. He was determined to keep a conversation going with her in order to learn more about the hostess. He shot another glance in the mirror and saw her talking on the phone, pencil in hand, apparently recording a reservation for someone. She was rather tall, something that was even more pronounced because of the way she wore her hair—rather big was how it looked to him. She was wearing a tight fitting dark green dress, somewhat low cut, all no doubt designed to captivate any man who walked in the door for lunch.

Natanya brought a place setting over to Leo and put everything in place. "I don't think I've seen you here before, this your first time with us?"

"Actually, yes. I live in Brooklyn and rarely get to this part of town."

"What brings you here today?" She asked, noticing some ink just under his collar.

Put off a bit by the question, he paused and searched his brain for a reply. He was not trained in the various arts of conversation in the pursuit of information, as was his friend Anna, but he needed to put forth a good effort. "Yes, well, I've got a meeting near here in a little while and I guess I'm very early, plus I've heard of this wonderful place for a long time, so I thought I'd try it for myself," he said, actually quite pleased with his ability to think on his feet—or on his stool, as the case might be.

"Well Leo, I'm sure you won't be disappointed and if you need anything just get my attention," Natanya said, with a flirtatious wink. Soon she was back with the borscht.

About halfway through his appetizer he looked up at the mirror and saw that the hostess was not there. His heart skipped a beat, but a second later he looked to his left and saw her standing at the end of the bar as if waiting for the bartender. When Natanya came over, she fixed a Diet Coke for the hostess without words being exchanged. The hostess grabbed the straw gently with two fingers and took a long sip, after which she made eye contact with Leo and smiled at him. He reciprocated.

"Not too busy here today," Leo said trying to engage the hostess in conversation—anything to help him get to know her and find Templeton Davis.

"Quite slow, in fact. Very rare. It'll probably pick up later."

"My name is Leonid," he said, deciding to go for broke.

"Hello Leonid, I'm Valeriya—nice to meet you."

"Beautiful name, Valeriya."

"Thank you, it was my grandmother's name."

At that Leonid, master of surveillance and the technical aspects of spying, was out of words. But the timing was alright, because Valeriya directed a teenage-type wave at him and made her way back to the hostess station. She came over a few times as Leo worked his way through the borscht, then the kulebiaka, another couple of drinks, and finally a strong cup of double espresso to counter the effect of several drinks. They exchanged more benign pleasantries, but nothing that gave Leo any clue as to who she was and what her connection might be to the man he and his comrade, a man now more than a little peeved at the idea that he was watching a building while his friend was dining in splendor and flirting with women at the *Russian Tea Room*, were trying to find. He had received the name of the girl in a text from Leo and had passed the information off to a friend in Brighton Beach, someone who had access to a fairly comprehensive database of Russian émigrés who lived in the tri-state area. A later text added the factoid that the girl's grandmother was named Valeriya, as well. You never knew with computers, he thought, any tidbit might become a key puzzle piece.

Shortly after two o'clock, and in keeping with his cover story about a meeting, Leo called for his check and pulled out a conspicuously large roll of cash, prominent with hundred dollar bills, and paid Natanya, leaving her a very generous tip. He left the restaurant after nodding goodbye to the hostess and was out the door.

On her next visit to the bar for yet another sip of a Diet Coke on this still sluggish day for the restaurant, Natanya brought up the subject of her recent customer. "Strange looking man. He tried to keep his collar up, but I could clearly see the edges of several tattoos, I think the guy was Russian mafia."

"Really? Wow!"

"And you should've seen the big bundle of cash he used to pay the bill. Had to be thousands of dollars," she said. "Only people I know who come in here and flash that kind of stuff around are men who are up to no good." They both took note and then moved on. It was just one of those things one ran into in the restaurant business in mid-town Manhattan. That and tourists. Mobsters were far more interesting—to a point.

Chapter Fifty-Four

THE MAN WITH the computer in Brooklyn hit what he hoped was pay dirt after using several different database search scenarios. He came up with sixty-seven women in the region named Valeriya (he was actually surprised at how common the name was), and narrowed it down by age to thirteen who possibly fit the bill. Then he added the *Russian Tea Room* to the equation and after he saw the result he uttered a curse—to himself—because he should have popped that fact in earlier. He contacted the man watching Davis's building and by the time Leo was back with him they were pretty sure they knew the identity of the hostess. She was Valeriya Kostitov. They knew that she was a graduate of New York University and had been working at the restaurant a little less than a year. But there was nothing in any file that suggested that she was involved in anything other than the normal, everyday pursuits of a young college graduate in the big city searching for a solid job in her chosen career of journalism. There was no address available for her and it showed that she received her mail at a post office box in Greenwich Village, not too far from NYU.

The information had been relayed to Moscow, where it was shortly after eleven PM. In fact, it would be the next morning before Vladimir Putin would be informed—and that was good news for Templeton Davis and Valeriya Kostitov, because once the big man himself picked up on this news alarm bells would start ringing. But this reality was several hours away as Leo and his comrade, Igor [really], waited and watched for Ms. Kostitov to leave work that day. They were pretty confident that she would lead them right to Templeton Davis.

Shortly before three PM, her boss letting her go a bit early due to the lousy customer traffic at the restaurant that day, Valeriya walked toward Sixth Avenue and then crossed over and headed toward 59th Street and the park. Leo and Igor followed about a half-block behind. Once on 59th, they saw her enter *Mickey Mantle's* restaurant and then talking with Templeton Davis.

Temp liked the place. Always had. He, like most men his age, grew up admiring the famous number "7"—a ballplayer who could do it all. Of course, also like all boys growing up near St. Louis, Temp was a life-long Cardinals fan, but that didn't keep him from being a Mantle fan, besides he played in a whole other league—literally and figuratively. So when Davis began spending time in New York earlier in his career—and eventually when he bought the place near Carnegie Hall—he became a bit of a regular at the restaurant once owned by "The Mick." In fact, every time Davis walked into the place and looked around at the memorabilia, he recalled that August night in 1995 when he and countless others held a vigil of sorts during the last night of Mantle's life.

He was sitting at the bar and had just been served a Guinness when he saw Valeriya Kostitov come through the door. He knew it was her. He recognized her from the restaurant, after all—having spoken to her many times. How could he forget a drop-dead gorgeous lady like that, he berated himself. She, of course, recognized him as well and sat down beside him.

"What can I get you?" Davis asked.

"Glass of wine, I guess, something dry—Merlot," she replied, while folding her coat a bit and laying it on the empty stool next to her. She looked around at the restaurant and noted that it was slow there, as well. "Must be some kind of restaurant boycott going on," she said smiling. "There was no one at our place today, either."

Leo and Igor decided not to go into the restaurant. That would be far too conspicuous, especially since Leo had lingered so long at the *Russian Tea Room*. So they took up a position on a park bench across the street with a great view of the restaurant door and because the bar was in the front of the place, they could actually see Davis and Kostitov on the far side of the bar facing the window, though barely. They would bide their time and make whatever move they could once the couple left the place. Their only challenge was the occasional horse and buggy pausing in front of them temporarily obstructing their view, but they managed to work around it. That, and the ambient smell.

"So, Mr. Davis how can I help with your article? I can certainly tell you that it's next to impossible for someone to break into the world of journalism these days. First, there's the whole revolution in media delivery. More and more Americans are getting their news on line—younger people hardly ever read an actual newspaper. And with so much free information available on the Internet, it's really hard to monetize the whole thing and that's the bottom line when it comes to jobs."

She paused and gave Davis a bit of an annoyed look that seemed to say, "Why aren't you getting any of this down?" And Temp then and there decided that he needed to be up front with Ms. Kostitov.

"Valeriya—may I call you that?"

"Yes, of course," she said, taking a sip of the glass of red wine that had been brought to her.

"Frankly, there is something else I'd like to talk with you about, first," he said, trying to ease his way into a conversational segue.

She was obviously taken back, but likely because Davis was a celebrity to her—at least to some extent—and that he might be someone with contacts in media for her to exploit, she disarmed him. "Certainly, Mr. Davis, what is it?"

"Well, first—you can call me Temp, all my friends do and I want us to be friends. The thing is, I *am* working on a writing project, but it's something bigger than an article on journalism and I know for a fact you can help me. I've been on a quest of sorts for the past week or so, one that has the potential to rock *the* world."

Not at all knowing what to make of such over-the-top language, Valeriya decided that she was indeed interested in what Davis had to say. "But what do I have to do with any of this?"

"Frankly, Valeriya, the trail has led me today directly to you."

"Me? Why? How?"

"I met with a professor at New York University this morning, fellow named Raspitov."

"Ah yes, I know him well. Brilliant man and in many ways a mentor to me. Did he point you my way?" she asked after taking a sip of wine.

"Yes he did, but I need to back up a bit and give you some background. I need to, as they say, 'read you in' to some things. Things that may make you uncomfortable. But if I have any discernment in the world, I'm pretty sure you're someone who's interested in the truth and this is what led you to journalism as a major and an ultimate career in the first place."

"Yes, you're right. And much of it goes back to my childhood."

"I know—and your relationship with your father, right?"

"My father? What do you know about him? Okay, Mr. Davis, what is this thing all about? I need you to tell me now!" she said in a way that seemed to attract attention their way. And Davis motioned for her to keep her voice down, which she clearly resented.

"Well here goes. I'm researching a book I plan to write, one that may blow the lid off how Americans view some crucial events during the Cold War. And what has led me to you is something I found out a few days ago in Oxford, England, when I visited a Dr. Clive Foyle on the faculty there."

Valeriya's eyes flashed instant recognition at the mention of Folye's name. "You met with Dr. Foyle? I tried to get information from him a few years ago while I was still in school, in fact, Dr. Raspitov ..."

"I know, Valeriya—your professor told me about it this morning after I showed him this." At that, he removed the letter from his pocket, the one written back in 2007 from Raspitov to Foyle on Valeriya's behalf. She looked at it and immediately recognized it.

"But what would your interest be in what I was working on with regard to David Ormsby-Gore?"

Templeton Davis decided to lay all his cards on the table: "My interest is in finding out if the late former British ambassador to the United States was, in fact, a Soviet spy." He paused. "There I said it."

Valeriya Kostitov looked deep into Templeton Davis's eyes as if trying to see into his soul. "Mr. Davis, if what you're sharing with me is on the up-and-up then I'm most happy to help you. In fact, I believe I can help you very much. But in order to do so we need to get out of here and go back to my place so that I can show you some things you very much need to see. And possibly, just possibly, what you have and what I have when put together may make for a much clearer picture. Why don't you pay the bill and we'll take a cab downtown. How's that?"

"Not so fast, Valeriya. I need you to know some other things, things that may upset, even scare you."

"I'm listening," she replied, as if bracing herself.

"Well in the past few days I've chased this story from Washington, DC, to New England, and then to the United Kingdom. And you need to know that some of those I have met with have, well, I don't really know how to say this ... they have ... they have ..."

"Mr. Davis, are you trying to tell me that something has happened to these people? Are any of them dead?"

"Yes," he said softly and in a way that almost brought him to guilt-induced tears. "Including Dr. Foyle. He was found dead on a sidewalk in Oxford—the television called it an apparent heart attack—within a few hours of our meeting and I heard about it just as I was getting ready to board the plane back to the States. But he's not the only one—frankly it all seems so surreal to me, like it's not really happening." At this, a tear flowed down his cheek and he grabbed a handful of cocktail napkins and dabbed it.

"Temp," she said, using the familiarity of his first name for the first time, "I doubt there's anything you could say that would surprise me. I've become well acquainted with the way death tends to be nearby when people begin to dig into things that involve my home country. Do you know why I was really so determined to get my journalism degree here in America?"

"No, I really don't know *that* much about you."

"Well, trade this glass of wine and that glass of stout for two shots of Russian vodka and I will, how did you say it? Read *you* in."

Templeton Davis waved to the bartender. Then, looking over the bartender's left shoulder and through the large front window of the restaurant, his eye caught the sight of two men sitting on a park bench on the other side of the street. They were too far away to be recognized, but there was something about them that caught his attention—or better—made a blip on his now near paranoid radar.

Chapter Fifty-Five

THEY CLINKED GLASSES and each of them took a short sip of vodka. "Do you know the name Anna Politkovskaya?" Valeriya asked Temp.

"Of course, I do. She was that journalist murdered back a few years ago because she was so outspoken in her writing, particularly her criticism of Vladimir Putin. Wasn't she shot execution style in the elevator of her apartment building in Moscow?"

"Precisely. I'm impressed that you know this because too many people here in the States either never heard of her or forgot about it all, or so it seems."

"Well, I can tell you that many of us here really did follow the story. I dealt with it on radio for quite a while. In fact, it was a great privilege to interview her on the air once by telephone—back in 2004, I think it was—and I've got an autographed copy of her book, *Putin's Russia*, in my library back at my place in Georgetown. Weren't you a student at NYU when all that happened?"

"Yes, I was. And I remember it as if it had happened just yesterday, but it was October 7, 2006. I was in my junior year."

"So this inspired you to become a journalist?" Just then, Temp glanced in the direction of the men on the park bench and had the thought that if these men were indeed following him, they were just about the most inept spies imaginable, allowing himself a bit of a reassuring smile.

"No," Valeriya responded, "I was already a journalism major. What it did was convince me that what I wanted to write about might one day lead me to a fate similar to Anna's. In many ways, her murder changed my life."

Temp was struck with the almost familiar way the dead journalist's name seemed to roll off Valeriya's tongue, prompting him to ask: "Did you actually know her?"

"I did. I grew up with her children, particularly her daughter, Vera. We were once very close, though I haven't heard from her in quite some time. Anna also knew my father. In fact, it was probably her relationship with my father that got him imprisoned by that tyrant, Putin. And I also have no doubt that at least one of the many reasons Anna Politkovskaya was murdered had to do with her relationship with my family and things my father may or may not have divulged to her. By the time of his incarceration he was pretty disillusioned with things in Russia."

"So, she inspired you long before she was killed—when you were a young girl?"

"Yes, and when I was ready to go to college she helped me get into the journalism program at Moscow State University, where she had studied years before. At that time, Anna was well into her work with *Novaya Gazeta*, one of the few publications willing to speak out against the increasingly Stalinist tendencies of the Putin regime. But then what could the nation expect, being governed by a KGB man?"

"How long did you stay at Moscow State?"

"Less than a year. It was becoming clear back around the time Anna had just published *Putin's Russia* that the environment for journalism in Russia was becoming less than inviting. So she wrote a glowing recommendation for me to the department at New York University just after father was arrested. It just seemed a good time to go abroad. My only regret is that I haven't seen my father in more than seven years and I frankly don't know whether he's dead or alive."

"Reading her book was a chilling reminder about how quickly things can move from what appears to be a trend toward freedom and democracy back toward tyranny," Davis remarked.

"Indeed," Valeriya said just before swallowing the last few drops of the vodka in her glass.

"Another?" Temp asked, while again looking at the men on the bench.

"No—at least not here. As I said I have things to show you at my place. Let's head there." And she reached for her coat and began to push away from the bar.

Davis put his hand on hers and said with sudden, yet quiet urgency, "Hang on for a second. Before we go, I need to be sure of something. Is there anyway anyone followed you from work when you walked over here?"

"Followed me? What?" She asked with a hint of panic in her voice and while quickly looking around the room.

"Steady, Valeriya—look at me. Look me in the eye. Calm down. Don't do anything obvious or abrupt. Just listen. I may be a bit on the paranoid side with all that's happened over the past few days, but I just want to be sure. Don't look now—don't even move your head at all until I say, but across the street there're a couple of curious looking fellows sitting on a bench and it could be nothing, but I want to make sure. So in a few seconds, I want you to continue talking to me about something—even laugh a bit—and glance quickly, but not for long, directly out the front window of the restaurant and see if those guys look familiar. Okay—go ahead, take your time."

After a few seconds, she put her hand on Temp's shoulder and glanced across the way. It didn't take but a brief glimpse to make her heart skip a beat. She looked back into Davis's eyes and said: "I'm pretty sure the man on the left was in the restaurant today and he tried several times to talk to me. After he left, the bartender told me that she saw a tattoo on his neck and that he paid his tab in cash from a large wad of bills. Said he reminded her of someone in the mob."

Templeton Davis needed no further convincing. He planned to operate on the assumption that the guys on the bench were unsavory, at the least. "Okay, let's just sit tight and figure out how to handle this." He looked around the room and saw an exit sign in the back and assumed that there was a door leading to an alley—had to be for fire codes and such. That was *where*—but now the question was *how* were they going to get out.

Just then, he glanced back at the men and noticed a livery carriage blocking the view and he had the idea to wait for the next such moment of inhibited view to exit the restaurant.

"Here's what we'll do. The next time the view is blocked we'll head to the exit and the alley back there and head back out on 58th Street and hope there is a taxi right near just waiting for us. That's my best thinking."

"Works for me, she said," as she watched Temp put two twenty-dollar bills on the bar and they continued making as-if conversation.

A few minutes later a carriage crept into view and when it began to obscure the view he said, "Okay, let's go!" They both bolted. But when he was halfway to the door he uttered a curse and ran back to grab his brief-case containing all the files. It had been on the floor next to his barstool. Then, within moments, they were out the back door of the restaurant and running through an awkward maze of alley toward 58th Street. Their best hopes were realized when a taxi approached within seconds. They hailed it and got in and began the trip toward Greenwich Village.

In a few moments, the horse-drawn carriage moved along and the men on the bench were instantly aware that their targets had given them the slip. Not knowing which way to go, they were at a loss. In fact, it would be several hours before the trail would be refreshed. And that would only happen from the top—when the men in the Kremlin gave the operatives a piece of the puzzle they needed and probably should have had all along. Vladimir Putin was a need-to-know kind of guy and he always needed to know more than everyone else. This misstep led to the loss of valuable hours.

"Now Valeriya," Temp said, while trying to catch his breath. "I've been trying to stay a step ahead of those guys and others like them for a few days and it's important that we think clearly. If they followed you to me, then that means they know who you are and presumably where you live. So we can't go there. Make sense?"

"Yes, certainly—but where do we go and how do I show you what I believe you need to see?" She asked with more than a measure of frustra-tion as Temp pondered it all.

After a few moments he asked her: "Have a roommate?"

"Yes, I do—Connie's her name."

"Do you trust her?"

"Of course, but we're not terribly close and I wouldn't want to put her in danger."

"Nor would I. But is she someone you could call and could she bring whatever you need to you somewhere?"

"I guess, but she'd wonder about it."

"Well, that's a risk we may have to take." He glanced at his watch and it was about 4:45 PM.

"Could you invite her someplace for dinner or a drink—have her meet you?"

"Sure, we've done that before. Good idea. I'll call her and ask her to meet me at a restaurant bar we've gone to a few times—she won't think twice about it, especially after she hears that I'm buying. I'll tell her I have some great news to celebrate. That girl will be out the door like lightning. She loves to party."

"And you can have her get what you want to show me."

"Leave it to me," Valeriya said as she speed-dialed her roommate. "Connie? It's Val. Yes, everything's fine—great actually. Hey, wanna meet me at *Knickerbocker's* for drinks in a few minutes? I got some super news today and feel like celebrating—my treat. Nope. I'll tell you when you get here. Oh, and could you do me a big favor? I need my laptop. It's on the table next to my bed, could you grab it? Thanks! You're a dear. See you in a few." After hanging up, she turned to Davis as the cab went over a pothole and said, "How's that?"

"Perfect. So the material's on your computer?"

"Yep, I have notes, files, and an assortment of scanned documents that you'll find of great interest. But most of all, I've got something written by my father. It's always been my plan to write the story myself—but not while he's alive, according to his wishes. You'll understand it all better when you read through what he wrote. I've just never been sure how or when to approach a publisher, or even a periodical for that matter. I just know that when that day comes, everything will change for me. It's not that I'm afraid, but I simply want to have it all prepared so clearly and accurately that it can never really be challenged. Now, before we get to the restaurant, why don't you tell me how you got involved in all of this? What's *your* story, Mr. Davis?"

Checking every few seconds to make sure the cab driver wasn't listening, he brought Valeriya up to speed about all that had happened. They had both drifted into silent thought by the time the driver, having fought traffic and hit just about every light along the way, pulled up to the restaurant on University Place in the Village. Connie wasn't there yet, so they grabbed a table toward the rear of the place. Soon she arrived, laptop computer in hand, and she shot a glance at Davis.

"Connie, this is, um, Dave Templeton," a friend from work. Davis looked at her as if to say: *That's the best you could come up with, Dave Templeton?*

"Nice to meet you, Dave. So it's a party, huh?"

"Well, yep, but turns out that it'll have to be a short one, Connie—sorry. We'll have a few drinks and then I've got an appointment in midtown. And that's the news. I'm going to be working on a big project with Dave, it's all just coming together now, but it could be a big deal. Isn't that right, Mr. Templeton?"

Davis smiled at both her wit and chutzpah and replied, "Yes, indeed. It's going to be a blockbuster and I'm sure glad to have this young lady helping with it."

"Help with it? Well, hell—I'm going to do more than that. You wouldn't be able to write it without me, now would you, Mr. Templeton?"

"I suppose not," he replied, smiling at how they were basically negotiating a book agreement in such an odd way.

Connie was clueless as to what they were talking about and a little disappointed that the party wasn't going to last long, but she rolled with it. She was used to making the best of things and this wasn't the first time that Valeriya had made plans and then changed them. But it never really seemed to bother Connie. At least she was out of the apartment. However, the next hour seemed a little like torture to both Temp and Valeriya as they killed a decent interval of time before they could get back to the subject uppermost on their minds. And while Connie was well into her third appletini and deeply engrossed in conversation with a guy named Chester who had joined her and bought her the most recent drink, Valeriya and Temp begged off and said good-bye.

Connie barely noticed.

Chapter Fifty-Six

AS THEY LEFT the restaurant, Valeriya Kostitov asked Templeton Davis the most obvious of questions: "What—or better—*where* now?"

"We need to find somewhere where we can work undisturbed for a while so I can review what you have on that machine," he replied fully aware that he was very unfamiliar with this part of town.

Valeriya came up with the ideal place and said: "Follow me." Soon they were walking into the NYU's Bobst Library at Washington Square. She had been part of a 'Friends of the Library' program, allowing her complete access since graduation; she occasionally visited to write and think. She led Davis to a quiet, even somewhat secluded, area on the third floor. They found a table and Valeriya sat down, back to the wall and able to see the room and door in the distance. She patted the chair next to her while drawing it closer to her, "Sit here."

She fired up her *Macbook* and typed a password to open a folder titled: *"For Anna."* There were several files in it and she clicked on one and brought up what looked to be an article or essay on the screen, but not one written on that, or any computer. It had been typewritten—looked like on an old manual machine and in Russian—and scanned into a computer file.

"I must tell you the story before I let you read this," Valeriya insisted and Temp nodded agreement, though he wondered how he would read something written in Russian. "My father—his name is Fedor, Fedor Mikhailovich Kostitov—was arrested shortly after Vladimir Putin was elected to his second term as president—what a joke—he's really like one of the old czars, or worse, that dictator Stalin himself," she said. Then as if catching herself in mid-drift, she continued. "That was early in 2004. Somehow he knew that once Putin won office again that old scores would be settled. My father served in the KGB for many years, but was then retired. He's much older than Putin and at one time was actually his superior officer. I don't know everything that happened between them, but what I do know for sure is that they despised each other. And with Putin holding supreme power, he was busy making sure that anyone who opposed him, or maybe had information about him, or anything for that matter that was unflattering, well it was just a matter of time before old comrades came knocking."

"One day, father called me into his room and asked me to sit down next to him on the bed. He'd been drinking very heavily, which was unusual for him. And I think he'd been crying, something even more unusual. I'd seen him weep at my mother's grave—she died of cancer when I was very young—but beyond that my father never showed much emotion. He had the stoic demeanor of a soldier. But since his retirement, and with all the changes in our country, he'd watched much of what he believed in and had fought for discarded, only to be replaced by the tyranny of a man he hated."

"Sounds like your father was a complicated man," Temp inserted.

Valeriya held up her hand in a gesture that seemed to tell Davis not to interrupt, and she continued without responding to his remark. "That day, he told me that he feared he was in danger and could be taken away from her at any time. I cried and hugged him. Then he reached up under the pillow and pulled out a large envelope, larger than I'd ever seen. It was filled, bulging really. And it was sealed—not only like normal, but with a large wax seal in the center and his signature over it. Very official looking. He told me to take it and hide it safely somewhere, but not to ever tell him or anyone where it was. Then he told me something that shook me to the bone. He said that upon his death, I was to deliver the envelope to Anna Politkovskaya and that she would know what to do with its contents. I assumed that whatever was in the envelope was pretty damaging stuff about someone—maybe even Vladimir Putin. As you know from reading her book about the man, Anna was very courageous in her unrelenting criticism." Temp wanted to interrupt with another comment—but resisted the urge and just nodded affirmatively.

"This, as I said, was all back in 2004. I was in the second semester of my first year in school, then studying at Moscow State University. I asked him if I could make Anna aware that I had the envelope and he was emphatic, angrily so, that under no circumstances was I to give it to her or in any way indicate that it even existed. In retrospect, I guess he was trying to protect her, as well. Two days later, men came early in the morning and took my father away."

"What'd you do with the envelope?" Davis asked.

"I'd already put it in a safe place and it was fortunate that I did, because other men ransacked our apartment and would surely have found it. I didn't know its contents, but I was pretty sure even then that whatever it was wouldn't have helped father's case with Putin's men. There was a little area in the basement of our building where a few of us would play years earlier and I hid the envelope behind some loose bricks," she said, as she found herself immediately lost in thought about being a little girl and playing with her father.

"I came to America in the summer of 2004. I tried to see my father before I left but to no avail. I imagine Putin's men were watching me some, but frankly if they were, they weren't doing a great job of it. My father often spoke about how incompetent and corrupt his old security service had become over the years. Anyway—I brought the envelope with me and was actually surprised at how easy it was. It was a pretty non-descript envelope and when one customs agent at Kennedy airport asked what it was, I replied: 'My father's will—he says I shouldn't open it until his death.' And that was that.

"Anna had given me some money before I left so I found a safe deposit box at a bank near New York University, where the envelope remains to this day."

"You're sure it's all safe?"

"Absolutely! No doubt about it."

"Okay," Temp said. "That's 2004—what happened next?"

"Well, I immersed myself in my studies and got to know a couple of profs pretty well."

"How well?" Davis asked, causing Valeriya to take slight offense.

"Not that *well*, Mr. Davis—get your mind out of the gutter!"

"No, no! Not what I was implying—please believe me, didn't have anything improper in mind at all," he replied defensively, while blushing a bit. "I'm just thinking about the body count up to now and wondering how many more might be in harm's way—that's all. Honest!"

Valeriya immediately saw believability in his eyes. "I understand. But what I mean by close is that a couple of the profs took me under their wings, particularly Dr. Raspitov, a wonderful man."

"That's fine, but did you read him in to your full story?"

"Oh no—not at all. You're the first person I've even told about the file from my father. Please know that. The only thing I asked Dr. Raspitov about was if he knew that man Foyle at Oxford. In my reading I came across his interest in the past about Ormsby-Gore."

"Got it. So, did you ever open the envelope and examine its contents—curiosity ever get the better of you?"

"No, it didn't. But I did eventually open the envelope and examine its contents."

"When? Why?"

"It was the day after I heard that Anna Politkovskaya had been murdered," she said with more than a hint of a heavy sigh mixed with sadness in her voice.

"I'm sorry. She meant a lot to you. It's all very sad," Temp said, trying to comfort her.

"You see," she continued, "My father gave me that material for her and her alone, to be passed along when he died. Now she was dead and frankly I had no idea whether he was alive or not, so I felt like maybe there was something in that old envelope that might help me make sense of it all?"

"Was there?"

"I'll let you be the judge," she said as she opened a file and turned the laptop screen toward him. "Read this and tell me what *you* think."

Chapter Fifty-Seven
Summer 1963—Washington, DC

DAVID ORMSBY-GORE liked Jack Kennedy. He really did. Not to the degree that Jack liked him, though. To the President, David was almost a member of the family and certainly just about as important to his administration as any member of JFK's cabinet or long-time staff. And this personal relationship was the cause of much internal conflict for the British ambassador.

When he had been recruited by the Soviets back in the 1930s along with many other young men and women from aristocratic homes, he was driven by idealism, having been persuaded that a world under communism, particularly Soviet-styled and dominated communism, would make for a better world. It would be more just than what he saw growing up with the inherent inequities between rich and poor, the haves and the have not's. This idealism was shaken early on in his relationship with Moscow, as was that of so many of the recruited spy harvest in that decade, with the non-aggression pact signed by the Nazis and the Soviets in August of 1939. But somehow David, along with fellow traveler's Philby, MacLean, Burgess, Blunt and several others, managed to see the tactical thinking behind Stalin's puzzling strategic move at the outset of the war. And of course, all of that changed in a moment of vindication once Hitler turned his war machine toward Russia in June of 1941. In fact, the next few years were fascinating ones for the young moles burrowing their way into the inner sanctums and upper echelons of British political life. After all, their home-land and the country of their real allegiance were, for a time at least, allies.

Then came the Cold War, with its nuclear threat. As the years wore on, David Ormsby-Gore worked more and more on the nuclear issue and within a decade after the end of World War Two he was a leading voice for nuclear disarmament and a significant negotiator on such matters for the United Kingdom. But of course, his real agenda—one furnished for him, first by Stalin and his men, but then carried forward by Nikita Khrushchev, was to work toward a world where the Americans and their allies reduced armaments as the Soviets gained operational superiority and thus the upper hand toward world domination. It was as simple and yet, as complex, as that.

So when the British Ambassador prodded his own Prime Minister, Harold MacMillan and the President of the United States, his stated reason was world peace. But his real role was to help effectuate a world dominated and controlled by the Soviet Union, via the specter of vast nuclear superi-ority and the capacity to enforce its will on the politics of the planet.

And, in the summer of 1963, it seemed as if his dream of being the great peace-broker for the West and chief agent of influence for the Soviets was all coming true. The relationship he had cultivated with John Fitzgerald Kennedy, since Scotland days long ago, was being manipulated in a way that would make the United States and her allies—including Great Britain—weaker at the expense of the Soviets. Having had his bluff called during the Cuban Missile Crisis, Khrushchev was now playing another card, and Ormsby-Gore was dealing the hand. It was the peace card—*you put down your gun and I will put mine down. You take your gun apart and I will destroy mine. You throw the parts away and so will I. I promise. You can trust me. Really.*

And there were other distractions that fateful summer—things that threatened to spin out of control—but if actually controlled and directed by a skilled manipulator could weaken the President of the United States at a time when negotiations about armaments were reaching the critical point. In other words, if John F. Kennedy was preoccupied with other issues and those issues could potentially threaten his very presidency, his power to call the shots internationally—especially to the Russians—would be seriously diminished.

And David Ormsby-Gore knew where his buttons were and just how to push. But again, this brought the British Ambassador no small measure of angst. And he knew that he was playing a dangerous game. It was also something quite unseemly for him. Ormsby-Gore was, among other things, a proper Englishman born to the manner. He knew very well all about extramarital activities, personally and observationally, but acting as a sort of purveyor (he despised the word "pimp") was beneath his aristocratic sense of dignity. Yet in the service of the great end of a world controlled by the good guys—in his deeply held view, the Soviets—he learned to hold his nose and found ways to place women in JFK's path. These particular women also had agendas beyond the mercenary—they traded not only in sex—but more importantly, in secrets. There were many along the way and over the years, but none more important than Ellen.

Ellen Rometsch bore a striking resemblance to Elizabeth Taylor. For a period of time she was President Kennedy's favorite party girl. Political fixer Bobby Baker had first set them up—as Ellen was a regular at a gathering at the *Carroll Arms Hotel* in Washington, DC called the *Quorum Club*, pretty much nothing more than a place for high-powered politicians to connect and cavort with high priced prostitutes. None of this bothered Jack Kennedy, he was well accustomed to the services of strange women; but there was something he didn't know about Ellen—actually a couple of things. First, though Bobby Baker had arranged their first meeting a while back, it was actually David Ormsby-Gore who made sure that Ellen Rometsch became part of the ambience at notorious *Quorum Club* gatherings. And there was one other thing that Kennedy didn't know. Ellen was a Soviet spy.

So while the British government was finding itself weakened by the Profumo scandal, the President of the United States was in a similarly compromised position. J. Edgar Hoover knew all about it and he made sure, via his boss, Robert Kennedy, the U.S. Attorney General, that the President knew that he knew. In fact, Ellen was tied in some ways to many of the key players in the dramatic story that was shaking the United Kingdom's political foundations. And before long, certain members of the press would be on to the story, encouraged by Mr. Hoover himself.

But before anything would be pinned on the President of the United States by the press or otherwise, he would be cut down by an assassin's bullet in a Dallas, Texas, street. And the trigger for that horrific event was one more conversation among many that John F. Kennedy had with his good friend David Ormsby-Gore. Only this one revealed a fact, something that the ambassador and Soviet spy would actually take a few days to report. Was this because deep down inside his heart he knew—he just knew—that the game was changing and becoming very dangerous for the world, and his friend, the President of the United States?

In the end, he indeed passed the information along, even though he feared that it was putting his long-time friend in grave danger.

Chapter Fifty-Eight

BEFORE HE LOOKED at the computer screen being turned his way, Templeton Davis stated the obvious. "You know I can't read Russian, right?" At this, Valeriya simply smiled and shot him a look that he interpreted as a non-verbal "duh."

"I've translated it into English, my dear. It's a part of the material I've been gathering for a book I hope to write one day. So don't fret. You'll be able to read it. I've actually edited and rewritten the phrases to make more sense to the American reader—where I'm sure any book of mine would be first published—but never at the expense of what my father was trying to say."

Davis sheepishly said, "Okay, thanks—just, well ..."

"Forget it, Mr. Davis, just please read what my father wrote. It's not all that long but it's very important that you read it and understand what he was trying to say."

At that, Davis pulled out his reading glasses and moved the laptop into his field of vision and began to read:

My name is Fedor Mikhailovich Kostitov. I am a retired KGB officer. If you are reading this, it means I am most likely dead. Long ago, I decided to try to unburden myself of the guilt of knowing certain things about certain events and certain people. I was in a position to witness important matters and at the time I thought they were of great benefit to Russia and the Soviet people.

I have now come to doubt that conclusion and wonder if everything we tried to do and had as our goals in another day was all a waste of time. I am convinced that what I know to be true needs to one day be widely known. I hope my courageous friend Anna Politkovskaya will be able to use her gift for language and the proclamation of the truth to the world so that everyone will know what really happened several decades ago.

I have furnished along with this note, a file of documents and records supporting the facts of what I am about to share. I know that in the hands of a skilled journalist such as Ms. Politkovskaya they will lead to further collections of records and that other people who share common memories of a world gone by will come forward to testify to the truth.

Temp looked up from the screen. "Was this originally written in Russian? It flows very well."

Valeriya replied, "Yes, my father was not a writer. The actual words in Russian were somewhat unpolished. What I've done is try to capture exactly what he was trying to say and translate it not only into English, but also into something readable. But rest assured, I have the original documents in the safe deposit box and scanned on that computer, so whenever this is published there'll be no doubt as to its authenticity. I'm a trained journalist, you know."

"I wasn't challenging that, Valeriya, I just wanted to compliment it," he replied noting her defensiveness. But then again, this was something anyone would likely be sensitive about. He continued reading.

In the early 1960s I was stationed in the American capital of Washington, DC. I was young, single, and serving during exciting times. President Kennedy was the leader of the United States and Comrade Khrushchev led the great Soviet Union. He seemed to be such a great commander compared to the young and inexperienced President, but living in the city at that time, I found myself very fascinated by Kennedy, his family, and America itself. I actually admired him when he finally stood up to Mr. Khrushchev on the issue of missiles in Cuba and felt that our leader was due the rebuke. But of course, I did not share these sentiments with anyone at the time.

I was in a position to observe and know certain things, particularly how it seemed that our nation always seemed to be a step ahead of the Americans when it came to information. And it was because of our very effective and highly sophisticated network of agents and spies. This was probably the height of our glory in such things. We had eyes and ears everywhere.

Most of these agents have long since been identified, but there is one man who remains hidden to history. He is dead now and it is likely that his death was due to his previous work and the long standing struggle he had in the years following, a struggle of emotion and conscience. For his betrayal was not just of his country, but two countries—and even worse, it was a betrayal of someone who regarded him as a best friend.

His name was David Ormsby-Gore and he was the ambassador sent from Great Britain to the United States. He was recruited by our intelligence services back in the 1930s, while he was a student at Oxford, one of a whole harvest of potential agents that came from a brilliant initiative envisioned by Comrade Stalin. This young man was particularly valuable at the time because his father was an important political insider privy to an abundance of information. The young man faithfully furnished us the information. His handler gave him the code name BUNNY, which was the name of a cartoon character at the time in a Scottish newspaper, the comic strip was called "Billy and Bunny" and it was about a boy who got in trouble and his rabbit friend helped him. From what I heard, David Ormsby-Gore hated that code name.

All was going well until the Americans managed to break some of our codes and learned clues that enabled them to identify several of our people. Of course, the most famous were Burgess, MacLean, and later Philby, himself (despicable drunk, that Philby). In the years following the flight of Burgess and MacLean in 1951 and that of Kim Philby in 1963, rumors have abounded about other high-placed moles in the west, but none were found. At the CIA, Mr. James Jesus Angleton spent his career tearing apart his agency to find spies and he had theories about several in the U.K. But he was never taken all that seriously by the British, which is too bad, because he was closer to the truth than he ever really knew.

But neither Mr. Angleton, nor anyone else ever came close to uncovering the most highly placed spy for us—that being British Ambassador David Ormsby-Gore. Was it vision or just luck that this young man as a recruit happened to strike up a fervent friendship with the son of the American Ambassador to Britain? I don't know, but it turned out so well. And by 1951, when the case against Burgess and MacLean was about to be broken by MI-6, a decision had to be made at the highest levels in our intelligence services.

Kim Philby was likely to eventually become the head of the MI-6 in Great Britain, giving us such an advantage over the rest of the world. We knew that the British and the Americans would continue to troll for bigger fish even after finding out about Burgess and MacLean, so the decision had to be made to protect one asset with every tool available. Would it be Philby—who was on a fast track to power? Or would it be Ormsby-Gore, who was still a low-level government functionary at the beginning of his political career?

The choice was to opt for long-term gain. Did our people have a sense at that time that John Kennedy, the dear friend of David Ormsby-Gore, would be a major political player one day—even President of the United States? Some would like us to believe that our leaders at the time had that kind of vision. But whatever the case—whether it was vision or luck—the dice were rolled and the decision was made to protect BUNNY at all costs, even if it meant sacrificing Philby. So Kim was compromised by circumstance. Our leaders were amazed and somewhat amused that it took so long for the west to figure it all out—more than a decade. Then Kim Philby boarded a Soviet vessel in Beirut in January of 1963 and came in from the cold.

Meanwhile, David Ormsby-Gore served our causes in the United Kingdom, rising in the ranks of politicians and diplomats, all the while furnishing us valuable information. Then after the American election in 1956 it became clear to some of our leaders that this young politician, Kennedy, might indeed run for and win the presidency. This led to Mr. Ormsby-Gore continuing to cultivate his relationship with Kennedy, while at the same time positioning himself to become an obvious candidate for the ambassadorship should Kennedy be elected in 1960.

And David Ormsby-Gore became Ambassador to the United States in 1961. He was more than that, however. He was almost a member of the Kennedy administration, if not family. He was privy to all the secrets and uniquely positioned to pass along the ultimate insider information to us.

"This is powerful stuff," Temp said, again interrupting his reading—something that Valeriya found quite annoying. "It's, in effect, a firsthand confirmation of just about everything I've been investigating. I can only imagine what will happen when all of this comes to light. You've clearly been sitting on one of the great stories of the last century—and this one!"

"I know that very well, Temp. I've just never been able to get to the place where I knew exactly what I wanted to do with this. I have to think there's some providence or destiny or some such thing in the fact that you contacted me."

"I agree. I very much agree." Then back to the screen.

We learned from him the time and location of the invasion to be known as the Bay of Pigs. We knew what he would say to Mr. Khrushchev in Vienna. We knew Kennedy wouldn't fire a shot over the Berlin Wall issue. We had eyes and ears in the White House during that fiasco over the missiles in Cuba. And we had a man of influence speaking in the ear of the American president back in 1963 about the ban of nuclear tests. This was all part of our strategy to get the west to disarm, while we continued to maintain—even grow—our arsenal of nuclear weapons. It was all designed to give us control of the world.

But it was what our agent, Mr. Ormsby-Gore, learned in the autumn of 1963 that changed everything and set that crazy madman Khrushchev on the path to something unspeakable. The chairman had always been volatile, sometimes unpredictable, and it would eventually be his downfall. Too bad that didn't happen a year before it really did, in 1964.

I imagine that because of his obvious friendship with and affection for President Kennedy, David Ormsby-Gore found it hard to betray Kennedy's trust, but he did so as a faithful comrade, someone committed to the cause of world communism and the Soviet Union. But it is likely the hardest thing he ever did—and we know that because of his later career—that was when he passed along some information directly from the lips of the President of the United States to his Soviet handler.

Templeton Davis paused when Valeriya returned with two bottles of water. She handed him one and he twisted off the top and took a long drink. After clearing his throat, he said: "This is very interesting. Your father was there back then? Fascinating!"

"How far along are you, Mr. Davis?"

"Well, it appears I'm about to learn a piece of the puzzle."

"Indeed you are," she said as she winked.

Chapter Fifty-Nine

DAVIS TOOK ANOTHER short swig of water and returned to
the computer screen to continue reading what Valeriya's father had written:

> Sometime in the summer of 1963, President Kennedy told David
> Ormsby-Gore about a top secret plan to assassinate the Cuban leader,
> Fidel Castro, as part of a larger coup designed to install an American-
> friendly regime in Havana. The plan was code-named AMWORLD. It
> was scheduled to take place around the first of December that very year.
> Kennedy had authorized it, his brother, the Attorney General oversaw
> its development, and the CIA would carry it out.

> This revelation startled our agent and according to the notes from his
> briefing on the matter, he tried to talk the president out of it. Kennedy
> was determined to remove Castro and his government, even though, in
> order to resolve the previous crisis over missiles in Cuba he had assured
> Chairman Khrushchev that he would keep his hands off Cuba.

"That's very interesting, because I've been a bit of a buff when it
comes to the Kennedy assassination and have probably read about every
conspiracy out there—and some of them are really 'out there,' if you know
what I mean. And a while back, I read a book by another radio talk show
guy—his name is Thom Hartmann, a little too liberal for my taste when it
comes to his on-air stuff, but the book was fascinating—not to mention
that it was about the longest, most detailed book on the subject I'd ever

encountered. Anyway, in that book—the title was something like, *Ultimate Surrender* or *Ultimate Sacrifice*, or whatever—he had a boatload of information about the whole 'AMWORLD' thing. Of course, his view was that the Kennedy killing was all about the mob—a mafia hit. I imagine that what I'm about to read will be a somewhat different theory?"

"No theory at all, Mr. Davis," Valeriya countered in a more formal and professional tone. "My father did not deal in theories. What he's written is the truth and completely factual!"

"Got it—Okay, I'm almost done," Temp said. And then he finished reading the memo.

Once our agent communicated with Moscow about this, the chairman was beside himself with anger and decided that it was time for Kennedy to go. And it was as simple as that. What happened a few months later, the assassination of President John F. Kennedy, was ordered by Moscow and carried out by an assassin named Lee Harvey Oswald, who had been trained by our intelligence services when he lived in the Soviet Union a few years before.

The KGB had also infiltrated elements of the American mafia, largely to keep an eye on its efforts to oust Castro for its own financial interests. This infiltration was used to make things appear to point to the assassination of the President of the United States by elements of capitalist organized crime. When Jack Ruby silenced the assassin Oswald, he thought he was doing so for his friends in the mafia, but he was really being directed by elements of Soviet intelligence. It was a classic case of compartmentalization.

Following the assassination of President Kennedy, the Americans did everything possible to avoid facing the possibility of any Soviet involvement. President Lyndon Johnson's Warren Report was largely designed to prove that Oswald acted alone. But many of us on our side, especially those of us who worked in Washington, DC at the time of Mr. Kennedy's death, knew enough of the truth.

As far as David Ormsby-Gore is concerned, the death of President Kennedy, especially at the hands of Soviet intelligence, was something he never got over. He was overwhelmed with grief and guilt. Within a year or so he walked away from his government work. And when Khrushchev was ousted several months later, in 1964, his work as a spy code-named BUNNY effectively ended. He had been cultivated and positioned largely to live and work in the orbit of his friend, John Fitzgerald Kennedy, and with the assassination his usefulness was hindered, as were his passion and commitment.

In the years following the killing of President Kennedy, Mr. Ormsby-Gore, who by then had inherited the title Lord Harlech following the death of his father, did his best to remain in Jackie Kennedy's life. At one point there were news items in the United States and the United Kingdom suggesting that they might actually get married, but that was not to be.

Then about 20 years after Kennedy died, Lord Harlech's remorse drove him to contact the American CIA. He indicated that he had vital information about the Soviet involvement in the assassination of the president. What he didn't know was that at the time we had a very highly placed and very effective mole working there for us. His name was Aldrich Ames and he gave the KGB information about how Lord Harlech had reached out and wanted to turn on the Soviets.

Before Lord Harlech could go into detail about what he knew with anyone from the CIA, he met with his death in January of 1985 at the hands of Soviet operatives. The car accident was brought about under the direction of KGB director Viktor Chebrikov. It was to silence Lord Harlech so that the story of how he, once one of the best friends of the President of the United States, had betrayed that friendship, his own country, and his own conscience leading to the death of his friend, and of course, our role in the whole affair would not be revealed.

I have known this story all along and believe that it needs to be made public so that something of this magnitude can never happen again. With the current regime and trends being what they are in my country, I am fearful that some of the very bad things we did in the name of world communism may be revived in the name of a new tyrannical czar named Vladimir Putin. The fact that my country is now being run by a very ambitious former head of the very KGB that killed President Kennedy and eventually also killed David Ormsby-Gore, one of the most important and skilled espionage agents ever, tells me that the world must know the truth.

I also know that telling this story is very dangerous. I have no doubt that great forces will fight very hard to prevent it from being told. But I am hopeful that people of courage will make the world at large aware of what happened during that crucial part of what was called the Cold War so that no regime can ever do such a thing again.

Along with this note, I have included in this package several items to verify what I have said. There are photographs, documents, and copies from the official file of the spy known as BUNNY.

When he was finished reading the essay, Templeton Davis took a deep breath and another drink from the water bottle before saying anything. The silence itself spoke volumes. He had known for a few days, at least he was pretty sure, of the fact that David Ormsby-Gore was a spy working for the Soviets. But this last part—the tie into the Kennedy assassination—this was what obviously was causing alarms to be tripped. He had known that he was in danger. Now he was beginning to understand the depths of that peril.

Finally, after several moments of pregnant silence, Davis simply said: "Wow," spreading the word out as he spoke it. "I now know two things for sure."

"What two things?"

"First, this story is more involved than I could've ever imagined. The tie-in with the Kennedy assassination should be, I guess, no surprise—but it still boggles the mind, frankly."

"You said two things."

"Yes, well—I guess the other thing is this: I'm in danger and now I think you are, too. I understand now what's motivating those who have followed me from New England to England and back. This is probably being directed by Mr. Vladimir Putin and his intelligence operatives—and I think their reach is very significant. I'm at a loss as to what to do, but I know this—if we don't watch our step and make a plan very quickly, we just may wind up like 'Wild Bill' Roberts and Dr. Clive Foyle."

They both sat silently for a few minutes, pondering their situation and fate.

Chapter Sixty

"I COULD USE a cup of coffee—you?" Temp asked Valeriya. She nodded affirmatively. It was time to take a break, or at least change venues. "We need to talk some things through. I know we just met a few hours ago, but the way stuff's been going the past few days in my life, a few hours seem like weeks."

"You've certainly gotten my attention Mr. Davis. I've got a feeling that I'm about to go through something that'll change everything in my life in a profound way. But then again, I guess I always knew that the story I hoped to one day write would shake my life, if not the world, to its foundations," Valeriya observed, as they gathered their things and made their way to the stairs and down and out the front door.

Soon they were in a diner a couple of blocks away. An all night kind of place, but few customers were there at the moment. It was about 9:30 PM, a little late for dinner and too early for any kind of bar rush. Actually, it was a near perfect place to continue their conversation. They ordered coffee.

"Like I said, Valeriya, you don't really know me, but I think we're both in grave danger, especially trying to hide in plain sight. Possibly those men on that park bench across from Mantle's place still haven't found the trail. But if they're at all connected to Putin, or if he has people in the Russian mafia that he can call on, then we're already, I fear, on borrowed time." He paused and looked over at his new friend and said: "I think we need an exit strategy."

"What do you mean—exit strategy?" she quickly asked.

"I think we need to disappear for awhile, either together or separately. But we need to completely drop off the radar. And I also think we both know deep down in our hearts that we have some work to do. We're now sitting on the story of the century, or at least the last century, and it begs to be written."

"I know," she replied. "You're right, but it's all so sudden. I know what Putin is capable of and I can't help but ask myself what my hero Anna would do," she continued, allowing herself to drift off into her thoughts for a brief and silent moment.

"Well, from what I know about Ms. Politkovskaya, I think she'd feel a duty to tell this story to the world. And if you had delivered these materials to her per your father's request, I think she'd drop everything else and make this story, with all of its potential ramifications, her entire focus. But this brings to mind another thought, Valeriya—what about your father? If he's alive, there'll most certainly be repercussions."

"Father's fate has, I fear, already been decided. He may be dead now, I have no way to know for sure. And besides, in a real sense, if this story comes out and its associated with his name in a highly public and high profile way, it may actually protect him if he is still alive. Does that make any sense to you?"

"Completely," Temp answered. "I think you're correct and I also think that the key to our future is the releasing of this information, but it needs to be done in a thorough way. We need to organize it and make sure that the presentation's flawless, because it'll be attacked with vengeance."

"It needs to be written in a book," Valeriya said, stating the obvious.

"Yes, but that'll take time to do. We have the key materials, but we'll need to be able to focus on it completely. I have a crazy thought. I think we need to disappear somewhere for a month or two, with no contact with anyone we know or love, and work on a book that will capture the attention of the world. With my contacts in publishing and track record as an author, not to mention the platform of my radio program, well, the sky's the limit for this thing." Suddenly both of them felt a rush of adrenaline, even excitement at the prospect. "But we need to think it all through—and quickly."

For the next two hours they sat in the diner, drinking coffee and making notes on napkins. They developed the most important "to do" list of
their lives, complete with the knowledge that evil people were looking for
them to do them great harm.

A little before midnight, they entered a parking garage near Valeriya's
apartment, hoping against hope that her car—a five-year old Toyota
Camry—was not being watched. They surveyed the area around where the
car was parked from a secure vantage point and both of them were pretty
sure no one was nearby. What was up with Putin's people—had they
already dropped the ball?

Actually, Vladimir Putin had been fully briefed only an hour or so earlier,
shortly after eight AM, Moscow time. And he was quite unhappy that the
news about the young girl, Valeriya Kostitov, had been kept from him
overnight. This was an incompetent thing and the Russian ruler was livid,
reminding those around him that this girl was related to an old nemesis by
blood, and that dead bitch Anna Politkovskaya by ambition. Losing the
night, allowing the trail to grow cold for eight hours before figuring out the
importance of the girl—this was unforgivable.

But by the time Temp and Val had formulated their plan of action at
that Greenwich Village diner and made their way toward the parking garage
for her car, the wheels were already turning. The girl's address and many
details of her life were now known by those who were tasked with finding
her, along with her new friend, and ensuring that both of them met the
same fate as Bill Roberts and Clive Foyle.

However, as chance—not to mention good fortune—would have it,
those tasked with locating her automobile were actually not in place when
Temp and Val found the Camry and began to exit the garage. In fact, the
two men assigned to the garage were just arriving at the scene and when the
Camry exited the facility. Unfortunately, one of the men recognized the
vehicle and the driver—Valeriya—from the information and pictures they
had received. They followed the car and fairly quickly made it clear that
their strategy was not covert surveillance, but rather a clear effort at termination right then and there, no matter what the collateral damage or how

much noise it made. These were not skilled covert technicians, but rather brutish thugs who viewed most every job as if they were working in a prison yard. Finesse was not part of their vocabulary.

Neither Temp nor Valeriya noticed the black Range Rover coming up alongside of them at a stoplight, but as the light turned green they couldn't help but see the gun and then they heard its report. As a bullet shattered the passenger side front window, Valeriya mashed her foot on the accelerator and began to move through the intersection. Then she turned suddenly left, while the Range Rover had committed to go through the intersection. The maneuver bought them a few seconds and Valeriya had the presence of mind to put half a block between the vehicles. And they were off on a high-speed chase. Not a word was spoken in the Camry.

Valeriya, it turned out, was a pretty good driver. Templeton Davis was certainly impressed—and grateful. She kept her head and navigated the streets of lower Manhattan with skill, hoping to alert a police squad car. Soon she did just that. After a sudden turn a patrol car parked in front of a coffee shop quickly came to life, complete with lights and siren. But by the time it had pulled from the curb it almost hit the Range Rover and the officers then and there sized up the situation as a big bad car chasing a tiny one and, having to choose, they chose to focus on the Range Rover.

Within a few minutes the officers had managed to cut the Russians off. The last any of them saw of the Camry was when it disappeared around a corner about three blocks away. And it kept going, heading toward the Holland Tunnel and eventually to the New Jersey Turnpike. At this point they had already improvised on the plan, which had been to wait for the banks to open in the morning so that Valeriya could get the actual file her father had given her from the safe deposit box, where it had been for so long. But now that was out of the question—they had already been burned. "At any rate," Valeriya told Temp, "I have copies of every last shred of paper in my computer. I scanned it all a while back, so maybe it'd be best left at the bank as a back up."

Temp agreed immediately and they proceeded south toward the Washington, DC area where he had some materials to pick up and a call or two to make. First off, they needed to somehow go by Estelle Ferguson's place down the block from his town home in Georgetown to pick up the parcel he had sent to her for safekeeping. He had not scanned any of the pages and the notebook was crucial if they were going to write a book about all of it. It would be around five AM by the time they were back in the DC area, so Davis let Valeriya drive the first leg. "Wake me up when you get to the Delaware Memorial Bridge, Okay?"

"Sure, get some sleep—mind if I play the radio?"

"Not at all, I love radio, didn't you know that?" They both had a mild laugh over that, one that seemed to release tension and relax both of them a bit. It was a satellite radio and Valeriya dialed it to BBC World News. Soon Temp was asleep and to the mild annoyance of his driver, he was snoring.

Chapter Sixty-One

A COUPLE OF hours later, they stopped at a travel plaza in Delaware and filled the car with gas. Temp suggested they use cash and handed Valeriya a fifty-dollar bill. Best to stay off the grid, they both thought. He bought an extra-large black coffee with two shots of espresso added at Starbucks and took his turn behind the wheel, while Val fell fast asleep. No snoring, just pleasant breathing.

On the list of things to do Templeton knew they needed cash—a good amount of it, as well as someplace to stay, and work. These things would be hard to do without involving yet another person. And then it came to him—he could talk to a lawyer friend. Not *his* lawyer, mind you—but another guy. After all, if people came looking for Davis during his time in hiding, one of the obvious things would be to ask his lawyer—Daniel Suffern. Too risky to use him. But there was another guy, Howard Taggart—they had worked together a few years back, but had not been in touch for quite some time. The lawyer had actually helped Davis when he published his first book, long before any literary agent would even look at the broadcaster. Temp imagined that with the right pitch and for the right fee (read: generous), he could persuade Taggart to represent him and help him hide for a while. After all, no laws were being broken—at least not yet.

As the mile markers raced by on Interstate 95, Davis's thoughts turned to his team. First, he scolded himself for not having them on his mind enough. They were like family. But any more contact or involvement with them at this point would just put them at risk. And that thought tore him up inside.

Then again, as he thought about the daunting job ahead—to turn out a world-class book in a short period of time—they might be helped along significantly with one more person to help. He began to wonder if maybe he should try to find a way to include young Gilbert Hobson in this. The guy was trained in research—it was his forte. But how to include him without putting the guy in danger? Or for that matter, how to communicate with him in the first place? When Valeriya awakened just as the Camry found the Capital Beltway, he brought up the subject to her and gave a little of Gilbert's background. She was impressed but they made no decision on it right then.

When they arrived in Georgetown it was still dark, which was good for cover. They could not risk using a cell phone, at least not theirs—likely they were being tracked—so Davis found a payphone at a 7-eleven about four blocks from his home. He dialed Mrs. Ferguson's number fully expecting to wake her. When she answered, however, she was clearly awake and sounded like she had been for a bit, bright eyed and voiced and all. "Estelle? Templeton Davis."

"Well, my word Mr. Davis what're you calling me about this early—you home now?"

"No, ma'am, I'm not, but I am nearby. I actually have to leave again right away, but I do very much need that package I sent to you the other day. You still have it, don't you?"

"Of course I still have it, what a silly question."

"I know, sorry about that. Well, I'll be by in about ten minutes—that Okay?"

"Certainly. Can I make breakfast for you?"

"Wow, thanks for that offer, Estelle and I'm tempted to say yes, but I gotta be on my way."

"You're ever the man of mystery, Mr. Davis."

"I know, and sorry for all the cloak and dagger stuff, but there's one more odd request—if you don't mind."

"Fire away with your odd request, young man." Davis loved it when she called him young.

"I need you to put the package on your back steps. Don't turn any lights on. I'll be picking it up shortly."

"You hiding from someone?"

"Mrs. Ferguson, yes I am, but you're going to have to trust me on this, it's nothing nefarious on my part. I just need to be invisible for a bit and I promise on my wife's sacred memory that when this thing is all over I'll explain it to you in detail. And you'll learn that you're a hero."

"Well now, you had me at 'wife's sacred memory,' Mr. Davis. I'll do as you say and please, please be careful, whatever it is you are up to."

"I promise Estelle, I promise and thank you so much for all your help!"

Fifteen minutes later, complete with the recovered parcel containing the Philby journal, the one-time pad, tapes and notes from the meeting with Bill Roberts, and the contents of the old man's BUNNY box that had been obediently placed on Mrs. Ferguson's back stoop, Temp and Valeriya were en route to Vienna, Virginia, where lawyer Howard Taggart lived and practiced law. Davis, using yet another pay phone in yet another 7-eleven this one on Route 123, just off I-66, got Taggart's home number from information and placed a call to his old acquaintance.

"Hullo …?" The voice was sleepy and raspy.

"Howard? This is Templeton Davis."

"Temp, what time is it?"

"Close to six AM, I thought you high-powered lawyers were up at the butt-crack of dawn, you sleeping your life away, my friend?"

"Funny, Davis. What in the hell are you calling me about this early? I haven't heard from you in, what, over a year is it?"

"Longer than that I'm afraid. But I need some help and I thought of you. I need your services and your absolute discretion."

"You can have both, I'm sure. What's the problem?" By now Taggart was wide-awake.

"Can we meet somewhere nearby, say, in 30 minutes? I've got a lot to tell you and some favors to ask."

"Certainly—you wanna come by here? I'm by myself—Melinda and the boys are at her mother's place in Florida for a few days."

"Sure, that'd work perfectly. See you in a few."

"I'll put the coffee on," Taggart replied, more for his benefit than Davis's.

Valeriya and Temp met with Howard Taggart for nearly three hours that morning. They described in detail everything that had happened and what they were working on. Taggart quickly recognized the severity of their situation—but also the potential, and it was the latter that really got him on board. He knew that this was going to be one of the biggest stories of the next year and he instinctively wanted to be part of it. So he offered all of his help—and that help was literally life saving. Temp asked him for some extra cash and Taggart pulled several thousand dollars from his safe in his basement. He also promised that he'd get more cash to them, if and when they needed it.

But the best part of the morning was when Howard Taggart gave Templeton Davis the keys to what he described as "his modest farmhouse" in Bedford, Virginia, about three and one-half hours away. "The place is secluded and beautiful. It's got Internet service, cable television, and you could pretty much hide and live there for who knows how long, virtually undetected. There's a phone there, too—landline, so you can reach out to me whenever you have need." He also gave them keys to a gray 2008 Ford F-150 pickup truck he kept down there at the house and suggested that they put the Camry in the garage there and leave it for the duration. Taggart suggested that they stop along the way for some new clothes and ample food and provisions for their stay at the farmhouse. In fact, he said that they should stop at several stores so as not to draw attention for buying a boatload full of stuff.

"One more thing, Howard, if I might be so bold," Temp continued, while wondering if this might not be the first time his lawyer friend had hidden someone from view.

"Fire away, I'm already on board and, frankly, a little excited about it."

"Well, there's a guy on my staff named Gilbert Hobson. Hired him to do research for me a while back and he has a real flare for it. Val and I have talked a bit about finding a way to include him in this—it'd sure be a big help. But how? Whadaya think?"

Pausing for a moment, Taggart thought and then responded, "You know, that might be a good idea. Hell, what's the difference between two people disappearing and three?" he asked with a devious smile on his face. "Tell you what. I'll find a way to contact him—off the grid, of course, would need to know where I might ambush him, though. You give me some kind of note in your hand—he would recognize your penmanship, right?"

"Definitely!"

"Okay, well, then I'll drive him down myself later today or tomorrow, depending on how it all rolls. How's that? Think he'll bite?"

"By the time he reads my note he'll be one salivating research geek!" Temp chuckled. Valeriya sort of rolled her eyes, still not completely knowing how to read this man who had so suddenly taken her life over and away. And while Temp worked on the note for young Mr. Hobson, he also came up with how Taggart could contact the young researcher.

"Here's the note for Gilbert and I think the best way to contact him is by staking out the little coffee shop in our building there in Rosslyn—you know the place?"

"Sure—we met there once, right—great cherry pie?"

"Yes—but it's blueberry."

"The team rolls in and out of the place all day—I think the phones in the office might be tapped, so you're just gonna have to watch and wait. There's a pic of him on the show's website, www.templetondavislive.com, so you can see what he looks like. And I guess I don't have to tell you to be discreet."

"Not my first rodeo, Temp—not by a long shot."

"I figured, but couldn't help it, sorry. Here, by the way, is the number to this disposable phone I've been using the last day or so, but I'm going to ditch it pretty quick. Can you pick up a couple of these for us along the way?"

"No problem. Got it. Now you two need to get on your way, let me take care of everything here, Okay?"

Temp and Valeriya felt very reassured for the first time since they ran out the back door of *Mantle's* place back in Manhattan. In return for all of his help, Howard Taggart agreed to work as their agent for the book they would be writing. They all knew that what he might earn from this would far exceed anything he could charge in fees. Fortunately, Taggart had some experience in the literary world, so this was far from foreign territory. The wheels in his brain were already spinning about potential publishers.

Chapter Sixty-Two

BY NOON, TEMPLETON Davis and Valeriya Kostitov were in her Camry heading down Route 29 toward Bedford, Virginia. The drive would take them by Culpepper, through Charlottesville, then Lynchburg and finally to the little town at the foot of the Blue Peaks of Otter. They stopped several times along the way, three times at grocery stores, and twice at Walmart stores for supplies. They also spent a little less than an hour at a mall in Charlottesville shopping for clothing and they grabbed a bite in the food court. The whole trip took nearly six hours.

Davis was excited when they passed by the *National D-Day Memorial* housed in Bedford because of the famous Bedford Boys, the group of young men who died on the beach at Normandy during the first minutes of that fierce and epic battle. But he realized that it was unlikely that he would have a chance to visit the memorial—at least not on this trip.

As they drove up a long driveway through the woods toward Howard Taggart's farm—the one he called "modest"—they were blown away. The house was beautiful and it was indeed secluded. Their safe house looked like it would live up to the name. They brought everything in the house and parked the Camry in the garage, where it would remain for the duration.

Davis, ever the gentleman, gave Valeriya first pick when it came to sleeping arrangements and she chose the obvious—the master bedroom, complete with a large bathroom outfitted with an oversized bathtub. He took a room down the hall, not as big as the master, but more than adequate. Temp scrambled some eggs and fried some bacon and they ate, while watching the news on CNN.

A few hours earlier, back in Northern Virginia, Howard Taggart had sipped a large coffee in the *Starburst Cafe* and savored the final bite of a piece of blueberry pie. It was about 2:30 PM and he was keeping an eye out for Gilbert Hobson. He continued through his copy of the day's *Wall Street Journal* and was about finished with an op-ed piece about something called a fair tax when Hobson walked in. The young staffer ordered a coffee and a muffin. He added cream and sugar—lots of sugar—to the beverage and made his way back to the door. Howard Taggart got up and followed him out, but not too closely.

Gilbert Hobson got into an elevator and Taggart joined him—just the two of them for the short ride up. The lawyer cleared his throat and spoke. "It's Hobson, right—Gilbert Hobson?"

Startled, Hobson replied, "Yes, who are you?"

"Relax, my friend—and I mean that, I'm a friend—a new friend. I have something for you from your boss."

"Temp?" Hobson asked excitedly while almost grabbing the envelope from Taggart's hand.

"Yes, Temp—he's your boss, right?"

Gilbert didn't answer, but was already well into reading the note. When the elevator door opened, Taggart hit the "Close" button and pressed the one marked "Down." The young researcher didn't notice—his eyes were glued to the page in his hand. It opened again back on the first floor and Taggart said to Gilbert, "Walk with me—let's find somewhere to talk."

"This for real, Mister?"

Taggart realized at that moment that he was, in fact, dealing with a geek of some kind, the query bespoke a kid asking an adult a question. But he ignored his natural urge toward sarcasm and measured his words. "Yep, it's the real deal sport and, frankly, you could be part of something gigantic. But the thing is that you've got to go with me right now. As in drop every-thing, don't go back to the office, don't go home, don't pass go or collect two hundred—that's the deal."

Gilbert Hobson was not the kind of guy usually comfortable with risk or adventure. His awkwardness with the girl up in Vermont demonstrated that. But for some reason he found a way to tap into his inner super hero or something and simply said, "Let's go!"

"Seriously?" a surprised Taggart asked. "Just like that?"

"Well, that's what the boss wants and I work for him, so—yessir—just like that."

In five minutes Howard Taggart and Gilbert Hobson were in the lawyer's Cadillac Escalade on I-66 en route to Rt. 29 and points south and southwest. Taggart dialed Davis's disposable phone and handed his smart phone to Gilbert. "Say hello to your boss."

Templeton Davis was washing down the last bite of eggs with a swig of orange juice when his phone rang. He answered it tentatively, "Hello?"

"Temp—that you? It's Gilbert! Boy, I'm glad to hear your voice. Everyone's freaking out back at the office."

"Well, Hobson it's great to hear from you and because you're calling me on this crap phone, I imagine you've met my friend Howard Taggart."

"Yep, met him and read your note and I'm at your service, boss. You can count on me."

"That's wonderful—great news. We've got a lot of work to do in a short time and you'll be great help. I have someone else here, too—someone trained in journalism. You'll enjoy meeting her, I'm sure." Temp smiled at that, recalling Hobson's brief encounter with another Russian girl up in Vermont. "Lemme talk to Taggart again and we'll talk more when you get here, or if that's too late, we'll chat in the morning."

Gilbert handed the phone back to the man driving the SUV and looked out the window at the countryside.

"Yeah, Temp, what's up—anything else?"

"Hey, stop in Charlottesville at the mall there on the main drag and get the kid some clothes, underwear, and such, we've got everything else covered here. Oh—and have him pick up another laptop computer and a very good printer, Okay?"

"Got it. We'll be in Bedford later tonight. You gonna wait up?"

"Dunno. Maybe. I'm beat, but I may get back up if you make enough noise." But by the time Taggart and Hobson arrived, Temp and Valeriya were deep in sleep and likely would have remained so during an earthquake or tornado. Conversation would have to wait until the morning.

Chapter Sixty-Three
Bedford, Virginia

VALERIYA AND TEMPLETON were both up well before six AM that Friday morning. Gilbert stirred about an hour later and when he met Valeriya he was immediately smitten and nearly speechless. He had been down in the dumps, having not heard from Anna, the Russian girl from the weekend before. She had given him a phony cell number that actually belonged to a deli in Brooklyn. After the third call from Gilbert looking for the girl, he was introduced to a particularly virulent string of Russian swear words and he got the message not to call back—ever. Of course, after reading Temp's note the day before, complete with the part about how that girl in Vermont was probably a spy, he felt kind of stupid about the whole thing. But that feeling was chased away at the first sight of Valeriya.

After coffee they fell into a work pattern that would be repeated over the next 26 days. Typing, dictation, re-writing, researching, and they all took a hand at editing each other's work. The first day they created more than 5,000 words to start the book. The story they were writing would also, of course, include the historic elements—all the way back to the 1930s, and the Soviet initiative at spy recruitment. Gilbert was tasked with organizing that material from Temp's notes as well as from sources on the web. But the narrative also included recent developments—including the deaths of Bill Roberts and Clive Foyle—this was Davis's assignment.

On the sixth day of their work, Howard Taggart called and told them that they should turn on *Fox News*. They did and they watched a story about their apparent disappearance. It mentioned that Temp's credit cards had been accessed for lots of cash and that his rental car had been found at the Boston airport. It was all presented in a dramatic way with clear indications of something sinister. The reports were soon all over the tube and also included interviews with the rest of the people from Temp's team. This caused him a sleepless night.

The story was breaking.

Estelle Ferguson grew concerned when she saw the television report and called the police. Soon FBI agents appeared at her door and heard her story, one of mystery about Davis and a package of some kind, all the cloak and dagger stuff. They did, however, manage to keep her name and story out of the news. By then, officials had a sense that the whole scenario held at least a hint of danger.

By the tenth day, the story had become a media obsession, which made them glad they had stocked up so much before getting to the farmhouse. To venture out by then would be far too risky. By the fourteenth day, the story of the disappearance of a radio talk show host, a Russian journalist, and a young research assistant was connected to the deaths of Bill Roberts and Clive Foyle. The mention of Foyle took the story international via *Sky News*, *CNN International*, and *BBC World*. They were hot. They were also about halfway done with the first draft of their manuscript.

Templeton Davis Live had turned into a national radio forum for people to call in and give their opinions as to what had happened to the missing host. In fact, during his absence the ratings spiked higher than ever. One caller actually suggested that the disappearance had something to do with UFOs. Meanwhile, Valerie Doling and Vince Benton had been interviewed several times by the FBI and though they had been reluctant at first, eventually they gave them the details about what Templeton Davis had been investigating. Before too long, it all got the attention of people at Langley and frankly was becoming one of the biggest mysteries in years. Where was Templeton Davis? Was he dead or alive? Was this a modern day spy story? Were the Russians involved? The Internet was buzzing with conspiracy theories. One site with the domain www.whereistemp.com received more than two million hits during one 24-hour period. The story had become an international sensation. All the networks led their evening news programs with the latest development or rumor and the cable shows dealt with it 24/7.

As for the men in the Kremlin, they pulled their teams back and gave up the search for Davis and Kostitov and simply waited for whatever shoe was going to eventually drop. To try to track the pair down was now far too risky. As it was, the global phenomenon had too many of their fingerprints on it. Vladimir Putin was sure that trouble was coming and was already at work concocting a narrative giving him and his security services plausible deniability.

Watching all of the speculation and viral news stories unfold on television only heightened the sense of urgency as the trio labored over the emerging manuscript. Finally, on the 26th day, the writers in hiding pronounced the first draft of the book finished. Of course, it would need all the polishing touches involved with professional editing and publishing, but the raw material was there in a form that would remain virtually intact.

And that was when they decided the time was right to come in out of the cold.

Chapter Sixty-Four
Washington, DC

DEMONSTRATING A REAL flair for the dramatic, Howard
Taggart secured an auditorium at the *Newseum* in Washington, DC for a
press conference. His cryptic invitation to news outlets gave just enough of
a hint that by the time it was scheduled—two PM on a Thursday afternoon—it had attracted major media attention. All he had to do was suggest
that there were now some clear answers in the case of the disappearance of
Templeton Davis, Valeriya Kostitov, and Gilbert Hobson.

All the major networks were there—cable outlets, too, as were several
international channels, including the *BBC*, *Al Jazeera*, and a crew from the
Russian network *RT*. This was the big time, so thought Taggart. He had
arranged for the writers to drive up under cover of darkness the night
before and they had been squirreled away at the motel in Fairfax waiting for
the appointed hour. He had one of his assistants book the rooms and get
the keys to ensure no one would see him or the mysterious trio.

And shortly after two PM that Thursday, Howard Taggart made his
way to the auditorium platform from a backstage area. This was the first
time most people were seeing the lawyer who had aroused such curiosity,
but they didn't dwell on it, because he was immediately followed into the
room by the three now-famous fugitives from publicity. There were obvious gasps and the assembled crowd almost erupted in a chaotic way.

"Ladies and Gentlemen," Taggart began, "First, I want to thank you
all for coming today. In a moment Templeton Davis will make a statement,

but we're sorry, due to the nature of what you'll be learning a little bit about, we'll not be able to take any questions today." There were murmurs from the crowd, clearly they'd want more. But Taggart ignored the rumbling noise and forged ahead. "I'm sure all your questions will be answered in sufficient detail very soon, but for now we want to make you aware of a story that's bigger than the mere and temporary disappearance of a broadcaster, journalist, and research assistant. It's a story that'll captivate the world. It's also a story that'll answer some long standing questions, yet it might also breed even more questions and speculation, that being the nature of news and history. This is what, I think, makes it such a potentially powerful story. We've chosen this setting today in this facility—the *Newseum*—because what you're about to hear is, in fact, the first words spoken in public about what will surely be the story of the century."

With that, Templeton Davis was introduced. He spent about fifteen minutes giving all in attendance and the multiplied millions watching on television a thumbnail sketch of what they had been working on in seclusion. He apologized to his friends and loved ones, but after explaining the real reason behind the deaths of Bill Roberts and Clive Foyle, he said he hoped that he would be forgiven. And he was. He had not only been trying to protect himself, he had tried his best not to put others in harm's way.

Valerie Doling was standing near the back of the room and about halfway through his remarks, Temp noticed his assistant and their eyes met. For a brief second Valerie just stared at the man who had not only risked her safety in a way, but also boxed her out of an experience she would have loved. But just seeing him safe and sound was enough to quickly melt away any real animosity or even annoyance. After a moment, she smiled at him and gave him a friendly, but subtle wave. Temp breathed a sigh of relief and noted that he felt a little like a married man being let out of the doghouse— *where the hell did that come from?* he wondered.

One thing Davis did not do was give away the key components of the story that day. He hinted here and teased there, but the full narrative wouldn't be told until the manuscript was published and he hoped someone would step forward to talk with Howard Taggart about just that.

And talk they did. For the first time in a long time—since before the economic crisis of 2008—the publishing world had a bidding war. In the end, though, it was one of the big boys who came through with an advance commensurate with the nature and scope of the book: 11 million dollars.

And a little less than four months later, after a frenetic period of editing and cramming all of the normal book promotion protocols into a much smaller time span, the book co-written by Templeton Davis and Valeriya Kostitov and with the added words "with Gilbert Hobson" hit the shelves. The title?

Camelot's Cousin.

They had a wonderful book launch party on an early spring Saturday at the home of Vince and Liz Benton in Clifton. There was a nice marker on the spot where Kim Philby's satchel had been discovered the previous October. Liz made a large batch of chili and several cherry pies. Of course, Templeton Davis also paid a caterer to make sure there was plenty of food and drink for the nearly 200 guests, but Liz's creations were clearly the crowd favorites.

Camelot's Cousin was an instant bestseller and Davis and Kostikov quickly became very familiar faces on all the major news stations and programs. Hobson became a bit of a celebrity himself, but tended to shy away from the camera and interviews. Temp was more than happy to let Valeriya be the chief spokesperson for the project and she demonstrated a natural gift for the art of the interview. Of course, the very fact that their book provided a plausible and credible explanation for the death of John F. Kennedy began a national discussion—it also reopened an old wound. After all was said and done, people now wondered: *Was it actually the Russians all along?* The clear fingerprints of Russian state security on the murders of Bill Roberts and Clive Foyle seemed to settle the issue for many Americans.

A poll taken a few months after *Camelot's Cousin* came out revealed that 73 percent of Americans in the survey now believed that Lee Harvey Oswald killed Kennedy, but had done so on orders from Moscow. Frankly, this turned the world of Kennedy assassination buff-ism upside down. But more than a few people found comfort in the revelation—almost as if to say, *I thought so.*

Epilogue

IN THE AFTERMATH of the publication of *Camelot's Cousin*, both Valeriya Kostikov and Templeton Davis enjoyed a sustained period of celebrity. They were also safe, and they knew it, because the story that people had murdered to see never come out was, in fact, out. And that was that. An attack on one of them now would draw lightning from leaders and media worldwide. There was no way Mr. Putin and company would take that bait.

Templeton Davis went back to his radio routine more popular than ever. Within six months of the release of *Camelot's Cousin*, nearly 300 new affiliate stations picked up his show and *Fox News* hired him to do a weekly show on Sunday evenings, one that he taped on Thursdays in New York—giving him a nice weekly scheduled respite at his place on West 57th Street. And, of course, most Thursday evenings, following the taping of his show, he'd meet his friend Valeriya Kostitov. She had come to see Temp as a father figure of sorts, certainly a mentor. Where did they usually meet? Of course—*The Russian Tea Room*.

And as for Valeriya, her celebrity star rose high in the media sky. *Fox News* rival *CNN* gave her a contract to cover Russia for them, so almost daily she had the chance to develop stories about Vladimir Putin and his gangsters (her word) for broadcast on *CNN* in the states and via *CNN International*. They would more often than not counter the clearly-propaganda material being put out by Russian network *RT*. And the New York *Daily News* gave her a contract to write two columns a week, which were picked up by 300 other newspapers. Early in the year, *Vanity Fair* did a feature on her, along with her stunning picture on the cover. She also spent much time trying to find out about the fate of her father—was he dead or alive? But reliable information remained elusive. This became an obsessive quest for her.

Time Magazine made Templeton Davis and Valeriya Kostitov its person(s) of the year that December, even before the book came out. That Hobson didn't share the limelight had no effect on him. He was happy as a clam. The book had made him moderately wealthy in a short period of time and he just wanted to keep working for Templeton Davis. The young man knew he already had it made in the shade.

Of course, Putin and his gang in the Kremlin downplayed the book in the international press and it was banned in Russia, but an ample number of copies managed to circulate in hard copy and e-book form. And there was little the would-be czar or anyone for that matter could do about it. There was an international outcry for the Russian leader to be brought to justice before the world court, but no such thing ever had much of a chance. The world would have to settle for the verdict of guilty in the court of prevalent public opinion. And that verdict was clear to people across the political spectrum. It was also very likely that Mr. Putin would have a very difficult time getting elected to a fourth term as President of the Russian Federation. His political opposition was stirring and organizing. It would just be a matter of time before the tyrant would be gone.

Templeton Davis made good on his verbal promise to Vince Benton. Even before the book was on a single store shelf, he made sure Vince's three little girls had nice little trust funds for their college education and then some. And he gave Vince and Liz a nice check for $1,000,000, telling them that now they could build that bigger house on the Clifton, Virginia property. But they chose to keep the old house as it was, complete with the dilapidated man cave. Instead, they bought a nice home in Stowe, Vermont—a place for fun in the summer and skiing in the winter.

In fact, Davis made sure that every member of his staff, from Valerie Doling on down benefited financially from *Camelot's Cousin*. And they were all very grateful.

Speaking of Valerie Doling. It was almost like a light had been turned on in Templeton Davis's brain the moment his eyes met hers, as he was speaking on that famous Thursday at the *Newseum*. Eventually, he began to pay more attention to his assistant and grew to realize that she had been more than that for quite some time. And, while their relationship didn't immediately erupt in romance or even morph into a full-blown affair, Temp found himself with feelings he had not known in years—since his wife died. He didn't quite know where to go with it all, but he began spending more time with Valerie—long, late, lunches, much conversation, teasing, even mild flirting. He invited her along when he was asked to return to Oxford to talk about the book and the story. They both visited Professor Clive Foyle's grave. Then they spent a day in London, highlighted by a luncheon with the top people at Thames House, headquarters of MI-5. But no matter the agenda for the day and evening, Temp and Valerie always stayed in separate rooms. He was fine with the pace, but Ms. Doling? Well, she took what she could get and yet still contemplated the nature of hope.

That next spring—actually it was late spring—Templeton Davis disappeared again, but only for a few of days. He told no one where he was going and this made some of his friends quite uncomfortable—and Valerie was livid. He wanted to travel alone, so he didn't use his private jet. This time he flew commercial to Denver, where he rented a car and made his way to a home in suburban Aurora. A few weeks before, he had asked Milt Darnell for help locating someone. It was a six-year-old boy named Anderson Watkins. His mom's name was Melissa, Melissa Watkins. Her grandfather's name was "Wild Bill" Roberts, but Temp wasn't sure she knew that.

He knocked on the door of a small bungalow and introduced himself to the young mother. She seemed to recognize him and invited him in. Melissa broke down in tears when Davis told her the story about her grandfather. "I've actually read your book, Mr. Davis, and I loved it very much. But I never knew all of that about my grandfather, thank you for telling me!" She had been going through rough times. Her husband had left and she was on her own as far as supporting her boy was concerned.

"Well, Melissa, there's more. He wanted to do something for your son and I want to follow through with that. I'm setting up a trust for him for his college education down the road. It'll cover everything. Also, I want you to have this now." At that, he reached into his pocket and pulled out a check made out to her for $250,000. "Your grandfather was an American hero, someone who helped keep the world safe in a day long since gone—but without people like him, we'd never know life as we know it. I know he'd be proud of you and your son," Temp said, with more emotion than usual.

He left the house in Aurora and caught a flight from Denver back to DC. Much later that night Templeton Davis fell asleep in the library of his home in Georgetown, while reading a book about the December, 1941 attack on Pearl Harbor. There was a half-eaten ham sandwich (with spicy mustard) on a plate on the table next to him and the ice that had chilled his ginger ale had melted away.

He was pretty much the happiest man in the world.

THE END

Notes and Acknowledgements

Camelot's Cousin is a work of fiction. The story is the fruit of the author's imagination. Most of the characters have been invented, but that said, there are several historic figures appearing in the book—some significantly— President and Mrs. John F. Kennedy, as well as his brother, Robert, for example. Other real-life characters include various nefarious spies from Cold War days, Kim Philby, Guy Burgess, Donald MacLean, Anthony Blunt, et al.

The most significant real-life character in this book is David Ormsby-Gore (later known as Lord Harlech) who became the British Ambassador to the United States early in the Kennedy administration. He was very real, but the story I have written about him is, indeed, fiction. I took a few circumstantial things and created what I hope is a compelling story. Of course, there is no actual evidence whatsoever that the British Ambassador to the United States during the Kennedy years was anything other than what he appeared to be—a well-bred British politician and diplomat.

Special thanks to legendary book editor, William G. "Bill" Thompson. He has helped me now with two projects and has been a wonderful mentor in many ways. Of course, Bill is a bit of a legend in publishing circles. He's well known as the editor who discovered both Steven King and John Grisham way back when. It worked out pretty well for them. I am grateful for the interest he took in this book and this author.

I am grateful to Karen Lieberman who helped so much with copy-editing and I am indebted, as well, to all of the people at *Telemachus Press* who helped bring this book to publication. Thanks also to Kelly Ablaza and Kathy Holland for proofreading the manuscript.

Without the support of my wonderful wife, Karen, who has believed in me for 36 years, and our three daughters, Jennifer, Deborah, and Brenda, I would not be capable of much. Then there are my seven grandchildren—but don't get me started.

Mike Zizolfo, a gifted artist, did the design for the cover. He also helped design three of my grandsons, with the help of my youngest daughter.

Regarding resources, I am indebted to Barbara Leaming and her excellent book, *Jack Kennedy—The Education of the Statesman*, for so much rich detail about the relationship between John F. Kennedy and his closest British friend—a relationship that began in the late 1930s and prospered during the era later branded as Camelot.

Of course, there *actually* was a spy code-named BUNNY, whose identity and activities remain a mystery to this day. Everything quoted as from a published work in my novel with regard to BUNNY is in fact *true*—every clue. This is what makes the story so fascinating, or so I hope. I have crafted a narrative around coincidence and circumstance. But again, please know—I made the story up.

Really.

In addition to Barbara Leaming's aforementioned book, I read and gleaned material and color from the following very real works:

A Death in Washington: Walter G. Krivitsky and the Stalin Terror, by Gary Kern

Walter G. Kritvitsky: MI-5 Debriefing and Other Documents on Soviet Intelligence, edited, with translations, by Gary Kern

Deadly Illusions, by John Costello and Oleg Tsarev

Mask of Treachery: Spies, Lies, and Betrayal, by John Costello

The Crown Jewels: The British Secrets at the Heart of the KGB Archives, by Nigel West and Oleg Tsarev

The Cambridge Spies: The Untold Story of MacLean, Philby, and Burgess in America, by Verne W. Newton

My Silent War, by Harold Russell "Kim" Philby

Treason in the Blood: H. St. John Philby, Kim Philby, and the Spy Case of the Century, by Anthony Cave Brown

Kitty Harris: The Spy with Seventeen Names, by Igor Damaskin

My Five Cambridge Friends, Burgess, MacLean, Philby, Blunt, and Cairncross: by Their KGB Controller, by Yuri Modin

The Crisis Years: Kennedy and Khrushchev, 1960-1961, by Michael Beshcloss

Ultimate Sacrifice: John and Robert Kennedy, the Plan for a Coup in Cuba, and the Murder of JFK, by Lamar Waldron with Tom Hartmann

Berlin 1961: Kennedy, Khrushchev, and the Most Dangerous Place on Earth, by Frederick Kempe

The Philby Files: The Secret Life of Master Spy Kim Philby, by Genrikh Borovik

The Master Spy, by Phillip Knightley

Spycraft: The Secret History of the CIA's Spytechs from Communism to Al-Qaeda, by Robert Wallace and H. Keith Melton

Spies: The Rise and Fall of the KGB in America, by John Earl Haynes, Harvey Klehr, and Alexander Vassiliev

Flawed Patriot: The Rise and Fall of CIA Legend Bill Harvey, by Bayard Stockton

Treachery: Betrayals, Blunders, and Cover-ups: Six Decades of Espionage Against America and Great Britain, by Chapman Pincher

My Five Cambridge Friends, by Yuri Modin

The Venona Secrets: Exposing Soviet Espionage and America's Traitors, by Herbert Romerstein and Eric Breindel

David R. Stokes
Fairfax, Virginia

About the Author

DAVID R. STOKES is a *Wall Street Journal* bestselling author, ordained minister, commentator, broadcaster, and columnist. His previous book, ***THE SHOOTING SALVATIONIST: J. Frank Norris and the Murder Trial that Captivated America*** (Steerforth Press/Random House, July 2011), is a narrative non-fiction, true crime thriller set in the 1920s. ***BOOKLIST***, in a starred review, says: ***"The book is engagingly written, in an immediate, you-are-there style, and the story is as compelling and surprising as any Grisham thriller. Top of the line."***

CPSIA information can be obtained at www.ICGtesting.com
Printed in the USA
BVOW081341011012

301743BV00002B/3/P

9 781938 701375